The Persian Precipice

Stoking the Flames of War

Niels Andersen

Niels Andersen

About the Author

Niels Andersen is a community college instructor and retired Air Force Lieutenant Colonel whose career took him to operating theaters around the world. From desert sands to the storied halls of the Pentagon, he taps a deep well of experience working national and military strategy. As an amateur military history buff he draws on past and current events to shape his stories and blur the lines between fact and fiction. His books highlight the extraordinary work of ordinary people in the relentless pursuit of our national defense, many whose accomplishments remain in the shadows and are known only by the ones who sent them into harms way, and those who fought by their side.

<u>Books by Author:</u>

Valley of Stars
The Persian Precipice

Acknowledgements

Writing is a work of passion for every author. Creating compelling stories that peek the imagination and pull the reader into the world we've created is the goal of every good storyteller. I hope you enjoy the story and I always welcome the viewpoints of readers to help improve my storytelling through your reviews. So, enjoy the book and let me know what you think. Happy reading!

All maps created using OpenStreetMap (OSM) data (openstreetmap.org/copyright) and is distributed under the Open Database License (ODbL). OSM data is made available under the Open Database Licence version 1.0 (the ODbL).

A special thanks to Yvonne Klocek and my dear friend Afsi Pouresmail. Yvonne is a colleague at Normandale Community College and a wonderfully creative artist who created the cover graphics. Her collaboration and ability to take the thoughts of this terribly linear thinker and mold it into thought provoking imagery was inspiring. Afsi was instrumental in helping with the nuances of Iranian society to shine a light on some of the challenges their citizens face under the radical regime.

I'd also like to thank the staff at Wordwise Media Services. Their insights and diligent editing comments have made me a better writer.

Lastly, to all the men and women who work tirelessly to protect this country and our way of life. These fictional stories don't even begin to tell the real story of the danger you face and the courage it takes to meet that danger head-on every single day. The public may never know of the awards earned or the names of the patriots lost. But hopefully through these works you know that even though we don't know who you are, we see you, and we honor you and your sacrifices.

The Persian Precipice

Stoking the Flames of War

Niels Andersen

Niels Andersen

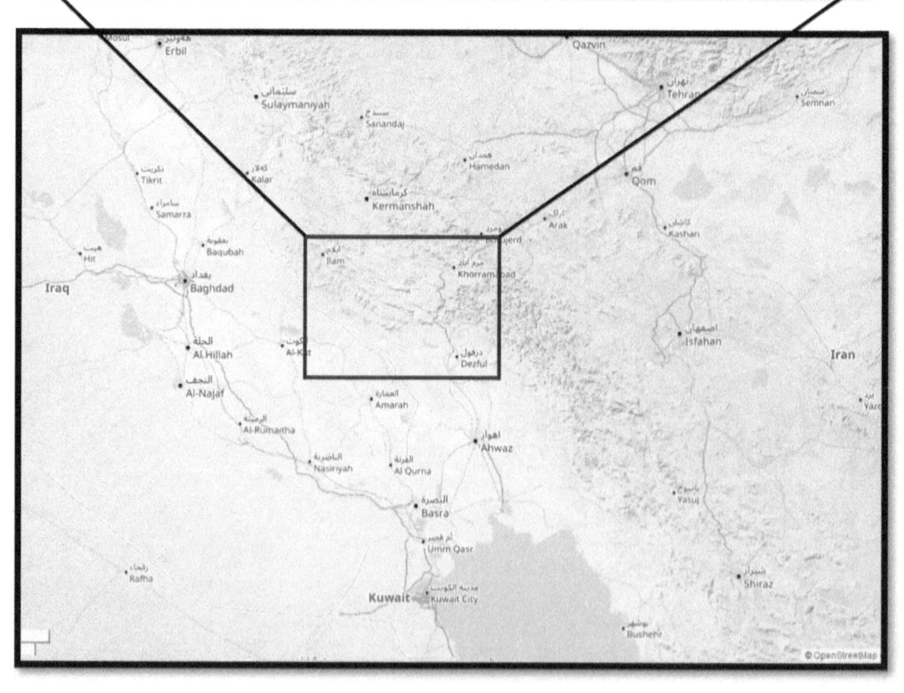

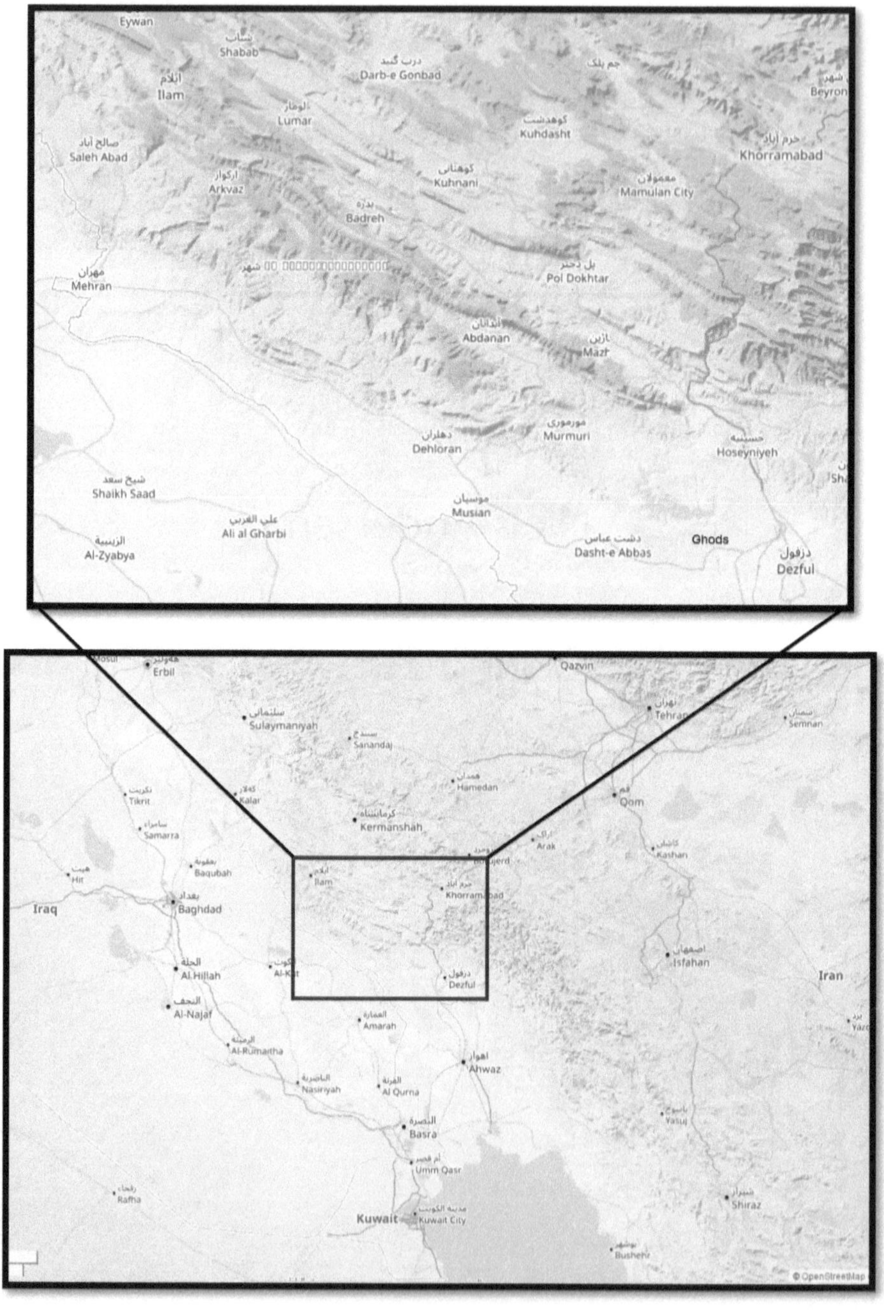

Eywan
Shabab
Darb-e Gonbad
Beyron
Ilam
Lumar
Kuhdasht
Khorramabad
Saleh Abad
Arkvaz
Kuhnani
Mamulan City
Badreh
Pol Dokhtar
Mehran
Abdanan
Mazf
Dehloran
Murmuri
Hoseyniyeh
Shaikh Saad
Musian
Ali al Gharbi
Ghods
Al-Zyabya
Dasht-e Abbas
Dezful
Mosul
Erbil
Qazvin
Sulaymaniyah
Tehran
Sanandaj
Semnan
Tikrit
Kalar
Hamedan
Qom
Samarra
Kermanshah
Kashan
Baqubah
Borujerd
Hit
Ilam
Arak
Iraq
Baghdad
Khorramabad
Al-Kut
Al-Hillah
Isfahan
Dezful
Iran
Al-Najaf
Amarah
Al-Rumaitha
Ahwaz
Yazd
Nasiriyah
Al Qurna
Basra
Yasuj
Umm Qasr
Rafha
Shiraz
Kuwait
Kuwait City
Bushehr
© OpenStreetMap

Prologue

The Arabella III slid gracefully into the boat slip at the marina adjacent to the Sheraton Dubai Creek Hotel. An elegant twenty-eight-meter Permare Amer 92 yacht, she was the epitome of modern sophistication for the ultra-wealthy. As the two male crewmen tied her off, a young woman sat at the stern talking on a cell phone.

The woman had the lithe body and elegance of a supermodel as her long black hair fell across the right side of her full bosom. The graceful lines of her figure were enhanced by the skintight, knee length, off the shoulder lime green dress she wore. Her olive toned skin literally glistened in the sunlight, reflecting off her thin, long face with pink lipstick and high cheek bones touched with a shimmering makeup.

"We just pulled into the dock," reported the woman.

A man's baritone voice answered.

"The scientist should be arriving shortly, you know what to do," he said.

"Understood," the woman said and ended the call.

A short, slightly heavy-set man approached the yacht. The scientist looked at his cell phone and then at the name on the stern of the yacht. He was in his fifties with a dark brown bushy mustache wearing a white, short sleeved Bahama shirt that fell loosely below his waist and casual navy-blue pants.

"Doctor Bashir, welcome to the Arabella three. I'm Sofia, I'll be your hostess for your voyage. Welcome aboard," said the woman and extended a hand to help the scientist aboard.

"Thank you, Sofia, it's a pleasure to meet you," Bashir answered.

"This is Captain Harsallah along with Qasem the First Mate and we'll be taking care of you for the next two hours. So, we can go below and get you comfortable while the captain takes us into the gulf," Sofia said with a big smile.

"Yes, that would be wonderful. It will be nice to relax before the conference and what better way than with such beautiful company," Bashir replied.

Sofia led Bashir down the short stairs to a small lounge just below deck. It had plush leather chairs and elegant teak cabinets stocked with any form of liquid enjoyment one could imagine. She pointed to a chair as the engines growled to life and the yacht began to slowly rock back and forth as the captain eased it away from the dock. The boat stabilized as it accelerated through the calm waters of the channel leading to the Persian Gulf.

"So, doctor, you mentioned you wanted a little relaxation and I understand you have a taste for scotch. Can I pour you one to get our...excursion going?" Sofia asked.

"Yes please," answered Bashir.

Sofia glided gracefully over to the glossy teakwood bar moving like a prima ballerina. She glanced over her shoulder and gave a quick smile to Bashir then bent down at the waist to get a bottle out of a lower cabinet, the outline of her thong clearly visible through her dress. She stood and turned around holding an elegantly curved clear crystal bottle of a deep rosewood colored scotch, the bottle neck slightly nestled in her cleavage.

She smiled when she spoke as her voice took on a soft, sultry, mesmerizing tone.

"Will a Macallan M Highland Single Malt do?" she asked.

It had the desired effect on Bashir as his respiration increased and his eyes fixated on her bosom, exactly where she wanted them to be.

"Yes, yes, that would be excellent, thank you!" Bashir said eagerly.

Sofia turned and got two whiskey glasses, then glanced over her shoulder with a slight smile. She saw Bashir fixated on the curves of her near perfect body as she poured two fingers worth into each. She turned and walked over to Bashir and bent over to hand him his drink. His eyes never left her cleavage.

"There you go doctor, Macallan neat, the only way a fine single malt should be enjoyed, don't you think?" Sofia asked.

"Yes, yes," Bashir said breathlessly.

They both took a long drink from their glasses. Bashir's eyes closed as the scotch whiskey burned slightly going down.

"Mmm, I get head notes of wood, spice, and smoke with a taste of dried fruit and orange zest," Sofia said in that same mesmerizing tone. "What do you think doctor, do you like it?"

She took a sip and ran her tongue along the rim of the glass as Bashir happily took another long drink of his own.

"Oh yes, this is exactly what I nee...." Bashir began before passing out and dropping his glass.

Sofia squatted down and grabbed Bashir's wrist to take his pulse. She picked up the glass then went through his pockets and removed his phone, wallet, and anything that could identify him. She strode over to the counter and dropped Bashir's things in a drawer then picked up her cell phone.

"The scientist has been neutralized, what are your orders?" Sophia asked the man.

"Execute the plan as briefed," he said. "Once you are in the gulf, send the coded message and a beacon will be activated to lead you in. Stick to protocol and I'll meet you in Bahrain upon completion of the mission."

"And the Iranian navy?" she asked.

"Our contact assures us it is all taken care of," the man replied. "Remember the challenge and reply code and everything should be fine. We've embedded a backstory in their systems just in case, so you have travel documents if needed."

"Right, I'll see you in Bahrain," answered Sofia.

Several hours later the yacht came to a stop about fifteen miles off the Iranian coast and rendezvoused with a small motorboat.

Two men boarded the yacht and were met by Sofia who was now wearing a loose, thigh length tunic, baggy cotton pants, and Muslim head scarf known as a hijab.

"The package is ready for transport. He's been sedated since we left Dubai and I administered the last dose twenty minutes ago so it should keep him out for several more hours. Do you have the destination instructions?" Sofia asked one of the men.

"Yes, and the phone so we'll take it from here," the man said.

With that the men lifted the scientist's limp body onto the waiting motorboat and sped away into the night toward the Iranian coast.

Chapter 1

The Mountain

Ebrahim Hamadani whistled as he strode past a fenced area full of spare parts and equipment with a heavy tool bucket slung over his lean but muscular five-foot-ten frame. His dark brown hair was wet with sweat despite the constant mid sixty-degree temperature of the underground facility. He was antsy with anticipation for his twenty-four hour shift to end so he could start his holiday to the coast with the woman he loved. While it was already a busy day maintaining the kaleidoscope of mismatched equipment in the facility, with the upcoming test it was sure to get busier.

The maintenance area was dimly lit and looked cold and grey under the fluorescent lighting. Buried deep inside the secret nuclear research facility, the racks of parts and equipment were its lifeblood. Purchased from rogue governments and smuggled from western nations, the black-market goods kept the facility as modern as many in the West. But it was dangerous business and came at a very high cost.

After more than thirty-five years of strict economic sanctions on the Iranian government, maintaining the facility demanded creativity, and more than a little risk. Oil they had plenty of. But without the ability to build refineries, shortages of diesel and gasoline made power and parts a major obstacle. The constant juggling of priorities and challenges in acquiring parts meant the facility operated in a constant state of chaos. The type of environment that gave Ebrahim job security and good pay.

The Iranians built the facility shortly after the revolution. Located 500 meters beneath the Zagros Mountains, it was carved out of the hard limestone of an old mine. Located next to an active gravel mining operation, any heavy equipment activity would appear normal, easily hiding its excavation and construction.

They cycled air through pipes buried into the limestone mountain using it as a giant heat sink. It cooled the air to ambient temperature well before it left the vents, hiding the thermal signature of the small underground city. And with deep shafts drilled into the bedrock to eliminate radiation leakage from their radioactive material, it was the perfect hiding place.

Ebrahim dropped his tool bag on a workbench next to Danesh Salahi, the senior maintenance technician on duty. Salahi was shorter and only five years older than Ebrahim but looked much older from the years of smoking and hard manual labor.

"Did you get that key card reader fixed in the research lab on Level 12?" asked Danesh.

"Ya, it was one of the old Chinese pieces of shit. The control board finally died so I just replaced it with one I use in my modules. We shouldn't have any more problems with it for a while," he replied.

"Well, we've got to start the test checklist in a bit," Danesh said. "You know the Commander has been nervous as hell about this guest coming in to observe so we don't want any issues today."

"Let's hope it's Allah's will that everything goes smoothly then!" Ebrahim responded with a chuckle.

"So, when are you going to marry that girlfriend of yours and make her a respectable woman?" Danesh prodded playfully.

"Come now, you know we are technically married already!" answered Ebrahim.

Danesh laughed.

"You live together under sigheh. You know that's only temporary," he needled.

"Maybe, but still within Shariah law!" Ebrahim replied smiling.

Sigheh is an obscure interpretation of the Quran popular with many young people in Iran. It's a temporary marriage contract under Islamic law that recognizes a man and woman to be married and therefore able to have sexual relationships. One of many loopholes common in Iranian life.

"Anyway, we're going on holiday for our anniversary after this shift and I intend to ask her to make it permanent. She doesn't have any family and my parents are both gone so we don't need anything elaborate, just a mosque. And I've picked out a small one on the coast if she says yes," Ebrahim said proudly.

"Good for you! Congratulations," answered Danesh slapping Ebrahim on the shoulder.

Just then the phone rang and Danesh answered.

"Maintenance, Salahi.... The master control panel you say?...But it's his day off.... Okay, okay, we'll get right on it."

Danesh hung up the phone.

"So much for everything going smoothly; the master control system failed a connectivity test with the initiator. Azad is having a fit and demands that we call in Massoud," he said.

"Such an asshole. What, we're just the dirt he scrapes off his shoe?" Ebrahim said derisively. "Unless it's one of Massoud's custom modules we can fix anything else in this place. And his never fail."

"I know, settle down. Let's start the trace in the relay room and see what we can find first," answered Danesh calmly.

As they maneuvered through the tunnels, a group of six soldiers surrounding the facility commander and another man moved quickly towards them.

"Out of the way, move!" ordered the guard in the lead.

Danesh and Ebrahim had to lean with their backs against the wall to let the group pass and heard the voice of the Commander talking to the VIP guest. Once the group passed the two technicians continued on their business.

"Who the hell was that the Commander was talking to?" asked Ebrahim.

"I don't know, but he was definitely nervous, so we better find this problem fast," answered Danesh.

It took thirty minutes to trace all the electrical connections and the two technicians were exasperated.

"Danesh, we need to call in Massoud," Ebrahim said a bit defeated. "I've narrowed it down to one of his modules that is integrating the Russian control board in the master control panel and the French capacitor bank that sends the initiator signal. I can get a positive response from each individually and all the relays before and after, so the problem has to be there."

"I'll let security know," Danesh answered.

An hour later the two technicians heard the beep of a failed door entry, then the metallic click of the magnetic lock opening as the facility's most senior technician walked through the door cursing out the faulty keypad. For a man in his mid-fifties, Massoud had broad shoulders, powerful arms, and a belly that slightly spilled over his belt. In short, he was built like a bull. The guards knew him as a jovial man carrying his heavy equipment throughout the facility. With salt and pepper hair and thick greying beard he could easily play Santa Claus in a different society. Today he was pulling a generator cart that looked positively ancient and as he opened the door Danesh and Ebrahim virtually accosted him.

"Massoud, thank God you're here. There's some kind of interruption in the wiring under the control room and Azad demanded we call you in," began Danesh.

"And we think it's in one of your interfaces, but we don't know how they work," interrupted Ebrahim anxiously. "The Commander is going crazy and threatened to have us shot if we didn't fix the electrical problem!"

"The Commander's got everyone on edge and the control engineers are even more obnoxious than usual. Sorry but we had to call," Danesh stated.

"All right, all right just calm down. The Commander isn't going to have anyone shot. We're the only ones keeping this shithole running. Now, tell me what the problem is and what you've tried already," answered Massoud calmly.

Although an old school tinkerer and fixit man, Massoud lorded over the patchwork of Russian, Chinese, Pakistani, and French equipment like serfs in his kingdom. He not only thrived in the chaos of the facility but was one of the most vital people in the organization. His tools were archaic, but he was an absolute magician with them. Somehow, he made an incompatible hodge-podge of an electrical grid compatible and kept it running.

The two technicians ran through all the issues and actions taken to narrow down the problem. Massoud listened carefully as he appeared to run the wiring in his head, tracing the thousands of miles of wires, tubes, and relays. Many of the relays and electrical interfaces he had to custom manufacture in the facility maintenance shop using scavenged parts to make the different systems compatible. His technicians never really understood what they all did, or how they worked. All they knew was his equipment never failed until today. Today of all days.

"Okay, I think I know where the problem is. I'll call the control room and tell them I'm on my way. And they better tell security this time or I'll make them sit there with their thumb up their asses," Massoud said loudly as he made his way to his office.

Massoud came out of the office with his tool belt slung around his hips. He packed up some parts in a canvas maintenance bucket, strapped it to the top of his generator on wheels, and headed out the door to the control room located deep inside the facility and one of the most secure places in Iran. Fifteen minutes later Massoud walked back into the maintenance room.

"Alright, problem is fixed," he announced.

"So, Azad is happy now?" Danesh asked.

"When I finished working on the master control panel, I bowed and told him, 'There you go Azad; your precious panel is now operational.'"

As Massoud spoke, he bowed and swept his right arm mimicking the veiled insult to the senior operations engineer as if the man were some kind of royalty.

"At which point he called me an asshole, so I laughed in his face," he said with a chuckle. "You should have seen the faces of the guards trying so hard not to laugh!"

This made Ebrahim laugh, only Massoud could get away with insulting such a senior staff person so publicly.

"You shouldn't have any more problems today," Massoud declared. "Danesh, don't forget you must check the cooling relays for the test today. Remember the protocol; the checklist says to run the checks two hours before the scheduled test so don't be late. Especially not today since the Commander has a guest.

"Those damn relays will get pretty hot," Massoud added. "You need to make sure when they need the cooling pumps, you're ready to turn them on. Oh, and I had a little trouble with the keypad at the entrance again. Once you're done helping run the tests on the relays and pumps, make sure you check that out. Alright, I'm going to watch my son's football game so no more electrical problems today!" he announced loudly.

As Massoud walked away, his laughter echoed down the tunnels as he left.

Nearly three hours later, Danesh and Ebrahim were finishing work on the cooling system. Only one pump malfunctioned but it was a relatively easy fix so fortunately didn't take too long to correct.

"If all goes according to schedule, they should be running the test in about 15 minutes. I'll handle the relays, go fix that damn entryway keypad. I get so sick of those things malfunctioning and the Commander will have a shit fit if his 'guest' is inconvenienced," directed Danesh.

"Are you sure you don't need my help down here?" asked Ebrahim.

"No, I've got this. Plus, it seems you have the magic touch with those things lately. And don't let those guards hassle you this time. I heard they pulled all the regular ones to the interior and posted a new shift on the outer perimeter. They're so paranoid about security with this guest it's crazy," ordered Danesh.

"Okay, call me if you have any other problems," answered Ebrahim.

He slung his tool bag over his shoulder and left. He made his way through the security checkpoints. He was glad the issue in the control room was resolved. He chuckled to himself at Massoud's insult to the senior engineer, they were all so pompous. Ebrahim was a hard-working man, and they never got their hands dirty. They were no better than him despite their fancy degrees.

He was happy Massoud took an interest in him and took him under his wing. He even helped Ebrahim work on his own electronic modules to fix some of the problems within the facility. As Ebrahim approached the entry checkpoint the guard stopped him.

"What are you doing up here?" the guard asked.

Ebrahim didn't recognize him, and his tone was more threatening than normal.

"I'm here to fix the keypad, I was told we've been having problems with it," replied Ebrahim.

"Alright, get to it. It took me three tries to get that piece of shit to work," growled the guard.

"Right, I'll just be over there at the access panel," replied Ebrahim as he moved to the corner just inside the security door.

He put his tools down and grabbed a custom screwdriver to remove the panel. With a few quick and skillful twists, he had the special screws removed. He snipped the security band on the latch, logged the time on his maintenance log with the identification number on the security band, then initialed the log entry. He pulled off the access panel and set it aside.

That's when he stopped and stared into the jumble of wires. There sat a custom-made module. But not one of Masoud's, one of his. It was tucked neatly into a corner of the space behind the keypad controller. Confusion was written all over Ebrahim's face.

"Something wrong over there?" asked the guard suspiciously.

"No, no, nothing wrong. Just have to trace this jumble of wiring is all," said Ebrahim as confidently as he could.

His mind was racing. Who put this here and what was its purpose? He started tracing the wires to and from the module. He didn't recognize some of them. A wire came out of the keypad into the module then back to the keypad. It looked like an electrical loop, but for what purpose, he had no idea. Another wire came from a group that was bundled with the security wires, but he had never seen this one before. Or at least he never had to fix it before.

Ebrahim heard a cell phone ringtone from inside his tool bag. It only rang once, as both he and the guard glanced at it. A few seconds later he heard a cell phone ringtone from inside the module followed by a violent shaking of the ground that knocked him and the guard over, spilling his tool bag on the ground. Smoke and dust started billowing up from the tunnels as alarms immediately sounded throughout the facility and blared overhead.

"What the hell did you do?" yelled the guard as the two men laid on the ground.

At that moment, both men saw a handgun laying on the ground with the spilled tools. The guard quickly rolled over and reached for his sidearm. As he drew, he swung around and took a hammer to his forehead thrown by Ebrahim. The blow to his head caused his shot to go wild, missing Ebrahim's head by millimeters. The guard fell backwards, drifting into unconsciousness. Ebrahim scooped up the gun and snatched the guards ID badge.

***

In the deepest part of the facility, the Commander escorted the special guest and his entourage into the master control room. The room was aligned theater style with a wall of large high-definition video monitors at the front showing camera views of the detonation chamber and data streams from all of the test sensors and equipment. A dozen technicians arrayed in three rows of computer workstations got quiet as the room was called to attention as the Commander and guest entered. The Commander escorted the man to the senior controller station in the second row just to the right of the center aisle.

"Sir, this is Azad our most senior controller, he will brief you on our progress," stated the Commander.

"Welcome sir," began Azad. "Over the past two years we have achieved a series of successful implosion tests. Today is the first test in initiating a fission reaction. It is a small-scale test, but an important one. If we initiate fission in this scaled down version, it will confirm the core design and we can move onto scaling it up."

The Commander spoke next.

"Our scientists say the math and theory shows it will initiate a small nuclear detonation and, on this scale, it would show as a small earthquake on the instruments around the world. Some may suspect, even possibly confirm a small nuclear test. But Intel says that given the number of earthquakes we've had here over the past several years, this detonation will register on the same scale as those. Would you like the honor of initiating the test?"

It was through the power of their guest's will that Iran's nuclear program had managed to come this far. A successful test would validate all the cost, in lives and treasure, it took to build it.

The Commander looked at Azad nervously and prayed that all went as planned. The video screens of the containment chamber, the scrolling lines of data that would indicate a critical reaction, and the constant hum of cooling fans couldn't break through his tension. Azad began the countdown.

"...Fourteen, thirteen, twelve, initiator switches on."

Azad initiated the final ignition sequence that would close all valves into the ignition chamber to isolate the test chamber and activate the trigger system for the implosion.

Beneath the control room, an electronic module silently autodialed a cell phone number.

"...Ten, nine, eight...," Azad counted down, "...three, two, one, zero."

As he came to zero, the guest pushed a red button on the console. In less than a blink of an eye an electrical pulse raced down wires, splitting into different directions. In one, small valves opened that should have stayed closed as the pulse continued to the test core detonating it. At the same instant, another pulse diverted to a box under the master control room detonating two-hundred kilograms of high explosives under the feet of the guest.

In a flash, the control room was vaporized along with nearly everything, and everyone in it. The test core exploded and some of that blast was diverted though a series of electrical pipes into several areas of the facility. The force of the blast spread radioactive material throughout the compromised air vent system.

As the alarms sounded throughout the facility, heavy containment doors and elevators automatically locked. People ran, desperately trying get to safety as radiation klaxons blared in areas that were no longer isolated. Overhead sprinkler systems that should have activated showers of water remained dormant.

The most secure area of the facility had become a tomb for any who still survived. But they wouldn't for long. The air was shut off and all external vents closed. No lights, no electricity, no air for the entire lower level. Completely sealed to try and contain the deadly radioactive gases. All but a few exhaust vents that is. Some evacuation vents inexplicably stayed open for several minutes and allowed contaminated smoke and gas to pour out into the Iranian sky.

Chapter 2

Wake-up Call

The pressure-controlled offices of the CIA's Southwest Asia section were eerily quiet. The purr of the air conditioning system cycling sanitized air and the blue tint of the LED lights made it feel cooler than it was. Within the shielded room, devoid of all radio or electronic signals from the outside, nearly all the workers in the section used earbuds attached to their personal iPods. It was their only escape from the drumming monotony of terrorist hunting.

Jake Thompson walked up to his cubicle next to the section's top computer expert and tossed his backpack in a corner. A tall and lanky junior analyst from a tough neighborhood in Kansas City, he was working on his Masters' thesis in International Relations at Georgetown. Ever since he threatened to kill his drunken abusive father, he had helped support his mom and four younger brothers and sisters. After joining the CIA, he lived modestly and had already put two of his siblings through college.

"Hey super snoop, I see you spent the night here again; you need to get out and have a real life," he joked.

"I have a life, it's these computers," responded Mo as she swept her hand in a broad semi-circle.

"Cyber-sex ain't real you know," laughed Jake as he plopped in his chair.

"Yah, but at least they don't cheat on me like the last loser I dated," she replied.

Dana "Mo" James was a middle-class black kid from Fresno with workaholic parents, a trait she seemed to have inherited. At twenty-seven, her round face and milk chocolate complexion held the faint telltale scars of the case of shingles she had in high school. The CIA recruited her after she eluded the FBI for nearly 3 years as a hacker, code named

"Mo." She did annoyance attacks just to embarrass the IT guys at her targets and was caught literally by accident. She was just seventeen.

She had infiltrated the Securities and Exchange Commission server when her cat jumped on her keyboard. Normally her timing was impeccable, getting in and out before anyone noticed. But the extra seconds it took to correct the code meant the IT guys noticed something. It was just enough for an FBI agent with a PhD from MIT to trace some of her code. Yet it still took six more months for him to catch her.

That's when a CIA recruiter stepped in. He offered to expunge her record and pay for college if she would work for them. Now she was the unit's best IT specialist, earning her own PhD in cyber warfare.

"By the way, *GillNet* sniffed out another plot in Germany just about to kick-off. Took some quick work but we managed to neutralize the threat," Mo responded.

"Ya, I saw on the news that the GSG kicked down the doors of several apartments in Potsdam last night. So that's the reason for another overnight stay?" asked Jake.

"Yup, they grabbed twelve of those Caliphate assholes planning a coordinated strike on the US and UK Embassies in Berlin. Caught them just after they loaded up their vans with explosives. These guys had body armor, lined the doors of the vans and two attack cars with Kevlar, had hand grenades and AK-47s with several thousand rounds. Looks like the cars would engage the Embassy guards, then the vans would plow through behind them for suicide runs on the Embassies. Would have been damned bloody," replied Mo.

"Damn, that was close," answered Jake.

"You got that right. We got live satellite video from the raid and spent several hours analyzing it," said Mo.

"Oh, so you spent the night talking with your little German boy-toy in the BfV, Her Ryker! Hattest du letzte nacht telefonsex, fräulein?" teased Jake in his best German accent.

"Du bist so ein arschloch!" Mo replied with a chuckle. "No, we definitely *were not* having phone sex last night. We were too busy taking down a terrorist cell you moron. Plus, he's probably married, in his forties, with two blond-haired, blue-eyed kids and a wife who could snap your sorry ass in half!" she said as the two friends had a good laugh to relieve the stress.

"Hey, hear anything from our little friend, *Hephaestion,* yet?" asked Jake.

"No, nothing. Last time he logged into the game was almost two weeks ago to tell *Wolfhunter* the resources had arrived. Then he went dark," Mo replied.

The section had uncovered a novel communications channel for a major terrorist network during a recent clash between Afghanistan and Pakistan. Mo's friend Karim, the section senior analyst, stumbled onto it while playing an online wargame called *Gods of Conquest*. In the game, a player named *Wolfhunter* was directing an attack when Karim realized it corresponded to one happening at the same time in real life. It turned out *Wolfhunter* was the leader of a dangerous Caliphate aligned terrorist group in Pakistan.

For the terrorist hunters, finding an enemy communications channel was like finding the holy grail. It was instrumental in preventing the Caliphate from controlling huge deposits of precious metals and gemstones that could have funded terrorist operations for generations. Mo deployed a worm program called *GillNet* that propagated through the enemy network as players messaged each other. The information it provided was invaluable as the team collected near real time intel on enemy targets and movements.

She'd mapped this branch of the Caliphate network over the past few months, but terrorist hunting was weeks of monotony interrupted by bursts of excitement and activity. Like a hunter in a deer stand waiting days to see his prey, the team had eliminated more than 100 terrorists either captured or killed. But there was one very important operation they hadn't figured out yet, and this made everyone very nervous.

"I'll tell you, ever since we intercepted that message about this potential attack in or around Shush, I haven't been able to find squat about it except that it's some kind of Iranian weapons lab," said Jake. "With the cutbacks on human intel over the years, and a lack of assets in Iran, we're virtually blind to its location."

"Well, I've got *GillNet* embedded on his computer and it alerts me every time he logs on," Mo responded. "I've traced his IP to addresses around Dezful, near Shush, but that's about it. An internet café, a coffee shop, never really in the same place but all in the surrounding area of the small city. Just some random game play and no more messages to the Caliphate leader, or anyone else in the game. He doesn't try to hide his location, but his other tradecraft is pretty good. No worries, when he does come online, I'll be able to track him pretty quick. He's not as careful as *Wolfhunter*."

Shortly after the communications method was uncovered, *GillNet* indicated a Caliphate target in Iran. The team had rumors about a facility but despite months of searching, they'd come up empty. And the Iranians were smart. They knew America relied on signals intelligence and space assets for most of their information.

They documented the inspection protocols used by America in the aftermath of Desert Storm. They analyzed American intelligence collection and the lack of information against the Iraqi regime. They had deftly placed spies in several of the region's intelligence agencies, and once the Americans "liberated" Iraq and got a Shia government installed, their assets were like kids in a candy store.

Mo rubbed her eyes and looked at the clock, a little after eight in the morning.

"Where the hell's KZ with that coffee? I've been staring at this damn computer screen for two hours and need caffeine and a good stretch."

She had just pushed away from her desk when the flash message came through her inbox. The message icon blinked red indicating an urgent incident message. Mo spun around and with a swift keystroke had the message system up and was reading the message.

"Global instruments indicate seismic activity 35.8 miles north-northwest of Dezful, Iran. Two seismic events were detected simultaneously about 11 miles apart. The larger event is located at 32°53'23"N 48°24'48"E, equivalent to a 3.4 level earthquake on the Richter scale. The second event was located at 32°47'25"N 48°15'47"E, equivalent to several hundred pounds of high explosive. Imagery shows smoke coming from suspected vents near the larger event. Satellites have detected a modest radioactive cloud moving Northeast toward Khorramabad. Winds from the Southwest at 8 miles per hour, expected fallout contamination for 20-60 miles extending from 30 miles southwest of Khorramabad, to 30 miles northeast."

Zack Gerlacher, the Southwest Asia section chief, burst out of his office at the center of the back wall of the section.

"Mo," Gerlacher called out across the room. "Are you seeing this?"

"Yes, sir," Mo answered.

"Pull up the coordinates on the big screen," ordered Gerlacher. "Jake, get on the horn to Ops and find out if we have any assets in the area. Okay Mo where is this?" Gerlacher asked as he walked up beside Mo and looked over her shoulder.

"I just pulled the imagery from NSA," answered Mo. "The larger event is 35 miles north of Dezful and 45 miles northeast of Shush. Satellites slewed to the location as soon as the event was detected and picked up smoke venting from areas along a ridge, here," she said pointing out grey-white smoke trails emanating from the side of a small mountain ridge.

"Looks like the closest major military installation located in Dezful is Vahdati Air Base, home of their 4th Fighter Wing," Mo continued. "Comments on the imagery indicate this is an active fault line with several small earthquakes over the last few years. Seems this wouldn't have caused anyone to notice if it weren't for the venting of radioactive material."

"Given the size of the tremor detected, that's most likely linked to a nuclear test chamber if the smoke is radioactive," Gerlacher said calmly. "Zoom in on the smaller event coordinates."

A nuclear event anywhere in the world was a priority issue, especially this part. Mo's fingers were flying across the keyboard of her computer. As the image moved east from the suspected test site, more smoke was noticeable coming from a smaller set of ridges.

"Black smoke, something's burning hot. Looks like more vents from an underground facility and there's a gravel road that dead ends there near the top of that hill," said Mo.

She traced a winding road that snaked its way up the ridge.

"Pull back a bit and follow that road," instructed Gerlacher.

As Mo zoomed out, a small group of buildings came into the picture along with what looked like an industrial site.

"Now that's impressive," he mumbled. "That's an active mine and gravel pit. Really great thinking if you're going to hide the construction of an underground facility with heavy equipment moving in and out. These guys were smart. Hide the building and maintenance in an active mining site and have your testing in an active earthquake zone.

"Mo, set up a video conference with Stu in Kuwait. I'll take it in my conference room," Gerlacher directed.

Mo opened an emergency channel to the station chief for Kuwait, the closest station with assets in Iran. Gerlacher moved quickly to the conference room. Without an embassy in Tehran the U.S. had to rely on allies for immediate information. The conference room was fairly small with a long eight-foot conference table in the center with an encrypted conference phone in the middle of the table. Gerlacher sat down at the head and punched the blinking button indicating the line that Mo had opened for him.

"Stu, have you seen the flash message about Dezful, Iran?" Gerlacher asked.

"Yes, we got it and plotting it out now. We have limited eyes in the area, our assets are further north with the Kurds and a couple in Tehran but haven't seen anything out of the ordinary lately. We're going through everything from the past month now to see if we missed anything," replied Stu.

"Okay, good. Contact your German and Afghan counterparts and see if we can get some help. Afghanistan's stable relations with Iran may give them an advantage for information gathering with less visibility. The German's relations are more strained since the recent sex scandal. But if we use the Germans as a decoy, maybe the Afghans can work under the radar. Given recent events along the Afghan-Pakistan border, I figure they owe us," instructed Gerlacher.

Karim Rezek came bounding into the section with a tray of coffee. As a senior analyst in his section, Karim had a reputation as one of the most accomplished analysts in the CIA. Tall and wiry with short dark hair like his Lebanese father, but jovial and outgoing like his Irish Catholic mother. Although he was raised Muslim, he went to a Catholic private school, a Catholic Jesuit university, and prayers at the mosque. It certainly made for an entertaining household, especially over holidays.

"Hey boys and girls, it's coffee time," Karim began and stopped dead. He looked at the big screen, "is that Shush?"

"Yup, close enough," replied Mo. "Now give me my coffee, quick, it's gonna be a long day."

Karim put the tray of coffee on a table, grabbed one for Mo and went to her station to look at the latest data on the terror attack.

"Here's your coffee, can't believe you can drink this mud. Okay, so what do we know?" asked Karim.

"You know me KZ, the blacker the better!" responded Mo.

KZ was an abbreviation of "The Great Kazam", a nickname she gave him as a result of his prowess at solving puzzles.

"So, there were two seismic events, several miles apart, virtually simultaneous. The geo guys are studying the signature of the larger one but it's pretty clear they tested a nuke. Not as big as the North Koreans first one though. The nuke cloud came from apparent vents near the site of the larger event and is drifting toward the northeast and populated areas. The area has had lots of earthquakes so if not for this nuke cloud, it might not have been detected for months, if ever," finished Mo.

"Well, I guess that treaty went up in smoke, just like their test. With a nuclear plume drifting toward the Iranian populated areas, it'll be a real wake-up call for everyone," stated Karim flatly.

"Ya, literally. And the Israeli's are gonna go berserk," added Mo.

"Not to mention the Saudis and virtually every Sunni government in the Middle East," answered Karim.

Gerlacher came out of the conference room next to his office and shouted across the room.

"Karim, get plugged into our ops guys in Riyadh. We need to know what the Saudis know and how they're going to respond."

"Time to get to work puzzle master," mocked Mo.

"Thanks," replied Karim sarcastically. "Hey, port everything we have for the last two months to my station and overlay the live sat feed. I need to get up to speed before calling Riyadh."

"You bet KZ. I'm still looking for something from *Hephaestion* on *GillNet*. Unfortunately, our friend has been silent," stated Mo.

"Take a look at our intercepts from when we first started tracking these guys. As I recall *Wolfhunter* sent a congratulations message in-game after the Waterloo Station attack. We should do the same here to put together a search grid on this guy for Ops," instructed Karim as he moved quickly to his desk.

Another flash message appeared on Mo's screen. She put it on the big screen.

"Satellites have detected trace radioactivity in the smoke venting from the second location at 32°47'25"N 48°15'47"E. The smoke has diminished but it has created a second radioactive cloud moving East/Northeast at 8 miles per hour."

"How the hell did they manage that? Zack, we need to talk to the Israelis right away. They're gonna get blamed for this," shouted Karim.

Gerlacher strode back onto the ops floor.

"Mo, tie into the Middle East section and let's get them talking to Mossad. We need to know what they know, and they don't like to share," he commanded.

"Zack, what are we allowed to share with them? You know they're going to ask," asked Mo.

"I'm calling the Deputy Director now to confirm that. But we need the name of who to talk to over there," he replied.

And just like that, monotony pivoted to crisis, activating intelligence assets all over the world.

***

Sitting in his fourth-floor office at CIA headquarters, Director David Anderson read through the live intelligence feed and ran his hand through his thinning grey-streaked blonde hair. He knew that some threats were more existential than others. And a nuclear capability in the hands of twisted zealots willing to kill millions in the name of their religion was definitely an existential threat.

In his world, every day meant a new crisis or threat that demanded his attention. As Director of Central Intelligence, DCIA, he was under constant pressure to protect the United States. A pressure that could crush a person physically and emotionally if they got too invested in every threat that even the rich mahogany and maple accoutrements that lined the walls and accented the furniture couldn't relieve. A lesson learned from more than thirty-five years in the agency but a stress that had taken its toll on his five-foot-seven, hundred-seventy pound body.

Anderson turned and looked out across the Potomac River through the bulletproof glass of his office. The specialized windows were comprised of two, polarized one-inch panes of laminated glass, with a narrow vacuum gap between them. The layers of fine copper mesh and polarization made it look like high-end sunglasses from the inside, but totally opaque from the outside. This made the DCIA's office impervious to external sound, visual, and electronic eavesdropping.

The warble of Anderson's secure phone broke the silence. He glanced at the caller ID as he picked up the handset.

"Hey Janelle, what's the latest?" he asked the Deputy Director for Intelligence.

"David, so you've already seen the flash reports, we've activated assets throughout the Middle East. I'm expecting to hear from our asset in Iran but nothing yet, and it could take a while as the Iranians will be on edge. Our contacts are hearing reports there's a major rescue effort going on right now and we've slewed our satellites to gather as much info as we can.

"The Iranians aren't being very discrete. Several unsecured radio calls have gone out for assistance and NSA's picked up urgent telephone calls to Tehran for medical experts. We believe we've identified the entrance to the complex from the movement of heavy equipment into the area where some of the venting was detected. Looks like construction equipment, so they might be mounting an effort to dig through rubble of some sort.

"I've called my counterpart at Mossad, he firmly denied Israel was responsible, but he seemed to know more than he let on. His voice had a bit of tension in it, though he was clearly trying to cover it up," stated the DDI.

"Well Janelle, I expect they're pretty rattled, and we already know this was a Caliphate op. Do you think Eitan's response was just surprise at the Iranian nuke test?" asked Anderson.

"David, I've known him for over 30 years. He wasn't lying, but he wasn't telling me everything either," stated Hayes. "We all knew they were working on it, but I get the distinct sense Mossad knows more about this than they are telling."

"Okay, I'll call Director Ariens. We'll have to give them something to get something though, so I'll have to think on this before I call. I'm about to head to the White House. What's the latest on the nuke cloud?" answered Anderson.

"SecDef probably knows more about this than anyone but looks like weather conditions may not be in their favor. It may be too soon to tell though, and they haven't made any announcements to their population yet. We're monitoring that as well. We've got satellites and sniffers online, so collection is maxed out. We'll have more info in about twenty to thirty minutes I expect," Hayes answered.

"Okay, contact me at the Situation Room with the updates," Anderson directed as he punched the phone dead.

Chapter 3

Fury

The explosion shook the ground in the shrouded cave that hid the secure entrance to the underground complex. The four-man security detail looked at each other and ran to the door.

"Explosion at the mine. Initiate mass recovery protocols now!" Captain Al Madani screamed into the radio to the command center a few kilometers away.

One of the guards swiped his ID badge and punched in the code to open the heavy door, but it didn't work. Just then the door opened, and someone stumbled out as they rushed into the tunnel. The guards quickly moved through the door and saw someone lying on the floor unconscious but swept past him to determine the status of their VIP guest. As they ran through the tunnels, other security teams joined them.

"Team 2, go secure the entrance. Take the portable handset and plug into the comm panel to communicate with command, our radios don't work down here. Tell them we need trucks to take survivors to the support base for interrogation. Make sure the troops responding know we're moving to the control room. Nobody leaves without being interrogated!" ordered Al Madani.

Emergency klaxons blared everywhere as the detail moved deeper into the complex. They moved swiftly and efficiently through the tunnels but were suddenly stopped by a sealed security door. The door that should have given them access to the most secure area of the facility was locked and nothing Al Madani tried would open it.

"Teams 3 and 4, start clearing each sector on this level working inside out from here. Send everyone to the cave but check them first, we need to search everybody who was down here. Move out!" ordered Al Madani as he turned back to the locked security door.

Beside the door was a panel that accessed the internal communications system. He slid his ID badge into a slot and punched in a code that gave access to the intercom system. Inside was a handset and he punched in another code to activate the intercom.

"Attention, anyone in Area 25 respond," Al Madani yelled into the handset. "Area 25, respond," he repeated after a few seconds and was met with silence.

A man answered in a raspy voice.

"This is Guard Station 24, Area 25 is gone," he said.

"Explain, what the hell do you mean gone?" demanded Al Madani.

"Sir, half my team is dead, the security door was blown off from inside the central control room. We are alive but barely. Hard to breathe through the smoke and dust," rasped the guard.

Al Madani immediately realized the control room was ground zero and the most senior personnel, including their visitor, were now dead.

"We're stuck at Door 17. Is there anyone who can open this damn thing, so we can get in there?" he asked, trying to be as calm as possible.

"Sir, the doors are automatically sealed when contamination is detected," the guard replied, coughing. "Our radiation detectors went off immediately and the system will isolate everywhere the detectors have been activated. The vents…(coughing)…the vents and HVAC systems have, have automatically shut down…and the electrical conduits are cut and isolated, sealing the entire contamination zone. (Coughing) Sir, (breathing heavily and struggling to talk) we are dead men in here (wheezing), and anyone entering will be dead as well," the guard said.

As emergency protocols were initiated throughout the facility, magnetic locks on the doors within the contaminated areas activated high strength tungsten carbide steel deadbolts. Six-inch diameter spring-loaded steel pins along the outside edges of the doors slammed into holes drilled into the bedrock preventing anyone from entering. Permanently entombing those behind them. The members of the security team gasped.

"That doesn't matter, we need to get in there and assess the damage. We need to find someone to open this damn door," ordered Al Madani.

"Sir, the maintenance technicians will have a panel in the equipment room that monitors the electrical, mechanical, and security systems. But if you are at Door 17, they are inside the contamination area," replied the guard, gasping for breathe.

"Alright, stay calm, you're doing great. Tell me what you can see," answered Al Madani to the dying man.

"Sir, (coughing) Area 25 has been…(wheezing) completely destroyed. I see, I see fires, but no fire suppression. The blast must have taken that system out. (Coughing almost uncontrollably) The smoke is filling up the tunnels fast, the fire will burn out as it consumes the oxygen. Ali…(heavy breathing) Ali, flashlights now," the guard said as his voice got raspier and his words became more labored.

"It looks like the blast was in the vicinity of the main control console, (coughing) and left about a 15-meter hole. The control room…(loud wheezing)…the control room contained most of the blast…but the heat and pressure would have vaporized anyone near it," the guard said as he fell into a coughing fit.

"You've done enough my friend," Al Madani said quietly. "Allah be praised, you and your men can rest now, your mission is done. Let us pray together and may we meet again in paradise," Al Madani said as he recited a prayer for the dying men behind the door.

After several minutes, there was no reply. Al Madani punched in the intercom code for the mechanical room…but got no reply. He tried three more guard stations inside the containment area, but no one answered. Only fifteen minutes had passed since the explosion and the battery-operated emergency lights started to flicker.

"You're kidding me. These damned safety systems are failing already?" Al Madani said in frustration.

With the power failing, the magnetic door locks would release trapping even more people inside the dying facility. He punched the code for broadcast on the intercom.

"Attention all personnel; evacuate, evacuate, evacuate. We are losing emergency power, move to the exits immediately and gather in the outer portico. Do not leave the portico. All security teams open all doors that give access to Door 17 and keep them open. I don't care what you use, just don't let them close. Once we lose power the magnetic locks will engage, and everyone inside will be trapped. Post security at every open door until power is reestablished," ordered Al Madani.

He then punched the code for the entrance. "Team 2 report," Al Madani ordered.

"Sir, personnel are already starting to get to the entrance and an emergency response team is 2 minutes out. They're bringing trucks to evacuate survivors, but the damn entrance door is stuck closed. We've tried to locate someone from maintenance to get this thing open but can't find anybody. They may be inside your position," replied the Team Leader.

"Radio command, initiate Emergency Protocol 10, we need a nuke team and bomb squad in here immediately," Al Madani instructed. "Area 25 has been destroyed by what appears to be a large bomb in the control room. All personnel inside there are dead. Radiation contamination detected inside Door 17 and containment protocols are preventing us from getting into the core of the facility. Tell them to get somebody out here with cutting tools to open that goddamn door and get us access into the core of the facility.

"We had trouble with the entrance keypad coming in, so it could have been damaged in the blast. But we're losing power to the security systems and are forced to evacuate the complex before the electricity to all the security doors are lost. So, we need generators for power. Coordinate the questioning of the staff, do not let anyone leave. Is that clear? No one!" ordered Al Madani.

"Yes, sir. Also, there's a guard here who was knocked unconscious and is just now waking up. He's not making much sense at the moment. He's mumbling something about a technician up here when the blast occurred. We've searched the entryway and found a tool bag and a cell phone on the floor by an open access panel for the electronic entry system," reported the Team Leader.

"Bag and tag it as evidence. And make sure no one touches that access panel until the electronics guys get here," Al Madani paused briefly as a memory shot through his brain.

"Son of a bitch, someone stumbled out Door 1 when we entered, we need to find out who the hell that was. Stay with the Guard and debrief him as soon as you can, but don't leave him alone," ordered Al Madani. "We have no idea who's involved in this."

"Yes, Sir," came the quick reply.

"Team 10, come in. What's your status?" radioed Al Madani.

"Team 10 reporting Sir. We're still evacuating the research sections and the lower levels are almost cleared. We've opened the door and cut power to the inner magnetic locks to activate the pins. Then we propped it open with the extended pins. Let everyone know it'll keep the doors from locking," replied the Team Leader.

That was an ingenious solution, Al Madani thought. By opening the doors and disabling the automatic magnetic locking mechanism, it would extend the steel pins outside the door frames. Once extended, the carbon steel pins would prevent the doors from closing.

"Excellent, Mohammed you're a genius!" Al Madani exclaimed. "Everyone, follow that lead and keep those doors open. Team 10, get someone into the auxiliary security control room and get the video feeds. You can access the main computer system from a terminal there. Do it now before we lose all power.

"The battery backup for the servers should hold long enough for a complete download if they haven't been damaged," he asid. "Make sure you get the entryway video first. Someone exited right after the explosion and we need to know who it was."

"Yes sir, we're on it," was the reply.

"Team 2, check the tool bag and the logbook if it's still there. Find out who was there with the guard. Then get with Team 10 to cross-reference with facility personnel," Al Madani demanded.

"Roger," was the reply.

Chapter 4

A Suspect

The mass of troops inside and outside the cave entrance to the facility were on edge and growing, filling the hot, humid air with choking dust. Trucks from the support base arrived within minutes of the explosion. Troops immediately secured the area around the entrance but were stopped from entering by the broken access panel sealing the entry door shut.

Twenty minutes after the explosion, a black BMW sedan pulled up. The mass of humanity parted like the Red Sea and snapped to attention as the tall thin man stepped out. At six feet two inches tall and 180 pounds, Colonel Jahan Mokhtari was taller than the average Iranian. His slender but powerful frame was clear under his crisp camouflaged fatigues, and his grizzled face showed decades of life at the point of the Iranian sword.

Mokhtari was an elite Quds Special Forces commander known as both brilliant and ruthless. His piercing steel blue eyes sent shivers of fear into anyone unlucky enough to fall under their gaze. Despite the short graying hair, neatly trimmed beard, and crisp clean uniform, he looked like he could kill without a second thought. Having risen in the ranks of the brutal and secretive Quds force, he clearly was a very dangerous man.

He strode into the cave to the sound of cutting torches struggling to slice through the tungsten carbide steel pins now sealing the entrance to the facility. The noise from the oxy-acetylene cutting torches sounded like a thousand hissing snakes as the blinding light of 6,000-degree flames and white-hot molten steel created a kaleidoscope of dancing shadows on the walls. The acrid smoke from the super-heated gases filled the enclosed space and hung thick in the air making the workers eyes water as others rushed to set up large exhaust fans to clear it. The lead engineer barked orders to the cutting team as Mokhtari walked up.

"Jabbar, move your torch 12 centimeters to the right. Stop floating offline dammit, there's people dying in there you jackass." the engineer bellowed.

"Sergeant Major, status," Mokhtari ordered as he walked up behind the engineer.

"Sir," the engineer replied as he snapped to attention and saluted. "The access panel has been deliberately smashed. Whoever did this either escaped or had an accomplice. We've just started cutting and we've got two teams working now so I estimate about an hour to get this door open, less if we get lucky.

"We have comms with the security team on the inside, the handset panel still works. We've plugged portable generators into the external system to keep power to the entryway, but the facility power systems are failing. If they go out, we don't have much time before things go very bad for those still inside as the air handling systems and security doors will automatically shut down."

"Let me see this smashed panel," ordered Mokhtari.

The engineer led him over to the disabled panel and handed Mokhtari a flashlight. The Colonel leaned in and looked closely at the smashed electronics. He pulled a sliver of black plastic lodged in the broken glass and inspected it. It was about an inch long, slightly rounded on one edge, with a slim line of raised texture along the other broken edge.

"Major!" Mokhtari called to his aid. "Look at this and tell me what you see."

"Looks like a piece of a gun handle sir," the Major replied.

"I agree. Bag it and get it to the lab asap. I want to know what kind of gun right away. Sergeant Major let's talk to the security team inside," ordered Mokhtari.

The Sergeant punched the code for the entryway, handed Mokhtari the handset and nodded to the Colonel.

"This is Colonel Mokhtari, what's the status in there?"

"Sir, Lieutenant Shahsani. Currently we have found a way to hold the security doors open should we lose power. We have all the levels above section 17 evacuated and all personnel are now in level 1 and 2. Captain Al Madani is at the entrance to security post 17 and can provide a full report from the affected area sir," the Lieutenant answered.

"Alright, all personnel are suspects. Do I make myself clear?" instructed Mokhtari.

"Yes sir. Be advised we have a guard who was at the entrance when the bomb went off. He says a maintenance technician was working on the door access panel and he heard two cell phone rings, then the explosion after the second. He's a bit fuzzy after that but he believes he saw a gun and a cell phone fall out of the technician's bag before he was hit and went unconscious. We have the cell phone but not the gun," the Lieutenant reported.

"Do we have a name yet?" questioned Mokhtari.

"The logbook shows a technician named Hamadani opening the access panel. That matches the name on the tool bag and we're cross-referencing with the personnel database in the auxiliary security control center," answered the Lieutenant.

"Alright, I want to know the minute you get that information, and we'll check from our side. Remember Lieutenant, no one is above suspicion. No one! Search everyone, bag and tag everything. Shoot the first person who resists, then the rest will be as compliant as little lambs," instructed Mokhtari coldly.

"Yes sir," replied the Lieutenant.

"Sergeant Major connect me to station 17," Mokhtari ordered.

The Sergeant punched in the code for door 17, the deepest in the facility that still had security.

"Captain Al Madani."

"Captain, Colonel Mokhtari. Status report."

"Sir, the explosion was centered in the main control room. We had a report from some survivors that there was a crater from an extremely powerful explosive that incinerated the control room and everyone in it. Radiation monitors detected radioactive materials and containment systems activated automatically isolating all levels below level 17. Unfortunately, all personnel in the lower levels are either dead, or dying sir.

"I initiated the evacuation and called for hazmat and engineering to get this door open so we can determine the extent of the damage," Al Madani continued. "I understand someone has smashed the entrance access panel blocking both entry and exit from the facility. The Sergeant Major assures us that the entry door will be open within the hour and we can get extraction teams down here.

"I've instructed that all personnel, including the normal security details, to be detained and questioned. Until we get access, I'm afraid there's not much more information from down here sir," finished Al Madani.

"I understand Captain. Tell me exactly what you know about the control room. Try and remember every detail," instructed Mokhtari calmly.

"Sir, the security Team Leader from station 24 said the control room was completely destroyed with the crater in the location of the main control console. I believe he said the crater size was fifteen to twenty meters wide?" Al Madani began hesitantly.

"Fifteen or twenty Captain. Details are important," urged Mokhtari.

"Fifteen as I recall sir," Al Madani replied.

"Go on," ordered Mokhtari.

"The blast blew off door 25 and the force of the blast caused severe injuries and fatalities into Section 24 as well. The Team Leader reported that their radiation badges went off almost immediately after the explosion so either something went wrong with the test, or it was a dirty bomb. Since door 17's locking pins activated, we assume radiation has contaminated everything beyond that point sir," Al Madani finished.

"Can the team leader describe the current situation?" asked Mokhtari.

"Sir, they are all dead, we lost comms with them several minutes ago. They were in bad shape but gave us everything they could," Al Madani replied sadly.

"I understand. Keep your team there and wait for the nuke teams to get to you. Send the rest of the teams to sweep the entire facility back up to the entrance. I understand you have someone in the aux command post. Have them coordinate the sweeps and try to get the video systems operational. We need a better look inside the contaminated areas," ordered Mokhtari.

"Yes Sir. It appears the duty maintenance technicians were all inside the contamination area except the one reported at the entrance during the explosion. But one of my guards used to work electronic security at the Bushehr Nuclear Plant. He just got internal comms back up and is working on video, though he could use some help. If you have a video tech out there that he can talk to it will speed up the process.

"Just a second sir. The aux command center reports the technician's name is Ebrahim Hamadani. His personnel record indicates he's an electronics technician and former EOD!" exclaimed Al Madani.

"Understood Captain," replied Mokhtari. Turning to his aide, "Major, I want the names of all personnel whether they were in this facility today or not and I want them all questioned. Send a car to Hamadani's residence and secure it. Arrest anyone who's there or nearby. Search the entire building, both inside and out. Also send out an alert to all units in the region to be on the lookout for him. Consider him armed and dangerous but take him alive! I want to know who helped him. Is that clear?" he ordered.

"Yes, Sir!" replied the Major as he quickly relayed the Colonel's instructions.

Chapter 5

Panic

E brahim had opened the entrance door with the stolen badge and stepped through as the external security ran past him. Turning, he swiped the card, closing the door, then smashed the keypad with the gun to lock it so it couldn't be opened. He jumped in the nearest truck, a pickup that had the mining company logo on it and sped off down the access road.

Ebrahim raced down the winding road away from the facility. He saw dust rising in a reddish-brown cloud ahead of him and knew that would be the responding security from the support base a few kilometers southeast of the facility. He took a quick right into a staging area full of mining trucks. Since the area was also an active gravel mining operation, it had multiple trucks moving material from the gravel pit to construction zones across the region. He slowed down and mingled with other construction vehicles. Ebrahim waited for the responders to pass, then nestled his pickup between two side-dumper trucks full of aggregate, and slowly drove away from the mountain complex.

His heart was racing as he constantly checked his mirrors to see if he was being followed. Panic and anxiety rose inside him as the emergency responders passed the small convoy of innocuous mining trucks.

"Dammit, why, why?" Ebrahim shouted as he pounded on the steering wheel.

"Stop panicking, slow down and think," he said to himself.

He took several deep breaths to calm himself and tap into his former military training to bring his heart rate down to something akin to normal. At eighteen Ebrahim entered the Army for his mandatory two-year military service. He was smart and had an aptitude for electronics, but he was a poor kid from a small village. Without family connections to get a job working with electronics, he was assigned Explosive Ordinance Disposal, or EOD.

He was trained to diffuse numerous types of military explosives, but it was the improvised explosive devices, known as IEDs, where his electronics acumen really paid dividends. IEDs were commonly used in Iraq and other hot spots in the Muslim world including the restive Kurdish areas inside Iran. The Kurds learned the craft well in their war with the Islamic Caliphate and Ebrahim quickly became one of the best EOD specialists in his unit.

"Okay, okay, so what do I know. Obviously, an explosion in the research facility. The gun, the cell phone…that call must have triggered it. But how did that equipment get there? Who was the last person to work on the panel?" he thought to himself as he wracked his mind to remember the log entries he had just seen.

He struggled to think of why someone would put a gun in his bag. And what was that cell phone. Then the realization hit him, he had left the cell phone on the ground.

"That phone. It must have been the trigger!" Ebrahim thought as his mind flashed back to IED's he'd disarmed.

"But why the hell two cell phones? Why not just call the one in the access panel?" he thought as he struggled to figure things out.

The side dumper trucks turned and headed into the small town where many of the mine workers lived. Ebrahim continued heading south and increased speed. He had about thirty minutes to his apartment and tried hard to drive normally, constantly checking for anyone following him. This was made easier since the highway was lightly travelled.

But the quiet of the road gave Ebrahim time to think as his EOD training kicked in. Every bomber had a signature, and it was his job to get in the mind of the bomber to figure out how they built the device, and how they protected it from being disabled. It was the second cell phone that garnered his attention, it was completely out of place.

"Why did that phone ring once? It wasn't mine, so someone had to put it in my bag. But it rang once, then the dialer in the module rang before the explosion," Ebrahim thought.

"Of course, it's the only thing that makes sense. I'm the perfect patsy!" Ebrahim exclaimed. "Who else but an ex-EOD to know about explosives, electronics, and how to wire them. The phone in the bag must have auto forwarded to the one in the access panel! They had to make it look like I dialed the trigger and had to have access to both. Son of a bitch!" he shouted slamming his hand on the dashboard.

"This took meticulous planning, access to the whole facility, and technical skill...it could only be one of the maintenance crew!" he thought.

A new wave of panic rippled through Ebrahim at the recognition he was in grave danger when a new fear gripped and angered him...so was his wife. While he was still frightened by the fact that the evidence would point to him, anger grew inside at the realization that one of his coworkers, who he trusted, would do such a thing. And worse, put the woman he loved in danger. His protective instincts instantly piqued, and his mind became clear and focused.

He checked his watch. Azar wouldn't be expecting him, so he prayed she'd be home. He thought about his cell phone, took it out, turned it off, took off the protective case, then threw it out the window, shattering it to pieces. He had to go dark and anything with a traceable electronic signal could be tracked.

"What day is it?" he thought. "Tuesday, that means she should be home in...15 minutes," as he checked his watch.

Ebrahim and Azar were active in the Parkour movement popular among Iranian youth. A cross between gymnastics and martial arts, Parkour includes jumping across obstacles like rooftops and martial arts fighting for exercise. Both found it exhilarating, and Azar took to it like a fish to water.

She was the best in the group, even better than Ebrahim. The group practiced every other day and today was one of them. Assuming she didn't meet friends afterward, she should just be finishing her shower when he got home, he thought.

"Please, please, please let her be home," Ebrahim said out loud.

Ebrahim's heart rate and anxiety rose as he passed the military storage depot just north of his apartment. His head was on a swivel looking for any sign of security coming after him. He was just minutes away from the apartment, located in the Koye Lour neighborhood of Andimeshk, a blue-collar suburb of Dezful,

Turning off the highway, he looped around residential streets and parked at a mosque four blocks from the apartment. He entered the mosque then quickly walked to a back entrance and left the building. He turned west and entered a small, wooded park a block away. He pulled off his jacket, donned a baseball cap with the mining company logo on it, and exited the park on the southeast corner.

The mosque had a camera for the parking lot but no others and the apartment complexes in these lower-class neighborhoods had none. With the tall park trees between Ebrahim and the mosque, his movements would be hidden. He exited the park and walked two blocks south, turned east for a block and a half and entered the apartment complex next to his. He moved down the hallway, picked up a paper bag left on the floor and stuffed his jacket into it. He stepped into the alley between the apartment buildings and tossed the bag into dumpsters shared by both complexes then entered his building next door.

Once inside, Ebrahim took the stairwell, bounding up the stairs two at a time. On the fourth floor he opened the door, just a crack, and peered down the hallway. Assured there was no one in the hallway, he swiftly entered his apartment about halfway down the hall and closed the door behind him.

"Azar, Azar are you here?" Ebrahim called out.

Azar walked out of the bedroom in a black sports bra with her iPod Classic tucked into the waistband of her black bikini panties. Her head bobbed in time with the forbidden rap music coming through her earphones as she dried her hair with a towel. She looked up and let out a startled squeal.

"Dammit Ebrahim, you scared the hell out of me!" she said as she yanked the earphones from her ears. "What are you doing home? I thought your shift didn't end until tomorrow morning."

Azar was petite yet powerful with a lithe but muscular body in a five-foot three, 110-pound frame. He was somewhat intimidated not only by her physical strength for a small woman, but her mental strength as well. He always marveled at his luck that such a strong, beautiful creature was in his life.

In his mind, she was perfection and could easily be one of those bikini models in that American sports magazine. The only flaw was the scar that ran from her right side, just below her rib cage, down toward her groin. A reminder of the auto accident that killed her family as a child, leaving her an orphan. But it gave Ebrahim great pleasure, playfully tracing its path during their intimate foreplay making Azar giggle with joy.

But now, it was a reminder of how much he loved her and the danger they were in. Ebrahim rushed over and gave her a big hug. He brushed a strand of her red streaked, dark brown hair from her face and kissed her.

"Praise Allah, I'm so glad you're all right," Ebrahim said breathlessly. "Azar, something terrible has happened and now we're both in danger. We need to pack some things and go right away."

"What the hell are you talking about? What could happen at the mine that would put us in danger? If this is some kind of joke to surprise me that we're leaving early for our anniversary trip, it's not funny," Azar replied as she pushed away from him, confusion clearly visible on her face.

"Look, we don't have much time, I can't explain everything right now, but I will, I promise. But we've got to go, right now!" urged Ebrahim in a panicked voice as he looked out the window.

She took a step back, threw her towel on the floor, and glared at him with her arms crossed. Her chocolate brown eyes focused like a dagger to his throat demanding answers.

"Go where? Ebrahim you're not making any goddamn sense. I'm not going anywhere until you tell me why," Azar said defiantly.

"Look, I don't work for a mining company, I work for the government. There's been an explosion at work and a lot of people have died. Someone went to great lengths to make it look like I did it. And to answer your question, no I didn't. But I need time to figure out who did. So, get some clothes on and let's move. I don't know when security will be looking for me," Ebrahim answered, in an urgent, and somewhat annoyed tone of voice.

"You're kidding...right?" Azar asked sarcastically.

The look on Ebrahim's face confirmed that he wasn't. Her defiance melted away into shock as the realization that they were truly in serious danger momentarily took her breath away.

"Oh my god, Ebrahim, you're not kidding! You know my company works with the government too!" Azar gasped as Ebrahim could see the wheels turning in her head.

Azar was a contract specialist for a big supply and logistics company supporting the military. The company held multiple military contracts with the airbase just south of Andimeshk, as well as the ordinance facility just north of it and was well connected. Her position allowed her to travel all over the country because she was exceptionally good at getting contracts. It didn't hurt that her stunning good looks were unmistakable even with a hijab, a head scarf required for females in public, and traditional baggy clothing to cover her feminine frame.

"Son of a bitch. Of course, they needed someone who could acquire whatever you needed. We're the perfect marks!" she said angrily as fear turned to rage.

"Oh shit, I didn't think of that! I was just hoping you loved me enough to believe me, but this is worse!" replied Ebrahim as the realization of just how deep the conspiracy might be.

Azar ran back into the bedroom followed by Ebrahim. She quickly pulled on a pair of black cargo pants, a lightweight loose-fitting thigh length cotton linen shirt, and pinned a hijab over her head. She shoved a few things into a small backpack and pulled on her running shoes as Ebrahim packed his own bag. Finally, she opened a drawer and pulled out a cell phone.

"No, don't," Ebrahim said as he grabbed her arm with the phone. "No phones. They can track us that way. We'll get a prepaid, but we need to go silent. I'll have to stop at an ATM and get money."

"This *is* a pre-paid phone. I carry it in case something happens when I'm traveling, I just never told you about it, so no one has the number. Plus, I already got some money for our trip, remember? I withdrew 250 million rial this morning. That should hold us for a bit." answered Azar as she shoved the cell phone into her back pocket then pocketed her iPod as well.

The amount was just over a month's combined wages between the young couple who were better off than nearly everyone in their neighborhood. Both had good jobs, and made good money even though as a woman, Azar was paid an average of twenty percent less than her male counterparts. By living modestly, they had accumulated a sizable nest egg, much larger than their peers.

But for their upcoming trip to the coast, they needed cash because of limitations on Iranian banking from the global sanctions. Despite the sanctions being lifted after the agreement with the Americans, the Iranian people were used to using cash for nearly everything. So, travelling with large sums of money was necessary, though dangerous, which spurred them to get into martial arts as they both loved to travel.

"Did you take that from your account or mine?" asked Ebrahim, suddenly quite concerned and glancing out the window.

"Yours of course, like we always do," answered Azar. "Shit!"

The realization hit her that she unwittingly made their situation worse if what he said about being a suspect was true.

"Police just pulled up outside, we've gotta go. Give me your personal and work cell phones and head to the roof," instructed Ebrahim urgently.

He took the cell phones to a small workbench he had in the spare bedroom. He removed the sim cards and smashed them with a hammer, then spiked the phones with a screwdriver to destroy the internal hard drives. While he knew they were innocent, every young person in Iran had something illegal on their phones. And the government would use anything, no matter how insignificant, to convict him and Azar. Then he followed her out the door and headed to the roof.

The couple ran up the stairs and were on the roof in a matter of seconds. They pulled their backpacks tight and ran full speed toward the edge of the building. Springing in one long step, they hit the ledge perfectly giving them leverage allowing their momentum to carry them across the gap to the next building. They let their legs absorb the impact on landing, did a tuck and roll back to their feet in a single motion, and kept running to the next ledge.

In less than 30 seconds they were across four buildings. They found a ladder off the roof of a corner building, slid down to the fire escape, and quickly scurried down to the street. Azar put her head down and grasped Ebrahim's hand as they walked casually down the street. Once at the mosque, they climbed into the mining truck and slowly drove away.

Chapter 6

The Situation Room

It was a hot, mid-September morning as Secretary of Defense Colt Jackson's three-car security detail moved quickly through traffic. The lights and sirens made the morning traffic part like the Red Sea. The cool air conditioning was in stark contrast to the stifling heat and humidity of DC's concrete jungle outside.

It was a welcome relief to Jackson who was confirmed just a week prior after being the second in command at the Defense Department for the past six years. But his elevation from Deputy to Secretary meant drastic alterations to his routine. Between the interruption of his workout routine, the elevated stress, and the constant meetings with all the rich food consumed at odd hours, he'd gained six pounds on an otherwise lean forty-nine-year-old, five-foot ten frame.

As the detail approached the corner of E Street and 18th NW, they radioed 30 seconds out. The lead car activated the encrypted challenge and response system as they approached the E Street Gate. The system automatically turned the stop light red at the corner of E Street and 17th, then lowered the first barrier. Once through the first barrier, the detail stopped at the second one as the cars, and identification of everyone, were checked. No one gets on the White House grounds without being thoroughly checked, not even Cabinet members.

It took 30 minutes for the Defense and Intelligence agencies to gather information for this meeting in the Situation Room below the West Wing of the White House. Jackson arrived with the DCIA and the Director of National Intelligence, DNI, close behind.

"Hello David, Jack, so much for having time to settle into the new job huh?" stated Jackson solemnly.

"Hi Colt, ah I mean Mr. Secretary. Sorry it's going to take me a while to get used to that I guess. But yes, these days it's a bit of trial by fire," answered Anderson.

"Hey Colt. And you can forget that Mr. Secretary BS from me, we've known each other too damn long and I'm too old to change," grunted DNI Jack O'Connor with a chuckle.

At six-foot-one O'Connor was a rotund man who enjoyed the fine dining establishments of DC more than he should. Sixty-six years old and more than forty years of government service at the Oak Ridge National Lab in Tennessee, the years of bad eating habits, long hours, and sitting at a desk had taken its toll.

"Don't forget, you used to work for me at Oak Ridge," O'Connor continued. "Besides, there's no one I'd trust more than the guy who literally wrote the book on detection and inspection protocols. There's a special place in history for the only leader of an international nuclear inspection team who had a bounty on his head!"

O'Connor slapped Jackson on the back. A former Nuclear Engineer on an Ohio class missile submarine, Jackson got his PhD in nuclear engineering after he left the Navy and worked at Oak Ridge specializing in nuclear weapons design. After Desert Storm, he became one of the most feared and reviled inspectors in all of Iraq.

"Well, I was hoping to have a breather to get my bearings after the Afghanistan-Pakistan dustup," replied Jackson. "But it seems Iran and the Caliphate have other plans."

"Don't worry my friend, you had a good teacher in Madeline Coltrain. Plus, this is in your wheelhouse, not hers. If anyone can give us guidance on a nuclear event in the world it's you," answered Anderson.

The threat from North Korea and Iran as well as the recent restart of nuclear development by China and Russia meant a new weapons race. If someone tried to hide a covert weapons program, Jackson would know how they were doing it. It was the reason former Secretary of Defense Coltrain insisted on Jackson as her Deputy. To President Saldana, it was a harmless demand. Little did Saldana know how important her insistence would become, until today.

Jackson settled into his chair at the head of the conference table as the new Secretary of State entered.

"Good morning, Adam," said Jackson.

"There's not a goddamned thing good about it," grumbled Secretary Griffin.

The seventy-six-year-old Griffin shuffled to the head of the table and plopped down into the chair across from Jackson. Once a tall man, Griffin's body was hunched over as rheumatoid arthritis attacked too many joints that left them inflamed and painful.

A retired UN Ambassador, he was called out of retirement to serve the remaining year and a half of the President's term after the previous Secretary of State, Jonathan Massey, resigned in disgrace.

"This just blew the President's Middle East policies all to hell," Griffin grunted in disgust. "Well, hopefully we can work together better than our predecessors Colt. The President's going to need our best advice on this. The Saudis, Israelis, Egyptians, hell the whole damn Arab world is having a shit-fit over this, demanding answers we don't have."

"I couldn't agree more Adam," replied Jackson as the room was brought to attention for the President.

The President strode to the head of the U-shaped table. Though moderately tall, his once dark brown hair had turned almost completely white and the dark, wrinkled lines in his olive toned face bore the trademarks of a man exhausted from the stress and weight of the past six years.

"Okay everyone, take your seats. David, bring me up to speed on the latest," ordered Saldana.

Anderson stood as satellite images were brought up on the giant video screens of the Situation Room and proceeded to brief the national security team on the nuclear event. The President visibly blanched. The controversial agreement with Iran was pushed through during the lame duck session after the party lost control of the Senate in the previous election. The former Secretary of State and party leaders loyal to Saldana virtually twisted the arms off Senators who balked at the deal. The President insisted Iran wouldn't be able to get a nuclear weapon for at least ten years. But with this intel, it had barely been ten months.

"The fallout cloud is moving Northeast toward Khorramabad, population approximately three hundred and thirty thousand. While the radiation is not that large, civilian casualties are expected. Estimates range from five hundred to three thousand depending on Iran's response," continued Anderson eliciting gasps from some in the room.

"How...why the hell didn't we know about this site?" Saldana stuttered.

"Sir, we have limited human intelligence assets in Iran. Finding a facility like this requires a bit of luck using electronic means. We must find the construction and support vehicles that indicate a detonation chamber is being constructed. Plus, we need information about the electronic systems required to conduct the research. But tracking where those systems are installed is near impossible once they are in country," answered Anderson.

"Sir," interjected Jackson as he pointed to an area along the mountains north of Dezful. "The research facility appears to be under this mountain range, here. Since this is an active mining operation, the presence of heavy equipment wouldn't set off alarms with our satellite imagery.

"The Iranians likely dug access tunnels to hide their movements and preparations. Given the size of the test, the tunnels would be very small and then filled in to seal them, easily hidden. I expect this test was to verify the design of the core to initiate fission; this is one of the hardest parts of the device. Once they have the core design, it's a matter of scaling it. That's the next huge hurdle for them," Jackson finished.

"Colt, you're the nuke expert, what are we looking at here?" asked the President as the political pecking order was clear.

"Sir, radioactive isotopes are like fingerprints, every processing facility will have methods that give their processed uranium a signature composition. The isotope expelled is enriched uranium the Iranians processed in the Qom enrichment facility prior to the deal. The radioactive gas is coming from vents positioned near the test chamber and the facility. Each section of the facility will have systems to automatically close those vents when radioactive gas is detected. There was an obvious failure of these systems. Whether accidental or deliberate is impossible to tell from what we know. But given the fact we have 95% confidence this was a pre-planned attack; my money is on deliberate.

"As for the fallout, the Iranians weren't so lucky. The weather patterns indicate a low inversion layer with low wind velocity. That means the air is stable and will allow for less dispersion of the radioactive cloud. Think of this pattern like putting a lid on a bottle and holding the smoke lower to the ground and moving slower allowing more fallout to return to earth. This is not good news for the cities in the smoke clouds' path as it will be more concentrated low to the ground. The good news is it won't drift as far, limiting the risk.

"Khorramabad is most at risk, especially to the elderly and children. There could be some lower-level radiation poisoning but limited. I would expect the Iranian defense forces to order people indoors to protect them from fallout. But it will be hard to hide the fact that the military is wearing anti-radiation suits.

"If it were me, I'd call it an Israeli attack against a civilian nuclear power plant. That way the Iranians might scare enough people to stay inside. They've run these kinds of drills before. Given their consistent rhetoric about the Israeli threat, and Israel's strike on a Syrian reactor in 2007, it's a plausible scenario for the population to believe. If they're successful in keeping people under cover, maybe a few casualties. If not, it could create a cascade effect of several thousand," stated Jackson matter-of-factly.

"So how do we know it was a terrorist attack at the same time?" asked Saldana.

DCIA Anderson answered. "Sir, if you remember during the events in Afghanistan, our analysts found a communications channel that Caliphate operatives used to coordinate ops. One of the messages intercepted from the leader in Pakistan indicated a target in the area of Shush Iran, located just 45 miles southwest of the facility. We believe the ancient city described in the message was this coded location. Despite searching for several months, we were unable to identify it until today."

"You mean we knew this was going to happen? Why the hell wasn't I told?" asked Saldana indignantly.

"Sir, we get hundreds of leads every day. Some lead to something, but most are nothing," replied Anderson.

Saldana wasn't happy.

"Goddammit, doesn't anyone know that the root of 'informed' is information? How the hell am I supposed to make informed decisions if I don't have all the facts?" Saldana said angrily.

The President's anger wasn't about the information. It was obvious he was more upset that the signature accomplishment of his second term literally just blew up in his face.

"Sir, our job is to bring you information that you can act on. Until today, there was nothing to present as we had neither confirmation nor timing of the attack. Look how much effort went into getting the intelligence you required for decisions about Afghanistan and the Valley of Stars. There was much less intel about this attack," began Anderson in a veiled critique of the President's hesitant decision making.

"Given the apparent capitulation on nuclear weapons development in the recent agreement, we had no indication this was a nuke facility. All our intel, as little as there was, indicated a conventional weapons facility. The bombing of which would have been problematic in the delicate balance of Mid-East relations but not catastrophic. This is a game changer, sir," Anderson finished.

Since the losses in the Afghan incident, Saldana wasn't just a lame duck President, he was severely wounded. This might cripple his party for years to come.

"Sir, the problem we face is that this development will launch a full-scale arms race in the Middle East. The Saudis and their Sunni allies are already waging a proxy war with Iran in Syria and Yemen, and this could erupt into a shooting one between them.

A complicated mess just got worse as Arab countries, who generally don't like each other, find themselves aligned with Israel against a common foe. The threat of war makes strange bedfellows," added Jackson.

Saldana turned to the Secretary of State.

"Jesus Christ...what's your take Adam?"

"Sir, Colt's right. We were already seeing relations thaw between the Saudis and Israelis before the attack due to their mutual hatred of the Ayatollahs. But this is more than just a power play in the Middle East, it's a rupture in the tenuous fabric of Islam. What started in Iraq in 2001 has ratcheted up dramatically since our withdrawal from there in your first term," began Griffin, who unintentionally threw the President under the bus.

"We all know the history in the fourteen hundred plus years of conflict between the Sunni and Shiite sects of Islam, so this is an extension of that conflict," Griffin continued. "But what complicates this is the infighting between the Sunni sects largely along tribal lines. Since the Shiite takeover of Iraq, and the Iranian influence in Syria and Lebanon, the Sunni sects have fought over who should be in charge. So, it may come down to who has the most money and influence. But the fear is that whoever's the most aggressive, just might win out in this Sunni struggle. And that may not be our allies."

"So, what's our response?" asked Saldana.

Everyone looked at Jackson.

"Sir, the first thing we need to do is find out the extent of the damage," he began. "To do this we'll have to work with our most trusted allies, and some we don't trust as much. We already know from satellite and geologic data what happened at this specific site, but we need eyes on the ground to evaluate the overall threat about how bad it is. How far along are they, who died in the attack, what's their backup capability, other nuke sites we don't know about, etcetera?

"Iran's next moves will be critical. We know the attack was carried out by the Caliphate, but they may not. I doubt they'll be quiet about who they think did this and the natural suspects are Israel and Saudi Arabia. The threat of direct retaliation is very real, so we need to evaluate military options immediately," Jackson said like the scholarly professor he once was.

"Lastly, Sir, and this will be the most difficult. What, if anything, do we share with the Iranians? Do we tell them that the Caliphate was responsible? They will want proof that would be very dangerous to give them. Plus, why would they trust us anyway? These are the questions that others in this room need to give advice on, not me," Jackson said turning to look at the two intelligence directors. "Sorry David and Jack, that's your call, but my vote would be no."

"As usual Mr. Secretary, your analysis is right on target," Anderson replied. "Mr. President, we've already started reaching out to our contacts around the world to coordinate information. I agree with Secretary Jackson about needing more human intelligence. But if we're putting boots on the ground, you'll have to authorize it.

"As for what intel to share with Iran, Jack and I will look at this issue in coordination with State and Defense and give our recommendation. But we should coordinate a statement to the press on this. We want to be out front and not wait for the rest of the world's leaders to comment before we do.

"I suggest we make a public announcement that we've detected a large explosion at an industrial area in Iran," Anderson suggested. "And we offer our assistance to them in the spirit of the recent agreement our countries just signed. This will serve two purposes. First it prevents them from being too aggressive in their immediate response by getting it into the public domain, maybe before they can block social media. Secondly, it gives us a little extra time to react. Not only to gather more information but to position our assets."

Jackson spoke next.

"Sir, I suggest Adam immediately contact their Foreign Minister and tell him in no uncertain terms that we know what they were doing. They've violated the terms of their agreement but in the spirit of trying to foster peace in the region, we'll wait until more information is collected before we act. Ask for their cooperation, though they will reject it. I'm already scheduled to meet with the Congressional leaders and will impress upon them this is all classified. We can't have them running to their microphones, though the opposition will revel in this development. We can reconvene this afternoon, sir."

Saldana looked down at the table for a moment in thought.

"I agree. Alright everyone, we have a lot of work to do to contain this. Shannon, you and Derek meet me in the Oval Office to formulate our press strategy," he ordered his Press Secretary and Chief of Staff. "Reconvene at 4:30 this afternoon before the evening news broadcasts. We all may have some fires to put out before the real story breaks."

Chapter 7

Calculated Risk

Ebrahim slowly pulled away from the mosque.

"Turn North, head to the munitions depot," instructed Azar.

"What? Are you crazy? We can't go to a military facility. They're probably looking for me right now," he replied panic stricken.

"Maybe so, but we need supplies, more than just these clothes and that gun you have under your shirt," she responded.

Ebrahim turned to her in surprise.

"How did you know I have a gun?" he asked.

"We live together. I noticed it when we were packing but didn't say anything because we had to move fast. Plus, I work with guns all the time and figured you'd tell me about it in due time. But right now, we need supplies before they get organized," she replied calmly.

"But what if they put out an alert?" Ebrahim asked.

"It's a calculated risk and since the explosion was near the mine I can use that. We're in a mining company truck, you've got a mining company ID, and you're dressed in mining company clothes. My company has a giant warehouse at the depot and has everything from clothing to explosives. Exactly the things they would need for a mine collapse," she said calmly but forcefully.

Ebrahim was caught off guard by Azar's commanding tone and made a feeble attempt at protest.

"Azar, it's just too much of a risk. I couldn't live with myself if anything happened to you," he insisted.

She turned to him with a bit of fire in her eyes.

"You're in my world now and you have to trust me as I trust you! I know virtually all the guards and it'll take time for the authorities to put the pieces together about us. So, just keep your mouth shut and follow my lead," she instructed.

Ebrahim was a little shocked by Azar's forcefulness, but thought her description of the situation was logical so followed Azar's instructions. Her inner strength is what attracted him to her. Although he knew she secretly participated in some recent protests, seeing that strength in action now both impressed and strangely bothered him. Ten minutes later they turned onto the access road to the munitions facility.

Ebrahim slowly approached the security gate as two guards came out of the guard shack and held up a hand for him to stop. His fear and anxiety threatened to burst into the open as he struggled to control his breathing. The guards came up on both sides of the truck as Ebrahim and Azar rolled down their respective windows.

"Hey Nasir, how's your day going?" Azar asked the guard.

"Hello Azar. What are you doing here? I don't have you on the list for entry today," the guard asked.

"Our company does business with the mining company up north and seems they had a cave-in at the mine and need supplies quick. They called me on my day off and said to get my ass over here to pick up supplies immediately. They sent this truck and a list of stuff they need," Azar replied in a slightly annoyed voice.

The guard nodded every so slightly to his partner at Ebrahim's door.

"Must be pretty bad if they called you in. Did they tell you what happened?" asked the guard.

"Hell no, they don't tell me shit, I'm just the mule! But, considering the list of stuff they want so urgently, it must be really bad," exclaimed Azar.

"Give me a minute to call this in then," the guard answered.

"Really?" asked Azar annoyed. "How many times have I been through here the past year, 200? Look, you can call it in, then your commander will call the Colonel, who'll call the base commander, who'll call the company, who'll call General Kamaliazad. But go ahead. It won't be my ass in front of a firing squad because it took so long to get these supplies up to the mine," she said with a wave of her hand.

Azar sat back, folded her arms, and looked straight ahead with a combination scowl and smirk, what western girls would call her "resting bitch face."

The guard paused for a moment. "Okay, give me your IDs."

Azar handed him her company ID while Ebrahim handed over his mining company ID. The local military and law enforcement officials didn't know the facility existed, so the cards maintained the cover story for those who worked there.

"Sorry Azar, you're cleared to go," the guard said handing back their IDs.

"Thanks Nasir. No worries," Azar replied.

"Hey, are you doing anything tonight? I hear there's an underground party at the hydroelectric plant on the river. Should be some pretty good forbidden dancing going on," the guard said with a wry smile.

"Nasir, you know I have a husband, right?" Azar replied with a wink and smile. "Plus, it's not fair to tempt Jabril here. What would his wife say? Unless you're both going too!" she added chuckling.

The second guard looked down at the ground.

"Aha! You are going! Well save some energy for when you get home Jabril. You know what happens when us women start that forbidden dancing! Nasir, text me the address and maybe we'll meet you there."

The guard opened the gate and smiled at Azar. She smiled and waved as the truck slowly pulled through. In the corner of the guard shack the combination laser fax/printer quietly whirred to life. It was a cheap Chinese knock-off of a popular western printer, but the paper catch tray was broken. The alert, with a picture of a man printed on it, fluttered to the floor in a graceful one and half flip. It landed face down and silently slid under the bottom shelf below the counter.

"Okay, turn right at the next road," Azar said becoming very serious.

"Are you always that friendly with men?" asked Ebrahim, suddenly jealous despite his fear.

"Being friendly makes me good at my job. I put these men at ease using whatever means Allah has blessed me with. But my heart belongs only to you, otherwise I wouldn't be here right now! If they let their guard down because they think I'm pretty, or available, or just someone they can talk to who won't judge them for being normal men, then so be it. I don't care if it means a better deal, more access, or more successful. And it damn well helped get us in here without being shot!" Azar said angrily.

"I'm sorry, I...I'm," Ebrahim stuttered.

"Look, it's okay, we're both on edge. Seems neither of us really knows what the other does. I love you, Ebrahim. We're in this together. Take the next right, and park in front of that building with my company logo on it," she said.

Ebrahim parked the truck next to the front door of the hulking warehouse surrounded by massive concrete bunkers. As the setting sun moved across the base, the bunkers lining the road cast shadows like the teeth of a gear sprocket. Ebrahim was sweating, and it wasn't just from the heat.

"We need to move fast. There's no telling how much time we have," Azar said urgently.

She glided over to a keypad next to a large door and swiped her badge then keyed in a numeric code to unlock and open the door. As the overhead door rose enough for her to walk under it, Azar waved for Ebrahim to follow her. Once inside, Ebrahim briefly stood in awe at the racks of equipment in the building.

"Food is the third aisle to the left. Here's a couple bags, grab whatever you can carry. There's ration packages and some buckets of freeze-dried food. Everything is pre-cooked so fill up the bag. Just a few inventions by the American doomsday preppers that others have copied," Azar said as she threw him a couple duffle bags then quickly moved to the aisles on the right.

Ebrahim looked at the cases of the prepared food. Containers smaller than a 3-gallon bucket held enough food for one person for a month. And a box of packets could feed a family of four for a month. He grabbed two of the boxes and stuffed them into a duffle bag. In addition, he grabbed packets of pre-made meals similar to the American meal-ready-to-eat. These contained high protein, high calorie foods to support troops in the field that he recognized from his time in the Army.

Next, he saw pouches of water and things that looked like small backpacks that were knock-offs of the hydration packs used by hikers and climbers. These carried water with a hose that allowed the wearer to drink while moving. Finally, he grabbed two field packs that they could use to carry equipment should they need to be on foot for any amount of time. After Ebrahim had filled the two duffle bags, he took them to the truck. If they had to survive in the field for any length of time, they had food and water to last a long time.

As he threw them in the back of the truck, he noticed two boxes of HMX military grade explosives. A chill ran down his spine and he froze for just a minute.

"What's wrong?" asked Azar as she threw a bag of tarps and rope into the truck.

"Why do we have HMX in the truck?" Ebrahim asked.

HMX is a highly stable military grade explosive used in weapons and missiles. More powerful than the RDX plastic explosive more commonly used by ground troops, it was incredibly deadly. This stuff could slice through many layers of solid steel like a knife through warm butter.

"Because we don't know what we'll be up against, and this is stuff they would need for a mine collapse. That's our cover story, remember? So, I figure we have five minutes, we need to get some more stuff and I can't carry it myself," replied Azar.

As he followed her back into the storage facility, she walked over to some boxes.

"Give me your gun," she demanded.

"Why?" asked Ebrahim.

"Because we need to switch it for something that I have ammo for. Here, take this PC-9. You should be pretty familiar with this one as I'm guessing you carried one in the Army," she said.

She handed him the nine-millimeter semi-automatic pistol used by the Iranian military. As Azar took the other gun from Ebrahim, she looked at it, then back at Ebrahim.

"Ebrahim, do you know what this is?" she asked as he shook his head no. "It's a Jericho 941. This is an Israeli gun, where the hell did you get this?" Azar asked surprised.

"It fell out of my tool bag during the explosion. I've never seen it before, but I grabbed it when I escaped! How do you know it's Israeli?" he asked sheepishly.

"Because I sell weapons to the goddamned military and need to know what's out there. We need to get rid of this," as she looked around the warehouse.

"Here, take two crates of 9-millimeter ammunition, there's a cart by the door. And this tent. I'll get rid of the gun and get us some more firepower," Azar called as she took off running toward the back of the storage facility.

Ebrahim loaded up the cart with the ammo, tent, and camouflage netting. As he was about to leave, he stopped, turned and grabbed some boxes of grenades and Primacord, a rope type explosive. Then quickly moved to the truck. He ran back in, grabbed some uniforms and boots. He looked for the smallest ones he could find that he thought would fit Azar and went back to the truck.

Azar came rushing out to the truck with four Heckler-Koch MP-5 nine-millimeter automatic submachine guns slung over her shoulder and two more duffle bags of gear.

"What's in the bags?" asked Ebrahim.

"Encrypted radio's, NVGs, binoculars, and a few odds and ends," Azar replied.

"Okay we need to get out of here," he said.

"When we exit the base, turn North," she instructed. "It's what the guards will expect based on our cover story and I want to get moving. We've already stayed longer than we should have. After that, loop Northwest. I'll explain on the way."

"But I want some answers and need to talk with my boss. So, we need to go into Dezful to his apartment first," Ebrahim answered.

"Ebrahim, that's a huge risk, do we really need to go there?" Azar asked nervously.

"I have to," he answered sternly, in a way that made it clear there would be no negotiation.

"Let's get the hell out of here, we can figure it out once we're on the road," she answered.

Azar stacked the boxes of HMX near the tailgate of the pickup and quickly covered the gear with a tarp. The two jumped in the truck and headed back to the gate. Ebrahim labored to control his hands as adrenaline flooded his system and his heart nearly beat out of his chest. As they approached the gate, the guards stopped them again.

"So, did you get everything on your list?" asked the guard.

"Yes, I did, Nasir, thanks," Azar replied.

As the second guard walked around the back of the truck Ebrahim reflexively moved his right hand off the steering wheel and rested it on his thigh to be closer to the gun he stuck behind his back. He watched the guard lift up the corner of tarp covering their gear.

"Hey Jabril, be careful back there. That's boxes of high explosives you're playing with. I wouldn't want you to lose anything important before tonight!" Azar shouted, chuckling.

The soldier dropped the tarp and took a few steps backwards as his partner had another laugh at his expense.

"Better get this up to the mine. Don't you need an escort for this stuff?" asked the guard.

"No. Besides us, you're the only other ones who know we're carrying it and the company felt it best not to advertise the movement in the open. Unless Jabril wants to come with us, but then he'd leave his wife all alone tonight and you never know what might happen then!" replied Azar, laughing again.

"Alright, go ahead you two. See you at the party tonight, Azar," shouted Nasir as the truck pulled away.

They turned north as Azar waved goodbye out the window.

Chapter 8

Quick Study

Jackson stepped out of the White House and saw his Chief of Staff, Victor Durchenko, standing next to the open car door.

Durchenko was a political juggernaut, feared by political allies and enemies alike. His nickname within the Pentagon was "The Czar." Strict, demanding, connected, and ruthless, as a political operative he had few equals. And he looked like a mob boss with his salt and pepper hair always slicked back as the years of heavy smoking gave his face an ashen, almost leathery look. Combined with his tall, lanky, yet muscular frame, and constantly bloodshot dark brown eyes, he looked every bit the political angel of death.

"Mr. Secretary, the Congressional leaders of both Houses are ready for us in the Speakers' offices. Do you have everything you need for your briefing?" asked Durchenko.

"Yes. DCIA will meet us there," Jackson said as he climbed into the back seat of the armored car.

Durchenko closed the door, moved quickly around the car, and slid in next to Jackson. The meeting was scheduled prior to the events of the day, but the potential nuclear disaster took priority over everything else.

"Are you ready for this?" asked Durchenko.

"I don't know Victor. I'm just a science geek, I don't have the political chops of Madeline," opined Jackson.

"Just take a deep breath Mr. Secretary, I've got your back. Stick to the points we talked about back at the office and leave the political hacks to me," replied Durchenko.

Jackson was a technocrat not a politician. When Coltrain resigned to run for Governor of Pennsylvania, she left behind Durchenko. Known as her consigliere by her political enemies, the message was clear, whatever the Czar did carried the political might of the queen of the party, Madeline Coltrain. And since the opposition-controlled Senate would oppose anyone deemed loyal to Saldana, Coltrain made a deal with the Majority Leader for Jackson's swift confirmation.

"If politics were only more like physics, I'd feel a whole lot better," answered Jackson.

"In many ways it is Mr. Secretary," laughed Durchenko. "Consider what happened between Secretary Coltrain and that asshole Massey. Massey was weakened after the total screw-up in Tripoli, then Madeline crushed him after the disaster in Afghanistan. A clear demonstration of when two particles collide, one is destroyed and the other becomes something better and brighter."

Now it was Jackson's turn to laugh, "I'd never thought of it that way. I guess you're right. Thanks Victor, I'll have to keep that in mind."

The drive to the Capital took just a few minutes. Durchenko dutifully followed Jackson and the DCIA into the Speakers' conference room and positioned himself along the wall behind Jackson.

"Ladies and gentlemen," began Jackson, "what you are about to hear is classified Top Secret and cannot leave this room. A couple hours ago, Iran conducted a successful test of a small nuclear warhead in violation of the recent agreement. DCIA Anderson will take you through all of the information we know right now, and we'll answer questions at the end. David?"

The statement elicited several members to curse under their breath as some minority party leaders shifted uneasily in their chairs. The Czar's eyes were like hammers on the heads of those who supported the shattered agreement so aggressively. The administration's assurances about the Iranian program were exposed as wishful thinking at best, and outright lies at its worst. As Anderson finished his briefing there were gasps at the extent of the damage.

"Thank you, Director Anderson," Jackson continued. "As many of you know, Secretary Coltrain and I objected to the analysis of the Iranian's progress. I testified that the intel could be interpreted more than one way. Despite the differences of opinion, the President, Secretary Massey, and some of you in this room, insisted on moving forward.

"But what is done, is done. We must respond to events on the ground as they are, not as we wish they were," Jackson said looking straight at the Senate Minority Leader. "We're pushing intelligence assets for more information and putting together options for the President. We are aggressively coordinating with our allies, therefore, we must insist you refrain from discussing this information until we are ready. Given that military options are likely I convinced the President it required full disclosure to Congress. You now have all the information we have. I open the floor to questions," finished Jackson.

Here was Jackson telling Congress that the worst-case scenario the administration labeled extremist, was reality. Those who argued for the administration to be cautious were marginalized and some retaliated against. Now, with the presence of the Czar, several people knew their heads would be on spikes in front of the caucus. They placed their bets on Saldana and lost. Especially the Senate Minority leader, Senator Goodnow, who led that putsch. After a short question and answer period, the group adjourned.

"Mister Secretary, I'll meet you after my meeting with Senator Goodnow," stated Durchenko. "Remember, just stick to what we discussed, and everything will be fine. Good luck."

"Thanks, I think I'm going to need it," answered Jackson.

Secretary Jackson was escorted into the Senate Majority Leader's inner office. A stunning mahogany desk sat in front of towering cathedral windows that framed the credenza behind it with a spectacular view of the Washington Monument. On one side was a floor to ceiling wall of bookcases surrounding a white marble fireplace, the same marble used in the original Capitol building. Several plush leather chairs faced the fireplace and had a small table between them with a bottle of a famous Tennessee whiskey and two glasses.

The Majority Leader shook Jackson's hand and directed him to sit. Senator Jonathan P. Stewart, the senior Senator from Tennessee, was a descendant of the state's highest-ranking Confederate general, Lieutenant General A.P. Stewart. A tall, slender 66-year-old man, he 'd been a Senator for nearly 30 years. Despite his age, Stewart had a powerful grip and a booming baritone voice that could carry in the Senate chambers without a microphone. He was a political powerhouse who outmaneuvered the President many times.

The meeting between Stewart and Coltrain a few short months ago was a meeting of political titans. Politics was Madeline's specialty, not Jackson's, so he was more than a little intimidated.

"So, Colt, how are you settling in? Seems the Iranians don't want you to get too comfortable," Stewart said.

"I'd have to agree with you Senator. Although we had some intel that identified this as a target for the Caliphate, we had no idea where the facility was or what it did. Needless to say, it's made everyone in the area very nervous and we need to get people on the ground to get more info," answered Jackson.

"Colt, please call me J.P. in here. I think we're of the same mind and you have nothing to worry about from the Senate. I promised Madeline, I'd give you all the support you needed as long as you kept me in the loop. I'd like to put one of my people from the Intelligence Committee staff in the Joint Intel Center to liaison for us," pronounced Stewart. "Madeline thought it would shorten the communication links so we can coordinate faster. You will have full veto authority over what they have access to, and they can advise the best way to get the support you need from us."

"Senator, I..." began Jackson when Stewart interrupted him.

"J.P., Colt, please," commanded Stewart with a smile.

"Sorry, J.P., this will take a bit of getting used to. Yes, I can make that work. But I prefer we speak directly about any important issues. No sense using intermediaries until this situation is resolved. I suspect the first order of business will be emergency funding through the black accounts to get people in-country as quickly as we can," replied Jackson.

Senator Stewart smiled and poured each a drink, handing a glass to Jackson.

"Well, Colt, we're in total agreement. Cheers," Stewart said

Colt hesitantly raised his glass in the impromptu toast.

"I'm told the Minority Leader will be more amenable to working together after today," Stewart said with a chuckle. "I was surprised to hear he is choosing to retire rather than run for reelection, though I'm certain he's not happy about it. Victor can be quite persuasive I'm told. Anyway, don't worry, I'll get the ball rolling with the Speaker for the funding. Just let me know how much you need, and we'll push it through."

"Well J.P., politics isn't my forte so I let Madeline and Victor handle that. As for the funding, I'll be meeting with CIA shortly and we'll put together a plan asap. Thank you for your cooperation," Jackson said.

"Colt, don't sell yourself short, you carry a great deal of respect from both sides of the aisle. So, we work together on what's important to both of us and be the leaders our people demand. Besides, you've already passed your first test, you're here against the wishes of the President. Knowing who holds the power in your party is the most important step to learn for self-preservation in politics my friend. Just ask that flaming asshole Massey and the soon to be former Minority Leader. We'll have plenty of things to fight about when this mess is resolved," he finished.

The neutering of President Saldana was complete, and Jackson needed to tread carefully.

"Thank you, J.P., I'll keep that in mind," replied Jackson as the Majority Leader escorted him to the door.

Jackson stopped just short and turned to Stewart.

"Remind me not to get on the bad side of you or Madeline, seems pretty dangerous to one's career," Jackson said with a slight smile to hide his discomfort.

"Then one last piece of political advice as a friend before you walk through that door and we become adversaries again," began Stewart. "Never tie yourself too tightly to one person, because when they sink, they'll take you with them. Even Madeline. That's a lesson you have to teach yourself I'm afraid, how to be your own person while using the power of others. Madeline is an expert at it, but even experts can falter."

And with that the Majority Leader opened his office door, "Thank you for meeting with me today Mr. Secretary. I appreciate your candor despite our differences and hope we can keep the lines of communication open between my office and yours," Stewart pronounced.

"Thank you, Senator, I'm sorry that I couldn't provide more information. I hope my offer to allow a member of the Intelligence Committee staff to liaison with the Joint Intel Center will demonstrate how committed we are to working with Congress," Jackson pronounced.

Senator Stewart smiled and slapped Jackson on the back like a proud father as he left the Majority Leader's offices with Durchenko.

Chapter 9

Conspiracy Theory

M okhtari absorbed information without emotion as he waited for the entryway to be opened. With two teams cutting the locking pins on the heavy steel door, work progressed faster than estimated. Less than an hour had passed since the explosion and the cutters were almost through the last pin.

The mass of soldiers in the portico were milling around waiting for the door to finally open when Mokhtari's aide walked up and saluted.

"Colonel, a security team from Vahdati went to Hamadani's apartment, but they must have just missed him," the Major reported. "There was a wet towel on the floor and women's clothes in the dresser and closet. There were two cell phones smashed on a workbench. Sim cards and hard drives were destroyed. They've found a laptop and a mining company jacket in the dumpsters behind the apartment. We have pictures of Hamadani and a woman and are working to identify her. The phones and laptop have been sent to tech for evaluation,"

"Any progress on the video feeds yet?" Mokhtari asked.

"They're trying to route power to the cameras inside the containment zone but most of that is being used to keep life support systems operational," replied the Major.

"Sergeant Major, how much longer on that door?" Mokhtari called out coolly.

"Another five minutes and we should be through sir," replied the engineer.

"Major, tell them to divert power to those cameras. Once the door is open, we'll have auxiliary power into the facility in ten minutes," Mokhtari ordered.

"Yes sir," he replied and ran off to relay the command.

"Sergeant Major, get your technicians to the aux security center and get those videos working. I want the stored video from the servers extracted immediately and sent to the base for analysis. The people inside Door 17 may be dead but those servers aren't," he added.

Six minutes later the engineer swung the door open as the security team on the other side cheered.

"Alright, security teams first. Take the survivors to the support base for interrogation. Move out!" ordered Mokhtari.

With that, a mass of armed soldiers entered the facility and started herding its occupants onto trucks. Of the 200 or so personnel inside the mountain during the test, only half survived. The roar of the huge portable generators reverberated off the walls of the portico entrance as an army of technicians and engineers unwound miles of cabling.

The cables were like umbilical cords, snaked into the dying facility to give life to its failing systems. Like the controlled chaos of a big city trauma center, the technicians moved quickly to stabilize vital systems. Cables were plugged into auxiliary ports and power cables were spliced to divert power to air handling systems that moved fresh air into the depths of the mountain.

Klieg lights turned darkness into daylight before emergency lighting systems failed. Another set of technicians rushed to stabilize communications and establish a direct link to the support base. Through this cacophony of sights, sounds, and activity strode Colonel Mokhtari.

He moved like a tiger stalking its prey. While he looked to be gliding in a casual stroll, his aides struggled to keep up with his long strides. It took just a few minutes to reach the auxiliary security center. The communications technicians had just started working while another plugged a power cable into the master control panel.

The control panel sprung to life as the fresh power connection snapped into place. Video screens flickered and images glowed as the dormant screens came alive. The security technician's hands moved quickly across the control panel as he initiated the download of all stored video to the auxiliary computers. The computer technician tapped him on the shoulder indicating the link to the external command center was connected and the transfer was initiated.

The upload of several terabytes of information would take more than half a day to complete. Then the security technician clicked on the live video feeds and the gathered soldiers gasped. Each infrared camera showed ghostly images of bodies, many trying to escape and huddled at each of the security doors inside the contamination zone.

"Bring up the cameras in zone 24. Start with the one at Door 24," ordered Mokhtari.

The security technician did as commanded. Mokhtari leaned into the large monitor as the technician cursed in shock as the image came onscreen then added a prayer to Allah.

"Swing the camera around toward zone 25," commanded Mokhtari.

The camera moved slowly as the image moved left to right. Door 24 was located at a T in the corridor going left and right to labs then down a long corridor to Door 25. The right corridor was filled with smoke and dust. Three bodies were clearly visible near the door. Down the corridor toward zone 25 the video showed blast damage along the corridor walls. Then complete devastation.

The technician moved the camera to focus on where door 25 used to be when Mokhtari ordered, "Stop."

"Zoom in here," he said pointing to an area just to the right of the center of the screen.

The camera focused on the edge of the blast crater. The room showed twisted and charred metal and wires where computer consoles used to be. Black scorch marks radiated like black rays up the walls as the telltale outline of a charred body could just be visible at the front edge of the room opposite the door.

"That floor is steel plate on I-beams. If reports are correct and the diameter was 15 meters, it puts it under the senior controller station which would be over here," Mokhtari said pointing off the right edge of the screen.

"This was a directional blast and would've taken a lot of planning and a very long time to set up. To get the device in there the saboteur would have to work piece by piece so as not to bring attention to himself. This would have taken months to put into place, not to mention getting it into the facility.

"Hamadani was an explosives expert, so this would be child's play for him. And as an electrical technician he could move around this facility at will. How far back do we have video?" Mokhtari asked the security technician.

"One week sir," was the reply.

"I see. It would take much longer than that. I need maintenance logs going back a year for when he worked in the control room. Look at all electrical anomalies that were reported in the last week and check the control room video feed for the same time frame. We might find out when he armed the device," Mokhtari instructed.

"Sir, communications restored, and a temporary encrypted wireless channel has been established; General Kamaliazad for you," stated Mokhtari's aide as he handed him an encrypted cell phone.

"Mokhtari."

"Colonel, status report," ordered the Commander, Sixth Special Forces Brigade, Iranian Revolutionary Guards.

"Sir, electrical and video systems restored. The stored video is being uploaded to HQ as we speak and my people are reviewing Control Room video here now. Directional high explosive blast under the control room, but everything inside door 17 is contaminated. Estimate about 100 fatalities and exact numbers will be given once we document the survivors compared to the personnel list of who was supposed to be on duty.

"Survivors are being transported for questioning. We're putting together a list of workers who were not working and sending security teams to bring them in. Nuke teams are making their way to the contamination zone, but we need to decontaminate each zone before opening the next one. Unfortunately, it will take time to get into the blast area to do a thorough EDA," Mokhtari reported.

The explosive damage assessment was one of the most critical phases of the investigation. It would provide crucial clues as to the components used in the bomb and any telltale signs of the bomb maker himself. Bomb makers considered themselves artists and always had unique design signatures that investigators could trace to other devices.

"How long before you get that damage assessment?" asked Kamaliazad.

"At least 24 hours. We must cut through each of the security doors first. That will be slowed down by the anti-nuke suits the teams must wear and the precautions for containing the contamination. Then the EDA team can get in, get residue for the explosive type, and evaluate the bomb details," Mokhtari answered.

"Colonel, we also need to find out how the radioactivity was released. A radioactive cloud was released from the blast chamber and our Russian friends tell us it's moving toward Khorramabad. We're taking measures to prevent significant loss of life there, but it appears to have been released into the facility as well. Our friends confirmed the isotope signatures are the same," Kamaliazad stated.

"Ah, so that means they sabotaged the air handling systems and the blast chamber itself. Obviously, this plan has been in the works for months, if not years. That's important information," Mokhtari replied.

"I agree, and unsettling that we were penetrated for so long. The cell phone recovered from the facility entrance had three calls to and from a Saudi cell number that is now offline. The last two cell calls pinged off towers in Iran, one on the coast and one in Shush. The final call came from a hardline inside the facility. That number is in the auxiliary security center," Kamaliazad said.

Mokhtari's head snapped around.

"Sergeant, open this comm panel immediately. Look for anything that's not supposed to be there."

Then turning his attention back to the General.

"How clever, the only direct hardline is from the support base. They must have tapped into it and may have triggered the device," he replied.

"The fragment from the gun handle you pulled out of the access panel has a texture pattern consistent with a Zionist semiautomatic. We're running analysis on the plastic now to confirm. If true, this means our two major regional enemies may be working together," Kamaliazad stated.

"We've activated all units in the area and secured the coastline. I've called in additional police units to reinforce the locals to maintain security and free up our people to sweep the countryside. The Health Ministry has activated emergency response teams to Khorramabad and your location. They should arrive at Vahdati Air Base in the next few hours. Colonel, everyone from inside the facility needs to be checked medically."

"Yes sir, I'll let the chief medical officer at the support base know. We'll keep gathering evidence but pretty clear whoever did this had outside help," answered Mokhtari.

"I thought you had a suspect Colonel?" Kamaliazad inquired.

"A suspect, yes, confirmation, no. We can't assume anything yet sir, too much we don't know. If Mossad and Al A'amah are working together, that is a very dangerous development," Mokhtari replied.

"Keep me appraised of your progress," answered Kamaliazad as the line went dead.

"Sir, there's a wire into the comm panel that shouldn't be there. It'll take a bit to trace it to its end," the communications technician reported.

"Do it. There needs to be an external source," ordered Mokhtari.

Chapter 10

Return to Dezful

E brahim checked his mirrors to confirm no one was following. As the military facility disappeared behind them, he took a right onto a side road that allowed them to loop back to the highway into Dezful. Once they were away from the danger, Azar broke the silence.

"Okay, so why do we need to go back to Dezful?" she inquired.

"We need answers. Massoud's been at the facility the longest and brought me into the group a few years ago; he's the only one I trust. His son was playing football today, so he wasn't at the facility when the explosion happened. Otherwise, he might be as dead as the others," he answered.

"Okay, so run through everything that happened. What the hell is this facility you're talking about and why do they think you did this?" asked Azar.

"I work in a military research facility as an electrical and mechanical maintenance technician. That part I never lied to you about, just where I worked. I'm sorry but it was a secret and I'd have been in real trouble if I told you," Ebrahim answered.

"What, more than you are now?" she asked.

He continued without acknowledging the sarcastic insult.

"We had a big test today and there was an important VIP there. Everything was hush-hush about that, and the facility Commander was on edge. Well, the systems are crap, and it takes a ton of creativity to keep things running. Massoud was the master at improvising using black market parts to make the whole place work.

"He was constantly building these modules that would make vastly different systems work together. French to Russian, German to Chinese; the guy's a genius. So, as I got more experience, he let me try making some modules of my own. I couldn't duplicate his, but he said 'everyone has their own signature way of doing things Ebrahim. Do them your way, not mine.' When the explosion happened, I saw one of my modules where it wasn't supposed to be. And I didn't put it there," Ebrahim said.

"You're sure it was one of yours?" asked Azar.

"It looked just like the ones I built. The casing and LED lights were from a batch I bought several months ago from a Chinese vendor. They were specialized to handle the cell phone sized circuit boards that I used as my base electronics. They have powerful processors and a bunch of universal controllers that I tapped into to control functions I needed. I had them locked in my locker in the maintenance room.

"And to answer your question, could someone break into my locker? We're maintenance guys... we can all pick a lock if needed. So yes, it could be anyone on my team. And the fact that whoever set me up used a cell phone trigger means I made it so damn easy for them," Ebrahim said angrily.

"Okay, so did anything odd happen today? Maybe it was small, so small you didn't even notice, but could be an indication of who did this to you?" she asked.

"We did our normal pretest procedures. Someone had to stay in the relay room during the test to make sure if one tripped it could be reset immediately. Because of the lousy cooling relays, it was normal procedure. So Danesh stayed in the relay room and sent me to the entrance to work on the entry system. It gave everyone trouble all day. It wasn't unusual, just bad timing. Or so I thought.

"When I got the access panel open, I saw one of my modules and stopped. It was long enough for the guard to become suspicious. Then suddenly a cell phone rang in my tool bag which caught the attention of the guard, then a ringtone from my module and the place erupted under our feet. Azar, someone wired a damned cell phone trigger into one of my modules and put it in the access panel," Ebrahim stated.

"Oh my god," she exclaimed. "But how did you get away?"

"The explosion knocked us off our feet, spilled my tool bag, and that gun fell out. I don't know how it got there because we're checked on the way in and the way out. Seeing the gun, the guard struggled to draw his gun and I hit him in the head with a hammer as he was about to shoot. I grabbed the gun, opened the entrance door and stumbled out as a security team rushed by.

"Once outside I smashed the electronic access panel and found the first truck I could find. They all had keys in them for when we went into the village for supplies, so we'd blend in with the mine workers. Then I drove to find you. All I could think about was getting to you and finding a way to get us somewhere safe," Ebrahim finished.

"But Ebrahim, how would someone know you'd be the one fixing the panel?" asked Azar.

"I'm not sure they did," he replied. "I haven't worked on that thing for weeks and it should have been Danesh, he was the senior technician. Monitoring the relays is scut work. You just stand there watching them; it's like watching paint dry. I'm almost always the one to do that."

"So, you and Danesh were separated when the explosion was triggered? Why did Danesh stay? Did he send you to fix the panel?" she asked.

"I don't know, I just don't remember. I know he said he'd monitor the relays while I went to fix the access panel but whose I idea it was, I just don't remember," Ebrahim answered, frustrated.

"Could someone from outside the facility trigger the explosion?" Azar pressed.

"I doubt it. They have a specialized cellular network inside the mountain to make communication faster. It's configured for our special phones and the outer areas are shielded to prevent electronic emissions from being detected by the Americans. So even if someone could trigger it from outside, they would need our phone and somehow get past the shielded perimeter.

"Plus, they wouldn't need to call the phone that was in my kit, they could have just called the trigger. That means there had to be an auto-dialer initiated from inside the facility. They did this to deliberately implicate me. My bag, my phone, apparently my gun. I don't believe I was supposed to make it out of there alive," replied Ebrahim.

"So, describe your modules. Maybe there's something you might think of that can help determine who did this," suggested Azar.

"They're made with cell phone boards we use in our special phones, and I order extra boards, controllers, and microprocessors to use with other electronics," he answered. "I use standard enclosures, the ones for those battery extenders, then I drill holes for port access, mounting of the board, and indicator lights. The module had the same enclosure."

"Couldn't someone else have built it? What about this Massoud guy?" she asked quizzically.

"Massoud's modules are completely different. He uses metal enclosures that have more mounting points. Mine are just simple, straight forward stuff. Use the clocks in the processors to turn switches on and off, activate relays, gather monitoring data and relay back to the maintenance room, that kind of thing. It's easy stuff so doesn't need much space. His have multiple boards and some even have their own power supplies. They have a bunch of other stuff in them that I have no idea what it does but somehow makes things that shouldn't work together, work," he replied.

"And no one else makes these modules?" Azar asked.

"No, everyone else is just about wires and machinery. I'm the one who's into the electronics stuff," Ebrahim answered.

"So, did you notice anything different about the module inside the access panel?" Azar pressed, playing half therapist and half interrogator.

Ebrahim sat silent for a few moments and used a trick from his time diffusing bombs. He'd force his mind to look at things in slow motion. It was his way to focus on the various tasks and prioritize them like a chess master.

In his mind's eye he unscrewed the access panel screws; they had normal wear. He looked at the security band, cut it, and looked at the logbook. There was his name less than a week before. He focused on the date; it was a date he worked, but he'd never worked on that panel.

"The date on the logbook, it's wrong. And my initials, they're close but not mine," Ebrahim said.

"Okay, what else?" she asked.

In his mind's eye he pulled the panel off and inspected the module. Same case as the ones he ordered, LED lights look the same, the screws...

"The screws are wrong," he said.

"What? What do you mean?" asked Azar.

"The screws are stainless steel. I always used brass; thought they were more elegant. Damn, why didn't I see that before?" said Ebrahim, exasperated.

"Anything else?" she asked.

"A module that looks like mine, my initials in the logbook, if they stole the module case and components from my locker, they'll have my fingerprints on them. Son of a bitch," Ebrahim said angrily.

"So, what are you going to ask your boss?" asked Azar.

"I need to know the backgrounds of the others on the team. He needs to know he's got a traitor among them," responded Ebrahim.

"But how do you know he's not the traitor?" she asked.

"He's been there forever. I've even seen his videos from government led demonstrations against the enemies of Iran. He's a true believer," he replied.

"But won't he turn you in if the authorities are looking for you?" she asked.

"Like the warehouse, it's a calculated risk," he answered.

The remainder of the drive was done in silence as Ebrahim rewound the last few weeks in his head to try and come up with anything else that seemed out of place. Driving past the Airbase on the outskirts of the city, the tension in the truck suddenly rose as numerous security vehicles appeared patrolling the perimeter of the base. Traffic began to get heavier as they took the expressway and passed under a roundabout. As they gently looped around a small park with an ornate fountain in the middle, the traffic crossing the bridge slowed to a crawl.

Ebrahim eased to the right and turned southwest as they exited the bridge. A half mile later, he turned into the parking lot of a transit station and parked. He pulled the mining cap low on his head to hide his face from the surveillance cameras. Together they took the pedestrian tunnel under the busy thoroughfare and exited on the other side heading east for a block then turning south. A couple minutes later they came to Massoud's apartment building.

The apartment complex was in a large, densely packed block with narrow passageways and alleys that seemed to be placed at random. The main streets had traffic cameras, but the back alleys didn't. Ebrahim led them past the building, down an alley to the south, then found a narrow passage to the back door of the building. He opened it, looked inside and waved Azar in. She took a step toward the door, paused and scanned up and down the alley, then moved quickly into the apartment complex as Ebrahim followed behind.

Chapter 11

A Kingdom on Edge

The big Y-shaped building west of Riyadh city center was buzzing with activity. Its white marble walls and ornate inlaid marble floors kept its occupants cool despite the 110-degree temperatures outside. Housing the powerful Al Mukhabarat Al A'amah, Saudi intelligence directorate, the complex was part of a larger walled complex within the city where the King resided.

Director General Bandar al-Jubeir gathered his senior officers to discuss the current situation. A second cousin to King Al-Faisal bin Saud, he was an imposing figure in his uniform with broad shoulders, dark hair with grey at the temples, and matching close cropped mustache and goatee beard. Being one of the King's relatives but far removed from the line of succession, he was responsible for the security of the royal family.

The conference room deep inside Al A'amah was deathly quiet as the senior analyst briefed the nuclear incident. The assessment of a successful nuclear test was the Saudi's nightmare scenario. Already fighting a proxy war in Yemen, the government was also battling a growing sympathy toward the Caliphate. But they had too many holes in the intelligence and no assets in the area where the incident occurred.

"What's this about a missing scientist?" asked Bandar.

"Yes sir, Doctor Husam al Din Bashir," the analyst answered. "He's an MIT trained physicist who was scheduled to give a presentation to the Nuclear Non-Proliferation conference in Dubai. He's our most senior scientist at the IAEA and an expert in nuclear inspection protocols. A vocal activist against nuclear weapons development by Iran, his disappearance at this time may not be a coincidence. We're still working through witness statements and have acquired the security video from the Sheraton Dubai Creek Hotel.

"His assistant had an unexpected change in his presentation to discuss but couldn't find him. When he checked with Bashir's security detail, they were unaware of his absence and immediately started investigating. After an hour of searching, they notified Emirates Intelligence and reviewed the security video of the hotel grounds," the analyst stated.

"The Hotel has a small fleet of yachts that host parties for VIPs and security video shows him boarding one of these alone. We're working to get the call logs to see if he received any calls. Emirates Intelligence is pressuring the service provider so we should have them later today. Finally, we have the name of the yacht he boarded, the Arabella three, and video shows it heading into the canal then out toward the Gulf. We caught images of a woman and two crewmen and are running facial recognition. Sorry sir, but not much to go on I'm afraid," the analyst finished.

"So, if we assume this disappearance is linked to the event in Iran, we need to look at all possible options to brief His Majesty on our next moves," instructed Bandar.

A vigorous argument erupted as the different departments fought over the options to respond. A few minutes into the discussion, Bandar's assistant came over and whispered in his ear.

"The American CIA Director is on the secure line in your office. He says it's urgent."

Bandar excused himself from the meeting and went to his inner office and picked up the secure phone.

"Hello David, how are you this morning?"

"Good afternoon, Bandar, though I suspect you already know it's not good. I'm sure you've seen the data out of Iran today. I just wanted to offer whatever assistance we can to you and your government," replied Director Anderson.

"Thank you, my friend. We've been told that this incident was a nuclear test that apparently went wrong. What can you tell me?" asked Bandar.

"I can confirm that we believe it was a successful nuclear test with a second large explosion at what we suspect was their research facility. We have an intercept from Iran claiming either Mossad or Saudi intelligence in this, or perhaps both. I have to ask my friend, did one of your citizens have something to do with this?" asked Anderson.

Bandar's thoughts were racing. Why in the world would the Iranians think they were working with the Israelis?

"I can confirm that my government had no prior knowledge of this incident," replied Bandar.

"Bandar, we're too old and have known each other too long for the parsing of words, though it's good to know this wasn't a sanctioned op. What can you tell me about the possibility of one of your citizens' involvement in this?" asked Anderson.

Bandar knew he had to tread carefully. It was clear the Americans knew about the missing scientist, but how much information they had, he didn't know.

"Yes David, we are too old to dance around questions and this incident is too important for us to have a misunderstanding. You obviously know of the missing physicist who is one of my countrymen. Dr. Husam al Din Bashir disappeared from the Nuclear Non-Proliferation conference in Dubai several hours ago. Since the incident occurred just a few hours before that conference was scheduled to begin, I don't believe it is a coincidence," Bandar began.

"We have quietly interviewed witnesses at the hotel with Emirates security and reviewed the security tapes. Bashir is seen boarding a yacht at the hotel docks that entered the Gulf. We are attempting to identify the owner of the yacht. The King has put our military on alert and is waiting for an update on the intel. Can you add anything to clarify the situation?" asked Bandar.

"It's our strong belief the Caliphate was behind this attack," Anderson began. "But they've been silent. Usually, they want to take credit immediately but right now nothing. We intercepted a Caliphate communication a while back that referenced something in Iran but given they've made threats before, it dropped in priority.

"Aside from the fact this was a nuclear incident in direct violation of their recent agreement, our concern was the apparent link to your country and Israel. So, if this wasn't sanctioned, and neither you nor Israel are admitting to an operation, then why are the Iranians mumbling about your collusion? But most importantly, could your scientist be working with the Caliphate?" asked Anderson.

"Until we find our missing scientist, I can only guess at this point. But you know we have some in the Kingdom who are sympathetic with the Caliphate's antipathy toward Iran even if they don't support their radical agenda. Are you absolutely certain this was a nuclear device and not a dirty bomb?" asked Bandar coyly.

"Given the estimated depth of the larger explosion and its predicted power, our specialists believe it was on the order of a small, half kilo-ton device. So yes, we are certain. This indicates they were testing a scale model of the initiator for a fission device, and appears they were successful. That's the bad news. The good news, I guess, is that the second explosion appears to have taken out their control facility and likely many of their top scientists.

"The radioactive isotope in both releases is consistent with material processed by Iran and not a dirty bomb. The release may have been engineered by valves that were deliberately sabotaged for maximum impact. It forces the Iranians to explain the deaths of those in the facility as well as those under the fallout. They won't be able to hide them," answered Anderson.

"I see," replied Bandar. "We're working to get assets into the area as we speak, but this facility seems to have caught us all by surprise. And with Iran actively looking for a Saudi citizen it will make it that much harder. It appears we must find the connection to this missing scientist. Either he's an important piece of the puzzle or a diversion to keep us looking in the wrong direction. Either way my government will demand an answer, as will yours I imagine," finished Bandar.

"The video of the yacht, can you send it to me so we can run an analysis on it as well? I'll have it run against our database of suspected Caliphate operatives to see if anything pops. Plus, if you send me the cell phone info for your scientist, we can help locate him. Did he receive any calls before he disappeared?" Anderson asked.

"We're working to track that down now, but I'll send everything we have. If we find him before the Iranians do, maybe we can limit some of the damage and get more answers. I'll have a copy of the video sent over right away," answered Bandar.

"Bandar, you know I must ask. Did your government know of this facility and what the Iranians were doing there?" asked Anderson.

Bandar paused, just briefly, as there was always some tension between the intelligence services of America and the Kingdom.

"David, we suspected they had a research facility in the area and like you, have spent the better part of a decade trying to get information on it. I expect you know as much, if not more than we do about it," he hedged.

"I see. Then please stay in touch old friend and I'll do the same," answered Anderson and ended the call.

Bandar sat back in his chair, deep in thought. The Americans were holding back information, though he knew the reasons why. It was well known that Saudi intelligence had Caliphate sympathizers in it much like Pakistan's ISI. But Anderson confirmed the event was a successful nuclear test and the release of radioactive gas may have been deliberate. This changed the dynamic if it was a Caliphate attack.

And Bandar had to consider that one of his countrymen was involved. Why else would Iran be implying Saudi Arabia was behind the attack and why link Saudi to Israel? If it were for propaganda, Iran would plaster that information all over the airwaves for justification to act. But why were they waiting?

More likely, they didn't want to bring attention to the fact it was a nuclear facility. But this missing scientist was still a mystery. And until Bandar could piece that part of the puzzle together, he had to assume the worst. That subversives within Saudi Arabia had something to do with this attack.

So, despite their wealth and power, there were members of the royal family who would use those divisions for their own personal gain. That's why Bandar headed the powerful intelligence agency. He and the King were like brothers. He was far removed from the throne but was closer to Saud than any of the King's siblings. They'd grown up together, went to the same schools, and had the same pragmatic view of the world. Therefore, the King's personal security fell to Bandar. He carefully selected men and women to guard the King and his family, even in his most intimate moments.

Bandar returned to the meeting with his directors.

"The Americans have confirmed the facility was a nuclear research facility and the attack on it was sabotage. That means whoever initiated it had an asset inside and been planning for a long time," Bandar said, withholding many of the details Anderson gave him.

"What of the nuclear gas release, what did he say about that?" asked the Director of Internal Security.

"They are working to determine if it was due to a dirty bomb or if the release was a result of where the explosion in the facility occurred given they clearly stored nuclear material there," Bandar lied.

If there was Saudi involvement, then it was very likely that someone in this room knew about it.

"So, our top priority is finding that missing scientist and confirming whether he had a role in this attack. Rajat, send the video surveillance of the yacht and cell phone info to our contact at the US Embassy. They know about our missing scientist, so we'll let the American NSA do the heavy work for us on that front," ordered Bandar.

Just then an aide came rushing into the conference room.

"Director," the aide said breathlessly. "The Iranians are claiming the Zionists have bombed a new nuclear power plant during its final certification testing near Dezful.

They've announced that a nuclear cloud is moving toward several Iranian cities and ordered those residents to remain inside until cleared by authorities. They claim the military found a small Zionist tactical boat and they may have been aided by us," he stated.

Bandar pushed a speed dial button on the phone next to him.

"Get the King to the bunker, immediately," he ordered.

Bandar thought he saw a hint of a smile on the face of his Deputy Director of Intelligence. The implication from the Iranians was clear. The Saudis had betrayed Islam by working with the hated Zionists to attack Iran. If this were a Caliphate operation, then they had made a masterful stroke. Unite the Sunni tribes against Iran, while sowing anger and distrust against the King.

Chapter 12

Steel Screws

Ebrahim and Azar moved nonchalantly through the apartment hallway. The carpeting in the dimly lit corridor was an ornate red and gold design reminiscent of a bygone era. But it was worn threadbare from the years of dust and foot traffic. The couple only encountered one person and hid their faces by playfully kissing as they walked by.

Massoud's apartment was a corner flat on the top floor of the six-story building facing northwest. The entrance was located at the end of the T-shaped hallway, hidden around the left corner. Ebrahim moved toward the door as Azar slid against the wall with her back to the main corridor.

She peeked around the corner to ensure they were safely hidden from view. With a confirmation nod, Ebrahim knocked on the door. After a few tense moments, the metallic sound of the deadbolt sliding free from the doorframe sliced through the silence. As the door swung open, the shock on Massoud's face was obvious.

"Ebrahim, what the hell are you doing here? You're supposed to be at work," Massoud said.

He then looked at Azar.

"And who is she?"

"Massoud, can we come in please? There's been an incident and I must talk to you...but not out here. Please!" implored Ebrahim.

"Yes, yes, come in," replied Massoud.

He took a step back and waved his hand to usher the couple into the apartment. Ebrahim stepped into the flat as Azar took one last peek down the hall then dutifully followed.

Massoud's wife came out of the kitchen.

"Massoud, who's at the door?"

"Someone I work with. Can you get us some tea?" Massoud answered.

"Thank you, Massoud. This is my wife, Azar. Is there somewhere we can talk privately?" asked Ebrahim.

Massoud's wife glided up next to Azar.

"Come with me, dear, you can help with the tea while the men talk," Massoud's wife announced.

She hooked Azar's arm and led her to the kitchen. Ebrahim followed Massoud to a sitting room. The room was located at the front corner of the flat. A wall of windows lined the left side, a gas fireplace sat in the center flanked by two floor-to-ceiling windows, and a wall of books on the right.

A fireplace was rare for a downtown apartment. Only well-off people had fireplaces that used propane tanks due to a shortage of wood and limited reserves of natural gas. As the senior maintenance technician, Massoud got his propane from the giant storage tanks at the support base. Just another benefit of working at the secret facility.

"Okay, so tell me what the hell you're doing here and not at the facility," ordered Massoud.

"There was an explosion during the test. I was working on the entry door, and it was such a powerful blast it knocked me and the guard off our feet. A cell phone and gun fell out of my tool bag and when the guard tried to shoot me, I panicked and fled. Massoud, I didn't do this. Someone has set me up," Ebrahim began.

"How do you know they were trying to set you up?" asked Massoud.

"Because I've never seen the cell phone or the gun, and someone used a module built from my components to trigger the bomb!" exclaimed Ebrahim, exasperated. "Massoud, I didn't do this, but I need your help to figure out who did."

"Well, I don't know how I can help, I wasn't even there," Massoud answered.

"You're a true believer and know everyone on our team. You brought almost all of us into the facility so you of all people know their backgrounds. Who else has electronics backgrounds that could wire the electrical system to trigger a bomb?" asked Ebrahim.

"Everyone had a background in some support system. And any of our electricians could have wired a trigger, you know that as well as I do. Out of the whole electrical crew, you and Danesh had the most electronics experience. Then Ghasem and Ozhan from communications. Hell Ebrahim, it could be anyone, even me!" Massoud replied.

"Yes, but it would have been someone who could roam the entire facility without being noticed. Not everyone had access to all areas. If there was a bomb, it had to be deep in the facility given the response I saw during my escape. That limits who it could have been, doesn't it?" asked Ebrahim grasping at any thread he could.

***

Azar and Massoud's wife walked down the short hallway from the kitchen toward the sitting room. As they passed an open door, Azar glanced in. The room contained a small workbench with a storage rack on one side containing a host of electronic parts and a soldering station on the workbench. Azar stopped and turned to take a closer look as something caught her eye.

"Come on dear, that's just my husband's work area. He tinkers a lot with electronic stuff. I try to stay out of there," she said as she touched Azar's arm.

"Ebrahim has something like this at our apartment, but not quite as elaborate. I was just marveling that he would love a workplace like this," Azar said turning and smiling at the wife.

The men stopped talking as the women entered the room with the tea. Massoud's wife poured a cup for Ebrahim and handed it to Azar to deliver to him. Then poured one for Massoud. Once the tea was delivered, she turned to leave and stopped at the entryway of the sitting room looking at Azar. Azar understood the not-so-subtle message and followed the wife back to the kitchen.

"So, do you work?" Azar asked the wife as they sat down with their own tea.

"No, I suppose I'm considered old fashioned. I follow the traditions of Islam and I volunteer at the local hospital working with women patients. I help the women navigate that path to stay true to the faith during their treatment," answered Massoud's wife. "Do you work?"

"Yes, I work for a company that supplies the government. I too must navigate a fine line to stay within the lines of the faith," replied Azar as she looked out the kitchen window.

Just then a green government car pulled up outside the apartment building. Azar's body tensed ever so slightly, and she quickly looked at her watch.

"Oh dear, I'm so sorry, I've lost track of time and I need to go across town for a meeting. We're going on holiday and Ebrahim surprised me by getting off work early. It was so romantic, but I still need to brief my boss before we leave. Thank you so much for the tea," Azar said as she stood and took another glance out the window.

The two women moved back down the hallway.

"I'm sorry to interrupt, Ebrahim we need to go right away, I'm late for my meeting with my boss," Azar said with some urgency in her voice as she nodded her head slightly toward the window.

"Right, I forgot," Ebrahim stuttered, after a fraction of a second delay in catching her meaning.

"Massoud, thank you for talking with me, I'll keep in touch."

As they walked quickly past the door to the workroom, Azar squeezed Ebrahim's hand. He turned his head and glanced in at the array of electronics.

"Thank you again my friend," said Ebrahim.

"I only wish I could have been more help," answered Massoud as he opened the door.

Once in the hallway, Azar leaned into Ebrahim and whispered in his ear. "Security just showed up. We need to get to the stairwell fast."

The two moved quickly in a few long strides. As they opened the door, they heard the security team moving up the stairs. They quickly but quietly went up to the roof. At the top they opened the door and left it open a crack until the team passed.

As the two-man security team entered the door to the hallway, Ebrahim and Azar rushed down the stairwell as quickly as possible and headed for the front door.

Outside Azar immediately turned to Ebrahim, "Split up and go in different directions. I'll meet you at the truck in 15 minutes. Walk a random route as they will be looking for a couple."

And with that she turned north and left without waiting for an answer. Ebrahim stood dumbfounded for a second staring after her, then started east. The sound of sirens rang out across the city a few moments later. Their high-pitched blaring seemingly screeched around every corner making his anxiety grow with every passing minute. Certainly, Massoud told the security team they had been there and Ebrahim prayed that Azar's love for him was stronger than her personal survival instincts.

Zig zagging around the busy city streets he ended up at the transit station. He walked around a bit checking for police. He'd spent the past 15 minutes nervously wondering if Azar was true to him or had just turned against him. After the third time circling the location of the truck, Ebrahim stopped at a corner about fifteen yards away. He was startled when he felt a hand on his back. He spun and reflexively moved his hand to his back belt.

"Hold on, it's just me," said Azar as she put her hand on his. "Did anyone follow you?"

"No, I moved back and forth and circled a couple times checking but saw nobody. How did you know to split up? I heard all of the sirens shortly after we left Massoud's," Ebrahim asked.

"I guess I watch too many of those American spy movies. It just seemed like the thing to do. Let's get out of here, there's something I need to show you," answered Azar urgently.

They returned to the truck and began to pull away from the station.

"Turn left and head across the Sasani bridge. We need to avoid the highways," she instructed.

Ebrahim merged into the night traffic and followed her directions. At the end of the bridge, they took a right then looped around and back under the bridge to cross a main thoroughfare. The road swept to the right heading north and west through an industrial area. They eventually turned onto a narrow street and into a burgeoning residential area.

"Ebrahim, pull over. I need to show you something," Azar said, breaking the tense silence.

"Okay," he replied.

"When we were at Massoud's, his wife showed me his work room. It had a bunch of electronic equipment, some I recognized, more I didn't. But I saw something you need to see," she began.

She pulled out the burner phone. Her fingers moved quickly across its face as the dull blue-white light of the screen lit her face in the darkness. After a few moments she held up the phone and showed Ebrahim a picture.

"I had to take this without his wife knowing so the positioning isn't great but look on the bench to the right of the solder station. Isn't that one of the cases you described?"

Ebrahim leaned in and took the phone. He moved his fingers to zoom in.

"What the hell? That is one of my cases, and that electronic board next to it is one of mine as well. Son of a bitch!" he exclaimed suddenly turning angry. "Massoud? This makes no sense, he's a zealot for god's sake!"

"Perhaps, but a zealot for which side? If the enemies of the Republic wanted to penetrate our most secret facility it would take years. More than the length of time you've worked there. If this Massoud did this, he was in the perfect position to set you up. He knew your background, your life before working the facility. And he apparently had the ability to move freely," Azar said logically. "Is there anything else in the picture that's useful?"

Ebrahim moved the picture around with his fingers.

"Son of a bitch, steel screws."

"I guess that's your proof, huh?" answered Azar.

"That bastard. I have to let the authorities know right away," Ebrahim said angrily.

"Are you insane?" Azar replied indignantly. "You have no proof and they have all this evidence. They'll shoot you the second they see you."

"Dammit, he killed my brothers and friends. The son of a bitch needs to pay for his treachery!" he said, his eyes burning with rage.

Ebrahims nostrils flared as he slammed his hand on the steering wheel. Azar lowered her voice and spoke calmly.

"Ebrahim, we have to be rational now, you're the suspect. We both are. He set us up perfectly. You have access, knowledge, skills, and you can bet Massoud has planted other evidence to implicate you. Even if they believed you, they'd kill us both out of pure chance we were co-conspirators. We're dead if we go back. Our only chance is to run.

Ebrahim closed his eyes, took a deep breath to calm himself and ran his fingers through his hair. She was right, of course. The military had their suspect; the setup was just too good. But where could they go? Yes, they needed to think about this and not make any rash moves.

"I'm sorry. Of course, you're right," Ebrahim replied.

"We need to get rid of this truck. The police and military are almost certainly looking for it by now. There's a car dealer not too far from here. Let's pull off the road somewhere, hide out until right at opening and get a vehicle. That will give us time to think of our next move. But we have to lay low and stay off the grid," urged Azar quietly.

"But how are we going to acquire a car?" he asked

"Remember who I work for so just leave that to me. I saw a pull-off about a half a kilometer back. Let's check that out and get some rest. The authorities are going to think we are running out of the city as fast as possible so will have the transit stations blocked. Undoubtedly, they'll have roadblocks set up on the main roads. Massoud no doubt has told them we were there, so we need to move deliberately," Azar said.

The calm in her voice reminded Ebrahim of his EOD instructor talking through disarming a bomb. The cool logic of it had the same effect on him. Instinctively his breathing and heart rate slowed as his brain pushed the anxiety of the situation away.

Within minutes they turned onto a dead-end road about 250 meters from the main road. The skeleton of a future housing project not yet started.

Azar got a duffle bag from the truck and pulled out four cylinders and placed them about 50 meters apart. She clicked on laser alignment beams from one cylinder to another to form a square. She then moved back to the center and pushed a button on a wireless remote. It turned off the lasers and activated invisible motion detectors creating an early warning system around the truck.

Ebrahim pulled the camouflage and tent from the truck. He tossed the camo netting over it then set up the pop-up tent. Finally, he moved some weapons from the truck to the tent. Azar joined him just as he finished, and they settled in for what he was sure would be a restless night.

"My dearest Ebrahim, we need to keep our heads clear," Azar said as she gently stroked his cheek. "There's no way we can stay here, and we have to find a way out of the country. If this facility was as important as you say, they will turn over every rock to find us."

"You're right. We'll need to move quickly but deliberately. Stay away from the larger cities. But do we go to Afghanistan or Iraq? I'm more familiar with the Iraqi border but that means moving through the Kurdish areas," he replied.

"Iraq is best *because* of the Kurds. They'll be slower to pursue us and risk contact with the Kurdish militias in the area," Azar replied.

"Azar, I'm so sorry for getting you involved in this. I'd do anything to protect you from this mess," Ebrahim said sadly.

"Ebrahim, I love you. Wherever you are is where I want to be. This isn't your fault. We've been betrayed but we're together and we're alive. We'll get through this, together," she said softly as she leaned in and kissed him.

"I love you too," he replied and pulled her closer to him kissing her deeply.

Azar rolled over and sat up straddling him.

"Like I said, we need to keep our heads clear," she said.

She pulled off her shirt and brought his hands to her body. Her beauty overwhelmed him, as he traced the scar on her side. It caused Azar to smile as the tension of the day began to drain away and his desire took over. The danger seemed to invigorate their passion for each other.

The physical exertion of their lovemaking grew in intensity as beads of sweat formed on their foreheads despite the cool evening air. The world disappeared at the power of their respective climaxes. With loud grunts of pleasure at their release, it was like every muscle in their bodies fired at once as they held each other tightly as if trying to merge their bodies into one. Ebrahim felt Azar's warm staccato breath on his neck and her muscles quiver as her orgasm subsided. Shortly after, his breathing shallowed as he drifted off to sleep.

Chapter 13

Tribal Mess

The smell of coffee and pizza permeated the conference room in the Southwest Asia section. The section's action group pored over reams of data from all over the world. Karim mentally catalogued each piece as Mo scooped up virtually every electronic intercept that referenced Iran. They plotted things on a virtual whiteboard to find connections. Any link, however tentative, was annotated. If links to other countries were uncovered, then data from them was pulled and added to the mix.

Mo and Karim scanned the information projected on the large screen. Mo just shook her head at the jumble of seemingly random events across the Middle East.

"Jesus, we don't know dick about this event," she exclaimed. "Except for the fact that it's a Caliphate op. They clearly knew where the facility was and what it did; it's really a stroke of genius. It lays bare the Iranian's lies about their nuke program and creates chaos within the Sunni countries. Not only because Iran appears to have a nuke capability but the alleged coordination between Saudi Arabia and Israel.

"Although Mossad immediately denied involvement after the event, they're clearly spooked, and coordination's been off the charts. Their analysts are begging for as much information as we can give them. It appears they knew less about what was going on than we did," Mo added.

Karim began thinking out loud, almost like a teacher working through a lesson with his class.

"I'm not convinced of that yet, which makes their reaction unusual. Most of our human intel on the Iranian nuclear program came from the Israelis. So, Mossad hinting they didn't know the details about this facility is a really scary thought, if true. We know the Caliphate is behind the attack, but did they have help from someone else?

"I mean, most westerners look at the region through the lens of western culture and the boundaries drawn on a map. But if we look at this from a tribal viewpoint the relationships in the whole region change. Tribal factions may fight each other or a common enemy, and seemingly switch at will for whatever is best for their tribe at that moment. Even the Arab/Israeli conflicts failed due to tribal divisions within the Arab states over control and dominance."

Karim paused briefly. As a third generation Lebanese American, Karim wrote his doctoral thesis on the tribal divisions in the region. It's what made analysis of the Middle East so challenging for so many in the west. The rampant tribalism made even members of the same religious sect act more like rabid enemies than allies.

"It's possible one of the conservative Arab states provided help. The Caliphate exposed the deep divisions within the Sunni community long hidden by the region's strongmen. When the Arab Spring raged across North Africa and the Middle East, it ripped minor cracks into gaping chasms exploding in violence. As protectors of the holy sites of Islam, and the largest population of fundamentalist Sunni Muslims, Saudi Arabia has always walked a political tight rope.

"The royal family used Wahhabism to bring the disparate tribes of the peninsula together," Karim continued like a professor lecturing his students. "But the ultra-fundamentalist form of Islam it wrought now threatens the very people who created it. Plus, the Sunni/Shia conflict has become more violent and extremist since the Iranian revolution. Given the proxy wars that link can't be ignored. But there's no benefit for the Saudis to work with the Caliphate, it would hurt their lucrative business operations around the world.

"The King's an Oxford trained economist with an MBA from Harvard. He's a free trader at heart and would much rather trade with the Iranians than fight them. But the bombing of a nuclear research facility certainly benefits them and others in the Gulf. So, if we look at this jumble of information as nation states, it makes no sense. But as tribal interactions, it becomes clearer. Mo, organize the information by their tribal affiliation, not by country," Karim finished.

Gerlacher came over to check on the progress.

"So, Karim, what do we have?"

"We're starting to look at things from a tribal perspective rather than nation states. We need to figure out the decision options for the various factions to try and get a picture of how we think the dominos will fall," began Karim.

"We know the Caliphate moved supplies out of Pakistan using Qureshi Farooq along with that Pak General who was executed after the Valley of Stars op. Both were getting orders from someone else, but we still don't know who. We have reports of a manhunt for an Iranian national and his girlfriend and NSA intercepted an unencrypted cell phone call from a Dezful policeman. It implied one of the workers at the facility was a Mossad agent and they have linked a phone number to a Saudi phone. Given the report of the missing scientist it doesn't preclude their involvement, but the Saudis deny an official op. Still no joy on facial rec from that video by the way."

Karim paused ever so briefly and tapped his coffee cup.

"You saw the Iranian's public announcement of an Israeli terrorist attack on a nonexistent new nuclear power plant within the last hour," he continued. "That will easily explain the radioactive cloud and their actions to protect their citizens. Even with the actions they've initiated there may be casualties, but it will limit them. They've said nothing more about possible Saudi involvement and there's no indication they know about the missing scientist."

Karim put his coffee cup down and folded his arms staring at the map for a second in thought.

"I'm still working out how this relates to the broader struggle with the Caliphate on the Arabian Peninsula though. Ideologically there's little difference between the Caliphate and mainstream Wahhabism; seems more of a power and control struggle. But the monarchy's lenient business dealings with the west have angered the Saudi clerics. Linking Saudi to Israel could isolate the King or initiate a broader Middle East war. Either way that would benefit the more fundamental elements in the region," Karim finished.

Gerlacher studied the map that showed a patchwork of colors representing the different tribal and ideological factions throughout the Middle East. He shook his head at the mess the region had become...or always was. Extreme interpretations of Islam combined with tribalist attitudes spawned a generation of feudal violence driven by ideological purity. And when the President allowed the ouster of several of those traditional strongmen, it opened Pandora's Box and the monsters were unleashed. Centuries of forced migration and arbitrary boundaries ensured there were few safe zones left for any populace.

"And we still don't have our own eyes on the ground in Iran," sighed an exasperated Gerlacher.

"Zack, that Army asset in Afghanistan, Sergeant Kirkorian, she's fluent in Farsi and helped break Farooq. She's good Zack, really good. Any thought of infiltrating from that side? It's a bit far but if they're looking for a Saudi, then infiltrating from the Gulf side is going to be high risk," responded Karim.

"The Iranians will lock down the area to the east because of the nuke cloud floating that way," answered Gerlacher.

"Well, I'm not an ops guy but if they're looking for someone who can handle themselves and blend in, I'd put my money on her," replied Karim.

"I remember her. Okay, I'll talk to the Directors," declared Gerlacher.

***

Gerlacher went into his office and punched the speed dials to conference the Deputy Director for Intelligence and the Deputy Director for Operations of the CIA.

"Director Hayes, Director Cavanaugh, the latest intel indicates a massive response," he began and briefed the two directors about the analysts' latest theories.

"Without boots on the ground, we're really hamstrung about what's going on especially given Mossad's apparent blindness in the area as well. My analysts believe we need to put our own people in there and need more information about that Saudi connection Iran may be looking for," Gerlacher stated.

"Seems they're in sync with the Situation Room but we've got damn few options for that Zack," replied DDO Cavanaugh. "Our pool of field operators with the skills and language is pretty small and we've already moved as many of those assets in country as we can. Unfortunately moving them to the area under such high security will be very risky. We can move a few but we could burn them," he finished.

DDI Hayes interjected.

"Well, we got a little lucky Silas, I was just told a deep cover operative is headed that way. But like you said, big risk to get information out with the security net they'll have around that place. So, Zack, do your analysts have any suggestions?"

"They worked with an intel asset from the Army on the Valley of Stars op. She's top notch, fluent in 10 languages, including Farsi, and skilled in combat. It means working with DoD but it's someone they trust," answered Gerlacher.

"Jesus, another interagency op? We saw how the last one turned out," answered Cavanaugh derisively.

"Silas, that was State, and those assholes burned DoD just as bad. They were the ones who screwed up Tunisia insisting it was a simple kidnapping for ransom that got our people killed. Don't forget DoD moved mountains to do the extraction and lost some of their own," stated Hayes.

The diplomatic compound in Tunisia was attacked by an Islamic militia group who kidnapped the Ambassador and killed several of his security detail. Cavanaugh scrambled a CIA tactical team to help recover the Ambassador, but when the mission went sideways, the CIA and Special Operations units had to fight a furious battle to recover the survivors. With a dead Ambassador, the lies, cover-up, and false narratives pointed the finger at the CIA team, yet everyone in the administration knew it was State's screw-up.

"Plus, Silas," added Hayes. "It's like you said, we have few options. So, in my opinion, if it means getting someone there to collect first-hand information, it's worth the risk. Zack is this the asset who did the interrogation of Farooq?" asked Hayes.

"Yes Ma'am. And we know DoD has some others who would have the tactical skills to do this," answered Gerlacher.

"Janelle, what would be their primary mission?" inquired Cavanaugh.

"Primary mission is intel gathering but we should try to locate and secure the two people the Iranians are looking for ourselves if possible. That means people with both intel gathering and ops experience. If we can find these two first, we do a snatch and grab and conduct our own interrogations. As for the Saudi scientist, if we assume there's a link, we need to be ready to act on that once we're on the ground. Otherwise, we're prepping for Iranian counteractions against Israel and/or Saudi Arabia. Silas, the Army asset proved very adept at getting information in Afghanistan that others could not," replied Hayes.

"Okay Zack, what's her full story?" asked Cavanaugh.

Gerlacher briefed the directors on her background and the company her family runs.

"Are you talking about SA2 Corporation? Those guys are unbelievable. Her parents own it?" asked Cavanaugh.

"Her father and uncle do. These guys are not who you want to meet in a dark alley," answered Gerlacher.

"Jesus Christ Silas, we've got to have this asset on this mission," Janelle said urgently. "I'm on my way to you right now to discuss something face to face, then we need to call DoD. Zack, thanks for the info. Silas, see you in five."

Chapter 14

Welcome to Kuwait

Sergeant Shirin Kirkorian only had time to grab her gear and hustle to Hangar 17. As a daughter of Iranian Orthodox Christian immigrants with dark brown eyes, chestnut colored hair, and high cheek bones, she was often mistaken as Hispanic. Despite her five-foot-six-inch athletic frame, her Army issued mollie pack looked huge as she ran across the hangar. There the intel chief had shoved a binder in her hands and pushed her onto the plane with a Chief Petty Officer from Seal Team 2.

The smooth flight of the nondescript, white business jet was a welcome reprieve from the gut-wrenching Humvee ride from Camp Wright to Bagram Air Base, Afghanistan. The hiss of the cool, dry air from the air conditioning system created the perfect white noise that had put her into a deep sleep. In a combat zone, soldiers know to sleep when they can because when the action starts, they may not sleep for days.

She was dreaming about hunting with her son when she felt someone touch her shoulder. Immediately wide awake, her hand instinctively moved toward her side-arm as the other came up defensively. There stood a soldier with short black hair, dark brown eyes, with a thick beard and mustache. The sleeves of his fatigues were rolled up and his arms looked like that of a weightlifter with dragon tattoos covering both forearms.

"Whoa Sarge, sorry for waking you. We've started our descent. I figured you'd want to review that binder before we land," stated the Petty Officer.

"Thanks. Guess I was more tired than I thought," replied Kirkorian.

"Darius Nasseri," the Petty Officer said.

He reached out his hand.

"My friends call me Naz."

"Shirin Kirkorian," she replied and shook it.

"Didn't know the Rangers had women now," he replied pointing to the Ranger tab on Kirkorian's shoulder.

"Yah, I'm the first. That's a nice Persian name you have Naz," she said.

He laughed.

"First generation. My parents emigrated during the revolution, but I was born and raised in south Jersey. Got harassed in school because of the name and had plenty of practice fighting. So, after graduation decided to join the Seals. Figured I'd use those fighting skills doing something good. What's your story?"

"Pretty much the same. I'm a Texas girl and my parents emigrated during the revolution as well. As for the Ranger thing, I figure I finally pissed off the brass so much they let me try it just to shut me up. So, I'm guessing you're fluent in Farsi too?" Kirkorian asked.

"Yup, parents spoke it in the house and English to everyone else. There's a pretty big ex-pat community in Jersey so everyone was bilingual," Naz answered.

"Well, no secret why we're both on this airplane then. I barely had time to take a piss before they strapped me in," she said.

"Sounds like me. My team leader grabbed me out of the chow line, told me to gear up and threw my ass in a chopper to Bagram. They shoved a binder in my hand and ordered me to get on this jet. Pilots aren't military, so guessing CIA," he replied.

"That's my guess as well. Worked with a couple of them during the recent fireworks back in Afghanistan. Interrogated that scumbag head of the Lashkar-e-Jhangvi, Qureshi Farooq. Managed to break the little prick in a couple days. He vomited information so fast the CIA guys were pissing themselves with joy," she answered with a chuckle.

"No way! I was on the team that did the snatch and grab on that asshole. Well, this is a small world," Naz answered laughing.

"So, anything in that package they gave us?" asked Kirkorian.

"I'm sure you know about the terror attack at an Iranian nuke facility?" Naz asked.

"Yah, I was briefed at Camp Wright before humping to Bagram," she answered.

"It appears the Iranians are looking for two people, a man and a woman. Plus, there's a Saudi nuclear scientist missing but there's no more information about that. In general, real light on details," he replied.

"Our HUMINT there really sucks. Congress seems to think we can get all the info we need electronically. Problem is that all our adversaries know it and know how to hide," Kirkorian replied, a little too sarcastically.

"Yah, well I'm just an ops guy, I leave the collection to the Intel guys. Give me a target and I'll snatch it, kill it, or blow it up," he answered.

"Well, I'm one of those 'Intel guys,' and my gut tells me we're not here for analysis. If this is a CIA op, I hope your Farsi doesn't come with that Jersey accent," she said smiling.

"Neguran nebashad, men faresa keamel aset," replied Naz.

"Okay, okay, you're right, your Farsi is...*almost* perfect," Kirkorian answered. "Sounds like the dialect around Tehran, right?"

"Yah, my grandfather was a finance minister in the Shah's government. He got my parents out, but the revolutionaries executed him and my grandmother. She was ill and he refused to leave her. They were defiant to the end though," he replied solemnly. "How'd you know about the dialect?"

"Linguist; pretty much my job to pick out the subtleties in language. That's why they put me in intel," Kirkorian replied.

"So, Kirkorian isn't a traditional Persian name, and the Ranger thing was it just for shits and giggles then?" Naz asked mockingly.

"Long story on both counts, I'll tell you sometime. But I had a leg up on most in Ranger school because I can shoot. Scored some shooting records during training," she answered.

"Damn, I know some Rangers and worked with a few who shot better than me. Now I'm really impressed. So, guessing that's the reason you're on this jet," he replied with admiration.

"Yah, I guess so," Kirkorian said laughing.

Two bells dinged over the aircraft's PA system.

"We're starting our approach. Please stow your gear and return to your seats," stated the pilot's voice with that tinny sound common from airplane speakers.

"Guess we'll get more answers in a few minutes," Naz said as he buckled himself back into his seat.

Ten minutes later the plane pulled to a stop inside a hangar at Ahmad al-Jaber Air Base where half a dozen men in blue jump suits swarmed the plane like a NASCAR pit crew. Located south of Kuwait City it was one of the U.S. military's main operating bases in the region. The pilot opened the aircraft door and as Kirkorian got to the top of the stairs, a booming baritone voice greeted her.

"Hey, candy-ass, welcome to Kuwait!"

Kirkorian looked down to see three men in khaki shirts, matching cargo pants, and tan combat boots waiting for her. Locking eyes with the man who called out to her, a sly smile came over her face.

"Jericho, you asshole, still the same sexist pig I see," she replied laughing.

She bound down the stairs and got a bear hug from the mountain of a man. Jericho had short, thick black hair with grey at the temples and a close-cropped beard to match. Telltale sunbaked lines radiated from the corners of his dark chocolate eyes that looked almost black against his tanned face. At six-foot-three, you could see the mass of muscles through the rolled-up sleeves of his shirt and fatigue pants. The smoothness of his skin belied a lifetime in the field, most of it spent in the brutal desert sun of the Middle East. Especially for a man who was well into the second half of his life.

"It's good to see you again Kirkorian, how the hell are you?" Jericho asked as he held her out by her shoulders. "Glad to see you still have all your parts after that shit storm in Afghanistan."

"Got a bit hot to be honest. Took a bayonet to the side but no serious damage. We had some damn good leadership and a lot of luck though. How're you Sergeant Major?" Kirkorian replied.

"Just Jericho now, retired two years ago and took over an ops team for the agency. You know me, couldn't sit behind a desk no matter how much you paid me. Plus, the kids are grown and the ex- remarried, so better to keep busy doing what I'm good at," he replied.

Naz stepped off the airplane stairs and extended his hand.

"Chief Petty Officer Nasseri sir, but everyone just calls me Naz. Glad to meet you."

"Just Jericho. That sir bullshit is for officers, I'm still a workin' man son," Jericho replied, grasping Naz's hand. "This is Moose and Hammer."

"Mustafa, but everyone calls me Moose."

Though not as tall as Jericho, Moose had a barrel chest and the arms and legs of an NFL nose tackle. His hand virtually engulfed Kirkorians when they shook.

"Hammersmith, glad to meet you both."

Hammer had brown hair and was just under six foot tall, about the same height as Naz. Like the other operators he was extremely fit and looked to be younger than Jericho but older than the rest of the group.

"Alright, time to go to work. I hope you got some sleep on the plane, a lot's happened since you left," Jericho announced.

Everyone fell in behind Jericho and tossed their gear in the back of a Humvee. As it pulled out of the hangar, the tread of the large combat tires growled a loud, deep guttural hum on the hot pavement. Even at night, the bright lights of the desert airfield shimmered through the thermals off the sunbaked concrete. After a five-minute drive the vehicle stopped in front of a sand-colored building at the north end of the airfield.

The solitary unmarked building was near several hardened bunkers. Moose and Hammer grabbed the soldiers' bags as the group followed Jericho into the building. The rush of air conditioning was a welcome relief from the thick, hot air outside.

Jericho moved quickly through the hallway to a back room. They stopped in front of a steel door with a retinal scanner and a keypad next to it. Jericho then punched in two sets of codes that entered setup mode for the system.

"We need a retinal scan, and a 5-digit number for an entry code. Start with the left eye then right, it will beep once between them when a good scan is accepted. Then when you hear a double beep, punch in your code and the red light will turn green to show it's set. Kirkorian, you're up," Jericho stated.

Kirkorian did as instructed, followed by Naz. Jericho reset the system then leaned in as the retinal scanner scanned his right eye. With a satisfying beep and a green light, he punched in his access code and the magnetic lock on the thick steel door opened with a clunk.

As the door opened, the team was greeted by a concrete stairway going down lit by the blue-violet light of LED tubes. At the base of the stairs was another steel door and another keypad. Jericho punched in his code and once again the clank of magnetic locks releasing allowed him to swing open the door and enter the underground bunker complex.

"Okay folks, ops center and comms to the left, quarters and armory to the right. Stow your gear, Moose and Hammer will show you to your racks. Sidearms stay with you at all times, even while you're sleeping. Get cleaned up and meet me in the briefing room at the end of the hall. Kirkorian, you'll be glad to know you've got your own showers so please don't put any of our own in the hospital this time," Jericho said with a smile and a wink to Kirkorian.

"Yes boss!" she replied chuckling.

Jericho walked away as Moose led the group into the living quarters. Steel twin beds lined both sides of the room with two doors to shower and bathrooms at the end of the barracks.

"Kirkorian, you're here at the last bunk on the right, Naz you're across the aisle," Moose said as he tossed her duffle bag onto the bed while Hammer did the same for Naz. "Stow your gear, clean fatigues are hanging in the locker next to your bunk, see you in ten."

With that, Moose and Hammer turned and left. Both soldiers stowed their packs, pulled out a set of tan fatigues and tossed them on the bed at virtually the same time. As Kirkorian started pulling off her pants, Naz turned his back to her.

"Don't worry Naz, I left my modesty behind a long time ago. When I volunteered for Ranger school, I told the powers that be that I wouldn't ask for or accept any accommodation. Whatever the men went through, I'd go through. No separate quarters, no separate nothing. Needless to say, it made a lot of people uncomfortable having a woman share shower and bath facilities. But I figured, if I was in the field with my team, there's not going to be any privacy there so why worry about it," Kirkorian said unemotionally as she pulled on the new uniform.

"I can imagine that was an odd situation for everyone. I know it would have been for me if a woman were in my squad for Seal training. So, what did Jericho mean back there?" Naz asked.

Kirkorian laughed, "Most of the guys reacted much like you just did, but there were a few who were extremely upset. They resented me being there and taking the place of 'others more deserving' as some of them said. One night two guys wanted to teach me a lesson and came after me in my bunk while everyone was sleeping. Unfortunately for them, they both had medical terminations from the program; one with a lacerated kidney and the other with a shattered nose. No one bothered me after that."

"Damn, guess I won't piss you off then," he replied. "How do you know Jericho?"

"He was the senior TI. He was the only one who knew I was gonna be in the class and tried every dirty trick to get me to self-terminate. Think of the most inappropriate comments you can make to a woman; he said every single one. He didn't push me any harder than the men, but he knows how to push buttons and pushed them all, against all of us.

"We started with 150 and graduated 62. I had some good teammates who helped me with the physical stuff and my shooting gave me a leg up. Jericho was the first to pin on my Ranger tabs and looked like a proud papa to boot. Lost two of those guys during the recent action in Afghanistan," she replied with a bit of melancholy.

"I know how that goes, lost one of the guys from my training squad on a mission with me. We had some bad intel and walked into an ambush. He took one in the face and ended up dying in the medevac chopper," Naz said. "Alright, let's go."

Chapter 15

Signals Intercept

"*Flash Message from NSA: An encrypted burst satcom transmission has been intercepted on a frequency associated with Mossad. Unable to confirm an exact location but triangulation indicates the general target area of the Iranian nuclear incident.*"

DDI Hayes pondered the conversation she was about to have as she savored her double-shot Mochachino. While she enjoyed the major chain's version, the CIA commissary had a pretty good imitation. Recent events meant late nights and 24-hour shifts were common and the extra shot of caffeine was a necessity these days. Gathering intel on the enemies of the West was stressing every Five Eyes country lately.

The highly secret Five Eyes alliance integrated electronic intelligence capabilities from the five English speaking countries of Australia, New Zealand, Canada, Britain, and America. Five Eyes shared collection in real time. So, when the burst transmission was intercepted; NSA, the Australian Signals Directorate, and the UK Communications Headquarters triangulated the signal to within a 50-kilometer zone around Dezful. Not GPS coordinates but in geospatial terms, a bullseye.

Janelle needed Mossad to tell her what they had held back and punched the speed dial for her Mossad counterpart. It took three rings before a familiar voice answered.

"Hello Janelle, I guess I shouldn't be surprised that it took you this long, well maybe a little," answered Mossad's Deputy Director of Collections.

"Hello again Eitan. So why don't you tell me what you left out of our first conversation. And don't try to bullshit me, the stakes are too high," replied Hayes with a skilled touch of annoyance.

"And what would you like to know?" asked Eitan.

"Who's the asset?" answered Hayes pointedly.

There was a pause on the line and the silence was deafening.

"Stop jerking me around Eitan, we know you have an asset on the ground near Dezful. We're about to send in a tac team so if you don't want your asset to end up dead, either by the Iranians or by us, tell me now."

While covert assets can be coordinated easily before going into hostile territory, once in-country, coordination becomes nearly impossible. The asset must make decisions that could mean the difference between peace and war with little guidance or help. Because of this, they react on instinct and any threat must be dealt with, creating a dangerous risk of deadly consequences.

"Yes Janelle, we had a deep cover asset in the area because we heard of the secret military installation somewhere near there. We narrowed down its location and have been trying to determine what the Iranians were doing there but had no definitive confirmation. We lost contact with the asset after the incident until a burst transmission indicated they'd been compromised. Protocol is to self-exfil, find a safe house, and call for extraction," Eitan replied.

"Compromised how?" Hayes asked curtly.

"Honestly Janelle, we have no idea. Nor do we know where the asset is. Just the message I've just relayed. We don't expect any more contact until they call for extraction," he replied.

"I take it the asset was in Dezful so I must assume they're working their way out and are still in the vicinity. Keep your extraction team away, my team will do it. We don't need any collisions and having Mossad and CIA shooting at each other will not go over big in either of our countries," she instructed.

"Janelle, my PM will not agree to that. You know how he feels about President Saldana," Eitan insisted.

"I don't give two shits how your PM feels; this isn't a political thing, and you goddamn know it. You should have told me about this before now. We know you've got better Humint in Iran, but we've got better Elint. Seems we've shared more with you than you with us.

"Look, I know we don't always share everything, but this is different. I've told you everything we know, and we need your support for this team. Keep in mind the Russians, Chinese, North Koreans, hell, all of Europe are involved on different sides. If you guys go rogue, we won't be able to control things. You have to trust the DCI and SecDef to steer this ship from our side. After the events in Afghanistan, they hold sway in the Administration right now," Hayes urged.

"I understand and I'll take this to the Director," he responded. "We've heard the intercepts as well, but I'm telling you, we had nothing to do with this. Tell Director Anderson he'll likely get a call from Ariens."

"If you want to prevent that regional war you've desperately tried to avoid, then hold your goddamn team Eitan, I'm dead serious. If your asset makes contact, tell them we're there to help. Infil launches in about fifteen hours. We'll keep you linked into what they find," Hayes replied.

"Alright Janelle, we'll talk again soon," Eitan replied, and the line went dead.

Hayes punched the speed dial for the DDO and conferenced in DCI Anderson.

"Okay gentlemen, as expected the Israelis held out on us. They've known about this facility for some time and have a deep cover asset in the area who's apparently been burned. No information as to who it is or how they were burned, and I have no illusion they won't send in their own extraction team. That means we could run into them, but I warned him if anyone gets hurt, it's on them. With that said, I say go on the op. The team has the latest and we'll update just before their jump," Hayes reported.

"What a load of bullshit! They knew and didn't tell us? I thought we were allies?" DDO Cavanaugh said with disgust.

"Well Silas, considering the President burned the PM by telling the Iranians about the Golan Heights advanced SAM battery, can you blame them? David, expect Director Ariens to call you. You need to impress on him we will operate with extreme prejudice against anyone who interferes with our op," Hayes stated solemnly.

"Janelle, you know the President will be hesitant to allow that," Anderson replied.

"It's that or World War fucking three. I doubt he wants that on his watch," she replied bluntly.

"Silas, what do you say?" asked Anderson.

"I agree with Janelle. If we go in, my team needs full operational flexibility. They're the best we have David, but they're gonna need solid backup," replied Cavanaugh.

"I've got confirmation from Secretary Jackson you'll have all the cover he can give you. I've made arrangements to have specialists on stand-by as a QRF," Anderson replied.

"Who? I won't have my people hung out to dry again David. I'll refuse to send them in without assurances that they aren't going to be sacrificed for some agreement the goddamned President makes," demanded Cavanaugh.

"Sorry Silas, you're just going to have to trust me on this, your team will not be left behind no matter what. If this goes tits up, we might have to do some things off-book and if anyone goes down for it, it'll be me. Plausible deniability Silas," the DCI replied calmly.

"To hell with the plausible deniability David, who's my backup?" Cavanaugh demanded.

"Silas, we've been spooks together for 30 years. If the tables were turned, would you tell me?" asked Anderson.

After a moment of awkward silence.

"That's what I thought. You can piss and moan all you want but you or Janelle would be acting DCI if this goes bad. So no, you don't get to know and neither does Janelle. You two need to keep working on the details and support our team. Make sure our assets are in position to provide whatever logistical support is required for this mission."

"David, we *can't* delay infil, everything's set up and ready to go. When will the President give the go ahead?" asked Hayes.

"I'm working on that. Secretary Jackson is on board so keep the ball rolling for infil and we'll get you the authorization," directed Anderson.

"Okay David, but if this goes sideways, you need to tell me the plan before you send in the cavalry so I can deconflict with the regional agencies. We can't do this in the dark," interjected Cavanaugh.

"Silas, you'll know when I know. You or Janelle need to be in the Joint Intel Center at all times. Plan out your schedules and coordinate with DIA, it's all-hands-on deck for this op," answered Anderson.

"Yes Sir," came the answer from both Deputy Directors as the line went dead.

Chapter 16

Escape from Dezful

Ebrahim's watch alarm went off, though he was already awake. He looked at Azar's dark hair splayed across her face and bare shoulder, and marveled at how lucky he was. While the tension of the previous day had melted away in the heat of passion, it wasn't long before reality invaded his dreams. Ebrahim leaned over, kissed her shoulder and she opened her eyes.

"Hey there beautiful. How'd you sleep?"

"About as well as you I suppose," Azar replied. "I felt you toss and turn all night. Can't say I wasn't doing the same. Has the sun come up yet?"

"No, sunrise is in twenty minutes," he answered.

"Then we better get moving and get this stuff packed up," she replied as she sat up.

Ebrahim perched himself on his elbow and watched Azar's tussled hair fall across her naked chest as the sleeping bag fell to her waist. She looked over at him.

"Now, now, as much as I truly enjoyed last night, we don't have time for that."

Sadness spread through Ebrahim like a wave.

"No, it's not that. I'm so sorry, all I ever wanted was to protect you and it turns out I put you in danger. You'd be better off if I'd died in the explosion."

"Ebrahim Hamadani, stop that," Azar said. "You are the best, most important thing that's ever happened to me. I was blessed the day you came into my life and there is no place, no place I'd rather be than by your side."

She reached up and gently held his face in her hands.

"Do you think for a second, I'd be safe? Even if you'd died in that attack, they'd have tortured and killed me just on the suspicion of helping. They don't care about the truth.

At least this gives us a fighting chance of both of us getting out of here alive!" she said softly as she leaned over and kissed him. "Now can we please get the hell out of here?"

"Yes," he replied.

Within fifteen minutes, they were back on the road.

"We need to avoid the major roads as much as possible. The car dealer is one I've dealt with before. I'm betting they haven't notified the suppliers that they're looking for me and this guy is a small fish. But the better reason is he's...discreet," Azar said.

"You mean he'll take a bribe," said Ebrahim more sarcastically than he intended.

"Call it whatever you want. By necessity I deal with people who are, shall we say, questionable. The IRGC needs things they can't get through normal channels, so yes, this guy is a smuggler, a thief, and a shithead. But that's exactly what we need right now," she snapped.

Ebrahim sat silent, embarrassed and annoyed with himself. Of course, Azar was right. But it made him uneasy how little he knew about what she actually did for a living. If not for her, he'd likely be dead already.

"Turn right and cut across the highway at the next intersection. Go past the Farmers Market and Mall then turn right, an immediate left, and then another left. That will bring us parallel to the street the dealer is on," Azar instructed.

"Okay," he answered.

The two looked straight ahead without talking for a bit before Azar spoke softly.

"I'm sorry I snapped at you."

"It's fine," Ebrahim said glancing at her. "As an Army grunt, I never thought about where our equipment came from. When you said you worked for a company supplying the military, I assumed you just did paperwork and deliveries. I had no idea what you really did or who you had to deal with. Had I known I might have quit my job to be your protection. But somehow, I'm guessing you wouldn't need it."

"Sweetheart, I've learned many things that help me stay safe. And trust me, most of my time was monotony and boredom. Plus, I had the backing of the IRGC, and everyone knew it," she answered.

Azar pointed across an upcoming intersection.

"Okay, see that parking lot with all those trucks?"

"Yes," he replied.

"Pull over there and park between a couple of those semis and wait for me. Leave the truck running and whatever you do, do not get out. Keep an eye on the door I go in. If

I come out and wave with my right hand, then pull the truck up to that door. If I wave with my left hand, get the hell out of here fast," Azar instructed.

"I can't leave you. I won't," replied Ebrahim sternly.

"My love. If we're burned, I'm already dead and the next thing you'll see is a bullet to my brain. You know as well as I the people we work for. There'll be no trial, we'll just disappear. So, if I have a chance to save you, take it. Get to the Saudis, the Americans, anyone other than these monsters and their allies. That's your only hope of staying alive," she answered.

She said it so calmly, it stunned him. Ebrahim sat frozen as Azar got out of the pickup and closed the door behind her. It took a second for him to get his senses back and by the time he looked up, she was already across the street headed down the short block toward the dealer. She walked with an air of confidence that exuded a "mess with me and you're dead" attitude.

Just then it occurred to Ebrahim, it wasn't just an attitude. Azar wasn't just good at Parkour or martial arts; she was the best. Given her work and who she dealt with in this male dominated society, she would have to command respect. Respect earned not just by using her feminine wiles to get what she wanted, but likely a few broken bones as well.

Her close combat skills and knowledge of all sorts of things that kill, plus the fact she worked for the IRGC, elevated that danger to anyone who crossed her to near certain death. And not a death that would be quick or painless. A shudder went through Ebrahim's body. How could he have been so ignorant!

Azar approached the door to the dealer and scanned the intersection in all directions. She glanced back at Ebrahim, and with a quick nod, grabbed the door handle, threw it open, and entered quickly. The minutes felt like hours as the adrenaline and anxiety coursed through him. Five minutes passed and Azar opened the door and waved...right hand.

Ebrahim let out a breath like a balloon losing air and put the pickup in drive. The uneasiness was still there but the anxiety had subsided as the tension of the situation with the dealer looked to be under control, for now. He pulled the truck up to a driveway and Azar pointed him into it. As he pulled forward, a powered steel and sheet metal covered gate slid open.

He pulled into a parking lot full of cars and trucks, both new and old. A man waved him forward then held up a hand for him to stop. Azar walked through the gate as it closed. She tapped the passenger window to have Ebrahim roll it down.

"Bring me the bag with the red tag on it," she ordered like she was talking to an underling.

Ebrahim instinctively obeyed. He pulled the tarp off the bed of the truck and looked around. He spotted the black duffle bag with a red tag and a lock on an oversized zipper assembly. He brought the bag to Azar who threw it onto the hood of the pickup. She pulled out a spring assisted combat knife and cut a plastic seal on the zipper then opened the small lock. As she unzipped the bag, Ebrahim almost buckled with surprise. It was full of money in nice, banded bundles. Azar pulled out ten bundles and zipped the bag back up, locked it, and threw it to Ebrahim.

"Here you go Zhubin, as we agreed. Two billion for the Nissan Navara, four hundred million for the demo of the pickup, and a little something to keep that lovely teenage daughter of yours from being a play toy for the IRGC," Azar said, handing over two and a half billion Iranian rial to the dealer.

The dealer looked nervously at Ebrahim and then at the money. "Who's this?" the dealer asked pointing at Ebrahim.

"Best not to ask questions Zhubin or do you want him to be your daughter's first of many?" Azar threatened.

The dealer dropped his eyes, looked at the ground, and shuffled his feet.

"Yes, yes, I understand," Zhubin replied nervously. "As always, a pleasure to do business with you Azar. I meant no disrespect of course."

"Remember, once this gate closes, General Kamaliazad wants this truck cut up, no traces. Give my best to your wife and daughter. There should be enough there to buy them something very nice to help you forget we were ever here. No?" Azar instructed with a smile.

Fear was written all over the dealer's face as his eyes darted between Azar and Ebrahim. Her smile was like a knife to his throat. The type of smile that only someone who holds ultimate power over another's life, or death, uses when asking a question that really isn't a question.

"Yes, of course. We'll take care of it right away. Please thank the General for his generosity," Zhubin replied.

Zhubin waved at one of his men to pull the new SUV up for his customers.

Azar turned to Ebrahim, "Load up the SUV!" she ordered.

Ebrahim nodded and started unloading the pickup and packing the large white SUV in silence. Azar opened the hood and pulled the communications computer from its

V-8 engine as the dealer handed her an after-market magnetic antenna. She disabled the factory datalink module, disconnected the GPS, installed an adapter for the specialized antenna, and reinstalled the computer. She plugged the antenna into the new adapter, pulled the antenna wire up along the frame through two sticky clips on the edge of the windshield, and stuck the antenna on the roof above the passenger seat. When she was done, Azar slammed the hood closed and looked at Ebrahim.

"All set?"

Ebrahim responded with a simple nod of the head and climbed into the driver's seat of the SUV. He pulled out a pair of sunglasses, adjusted the seat and mirrors, then looked straight at the dealer with the kind of neutral face he would get when focused on diffusing bombs. Just a simple blank, expressionless stare, made more menacing when the target couldn't see his eyes.

Azar got into the passenger's seat and rolled down the window.

"Zhubin, I'll see you in a couple weeks. I see you have several of those small pickups and I'm expecting an order for about half a dozen. But here's the hard one, I need two American heavy-duty pickups with diesels and full tow package. Our normal agreement applies; give me an estimate of time and cost when I come to see you."

"Yes Azar, I look forward to it," the dealer said, finally smiling. His demeanor changed dramatically with the thought of getting several billion rial in the next few weeks.

"Head back to base," Azar instructed turning to Ebrahim who nodded acknowledgement.

The sliding gate opened and Ebrahim eased the big SUV out of the driveway and turned back in the direction they came from. He made a right turn and headed north along the road paralleling the main street.

"Where to boss?" he asked.

"There's a large industrial complex three blocks up; pull in there, I need to get something from the back," Azar answered.

"By the way, I thought that guy was going to piss his pants. I almost did! So, what's your 'normal agreement' with him?" Ebrahim asked.

"It means absolutely nothing in writing and no phone calls. We do the business face-to-face or not at all. It's to protect him, and me. Despite the fact that smuggling is the only way for us to get the equipment we need, officially it's still illegal. We order stuff and pay in cash just like we did for this vehicle. I tell him what I need and don't ask how, or where he gets it. If it's equipment from a country with sanctions on us, we pay in hard currency, either US dollars or Swiss Francs," she answered.

"So how much money do you have in that duffle bag?" he asked.

"About eight billion rial and 250,000 US dollars," Azar answered casually as if it was no big deal.

Ebrahim nearly choked. "Do you always carry that much money?"

"More or less," she answered. "I actually just grabbed a medium sized bag; it's easier to carry. I kept the equivalent of five million US at the warehouse. If I needed more, I just called the home office and a truck brought it to me."

Ebrahim sat stunned.

"Pull in here and park for a minute," she said pointing to an industrial lot.

He pulled into a lot that had several trucks loading or unloading. Azar got out and went to the back of the vehicle. Within a minute she found what she was looking for and climbed back into the passenger seat with a small drab green military radio. She connected it to a module that plugged into the USB port of the car, turned it on, and tuned it to a frequency that came alive with military chatter.

The scale of the devastation at the research facility was immediately apparent from the volume of requests for more engineering and nuclear decontamination equipment. It also meant that the demand to find the two of them would be intense and nationwide.

"They're dealing with radiation fallout in Khoramabad! Was this a nuke facility?" asked Azar with surprise.

"Yes. There was a test yesterday when the explosion happened. But there is no way that the test could have caused the explosion at the facility; the test chamber was completely isolated," replied Ebrahim.

"But they're talking about nuke teams to decon *inside* the facility!" she exclaimed.

"I know, but it makes no sense. The only connections were electrical through a conduit that was filled with...oh my god!" he blurted.

"What?" she asked.

"Massoud," Ebrahim replied almost hissing.

His eyes narrowed and his lips pursed just a bit as he said the name.

"That son-of-a-bitch laid out all the connections to the blast chamber and oversaw all the drilling and sealing of those conduits. Only he would know the location of every pathway and electrical system, as well as all the fail-safe systems that are supposed to be in effect.

"Whenever there was a test, we always had automatic cutoffs as soon as the trigger impulse was sent to isolate any relays and junctions that couldn't be filled with concrete. Massoud would've had to ensure some of those conduits remained open and disabled the fail-safe mechanisms to allow radiation to get in. Given the force of the explosion, it would push that radioactive dust into the facility before anyone could react. Oh my god!" he said in horror.

"But won't that implicate him?" asked Azar.

"If he set me up for the trigger in the entryway, he could easily do the same anywhere and anytime I was in the facility. Only three people knew the overall map of the connections: me, Danesh, and Massoud. I bet Danesh is dead, and I was supposed to be a martyr for the cause. Oh, Massoud would get an uncomfortable interrogation, but without any evidence pointing to someone else, he'll survive," Ebrahim replied angrily.

"Right, Occam's Razor," Azar said.

"What?" he asked.

"It means the simplest, most obvious explanation is the right one," she answered. "If all the evidence points to you and me, that's their truth."

"The bastard, I feel like going back to his apartment and putting a bullet in his brain," Ebrahim replied.

The calmness of his voice belied the fury he felt inside.

"I agree, and that condescending bitch of a wife too. You know she's as involved as he is," added Azar.

Ebrahim seethed with rage, his knuckles going almost white gripping the steering wheel. Azar leaned into the radio to listen intently to someone complaining about the police.

"Ebrahim, did you hear that?" she asked.

"Hear what?" he replied, snapping his mind back to the present.

"There's a lot of confusion and coordination issues between the military and police. We need to move before they get organized," she stated urgently.

Azar grabbed a handheld GPS and pulled up the map.

"Okay, so we should head toward Dasht Abbas," instructed Azar. "I know that area, but it's been some time since I've been there. There's a checkpoint here at the roundabout for the Dezful-Andimeshk Highway north. Only one local police unit and they're looking for a mining company truck with a man and a woman. There's a military presence at the access road to the military airbase but we'll be turning away from them.

"They won't be expecting us to move so close to their armed security and this road loops back up to the Andimeshk-Shush Highway avoiding another, more heavily armed, checkpoint where the two highways meet. After that there's not another one until it splits to Highway 64. That gets us a straight shot to Dasht. We can't move too fast; likely have to stop for the night in Dasht and then make our way to Ilam. I have friends there from the orphanage," Azar stated.

"Alright boss, slow is steady, steady is fast," answered Ebrahim.

He pulled out of the parking lot and turned north as Azar had directed.

Suddenly the radio crackled with traffic when a particular transmission caught Azar's attention.

"*Dispatch, X-ray 26, a white pickup truck, license AQ67553 headed north on the Dezful-Andimeshk Highway toward Andimeshk-Shush Highway with a male and female matching the description of the suspects,*" called a police unit.

"*Roger X-ray 26, hold position, do not pursue. X-ray 55, take a trail position, all units, do a box takedown after Azadegan Road,*" replied dispatch.

"Shit!" exclaimed Azar.

"Turn right at the next intersection and pull into the Mall parking," she said. "There's something we need to do."

He quickly did as she asked.

"In the parking garage, park at the highest covered level," she instructed.

Chapter 17

Ops Planning

Naz and Kirkorian entered the small briefing room with a set of 80-inch, high-definition screens and theater seats in a semi-circle in front of them. To the left was a rectangular table with two computer stations. Jericho, Moose and Hammer were already seated in the front theater seats.

"Good timing just got the sat link with Langley. Si'down," ordered Jericho as Kirkorian and Naz took their seats. "Go ahead Langley."

"Hey Kirkorian, nice to see you again," the man on the video link said.

"Hey KZ, how's DC?" she replied.

"I'd say it's hot but then you'd just think we're a bunch of pansy asses considering it's 110 in the shade there," Karim replied.

"Mr. Rezek, what have you got for us?" interjected Jericho.

"Right, there's a massive manhunt going on for the suspects in the bombing. The Iranians are looking for a maintenance worker from the facility named Ebrahim Hamadani and a woman named Azar Barghani. He's ex-EOD and she works for a government contractor with access to all sorts of nasty military equipment. It appears she's his girlfriend, so together they could be very dangerous. But something strange happened, they were spotted at the apartment of the lead electrician.

"The reason this is strange is that we know the Caliphate was behind the attack and planted someone deep on the inside. Given the extensive planning for this operation, they would've had an exfil plan, so why meet with a coconspirator immediately afterward? If he's not the bomber, he might have been set up. Either way the Director wants them found and brought in by us. Priority is to gather intel and find out what damage has been done and second is to find these two people," Karim finished.

"If the Iranians are looking and can't find them, how does DC think we can do better?" asked Kirkorian. "They'll have that place locked down tighter than a drum."

"We're scanning all frequencies on the cell networks and known satellite comms from every country in the region. If we get something, NSA will triangulate and lock down a general location. Then we'll start satellite scans 24/7. The Iranians will likely ask the Russians for help, but they don't have the real time capability we have," answered Karim.

"What's the status of forces in the area?" asked Naz.

"Expect Quds Special Ops troops backed up by regulars from the airbase in Dezful and local LEOs. They're already flowing additional troops and law enforcement for the search and the LEOs are manning roadblocks and checkpoints. Their Navy has launched nearly every gunboat they have to cover the coastline, so infil will be a challenge but Jericho has a plan for that. As requested, we've been running C-17s and -130s between Kuwait and northern Iraq every couple hours to help your cover Jericho," Karim answered.

"Excellent. How far from the border are they flying?" asked Jericho.

"Five miles and randomly vary about a mile and a half either side like you instructed, but clearly remain in Iraqi territory. You have F-22 and F-15 CAP with alert birds for aircover. The Iranians have launched their own CAP but with the F-22s and Saudi F-15s on station, they've kept to themselves," answered Karim.

"And the Kurds?" asked Jericho.

"The DDO is working with our assets embedded with them to coordinate the linkup once in-country. They'll provide security for the LZ. Your linkup procedures will be sent in a few hours," replied Karim.

"Okay, good. That gives us time to go over the plan and do a walk-through of the infil. I'll check back for last minute intel before we go airborne," Jericho said.

"Sounds good. Langley out," replied Karim and the link went black.

Jericho nodded to the computer tech who punched some buttons on the computer and a map of the border between Iran and Iraq flashed on the center monitor. While the map flickered onto the screen, Hammer moved to the corner of the room and picked up a black duffle bag and brought it to the front of the group.

"Alright people, I've read through your files, and I know you're both jump certified. So, the infil will be a HALO jump with a twist. DARPA's been working on new wing suit tech, and we're the first ones to have it. Hammer?" Jericho began.

He waved for Hammer to take over the briefing.

"This is the FSX-10 integrated Wingsuit. The suit has some modifications to make it more rigid and aerodynamic. I'm told when you both went to the spec ops jump training you used a flying suit, this is that on steroids. The gloves have controllers that will adjust the rigidity and camber of the suit.

"As you exit the aircraft, the suit will deploy like a normal one. When you push the button in the right palm, the suit will expand with compressed air. Actuators behind the arms will expand like jaws opening to form a more rounded rigid leading edge. Carbon fiber rods in the web are attached to actuators controlled with the left palm plunger to increase or decrease camber. Think of them as flaps for adjusting lift at lower speeds.

"We've got an aero training area, and we'll get one live jump tomorrow morning to get used to them. Helmets have encoded RFID so the head up display will show where everyone is. Comms are Ultra-Wide Band so are untraceable and can't be jammed. The operational jump will be a HALO, so our practice will mimic the distance we have to go. Just so you know, it's a lot further than a regular Wingsuit," Hammer finished.

High altitude, low opening parachute jumps are some of the most dangerous tactics ever done, especially at night. With horizontal wingsuit speeds in excess of 125 mph, any misstep in timing of any kind over the rocky terrain could be fatal. Their specialized helmets showed airspeed, altitude, positions of team members, directional heading, and GPS. The stealthy radios used a one gigahertz wide band of frequencies enabling the team to hide their transmissions among thousands of normal ones. Transmitting over so many frequencies, even if the enemy could detect them (which they couldn't), they wouldn't be able to triangulate a location.

"Okay, elite Wingsuit flyers have a max glide ratio of up to 4 to 1," Jericho said. "This suit gives us between 5 and 6 to 1 and we'll need every inch of it. Moose, bring up the infil track."

Jericho stood and pointed to the lines on the map indicating their infiltration route and continued his briefing.

"We're going to fly this corridor along the border with one of the recent diversion flights. Our jump point will be here then we'll fly northeast for 30 miles to this valley, then turn southeast and follow it for five miles to the LZ."

"Holy shit," mumbled Naz under his breath.

"So according to your numbers, we'll be jumping from about 35,000 feet then?" asked Kirkorian.

"That's right. It means we have to manage our speed and glide ratio very carefully. We'll be crossing several ridgelines and should get some updrafts to help us given the prevailing winds. Weather predicts winds coming from the southeast, so at a slight angle to the ridges, but should give us some leeway.

"The LZ is a mile west of Blyeen, here at the mouth of the valley we'll be following, on the edge of Kurd controlled territory. The terrain's pretty flat but hidden from any populated areas," Jericho answered.

"If the wind changes and comes from the northwest, we'd have problems getting to the LZ. Do we have a backup plan?" asked Naz.

Jericho pointed to a new position on the map and circled it with his finger.

"There's a Y-shaped valley here, three miles due west of Blyeen. If the wind isn't favorable, we should still get some updraft, but glide ratio drops to 4 or 5 to 1 on a direct line. This is the alternate LZ, then we have to hump about 3 miles to the link up," he replied.

"That's a long way from the target area," stated Kirkorian.

"We'll get supplies and vehicles at the linkup. Hopefully we'll have some additional info about possible locations from our electronic sweeps by then. Moose will run comms, Hammer and I fire support. Kirkorian, you and Naz are the most natural Farsi speakers, so you'll pose as a married couple and be our eyes and ears," Jericho answered.

"Passports and travel papers are complete for everyone so get your cover stories memorized. We've begun inserting your back story in their computer systems but since you're coming from small villages their records suck, so back story isn't as complicated," he said as he pushed large envelopes toward each person on the team. "Alright people let's get to the training room. Each of you have your own custom suit, and it's time to get used to operating them."

With that, the meeting moved to a room just down a short hallway to the right of the conference room. There, five wing suits hung in a row, each with a name on it. Kirkorian and Naz spent about an hour mastering the operation of their new wing suits then moved to a training tank. It was a fifteen-foot diameter vertical tank with a giant fan at its base that allowed the skydiver to maintain flight position suspended on a column of air that simulated freefall.

"Okay Naz, get into free fall position and initiate the compressed air. You'll feel an immediate gain in lift so watch your head. You'll need to compensate for the airflow by positioning your arms and you'll start to move forward. Once you find a neutral position, you'll be able to hold it pretty easily due to the carbon fiber ribs in the suit," coached Jericho.

"Whoa!" exclaimed Naz, almost losing control as he initiated the inflation of the wing suit.

The compressed air inflated baffles in the suit which enhanced the rigidity of the carbon fiber support structure. The increased lift threw him toward the top of the tank, and he nearly spun out of control as he compensated for the sudden change in aerodynamics.

"That was a big surprise, damn near lost it completely. You weren't kidding about watching my head. Kirkorian, it's a lot more sudden than you expect. Use down pressure on your arms as you initiate, almost like you're flapping your wings down and it should help smooth out the aero. You'll still go up but should minimize force on your shoulders. Hope you worked pecs today," Naz said with a chuckle.

"Alright hotshot now let's do some turns," instructed Jericho.

"Yes Boss," replied Naz.

After about fifteen minutes of flight, Kirkorian got in the wind tunnel tank and worked through the same set of routines as Naz. She took his advice and managed to have better control during the inflation of the suit and a smoother transition to flight. They did their live jump at sunrise and moved through various formations.

At the completion of training, Jericho was satisfied. Parachute specialists met the team as they returned to ops and took the suits for a complete system check and repack. The five operators grabbed some food and drinks and headed back to the conference room for the mission update.

"Alright Langley, what've you got for us?" asked Jericho as the team settled into the seats in front of the large monitors.

"Okay, the LZ is confirmed with the Kurds," Karim began. "Your equipment is on its way and should be positioned when you land. The Kurd team will be positioned east of the LZ and will flash one green light, then two red, and one green every 30 minutes from scheduled RZ and continue for 4 hours. You'll answer with three infrared flashes in response. If you miss the window, send a burst message with location and we'll try to do a reset, but you might be on your own."

"The LZ is about 150 miles from Dezful. The Kurds have vehicles for you and once in-country we'll sat-link the latest intel to you. Because of the heavy military presence, we felt it best for you to figure out your own path based on what's current on the ground and what the eyes in the sky show us.

"You'll have to balance speed with stealth and make sure you have commlink the whole way. That's up to your discretion Jericho; the DDO says that we're to give you whatever you want without question. Right now, heading slight east then due south looks good, but roadblocks are being moved constantly so we'll try and guide you in once you decide your route," Karim finished.

"Alright, thanks. We'll do some map and terrain study with the team and have a couple options to discuss with our Kurdish contact," replied Jericho.

And with that the satellite link was terminated.

"Jerry, pull up the terrain maps and overlay paved roads in red and any known unpaved ones in yellow," ordered Jericho.

Satellite imagery came to life in graphic detail on the large monitor. Red and yellow lines appeared crisscrossing the arid landscape projected before the team. Jericho used a wireless mouse and keypad to maneuver the image around and zoomed in on the landing zone and the surrounding areas.

"Jerry, do we have any real time video?" Jericho asked.

The screen flickered showing a narrow valley with steep ridgelines rising on both sides sparsely dotted with scraggly trees and large boulders. The floor of the valley was flat with a narrow dry rocky creek bed that meandered along it. The team instinctively leaned into the images as each member memorized the location and surrounding terrain.

Kirkorian pointed to a spot on the screen.

"When we get to the LZ, I'll position on this ridge here, south of the LZ. There's a good outcropping of boulders that will give me overwatch to see all approaches directly from Blyeen," she announced.

Naz pointed to another area.

"Here's a large clump of trees that looks about 100 meters southwest of the LZ, just the other side of this road. It has good cover and a great defensive structure with the trees and large boulders. We can arc in a semi-circle under cover with a direct view of where the Kurds should be and still maintain clear satcomm sight lines," Naz stated.

"Kirkorian, drop your gear here and we'll take it with us. Then hustle your ass up to the overwatch location; it's a 200-meter sprint, uphill," Jericho instructed.

"Wouldn't be the first uphill sprint I've done in the last few months. At least this one's not at 8,000 feet!" she replied.

"I know, I know, I read the after-action report. Let's hope we don't need it but glad to know we're good to 1,300 meters," replied Jericho.

Naz had the look of confusion on his face over the interchange between Kirkorian and Jericho when Hammer leaned over and whispered in his ear.

"She took out a Pak sniper and his spotter at 1,300 meters. Saved an Afghan Army platoon from being annihilated during the Valley of Stars campaign."

Naz's confusion turned to admiration. "Damn," was all he could muster.

Jericho continued.

"Okay, once we connect with the Kurds and get geared up, we'll move east to Aseman Abad, then head south on this road to pick up Highway 21. We take that south to Zirkhaki to pick up Highway 19 to Vareh Zard, then 37 into Dezful. Expect everything within 15 miles of Dezful to be crawling with troops and checkpoints so sticking to our covers and backstory is critical.

"Naz, Kirkorian, remember you're a merchant from Ilam heading to Dezful with your wife to secure supplies and customers for your business. We've secured you a hotel reservation in the center of the city so if they check, it will match the story. The rest of us will be laborers looking for work there. We've got a room about five blocks away at a low-end hotel, that will be command center. There's fewer prying eyes and more people to keep their mouth shut with the right financial incentive.

"Ilam is large enough that if you run into someone from there, they aren't likely to know everyone, but small and out of the way enough as not to raise questions about your business. You have the information on both targets. The girl works for the major supplier to the military for that region so try to arrange a meeting with their local sales rep to sell them stuff. Hopefully we can find someone who likes to gossip," Jericho stated.

"Lastly, you've all been hand-picked because you have unique skills, and can all think on your feet. There's a lot more unknowns in this mission than knowns so be flexible and adapt to what's on the ground. You're going to be put into situations where you have to make decisions without asking 'mother-may-I.' Do it.

"It doesn't matter what I think or what any of those douche bags in DC think; they're not there. You are. We're officially ghosts, so whatever happens to us, no one will ever know. Your life, and the lives of everyone on this team, depend on trusting each other to do what's best for all of us.

"Naz, you don't remember but we've met before in Tunisia. I was leading the CIA team you guys helped extract. I heard it was your idea to fast rope a squad behind the enemy lines and take out their commander," Jericho finished.

"That was you?" exclaimed Kirkorian. "That was really ballsy. You were lucky to get out!"

"I concur Chief. The survivors of my team and I thank you for that. It was looking pretty grim until that point," answered Jericho. "And that's the kind of initiative that shows how people think when the shit hits the fan. Get some chow and hit the range. Kirkorian, get your CSR to the chute specialists so they can pack it in the suit. Moose, we need to go over the comm protocols, everyone else is dismissed."

"Will do boss," she replied.

And with that the planning meeting was over. Naz and Kirkorian headed to the sleeping quarters where she pulled out the Remington CSR sniper rifle to bring it to the parachute specialists.

"Is that what you used for the pair of kills in Afghanistan?" he asked.

"Yes. It's a lot like the Mark-13 your guys carry, and I shoot .300 Winchester Magnum rounds. It has good balance for a modular rifle, and I get 900 meters per second out of the ammo. I like the .300 versus the Lapua .338 as I find I get less drop with this gun," Kirkorian replied as she pulled it out and had it together in less than 30 seconds.

Naz admired it like a giddy fan boy. He pulled back the bolt and lifted it to his shoulder as if aiming at a long-range target. He took in a breath and stopped exhaling halfway through, then pulled the trigger with a satisfying clank as the firing pin slammed forward into the imaginary bullet.

"1,300 meters huh?" Naz asked admiringly.

"Yup. Told you I was a better shot than you. Now give me my gun back and stop drooling on it!" she replied with a laugh.

Chapter 18

New Identities

Ebrahim maneuvered to the top of the parking ramp and pulled into a space in the corner of the highest level. Azar jumped out and opened the rear hatch. She pulled out a piece of blue fabric and wrapped it around her head as a hijab. Next, she pulled out a tube and then something that looked like a suitcase and closed the hatch.

"Come on, we need to go shopping," Azar urged. "There's a store in here with individual dressing rooms, take this case and I'll carry the tube. We'll tell the clerk you're a photographer heading to a wedding and my dress was accidentally ruined and needs to be replaced. We're married and you must approve the dress."

She spun and started walking quickly toward the stairwell door to enter the Mall.

"Wait, this is crazy. We need to get out of here," Ebrahim exclaimed.

Azar stopped and turned around and took a few steps back to face him.

"You're absolutely right. Except they know who we are, we have no travel documents, our original route is blocked, and they've just enhanced their security checkpoints," she replied talking quietly. "So, we need new travel documents few will question, right?"

"Yes," Ebrahim answered quizzically.

"So, let's get new travel documents," Azar answered.

"But how?" he asked.

"Who do you think provides the IRGC with all their equipment? Including their identification gear?" she asked with a wink and a smile.

"Damn!" Ebrahim responded with a smile. "I never thought of that."

He followed quickly behind. As they got to the door leading to the entrance to the mall, he put his hand on Azar's shoulder.

"Hold it, let me get ahead of you." Then he turned to her, "I love you with all of my heart so please know, whatever happens after we open this door, it's not me."

"I know my love," she replied.

"Good," Ebrahim answered then turned and yanked the door open.

"You ignorant cow!" he shouted as he took long strides forcing Azar to almost run to keep up with him. "How could you let that happen? If I find this was deliberate, I'll take my cane to you again."

Azar was surprised and a bit shocked at the dramatic transformation in Ebrahim. Shoppers looked at the two of them. Several women just looked down and scurried faster to get away from the angry commotion while some of the men smiled with approval.

Azar looked down and replied meekly, "I'm sorry."

"I didn't say you could speak woman," he hissed.

They walked another thirty feet.

"Where's that store you said had the dress?" Ebrahim demanded with disdain.

"Top of the escalator first store on the right," Azar replied, making her voice quiver with fear.

Ebrahim walked straight upright showing every inch of his muscular five-foot ten frame. Not once did he ever look back at her. At the top of the escalator, he turned and entered the first store on the right. He stopped dead a few feet inside the door as Azar almost ran into him.

"Alright, where's that dress you said will replace the one you butchered?" Ebrahim growled.

Just then a saleswoman approached.

"Can I help you find something?"

"This bumbling idiot needs to replace a dress she ruined," stated Ebrahim angrily. "Show me to a dressing room then bring her and the dress to me."

The saleswoman was taken aback but could not argue with this angry man in front of her. She looked at the man and then the quivering fear on Azar's face.

"Yes...yes, of course sir. Right this way," the saleswoman replied.

She escorted Ebrahim to a dressing room and closed the door behind him. She then turned and hooked Azar's arm as they walked to the racks of clothing.

"Who is that man?" the Saleswoman asked.

"My husband. He's a photographer and we're headed to a wedding. On my way out the door my dress got caught on a hook and ripped. He's very particular when he works and always must approve what I wear. It must blend in with the wedding party. I'm sorry if my clumsiness has caused you pain," Azar replied.

The saleswoman put her arm around Azar.

"Nonsense, I'm sorry you must endure this abuse. I wish we could control our own lives and divorce bastards like that!" the saleswoman said.

"Oh no!" Azar replied with the look of horror. "He would kill me first. And I could not leave my children. I can endure for them."

"Well, you shouldn't have to," the saleswoman replied with disgust. "Okay, let's find that dress."

After a few minutes, Azar picked out three long, colored dresses, each with a matching overcoat and hijab. The saleswoman took her back to the dressing room where Ebrahim was waiting and knocked on the door.

"Come in," he bellowed.

Azar entered with her shoulders slightly slumped forward and her head down. Once she was in, the saleswoman closed the door behind her.

Ebrahim leaned into Azar and whispered, "I'm so sorry."

"It's okay, I understand what you're doing," she whispered back. "But if you ever do it for real...I'll kill you," she added with a wink and a smile.

Ebrahim smiled back, though after the past 24 hours he was pretty sure she could.

"Okay, we need to work fast. Open the case and get out the camera in the top left corner," she instructed.

Ebrahim opened the large case as Azar pulled out a small screen stand from the tube. She had it set up in less than a minute and hung a black and gold banner on it. She plugged a cable into the camera and turned on the computer in the case.

"Okay, sit in front of the banner and don't smile," she directed.

Ebrahim sat straight with his arms down at his side with his blank, EOD face as Azar took his picture. She looked at the computer, made some quick adjustments, then grabbed the image and placed it into a small box on the screen.

"What name do you want?" she asked.

Ebrahim thought for a moment, "Hasan Rahimi."

Azar quickly typed the name and hit print. The small printer whirred to life and a plastic card popped out. She swapped the backdrop and hung the blue fabric. She put on the gold dress with a black overcoat and black hijab and sat in front of the screen as

Ebrahim took her picture. Once again, Azar made some adjustments, typed a name in and hit print as another plastic card came out of the printer.

"What name did you pick?" asked Ebrahim.

"Gulshan Habibi," Azar answered. "Okay, let's pack it up and get out of here. We're IRGC security so we shouldn't get too many questions."

They repacked the equipment and Azar changed her outfit. The two looked at each other and nodded. Ebrahim threw open the door and strode to the sales desk with Azar shuffling behind him.

"We'll take this rag and the green one," he barked at the saleswoman. "Go stand by the door while I pay for these," he said derisively.

Azar moved off as instructed with her head down. The saleswoman rang up the outfits and Ebrahim threw the money on the counter, turned and walked away without saying a word. Azar looked at the saleswoman who gave her a sympathetic look and mouthed "I'm sorry." With a nod of acknowledgement, she turned and followed Ebrahim out of the store, down the escalator, and out to the parking garage.

At their parking level, they saw no other people and walked quickly to the SUV. Ebrahim opened the rear door, put the equipment into the back, and jumped into the driver's seat. Azar got in, grabbed the GPS, and looked at the map.

"Okay, look at the map. If we head back to the southeast, we can pick up the highway here, then loop back around Dezful University. We take Azadegan to this road that parallels the Andimeshk-Dezful Highway and pick up this road that will loop around to the north and connect with the Andimeshk-Shush Highway. There's a local checkpoint here so they won't mess with anyone from the IRGC. Especially if you repeat the performance from the store," Azar suggested with a side glance at Ebrahim.

"Okay, got it," he replied.

He put on his sunglasses, not because he needed them under the partially overcast sky, but because it made him more sinister looking. He'd memorized the route using another trick diffusing bombs. It helped him remember complex wiring schemes and "build" the bomb in his head so he could retrace things without having to look again.

They drove in silence listening to the radio chatter, constantly checking for anyone following them. They passed a commercial zone across from a sprawling residential area that swung in a wide sweeping circle. On the northern side of it they took a roundabout and headed north. As they approached a canal, there was a construction crew where the GPS indicated a bridge.

They pulled up to the barrels blocking the road and, to Azar's surprise, Ebrahim honked his horn to get the attention of one of the workers. A worker approached with an angry look on his face waving feverishly for them to move on.

Ebrahim glared at him through his sunglasses, pulled out his gun and put it on the dash. The man's face went white and he stopped dead in his tracks. Ebrahim rolled down his window and waved for him to come to the car, then pulled out his IRGC ID.

"We need to get across this canal now!" he said in a calm, dangerous tone. "Where's the nearest crossing?"

The worker swallowed hard as he looked at Ebrahim and then at Azar who stared at the man, increasing his anxiety.

"There's, there's a temporary bridge about a kilometer northeast of here. This road parallels the canal and will take you right to it," the worker stuttered.

"Has anyone else come this way today?" asked Ebrahim.

"I...I don't think so," answered the worker haltingly.

"You think or you know?" hissed Ebrahim.

The worker cleared his throat, "No, no one has been by here since we started working."

"Good. If anyone, and I mean anyone comes by here, contact the police immediately. Now get back to work," Ebrahim commanded.

He rolled up the window before the man could answer and threw the SUV into reverse. He put it into drive and floored the accelerator sending sand, dust, and gravel flying as the powerful SUV sped off in the direction the worker directed. A minute later they took a left and crossed the temporary bridge. They looped around a soccer stadium and two minutes later, they maneuvered around a traffic circle then finally headed southwest on the Andimeshk-Shush Highway. A few minutes later the traffic came to a stop.

"Checkpoint ahead. Local police only but they are being pigs about things, boasting about how they're checking every car. How do you want to play this?" asked Azar.

"You've got those HKs in the back, right? Looks like we need to get them out and get into those uniforms as well," Ebrahim answered.

He eased over to the right lane and after about 500 feet took a turn off the highway. He pulled into an empty gas station and maneuvered around to the side. He parked in the blind spot of a video camera on the corner of the building. Azar opened the rear hatch and pulled out the uniforms and the machine guns. She tossed them into two bags, each having a uniform and an MP-5, and threw one to Ebrahim.

They entered the station and headed for the restrooms, avoiding the cameras inside. A few minutes later they emerged dressed in their uniforms, carrying their machine guns over their shoulders. With a nod, Ebrahim grabbed a couple bottles of water and went to pay for them, keeping his back to the camera inside the station.

A few quick steps later they were back in the SUV and pulled out of the station. If anyone looked at the video feed, they would see the SUV pull in and then a soldier buying water. A pretty good cover Azar thought. Ebrahim followed the frontage road and pulled back into the traffic jam. It took nearly an hour before they saw the roadblock.

"Ready?" he asked.

"Let's do it," Azar replied as she racked the HK to chamber a round.

Ebrahim pulled onto the shoulder and sped up. A couple hundred feet later they came upon the checkpoint. One of the policemen aggressively waved for them to stop, pointing his own machine gun at the SUV. Ebrahim stopped and calmly rolled down the window.

The policeman began walking toward them and waved for his partner to follow. As they got close to the SUV, they stopped briefly upon seeing the uniforms Ebrahim and Azar were wearing. The policeman called for another to join them as the three of them cautiously walked up to the SUV. The third policeman moved around to the back of the vehicle while the other two went to each window.

Ebrahim said nothing but glared at the policeman through his sunglasses. Once again, he had that blank, expressionless face even though he had to use every technique learned from diffusing bombs to keep his heart from racing.

"Who are you? We had no call that any military units were out this way," asked the policeman in as threatening a voice as he could muster.

Ebrahim pulled out his IRGC ID and handed it to the officer without saying a word.

The policeman took it and looked at his partner. "IRGC," he said handing the ID back.

"I didn't know they had women in the IRGC," said the other officer at Azar's window. "Get out of the car so I can search you."

Ebrahim looked at the man as Azar answered.

"I'll tell you what, I'll get out of this car and give you one chance to kill me. I'll even make it interesting and let you keep your gun while I'll just have a knife. But you better make sure you kill me with your first shot, or I'll slit your throat and string you across the hood of your car as an example for everyone to see."

The policeman went pale as he looked at Azar then his partner on Ebrahim's side of the car.

"And tell your partner there in the back that if he doesn't get his hands off our vehicle, we'll kill you all," she hissed coldly.

The policeman on Ebrahim's side of the car cleared his throat and waved his arms.

"All right, all right everyone, calm down. We're all on the same side here." Turning to Ebrahim, "Where are you headed? We haven't had any notification of the military coming our way."

"None of your damn business asshole," Azar shouted from the passenger seat.

Ebrahim put up his right hand to quiet her and turned to the policeman, "Forgive my partner, she's eager to capture the suspects and get a chance to interrogate the woman. She can be quite...persuasive. We're headed to Ghods. We got a report the suspects may be moving west so we've been sent to coordinate with the locals there. The backgrounds of the suspects make them extremely dangerous, especially the woman. Have you found anything suspicious yet?"

"No sir, not yet. Just the usual traffic but you can report how thorough we're being, I hope. And by the way, when you do catch them, that woman's interrogation is one I'd like to see," he said with a nervous chuckle.

It was a vain attempt to make light of the encounter, but Ebrahim just stared at him. The policeman cleared his throat and took a step backwards.

"Okay, let them through. You two get back to the checkpoint," he ordered.

The policeman waved for Ebrahim to proceed. He slowly pulled forward and rolled up his window. Once past the police cars, he moved back onto the road and drove away from the checkpoint.

Chapter 19

Uncomfortable Interrogation

Mokhtari stared through the one-way mirror at the man in the interrogation room. He'd watched him shift nervously for an hour and occasionally look at the handcuffs and chain looped through an eye bolt on the table. Restrained like an animal the man was clearly uncomfortable in the unpadded solid metal chair with a straight, flat back.

The room was dimly lit except for the high intensity light glaring in the eyes of the restrained man. The concrete walls were cold but stained from the interrogations of hundreds of people who came before him. The faint smell of chlorine emanated through the room reminding all that the Islamic Revolutionary Guard Corps wasn't shy about using violence to get what they wanted. In here, civil rights were whatever the IRGC said they were.

There was a knock on the viewing room door.

"Enter," ordered Mokhtari.

"Sir, I have the dossier on Hamadani and the woman," the Major said, handing Mokhtari a folder. "The woman's name is Azar Barghani and she works for Khavari Industries."

Mokhtari's left eyebrow rose as he scanned the dossier.

"She's worked there for about six years and become their top salesperson. Sir, she's acquired equipment for us that no one else could. She and Hamadani have lived together for three years and have clean records. We dug into her background. Her family was killed in an auto accident when she was nine and she was raised in a small village orphanage a few hours northwest of here. We're sending a team there now in the event she tries to make contact with them.

"She had access to a large warehouse at the munitions depot and they showed up there last night. She told the guards she was sent by her company to get supplies to support the recovery effort. We checked with the company and that was a lie. They were in the warehouse for less than ten minutes and drove off heading north in a mining company truck. We've confirmed they had a load of supplies, including HMX," added the Major.

Mokhtari's head snapped around to look at the Major.

"So, we have a bomb expert with full access to our facility and a background in electronics. And a person who can get her hands on every piece of equipment he would need to build a bomb, plant it, and make his escape. Someone who likely has contacts all over the black-market world and who has a storage facility packed with our most dangerous weapons that we let have ten whole minutes to gather supplies. That's who we're hunting?" he asked in his calm, threatening voice.

"Yes sir," stammered the Major.

"And what of this man?" Mokhtari inquired, pointing at the man fidgeting in the interrogation room. "He was Hamadani's supervisor; he would have hired him. Tell me why I shouldn't assume he wasn't involved."

"Sir, we're still gathering information, but he's been a loyal follower for over a decade. He insisted on extra background checks for everyone he hired. Every person under his control went through an extensive workup, even going back to verify details from birth and cross referencing with death records of infants. He's cooperated fully and given a full statement about his unexpected contact with Hamadani and the girl at his apartment before security arrived," answered the Major.

"What did tech find in his apartment?" asked Mokhtari.

"They found similar equipment to the module we believe was the trigger mechanism. He stated that Hamadani ordered the equipment and asked him to help with some configurations that could be used to automate some of the things they had to do in the facility. We're confirming the purchase orders through the supply system now, but we did find one recently that showed a set of components ordered by Hamadani that includes the serial numbers of those found in the trigger unit. So far, everything this man told us checked out," replied the Major.

Mokhtari grunted in acknowledgement, though deep in thought.

"What about the arming of the bomb, any progress on that front?" he asked.

"We're still looking at logs but that's taking time. Hamadani signed out to the control room several hours before the test and that information was supported by this man. There was an anomaly reported and Massoud here, was called into the facility on his day off.

"The guards confirm he entered the facility and left about an hour later. According to his earlier interview he went to the main electrical control and sent Hamadani to the control room. He said Hamadani was only supposed to work on the master control panel as he traced the anomaly to find a work around. Our techs confirm that was a reasonable explanation based on the wiring diagrams of the facility," replied the Major.

"Can anyone confirm it was Hamadani who worked in the control room?" Mokhtari asked with virtually no emotion.

"No sir, the anomaly affected the control room camera and everyone who would know what happened beyond checkpoint 17 are dead," was the reply.

"How convenient," Mokhtari said more to himself than to the Major.

"Sir, are you suggesting it wasn't Hamadani who did this? Every shred of evidence we've collected points to him," the Major said.

Mokhtari turned and stared at the Major for a few seconds before he replied, making the Major drop his eyes.

"Major, I didn't *suggest* anything. You're correct, all the evidence points to this Hamadani and likely his girlfriend. You've tied this whole event up with a big, beautiful bow and think it's done but you have no idea who sent this man, what was the motive, if he had accomplices, hell, if he is an enemy zealot then why is he still alive? There's been no claim by any country or known organization. Don't bring me shit and tell me it smells good. I need facts I can turn into *actionable* intelligence."

"Yes Sir, my apologies," the Major answered sheepishly.

"Have they traced the external phone line yet?" Mokhtari asked, returning his attention back to the ever-expanding investigation.

"Yes Sir, it went to another cell phone module placed down at the mine area located in an electrical box. Same batch as the trigger mechanism. It looks like the wire was run some time ago, but the module was placed recently given the lack of weathering on the unit," replied the Major. "Tech has analyzed the call log and found that there was just one incoming call from the same Saudi burner number we found before. It auto forwarded to the phone recovered from the toolbag."

"I see," replied Mokhtari, staring at the man in the interrogation room again. "And what about the interrogation of the surviving guard from the entrance that fought with Hamadani before his escape?"

"He stated that Hamadani came to work on the entrance door access panel. The guard mentioned he was acting strange once he pulled the panel off. The interrogator believes he was to trigger the bomb and then escape. Seems the cell phone trigger was the backup plan to detonate the device from outside if Hamadani got cold feet or was unable.

"Once the device detonated, they were knocked to the ground from the blast and that's when the guard saw the gun and tried to engage. Hamadani apparently threw a hammer at him, hitting him in the head and he blacked out. Doesn't remember anything until the medic was treating him," answered the Major.

"Supposition and guesswork are not facts. What exactly did the guard see; 'acting strange' doesn't tell me anything," Mokhtari answered.

"The report says that Hamadani took off the panel and paused briefly. The guard asked what was wrong and was told nothing. So, whatever he saw, Hamadani lied to the guard. The guard then said he heard a cell phone ring once, then another ring a second later and the bomb went off," answered the Major, handing Mokhtari the folder.

Mokhtari stared at the report in silence, deep in thought.

"Major, if you had set this all up and placed the devices where they were supposed to be, why would you pause once you opened the panel? And why have someone initiate the bomb from the outside when you are at your escape door? It's clear the bomb was somehow connected to the activation of the test due to the diversion of radioactive materials, so all he had to do was arm it, then escape. Why wait?" asked Mokhtari.

"Maybe the call to his cell phone was the signal to arm the bomb? It would imply he was just the bomb maker and had no authority to initiate it. Or he got cold feet because he felt it was a suicide mission and had to pause to take a breath? We've seen that kind of hesitation before with martyrs from our own supported groups," the Major answered.

"Perhaps," grumbled Mokhtari.

"Sir, we have no evidence of anyone else involved and the most straight forward answer is usually the correct one," replied the Major.

"The key word in your statement is 'usually,' Major, and you forget the rest of the theory," Mokhtari answered calmly. "If you have two competing explanations that fit all the available evidence, the least complex one is normally best. You're correct, we have no other evidence, but we're not even inside the facility core to gather it yet either. This required extensive planning and patience. And whether this Hamadani was involved or not, he and his girlfriend are a serious threat that must be dealt with quickly."

Just then a soldier knocked on the door.

"Enter," Mokhtari bellowed.

"Sir, they've set up a containment perimeter and breached door 17 at the facility."

"Tell them do not decontaminate until our people get in there and look for evidence. Tell them anti-nuke suits only, no decon until I say so. They start spraying that place down they could ruin the evidence needed to solve this puzzle. And have the nuke team commander call me immediately," commanded Mokhtari.

"Yes Sir," was the reply and with a crisp salute, the soldier ran down the hallway to pass along the order.

"Major, I want you to dig deeper into all of the maintenance crew. They're the only ones outside of the commanders and security who have access to the whole facility. Plus, whoever was behind this needed electronics training and access to locations without calling attention to themselves for being there."

"Yes sir."

The Major saluted and left Mokhtari to stare at the electrician deep in thought. A few minutes later his cell phone rang.

"Colonel Mokhtari."

"Sir, this is Lieutenant Colonel Shirazi, commander of the nuke team. How can I help you?"

"Colonel, have your men gone into the facility yet?" Mokhtari asked.

"Yes, but just to evaluate radiation levels through section 17 first and search for casualties. They're moving at a steady pace," Shirazi replied.

"What are the levels you're seeing right now?" inquired Mokhtari.

"Looks like lethal levels could be reached in a few hours of unprotected exposure. We found higher levels near HVAC vents. The dust from the explosion will carry more fallout with it to areas closer to the detonation point due to the apparent delay in the isolation systems from activating. I'm rotating my people every hour to prevent over exposure," the commander replied.

"I need a few of my security people in there to assess evidence. What would happen if they were there more than an hour?" Mokhtari asked.

"Sir, radiation poisoning and lethal exposures will depend on the health of the individual even with anti-radiation suits. I would guess at the rates we're seeing now, maximum exposure should be three hours to limit permanent health effects. The suits will reduce some direct radiation exposure, but a fairly high percentage of the most damaging gamma and X-Ray particles will still get through. The suits are very good at filtering dust and fallout that could be ingested or inhaled which would be impossible to decontaminate but give only modest protection from actual radioactivity," Shirazi explained.

"I thought we had those advanced suits from Germany. Doesn't that give our people more time?" Mokhtari asked quizzically.

"Sir, the best suits in the world only limit exposure, not prevent it. I'm trying to keep our people below 750 millisieverts to avoid significant and damaging health effects. While we can treat radiation poisoning for exposure levels above that, an exposure of 4,000 millisieverts is generally lethal with increasing levels of debilitating health effects over a lifetime up to that point. Even with the suits, at three hours of constant exposure your men could reach levels of 900-1,200 millisieverts and radiation sickness symptoms would almost certainly be felt. Anyone you send in needs to understand these risks, sir," answered Shirazi.

"Alright, let the on-scene commander know and get a team in the facility areas as they are opened. Once you get an assessment of the contamination, give me an estimate of how long before we can open the facility again," commanded Mokhtari.

"Sir, I don't think you understand. We may never be able to open this facility again. We're only seeing the contamination levels on the outer areas. The closer to the explosion site, the more dust and contaminants will have settled irradiating everything. We can decon some areas but others with heavier fallout cannot be decontaminated, only encased. I would expect that the inner 5 levels may never be habitable again," replied Shirazi bluntly.

"I see," Mokhtari answered thoughtfully. "I need to get those areas open anyway to get a team in there to do the damage assessment and recover our fallen martyrs. We'll figure these things out as we go."

"Yes sir," Shirazi replied as Mokhtari punched off the call.

The Colonel stood for a minute then turned and entered the interrogation room.

***

Massoud sat nervously, the discomfort of sitting in the hard metal chair and chained like an animal to the table for so long proved challenging to maintain his composure.

Mokhtari entered and sat across from the electrician just staring for a few moments. His cold steel blue eyes made Massoud shiver and sweat at the same time. For the first time, Massoud felt fear as his eyes tried to make contact but fell to the metal loop his hands were chained to.

"Massoud, they tell me you are a zealot. Tell me why you weren't at the facility during the test given the intense level of interest this event had," Mokhtari inquired.

The calmness of his voice had a dangerous tone that made the stare of Mokhtari even more threatening. To Massoud, having this man question him was like being thrown into a tub of ice water. His brutal reputation was legendary, but Massoud had always assumed it was more bluster than reality. He was wrong.

This was a man who wouldn't think twice about executing Massoud's wife or take a drill to his son's legs while he was forced to watch. Mokhtari had done it before. Massoud had to be very careful.

"Sir, my leave was approved several months before this test was planned. You see, my son is on a traveling football team in the premier junior national league. They had a game that day and I was on call, so everything was covered. I had my two most senior electrical technicians cover the interior systems and felt they could handle just about everything that came up," Massoud began.

"But they couldn't," interrupted Mokhtari.

"Well, no. There was an unusual anomaly that popped up in the master control panel that they couldn't trace right away so they called me in to help. The facility commander ordered it due to the guest that was scheduled to observe, and he wanted it fixed immediately," Massoud replied.

"You've stated that you sent Hamadani to the control room. Why didn't you go yourself if the commander was so concerned about this? I would have demanded the most senior technician to do the repair on such a critical system," Mokhtari pressed.

"Well, yes, I see what you mean. But there were several hours between the anomaly and the test. Hamadani had worked on the console several times and knew it like the back of his hand. It made sense for me to trace the circuit at the master panel while he reported what he was seeing directly under the console. Danesh was a relay and comms guy; Hamadani was more an electronics expert which made him the better choice," Massoud answered.

"I'm also told you had extensive background checks on all your people. How do you explain Hamadani slipping through the net you cast to prevent this?" Mokhtari inquired as he leaned in just a bit.

Massoud felt the pressure as this was a crucial piece of his carefully built backstory. It was now or never to see if he was successful.

"Well, I knew my people would have the greatest access within the facility. And they would likely be in positions and locations that could be the most vulnerable. I wanted to make sure they were completely vetted and trustworthy," Massoud began but was interrupted.

"So, you are to blame for this Hamadani getting access to plant his bomb?" Mokhtari insisted, now more threateningly than before.

"No, no, I tried to prevent this," Massoud stuttered. "I demanded the security assets look at everything, more than once, to confirm their backgrounds. They came back with nothing!"

"So, it's my fault?" Mokhtari asked more forcefully.

"No, no sir, that's not what I meant..." Massoud stammered.

Mokhtari leaned in slightly and his voice became increasingly accusatory.

"You were their leader; how did he get the explosives in the facility and wire the systems required to detonate them without you noticing?"

"I, I don't know. There were several layers of security that were in place to prevent unauthorized materials from entering. I'm not an explosives expert so I don't know what's required to do this," Massoud pleaded.

"But you blame my people for this event. Why shouldn't I execute you and your family for your recklessness in bringing Hamadani into my facility?" Mokhtari growled.

"No, no, I'm not saying that. I'm saying we did everything possible to ensure the security of our work. We followed every protocol and exceeded them. What more could I have done?" Massoud stuttered as his mind was racing to come up with answers.

Though he'd anticipated this interrogation, Massoud began to worry. It was one thing to think through the role he had to play; another with this man who would kill him or his family just for sport actually pressing him. His heart was racing, and sweat was soaking his shirt.

There was a knock at the door and the Major opened it.

"Colonel, we have a development."

Mokhtari nodded without taking his eyes off Massoud. After a few seconds he slowly rose, turned to leave the room and stopped.

Turning to Massoud, Mokhtari spoke in a quiet, inquisitive voice.

"Tell me, if it were you, how would you have smuggled the explosives into the facility?" he asked.

The question and the tone took Massoud by surprise, and he answered quickly.

"I'd bring it in hidden in equipment in small amounts I suppose."

His mind started racing, did he answer too fast? He desperately tried to gauge Mokhtari's reaction, but the man just stood like a statue. No emotion, no reaction at all. Mokhtari just turned and left the room as panic and anxiety rose in Massoud.

***

Once the door closed the Major turned to Mokhtari.

"Sir, technical branch has broken into the laptop they found outside of Hamadani's apartment building. We had to employ the Russians to help us get into it, but it was an older version of Zionist encryption they've dealt with before. It had a secure email application showing an email chain with someone codenamed Perseus.

"They traced the metadata to a server in Israel. The message itself is also coded but there was an email sent to this Perseus the day the facility was informed of the test. There was another the day before the test with a return message. But the computer was completely wiped clean of fingerprints.

"Also, we have a report of a pair of IRGC passing a checkpoint northwest of the city who said they were being sent to Ghods to coordinate with local police. And sir, it was a man and a woman in IRGC uniforms and IDs. They told the checkpoint they had reports of the suspects moving west. Their story makes sense with where we expect them to move, but I've found no one who can recall giving such orders."

"How long ago did they pass the checkpoint?" asked Mokhtari.

"Over two and a half hours. The checkpoint had vehicles backed up for miles so were delayed in reporting in," replied the Major.

Mokhtari stared ahead for a few moments deep in thought.

"Contact the police commander in Ghods and find out if these two actually made contact. If they passed the checkpoint nearly 3 hours ago, they may have been in Ghods for some time. And get a company of troops moving that way. Did they give a description of the vehicle?" he asked.

"Yes sir, a white Nissan SUV just like hundreds of others we drive," came the answer.

"Well, that makes sense. The woman has the means to get whatever equipment they would need. They may have counted on this getting buried with the hundreds of other moves," Mokhtari replied, thinking out loud.

"Sir, we've had sightings all over the area, and reports of suspicious movements in multiple directions. If they have the type of gear you're suggesting, they could be sending us on false trails all over the place," the Major stated with a touch of frustration.

"Yes, that's exactly what I would do," Mokhtari mused. "Have we cleared that security team and completed the interviews with the facility personnel?"

"Yes sir," came the response. "There's a clerk from the mining company missing. She was at work the morning of the test but has disappeared since. Security is sweeping up her known associates but nothing yet. We're checking extended family now."

"Give that Captain who led that security team command of the Company to Ghods," Mokhtari ordered. "And issue them those new radios we got from our friends."

With a crisp salute the Major moved quickly to the execute the orders.

Chapter 20

Hiding in Plain Sight

Azar glanced at Ebrahim, "they'll be expecting us."

"I know," he replied. "But we need to play this out. The more we delay the IRGC response, the further away we get."

"But they'll send people here once they figure out no one gave us orders," she said.

"Yes, so we have to be convincing," he answered before pausing for a few moments. "You know the one thing that was most dangerous about EOD? It wasn't the bomb you saw that killed so many people, it was the one that exploded when everyone responded that did the real damage. It's like those spy novels you love so much, misdirection causes confusion. I assume that's why you suggested Dasht Abbas, right?"

"Well, it crossed my mind," Azar replied looking quizzically at Ebrahim. "It gives multiple options for escape and a place to hole up."

"True. This road goes to the Iraq border, or we can go south just past Ghods to the Iraq border, or north near Dasht Abbas. They'll expect us to run to the border and that's why you want to go north into Kurd territory." he said unemotionally.

His face was locked in the bomb diffusing deadpan Azar was becoming accustomed to. Once he went deep in thought it was like he was in a trance, quietly tracing the options in his head. But this was a whole new level of focus. He had only glanced at the map yet seemingly memorized the whole route structure and its offshoots.

"You're right, Kurd territory will be dangerous but will slow them down more. We can blend into the small towns and villages. The small local police are less sophisticated than larger cities making coordination more challenging. But any move by regular IRGC forces will get the attention of the Kurds," Azar replied.

Ebrahim didn't speak for several minutes, so she went back to monitoring the radio.

"What business was your company doing in Ilam?" he finally asked.

Azar turned, surprised by the question.

"What?"

"What business did your company do in Ilam? There's no IRGC base there and though you said you have friends there you know the less direct backroads. You'd only take backroads if it was necessary. So, who were you selling to?" he asked again looking straight ahead.

"Ebrahim, we do business with more than just IRGC, you know that. We supply the police as well as..."

"The Kurds?" he interrupted her.

Ebrahim looked at her with that blank gaze that was no longer cute, but increasingly maddening.

"When we started out you immediately thought of Kurdish territory. Extremely dangerous for anyone supplying the IRGC, especially operating alone. I believe you when you say you have friends from the orphanage there. Are those friends Kurds?" he asked.

"Yes," she said, almost whispering.

"Company sanctioned or off-book?" asked Ebrahim.

"Both," she replied. "Selling to the Kurds is lucrative not only for the immediate sales, but for generating IRGC contracts to counter them. But for me personally, I don't like the IRGC, so this was my little rebellion. All officially off-book of course."

Ebrahim didn't immediately respond and just stared ahead.

"You're angry with me," Azar said quietly.

"No, just the opposite," replied Ebrahim. "We've both done things for our own survival and if not for you I'd be dead. It can't be a coincidence that Allah has put our skills together. I'm certain we'll get through this."

He gently caressed Azar's cheek. Her eyes watered up. It was the first time that she felt the emotion of everything. Ebrahim was panicked when it started, but now he was...calm.

"Ebrahim, I...I need to..." Azar began but choked up.

"I know my love. No more secrets. We face everything together, no matter the outcome," he interrupted.

"But I..." Azar struggled to get words out when the radio call broke in.

"Sergeant Rahimi, this is police Commander Soleimani, come in."

Ebrahim unhooked the microphone from its bracket.

"Rahimi, go ahead."

"Sergeant how far out are you?" the Commander asked.

"Ten minutes," Ebrahim replied.

"Copy, we're ready for you. You'll see a car in a little bit; one of my officers will lead you in," the Commander answered.

"Copy, out," radioed Ebrahim. "Well time to get our game faces on. You ready?"

Azar wiped away a few tears, "Ready."

Ebrahim saw the police car on the side of the road with lights flashing. He flashed his headlights and slowed down as the cruiser pulled out in front of him. A few minutes later they pulled into a parking area as a metal gate closed behind them. Nervousness rose in Azar as she tightened her grip on the gun in her hands.

"Easy, we have to be cool headed now," whispered Ebrahim. "If it were a trap, there would be fifty guns on us right now."

She knew he was right, but all her senses were on high alert as she scanned the shadow areas of the building for threats. The two slowly climbed out of the SUV as a door opened on the side of the building and a man stepped out. Azar immediately profiled him; average height, mid-forties, slightly overweight but athletic build wearing a commander's uniform and a side arm on his right hip.

"Sergeant Rahimi, I'm Commander Soleimani."

Ebrahim gripped his hand with a quick shake.

"Commander, things are moving fast so we need to get right to it. How many men do you have?"

He swept past the Commander and headed for the doorway. Soleimani cleared his throat.

"Uh, yes well, we are a small force of about fifteen. Five cars and the command vehicle with two dispatchers here in the building. When we got the call from Dezful I called in our off-duty officers. This way," Soleimani said.

He led the group down a hallway and through a door on the left. The station was typical of many small-town police stations in Iran. Cracked and peeling green wall paint, dingy grey linoleum tile floors with years of scuff marks, with the heavy smell of cigarette smoke and lousy coffee. Ebrahim and Azar kept their assault rifles slung across their chests with their right hands on the pistol grip handles, like all soldiers in the field do. Just a reminder to the local officers that these were professionals who were ready for any action, anywhere.

The group entered the ready room as a police sergeant called the room to attention. Ebrahim moved through the door, looked at Azar, and gave her a head nod toward the corner next to the door. With a nod, she turned and took a position with her back to the corner. The crisp movement of the two uniformed soldiers, the black and gold emblem of the Revolutionary Guards, and the deadpanned look on their faces, had the effect Ebrahim intended...fear.

"Gentlemen be seated. This is Sergeant First Class Rahimi and Ranger Habibi. Sergeant Rahimi was sent to coordinate the response to the recent terror attack in Dezful. There are reports the suspects might be headed our way so pay attention. Sergeant Rahimi," the Commander announced as he stepped aside.

The policemen looked at Ebrahim, then at Azar. Though petite, she looked imposing in her green and grey camouflaged fatigues, snug fitting black hijab covering her head, and matching black beret. Most police knew the IRGC had women called Rangers. Their official reputation was one of highly skilled killers, and with Azar's side arm on her right hip, combat knife on her left, and the HK slung across her chest, it certainly reinforced that impression.

Ebrahim walked over to a map of the local patrol area. The small force covered Ghods and some villages nearby.

"The individuals we are looking for are a man and a woman last seen in a white pickup truck and considered armed and dangerous. The two are similar height and build as we are," Ebrahim stated pointing, at Azar and himself.

"There have been reported sightings in multiple directions from Dezful, so resources are stretched thin. We believe they're headed to the Iraqi border, so we need roadblocks on all roads across the river. I need two cars to the north here at the dam and two here just east of Ghods where these highways split north and south. That checkpoint covers two bridges.

"My partner and I will position just west of town at this highway from the north. The last car will remain here as a fast response team with the command vehicle. Commander, you'll coordinate everything from here. Gear up with vests and full weapons kits.

"Check every vehicle no matter the type or the occupants, and above all be careful. Maintain a two-deep posture; one team approaches and the other provides cover. The suspects are smart, they have skills, and trust me, they've killed many of our countrymen including friends of ours. If you see anything suspicious, call for backup immediately. Commander?" Ebrahim stepped aside.

"Alright, you heard the Sergeant. You four take the dam, you the split, the rest of us are backup. Gear up and move out!" Soleimani ordered.

As his men moved off quickly, Soleimani turned to Ebrahim.

"Sergeant, are you sure you don't want to stay here at command center to work this? I can send my other patrol car to your deployment point."

"No Commander," answered Ebrahim. "Ranger Habibi and I have much more training to handle these suspects by ourselves than your men. I'd rather no one gets killed unnecessarily; we can manage by ourselves."

"Yes, yes, that makes sense. Thank you, Sergeant," replied Soleimani.

With that Soleimani was off to coordinate the movements. The whole department was buzzing with tense activity. Ebrahim and Azar started down the hallway when one of the officers came up behind them. The man was about Ebrahim's height but thinner with slicked back black hair and a slightly crooked nose.

"Hey Sergeant," he said.

Ebrahim and Azar stopped and turned around.

"I'm former Army and know how to handle myself. If these two are as dangerous as you say, maybe you could use a hand. I just got back from Iraq fighting the Caliphate and, well, there's nothing like combat to hone your skills," he said looking at Azar.

"I already have a partner," Ebrahim answered in a deadpanned voice.

"I know, but I figured maybe you needed someone with a little more...experience in these kinds of things," the officer said as he tilted his head toward Azar.

Before Ebrahim could respond, Azar had her knife at the officer's throat pushing him against the wall.

"What makes you think you have more combat experience than me?" Azar hissed as she pressed the blade against the man's jugular. "Tell me why I shouldn't gut you like the pig you are."

Fear was written all over his face.

"Habibi, stand down," Ebrahim ordered softly as he put his hand on her shoulder. "Officer, I'm sure you're good at something but if you interfere with us again, I won't stop her next time. Do you understand?"

"Yes, yes Sergeant," came the reply.

Azar sheathed her knife as Soleimani came into the hall to check out the commotion.

"Sergeant is there a problem?" he asked.

"No Commander, just a little misunderstanding. Right officer?" replied Ebrahim.

The officer nodded, not taking his eyes off Azar.

"Good, Zahiri, get to your post and leave them to their work," Soleimani ordered.

The officer slid with his back along the wall to get away from Azar, then turned and disappeared through an open door. The Commander glared at him, then waved to Ebrahim and went back into the command center. Once the two got to the SUV and slid into their seats, Ebrahim turned to Azar.

"So much for hiding in plain sight. You know, killing a policeman is a very quick way to get attention."

"It was a reaction. We couldn't afford to have anyone come with us or follow us. I just figured a little 'street theater' would deter him from trying," she replied.

"Well, he looked like he pissed his pants when you had that knife against his throat. I'd guess that's not the first time you've used 'street theater,'" Ebrahim said.

The powerful V-8 engine came to life with a growl, and they followed two of the patrol cars out of the secured parking area. Ebrahim scanned his mirrors and headed west-southwest. Azar listened intently on the radio for any information about those who would follow. They arrived at the assigned checkpoint and Ebrahim pulled over to the side of the road.

"Why are you stopping?" she asked.

"We need to keep up appearances until we're absolutely certain no one is following us or watching us. I didn't see anyone but if we sit here and stop a few cars, if someone is watching they'll report we're doing what we said we'd do," he answered.

"Got it," she said.

"I figure we have less than an hour before we need to move. That checkpoint in Dezful has reported in by now and it'll take a bit to get someone to check us out. We need to be gone before then," Ebrahim replied scanning outside the car.

Azar looked at Ebrahim with the realization that this was not the same man from the previous day. At the apartment he was the panicked, frightened man just trying to do anything to protect her. Now he was logical and calculating. The more complex the situation, the calmer he seemed to become. It was a side of Ebrahim that Azar hadn't seen before and found herself loving him even more.

For the next thirty minutes they dutifully stopped several cars coming from the north and searched a few. As they walked back after inspecting a blue Toyota sedan Ebrahim gave a nod to Azar.

"You ready?"

"I thought you'd never ask. Can we get the hell out of here now?" she asked.

"Pretend you just got a cell phone call and point to the west," Ebrahim said.

Azar feigned the call. They sprinted to the SUV, and he gunned the engine with a spray of gravel.

Ebrahim grabbed the radio microphone.

"Ghods command, Rahimi, come in."

"Go ahead Sergeant," the dispatcher replied.

"Roll the backup car to replace us at the western checkpoint. We've been ordered to check something out west of town," Ebrahim replied.

"Roger," came the reply.

"Sergeant Rahimi, this is Commander Soleimani, is there something I should know?"

"Commander, this might be nothing, but we have to check it out. Keep your checkpoints in place and stay vigilant. I'm sure the suspects haven't come our way, but every lead must be investigated. If you see anything suspicious, call Dezful for backup immediately. Don't wait as things could escalate quickly," Ebrahim ordered.

"Good luck Sergeant, you can count on us. Ghods command out."

"Okay, twenty minutes to Dasht Abbas," Azar stated.

"We can't stay there. We need to start north and get out of these uniforms. Once the IRGC gets to Ghods they'll be looking for a white Nissan SUV with two soldiers. The white SUV isn't a big deal, but we need to change our story now. If we stop in Dasht Abbas, they'll catch up to us. We need to cause confusion; did we go west, south, or north. So, we need to leave there quickly," Ebrahim reasoned.

"I agree. Just past the town there's a road that goes north. That's where we want to turn. There's a dirt road coming up on the left, turn there and we can pull off to change," Azar answered.

Ebrahim made the turn and pulled to the side of the road. Both got changed, then continued to Dasht Abbas.

"So, what's our story?" Azar asked.

"Simple, we're on vacation and we're headed to Ilam to visit friends, just like we were supposed to do before this all started. Just a little different direction my love," he answered with a smile.

"And how do you explain us going through small towns?"

"Easy, we're coming from a small town south of Dasht Abbas. It's the most direct route."

"Sounds reasonable enough, I guess. And easy to remember. You must have been reading some of my spy novels," she said, impressed.

"I just figured we should keep as much of the truth as possible to make it easier to recall. And since we're going north from Dasht Abbas, well, it really isn't a lie so all in all, it's all true...more or less," Ebrahim said.

"Always the logical one, that must be why I love you so much," she replied.

Chapter 21

The Hunt Begins

Captain Al Madani and his three platoon leaders approached the policeman who appeared to be the team leader manning the checkpoint. He scanned every member of the team and immediately identified him from the way the rest of the police acted around him. He wasn't the most vocal but when each team member did something or said something, they looked at this man for non-verbal affirmation.

Al Madani pulled out his ID.

"Captain Al Madani, are you in charge here?"

The policeman straightened up to near attention, "Yes sir."

"Tell me about the IRGC team that came through here a few hours ago. Were you and your men here?" Al Madani asked in more of a command than a question.

"No sir, we just took over about 40 minutes ago, but Officer Adinejah was. He's just about to leave. He stayed a bit longer because we had a rush of cars right at change-over," the team leader replied.

"Get him, and make it quick," Al Madani ordered.

Officer Adinejah approached and came to attention in front of Al Madani with a crisp salute. Clearly this man was prior military, thought Al Madani.

"Sir, Officer Adinejah as ordered."

"You were manning this checkpoint when the IRGC team came through correct?" Al Madani inquired.

"Yes sir, but I didn't interact with them, I was at the inspection point questioning another traveler. Their vehicle came up on the side and was engaged by Officer Saleh and two others. From what I saw, the interaction got a little intense, but Saleh kept everything in check," answered Adinejah.

"Can you describe the man and woman?" asked Al Madani.

"I didn't get a good look at them. They were both in uniform and the man was wearing sunglasses, like his," Adinejah responded pointing to one of platoon leaders. "The man was built a bit like you, and the woman seemed petite but clearly was a threat."

Al Madani held up a picture of Ebrahim. "Was this the man?"

Adinejah leaned in to get a closer look.

"It could have been, the facial features are similar but like I said, I was working with another car and didn't get a great look. Sorry I couldn't be more helpful sir, but Saleh spoke with him up close."

"Why did it take so long to report the interaction with the IRGC team?" quizzed Al Madani.

"Sir, we were busy with the traffic that was backed up but radioed ahead to Ghods to let them know the team was headed their way. They seemed surprised to hear but Saleh figured it was just the confusion of all the commands flying around. We reported the contact during our normal reporting time a bit later," Adinejah replied.

"Thank you, Officer Adinejah," Al Madani said.

The officer dismissed himself with another crisp salute.

"Lieutenant, take a squad and interview this Saleh. He'll be back at the main station filing his paperwork on the checkpoint. Show him the picture and contact me immediately."

"Yes sir," replied the Lieutenant.

"The rest of us will head to Ghods. Let's move," ordered Al Madani.

It was early evening and Al Madani was frustrated. With all the checkpoints around Dezful, maneuvering his large force was challenging and excruciatingly slow. And now his convoy was just a few kilometers from Ghods when another checkpoint choked the lone highway heading west. He slowly led the convoy down the side of the road, angry that his prey may be eluding him.

As he approached the checkpoint, Al Madani saw the police cruiser blocking their path. He climbed out of his vehicle along with his Command Sergeant and the two walked directly to the policemen talking to the occupants of a stopped car. Al Madani noticed a second patrol car with its two officers standing in cover position. *Smart positioning*, he thought.

"Who's in charge here?" Al Madani asked the nearest officer.

"Sergeant Namdar sir, he's positioned over there in the cover car," the officer replied.

Al Madani pushed past the officer and headed towards the checkpoint's team leader. When they got within a few yards, the team leader came out to meet them.

"Hello Captain, Sergeant Namdar sir, glad to meet you." he said. "Did Sergeant Rahimi find something and call for backup? When we saw your convoy approaching, we figured he used military channels to call for reinforcements."

"Sergeant Rahimi?" Al Madani asked.

"Yes sir, Rahimi and Ranger Habibi, the two IRGC who came and set up our checkpoints. They were manning a checkpoint to the west and got a call to check on something then had our backup patrol takeover their position," Namdar answered.

Al Madani looked at his Command Sergeant then pulled out a picture.

"Is this Sergeant Rahimi?" Al Madani asked.

"Hmmm, looks similar but he had a uniform just like you, had your features and was maybe about the same height. Could be him but sorry, I was called into the station on my off day and was excited that we had a part in the search for such high-profile suspects," Namdar replied. "You should speak with the Commander; he had the most interaction with Rahimi."

"Thank you, Sergeant, where's the station?" asked Al Madani

"Two kilometers straight ahead. It'll be on the left across from the mosque," Namdar answered.

Al Madani returned to his vehicle as the patrol car moved out of the way.

"Call command and have them check for these two individuals in the personnel database. Let them know we're going to talk with the police commander," Al Madani ordered the Comand Sergeant.

With a wave of his hand the column was moving again. They pulled up in front of the police station a few minutes later as Soleimani came out to greet them. Al Madani motioned for the Company to secure the area.

"Captain, welcome to Ghods, I'm Commander Soleimani. We got a call from your command center and are ready for you. Are you certain the two IRGC soldiers were the suspects?"

"Hello Commander, that's what I'm here to determine. Where can we talk?" answered Al Madani.

"The ready room. I've got a couple of my officers who spoke with both up close," Soleimani replied.

The Commander led the group to the same ready room Ebrahim and Azar were in several hours earlier.

"Tell me about the man and woman who said they were IRGC," Al Madani instructed.

"Both were highly professional. The man who called himself Sgt Rahimi spoke confidently and logically. He spelled out the situation and said the suspects were expected to try and make it to the Iraqi border as quickly as possible. He said we needed to cover as many routes between Dezful and the southwest as possible.

"Rahimi positioned every checkpoint and instructed us to use the two-deep cover as the suspects were considered very dangerous. Everything he said was spot-on, from the positioning to cover alternative routes, to the reports we received once he put us on the radio channels for the network, everything. Ranger Habibi was equally professional, though seemed a bit of a hot head. She didn't say much as Sergeant Rahimi was obviously in command," the Commander answered.

Al Madani got the picture of Ebrahim out, "Is this Sergeant Rahimi?"

Commander Soleimani took the picture and looked at it for a moment.

"It looks like him. His hair was shorter and pulled back...like yours, and he had a very trimmed beard. Yes, I'm confident this is the man called Rahimi."

"Was this the woman?" asked Al Madani as he switched to a picture of Azar.

"Hmmm, I'm much less sure of that. She had a tight hijab and beret and never took off her sunglasses. Seems to have the right height and build, but she was very fit and seemed very skilled. She had an encounter with Officer Zahiri, and he saw her up close. By the look on his face when I saw them in the hall, it wasn't a pleasant encounter," answered the Commander. "Zahiri, come here immediately."

Officer Zahiri turned into the ready room and stopped in the doorway, his eyes moving back and forth from Al Madani and the Commander.

"Yes, sir."

"This is Captain Al Madani. He has some questions for you," the Commander said.

"Sir, I'm sorry for insulting Ranger Habibi but she over-reacted. She put a knife to my throat and threatened to kill me. Rahimi stopped her but she went too far. Yes, I followed them in my own vehicle because something just felt off, but they manned their checkpoint and stopped several cars just as they were supposed to. When they called for the backup patrol car to take their position, I came back immediately. I promise, the mission was never compromised," Zahiri said nearly babbling.

Al Madani held up the picture of a woman.

"Was this the woman you call Habibi?" asked Al Madani.

"Sir?"

"Look at the picture Officer Zahiri. Is this woman Ranger Habibi?" asked Al Madani more forcefully.

Zahiri's eyes darted between Al Madani and Soleimani as beads of sweat formed on his brow. He leaned in to look at the picture.

"I believe so sir," Zahiri replied swallowing hard. "It was a little challenging focusing on her looks when she had a knife to my throat. But yes, I'm certain that's the woman."

"You said you followed them to the checkpoint. Tell me everything you saw, do not leave out the slightest detail," Al Madani ordered.

Officer Zahiri recited what he'd seen; the pair took up their post, Habibi was the cover officer and Rahimi searched the cars, there were ten of them. They remained completely calm and professional as far as he could see. Then he saw them get a phone call, then the radio call for the backup patrol car, then they headed west, southwest on Highway 37 and he returned to the station.

Al Madani listened intently, absorbing each detail for his report to command.

"They knew you were watching. You're lucky they didn't loop back and finish the job the woman started. Commander, what time was their call for the replacement car?" Al Madani asked.

"15:38 Captain."

"Over two hours ago," Al Madani replied looking at his watch. "I need a phone and privacy."

"Yes Captain, you can use my office, this way," the Commander replied, pointing down the hallway toward the command section.

The group moved quickly to the Commander's office and Al Madani called Mohktari.

"Sir, they were here," he reported.

"How sure are you? We've had multiple reports all around Dezful, but most have been false trails," Mokhtari replied.

"One hundred percent. But these two are incredibly smart and very patient. They played the IRGC role perfectly, including setting up the checkpoints and even manning one themselves for a while. Sir, they are not panicking, and are working deliberately. This feels like a preplanned escape. I feel they are more dangerous than we first thought," Al Madani answered.

"I see. It's possible this was their plan, but it might just be training and instincts," Mokhtari said thoughtfully. "Hamadani is former EOD, so he knows how to keep his cool. And I've been told the woman has extensive black-market contacts. But yes, this does make them very dangerous. Tell me everything you've found since they passed the Dezful checkpoint."

Al Madani recited everything, making sure to get every detail. He had the feeling that Mokhtari knew some piece of the puzzle he didn't, but in his mind, he was positive they had their traitors. Now it was a matter of tracking them down.

"The woman put a knife to a policeman's throat you say. Seems she has skills we weren't aware of and knows how to use fear and intimidation to get what she wants," Mokhtari stated with a hint of professional admiration. "So, what is their most likely direction of escape?"

"Sir, that's the problem. Just to the southwest of Ghods there are six separate routes they could take to go west or south to the Iraqi border," Al Madani answered.

"How many routes north?" Mokhtari asked.

"North sir? That just gets them further away from escaping, why go that direction?" Al Madani asked, confused.

"Captain, until now, they were being reactive and likely to make a careless mistake. Hamadani made a clumsy escape from the facility. We just missed them at their apartment, we barely missed them at the apartment of Hamadani's supervisor. And they left behind incriminating evidence. But they are smart, calculated, patient, very good under pressure, and have likely acquired resources to escape and evade.

"They went through a checkpoint and into Ghods, in IRGC uniforms and identification, not only set up a perfect checkpoint plan but interacted with the officers, threatened some of them, manned a checkpoint, and went so far as to feign a callout to continue on the escape route. They are acting deliberately, not reactively. So, do I think they'd go north? Absolutely. It makes our job infinitely more challenging. Why not escape toward the one area where we could encounter armed resistance?" Mokhtari answered more like a teacher than a commander.

"The Kurds!" replied Al Madani as the realization of the danger swept over him.

"Yes, the Kurds. Okay, so there's three main routes to the Iraqi border. Send teams down each all the way to the border. I'll notify the border guards to be on the lookout. Tell them to move fast. I'll get our Russian friends to get us some satellite coverage to sweep the area. I've already flown a team to Mehran, but that's the obvious place to run and on the main highway. These two are too smart for that but it's covered.

"There are cutoffs to the north at Dasht Abbas, between Mousiyan and Dehloran, and just past Havian. You need to split the remainder of your company into three and check each out. I suspect they'll try to avoid the main roads so we concentrate on the less travelled with more challenging terrain. It will slow them down, but us as well. But all routes will converge at Ilam; I'll send a special ops team there," ordered Mohktari.

"Yes, sir. I'll check in as we move through each town and village. As you said, it will be slow going but if you put a team in Ilam that will block at least one route," Al Modani replied and with that Mohktari ended the call.

As the IRGC company moved out, Soleimani radioed an all-points bulletin to police stations in the area.

Chapter 22

Go – No Go

D CIA Anderson drained his sixth cup of coffee of the day. The high-level coordination of the Iranian operation was stressful but came together quickly. He leaned back in his chair and slid the non-descript memo into a folder. It had a red and white slashed border like a barber pole and the words TOP SECRET SCI marked in bold letters on the cover. He slipped that into a Kevlar bag, locked it, and then put the bag into his briefcase.

With the document secured, he punched the speed dial for the Secretary of Defense on his secure phone.

"Colt, are you ready?"

"All set David. Do you have the memo?"

"Got it. I'll meet you at the White House in fifteen."

"See you there."

Fifteen minutes later Anderson was outside the Oval Office. Jackson strode up beside him as the President's Executive Assistant nodded to the Secret Service Agent who opened the heavy bullet proof door to the President's inner sanctum.

"Come in gentlemen, have a seat," President Saldana said.

He motioned to the two sofas facing each other across the half-moon carpet with the Presidential seal on it.

"So, what the hell is so important that I had to postpone my meeting with the Chinese Premier? Is it Iran?"

"Yes, sir, it is," began Anderson. "We have a joint CIA/DoD team ready to be inserted into Iran to gain information and possibly extract a valuable intel resource. I forwarded the latest brief; did you get a chance to read it?"

"Not entirely, but I scanned the summary. Are you talking about the suspected bomber?" asked Saldana.

"Yes sir, but there's more. We found out that Mossad has a deep cover agent in the area we were not aware of...," Anderson began.

"They lied to us? Again? Meier, that slimy son-of-a-bitch, I knew I couldn't trust that asshole," raged Saldana.

"Sir, Prime Minister Meier likely didn't know about this asset until now. They are deep cover which means they were inserted long before Meier took power. Just as you don't know where all our assets are, neither does he. And Mossad didn't exactly lie, they just didn't tell us everything until now," Anderson replied.

"Right, and unicorns are real. Christ David, you give him too much deference. He's probably the one who put the asset in place," Saldana seethed.

Jackson spoke next in the calm tone of a professor tutoring a student.

"Sir, despite your antithesis toward the Israeli Prime Minister, both the suspected bomber and the Mossad operative will have extremely valuable information. The suspect and his girlfriend not only know about the facility that was sabotaged but have extensive knowledge of the Iranian forces and their support assets in the area. If we can find them before the Iranians do, it would be a coup for our understanding of how far along they are with their weapons programs.

"As for the Mossad agent, we need to be the ones to find them and extract them. Iran already believes Israel and Saudi colluded in this attack and if Israel sends in a team and engages the Iranians on their soil, then all hell will break loose. Sir, I cannot stress the military implications of this strongly enough. This could ignite a war with potentially global implications. With the proxy wars in Syria and Yemen already threatening to expand, this would be the last straw. Plus, we know Iran now has a nuclear capability, but we don't know where all their facilities are," Jackson concluded.

"That's why we need our team to do this and keep the Israelis and the Saudis out of it," added Anderson. "The planning and preparations are done. We just need your order to execute it. This is an executive order giving authorization for CIA and DoD assets to conduct operations on Iranian soil.

"But one important thing Mr. President, you must give full autonomy and authoriza-tion to use whatever tactics and force is necessary to accomplish this mission. Make no mistake sir; if the team is caught this is an act of war. But given recent Iranian aggression in the Strait of Hormuz and their violation of the nuclear agreement, we have firm justification for action."

"How long do I have to think about this?" asked Saldana.

"You have four hours sir," replied Jackson.

"Christ, you don't give me a lot of options here boys. Can't we do this through electronic intercepts or someone else's assets?" asked Saldana.

Jackson responded with the cold hard logic that always made the President uncomfortable but unable to refute.

"And who would you trust, Sir? The Israelis have the most robust Humint network, but you just indicated they are not an option. And the French and Germans have been tripping over each other to do business with Iran since the JCPOA agreement was signed. Sir, you have no options."

"What a goddamned mess," Saldana grumbled under his breath. "So, give me the Reader's Digest version of this Executive Order."

"Sir, you give authorization for us to use whatever means necessary to gain intelligence on the Iranian nuclear program and the recent incident in Dezful. In addition, you give preemptive authorization to destroy their nuclear capability if found to be in violation of the Joint Comprehensive Plan of Action," answered Anderson.

"Military action? Are you two crazy?" blurted Saldana in exasperation.

Secretary Jackson didn't wait for Anderson to answer.

"No Sir, we are not. If we do nothing the Iranians have the technology to build another nuke and God knows what they'll do with it. And you can be damn sure neither the Israelis nor the Sunni Arabs will wait around to find out. If they get involved, the Russians and Chinese side with Iran, then we have a real shooting war we can't control.

"If we intervene, then we control the situation and keep the others on the sidelines. It's our people at risk and our advantage if we succeed. But without this authorization, our people won't go in, and you lose on all fronts. You'll be seen as selling out our allies and weak in the eyes of our enemies. You may not even make it to the end of your last term if you fail to act after Tunisia and Afghanistan sir."

Saldana was visibly shaken, and his hands trembled.

"Is this Madeline's plan, Colt?" he hissed angrily.

"Sir, I'm the Secretary of Defense, not her. And you are the President of the United States, not her. I'm the technocrat, not the political guy. I don't know the politics; I just know the real-life ramifications. This is the plan David and I agree is the best option; politics be damned. Sir," Jackson answered bluntly.

Saldana glared at the two men, his hands shaking just a little then looked down, silently staring at the Executive Order in front of him. It was DCIA Anderson that gave the President a lifeline.

"Sir, may I suggest you go over this with Garver and McIlvoy. But understand, this must be signed in the next four hours, or we lose our window of opportunity," he suggested.

"Yes, yes, that's a good idea," said the President as he got up and punched the intercom for his assistant. "Paula, get me the White House Council and Chief of Staff, asap."

"Yes, Sir," came the slightly tinny female voice.

"Alright gentlemen, I'll call you with my decision."

As the two men made their way out of the White House, Anderson leaned over and spoke quietly.

"Jesus, Colt, nothing like taking your rhetorical knife and slitting his throat. I thought you said you weren't the political guy."

Jackson laughed.

"I had a little advice from a friend who's played these games a long time. He told me I should treat politics like a no-notice nuke inspection. Know the answers before you enter, then box them in with their own words and actions. Unfortunately, the President made it easy."

"Well let's hope to God he doesn't get wobbly, for both our sakes. I'd hate to have to go rogue, but I will if I have to," Anderson said with more bravado than he felt.

"Don't worry David, we're in this together. If you go rogue, we both do. I'll be damned to have a repeat of that cluster-fuck in Tunisia," Jackson replied as they arrived at the entrance where their cars were waiting.

***

A few hours later Jackson paced nervously in the conference room of the Joint Intelligence Center while DCIA Anderson sat calmly at the conference table. Jackson had been through these operations before but never as the one sending people into harm's way. It was a new, and uncomfortable sensation for him. He'd been in dangerous situations before, but this was different. Once the orders were given, he was just an observer.

"How the hell can you be so calm David? I'm so damned jittery I feel like I downed an entire pot of coffee. And why hasn't the President given the execute order? We're going to lose our window for Christ's sake," Jackson lamented.

"We've all been there. The first infil I ordered I chain-smoked a pack of cigarettes until the team was safely inserted. This really isn't much different than sending an inspection team on a no-notice inspection," suggested Anderson.

"A lot more dangerous, and not at all the same. But thanks for trying," Jackson replied.

There was a knock on the door.

"Enter," announced Anderson.

"Secretary Jackson, Director Anderson, any word from the President yet?" asked Jeremy Stroika, Senator Stewart's hand-picked liaison.

"No, and we're running out of time," answered an annoyed Jackson.

Stroika went to a secure phone and spoke in hushed tones. A few moments later he turned to Jackson.

"Secretary Jackson, Senator Stewart would like to speak with you."

Jackson grabbed the phone. "Yes Senator?"

"Colt, I know what you and David are trying to do, and you have my full support regardless of the President's decision," Stewart began as the implication became clear. "You two keep going, I'll get you your authorization, no worries. Do not, I repeat, do not miss this window. There will be no repercussions. Do I make myself clear?"

"Yes Senator, I understand. I'll let Director Anderson know," Jackson replied.

With that the line went dead.

"Jeremy, please excuse us and close the door." Jackson requested.

"Yes Sir," he replied and left.

"Well, what did the Majority Leader say?" asked Anderson.

"He said we're covered, no matter what. I guess Jeremy is more observant than I expected, or Stewart is a bloody mind reader," Jackson answered. "He said he'll get us our EO."

"I'm sure the White House Counsel had a fit over the wording," replied Anderson. "But with Stewart's backing, I really don't see that Saldana has much choice. You're sure you're in with this plan?"

"Yes, my friend, I am. I guess that's what's got me so damned jittery. I know it's the right thing to do but the thought of the AG sending the FBI to my door is a bit unsettling," Jackson said nervously.

"Don't worry about the Attorney General, he's a political hack and Durchenko has him by the balls. And the threat of both Coltrain and Stewart going after their political enemies should make them piss their pants right now," replied Anderson.

But the slight nervousness was apparent even in his trained voice. There was a knock at the door.

The Senior Operations Officer opened the door. "Gentlemen, five minutes."

"Here we go," stated Anderson.

He stood up and led Jackson onto the operations center floor.

"Sir, we don't have Presidential authority yet," whispered the officer.

"How long can we delay and still make the LZ?" asked Anderson.

"Two minutes, tops," the officer answered.

To Jackson, time seemed to stand still as virtually every member of the ops team stared at the clock. It was an excruciating wait.

"Send the execute order," ordered Anderson two minutes prior to the scheduled time.

Every member of the Joint Intelligence Operations Center looked at the two senior members of the Administration.

"Execute the order Colonel," added Jackson with authority.

Suddenly the tension in his shoulders completely evaporated. The deed was done and there was no going back now.

"Castor 21, execute, execute, execute," ordered the Senior Operations Officer over the satellite radio.

Two minutes later, the secure fax machine in the corner of the ops center whirred to life.

Chapter 23

Infiltration

Kirkorian walked out of the shower room drying her short chestnut brown hair wearing just a pair of cranberry boy short panties and matching sport bra. Naz tried to look away but noticed a thin red line on her left side just above her hip. He immediately recognized it as a healing wound.

"Does it still hurt?" Naz asked, pointing to the wound.

"No," she answered looking down at the scar. "Just feel a little tightness sometimes when I'm working out hard or doing crunches. Happened during the Valley campaign. A Pak bayonet got me during a big rush against our position. Got four of his friends before he hit me, unfortunately for him he took a few SAW rounds to the chest and head.

"The medic glued it closed but the surgeon had to tidy up the cut in the muscle. Couldn't do shit for workouts for five weeks until the internal stitches dissolved. The second time doing ab work, two of them let go and pulled back through the muscle and holy shit, it felt like that bayonet hit all over again," Kirkorian finished.

"Mind if I get a closer look?" asked Naz inquisitively.

"Sure, go ahead," she replied.

"Damn, you had a good surgeon," Naz marveled as he traced the healing wound with a finger. "Nice clean line, looks like he never put any stitches in it!"

"Yah, no kidding! He was a plastic surgeon in the real world and told me he'd make sure I'd get to keep my bikini bod. Not exactly a PC thing to say but he was great," Kirkorian chuckled.

"For my two, had an OB/GYN stitch my ear back on," he said as he leaned in and pulled his ear forward to show Kirkorian the scar behind it. "And a cardio/thoracic repaired my right shoulder," he added, pulling off his shirt.

"Nice, what got you?" Kirkorian asked as she leaned in to inspect the scars from the bullet wound.

"A 5.56 from a Russian light machine gun. Went right through the mud wall of a house we hit in Helmand province," he replied.

"A through and through, damn you're lucky. It would have crushed your shoulder had it hit bone. Must have just clipped the vest, right?" she asked.

"Exactly, took a chunk out of the edge of the plate and ricocheted under the armpit. It nicked the artery and was a little touch and go, but fortunately we were close to a field hospital. As for the tightness, I know what you mean, I still have a bit from the scar tissue," he replied.

"Alright you two, enough with the war stories," Jericho bellowed from the doorway of the sleeping quarters. "Gear up and meet in the conference room in five."

"Yes, Boss," came the reply as the two operators quickly got dressed and gathered their gear. Minutes later the team was in the conference room watching the datalink from Langley.

"Okay, go ahead Mr. Rezek," Jericho ordered.

"DCIA is still waiting for the EO from the President," began Karim. "But we'll go all the way until drop time for it. Jericho will be on comms the whole flight and we've confirmed the required supplies have been prepositioned. The Kurds encountered an Iranian patrol, but they made diversionary attacks 15 clicks northeast to draw them away. They've got everything you asked for."

Jericho interjected. "Everyone but Kirkorian will be carrying the MK-17 SCAR-H with an extra swappable barrel, and suppressor. Hammer and Naz will carry scopes while Moose and I will have reflex sights. Kirkorian, your CSR is packed with your .300 Magnum Winchesters, and we'll have extra MK-17s at the RZ so everyone is shooting the same ammo. Mr. Rezek, please continue."

"Right. The LZ has constantly been scouted for the past 12 hours. Vehicles, equipment, and native clothing will be waiting for you. The latest intel is that the intense manhunt surrounding Dezful continues. Local LEOs have multiple roadblocks and are conducting 100% ID checks. We've double checked your backstops. I hope you studied them; expect to get questioned rather intensely if stopped. From our latest intercepts, the couple was reported at the residence of another worker at the facility. He and his family have been detained for questioning, but apparently is cooperating.

"From their logistical movements, the IRGC have moved a lot of heavy equipment and nuclear decon gear. It appears there was some leakage of radiation into the facility and their medical teams are treating people for radiation poisoning. And one last thing. There is a deep cover Mossad agent in the area who's apparently been burned. They've gone silent for a self exfil and you are to try to extract them if possible."

"Do we know where the extraction point is?" asked Jericho.

"No, all we know is they will lay low, self exfil, and call with extraction details when they reach someplace safe," Karim replied.

"Alright, thank you Mr. Rezek. And tell DCIA to stick a hot poker up the President's ass to get him to make a goddamned decision. I'm not gonna have a repeat of Tunisia," Jericho responded.

He drew a finger across his throat as the communications specialist terminated the link.

"Suit up, launch time in 45 minutes. You'll each have a chute specialist to help. We're expecting clear skies and full moon so we're going in with minimal gear for max aerodynamics and weapons are already stowed in the suits. Okay, move out," commanded Jericho.

The five operatives strode down the hall to the parachute shop. Like all warriors about to go into battle, they used jokes and friendly banter to push the tension of the upcoming mission away and try to stay loose. Naz told a story of a Marine who set off a grenade launcher by accident while getting into a helicopter. His acting out the chaos of the event had everyone howling with laughter.

But with each tightening of a strap, securing of Velcro, and rechecking of equipment the room got quieter. Each donned their helmet, checked for oxygen flow, did a comms check, and the team was ready. As they walked to the Humvee for the short trip to the flight line, the mood turned solemn as each person began their mental preparation.

They were like shadows moving to the C-130H transport in the darkened corner of the airfield. Dressed in black with their faces painted with camouflage, their movement barely registered in the darkness of the night. Even the lights of the big cargo plane were turned off so no one at the airfield even noticed them.

The team settled into the web seats along the sides of the plane as the cargo ramp of the C-130 slowly raised. The engines growled with the sound of chainsaws as the aircraft started moving. A minute later, they roared to full power for takeoff, so loud that it would be deafening if not for the earplugs the team wore. The acceleration pushed the team members sideways toward the back of the aircraft, they held onto the seat webbing to brace themselves as it lumbered off the runway and climbed.

Thirty minutes later, Jericho spoke into the green headset he wore. He looked at his watch, took the headset off, and put his helmet on. He gave the signal for the team to stand. There was no talking as each person did a final check of their equipment, secured their helmets, and prepared to jump.

The cargo ramp of the C-130 was lowered and the team walked onto it with Jericho in front and the other four forming two lines either side of him. The red light on the bulkhead next to the ramp was bright as Jericho held up a finger indicating one minute to jump. The light turned green and Jericho took three running steps and dove headfirst out of the airplane followed by the rest of the team.

As Kirkorian exited the airplane, she activated the compressed air channels in her wing suit. The team was positioned in a V formation like a flock of geese with Jericho in front and Kirkorian to his right. It allowed the trailing wings of the formation to get added lift from the person in front.

The flying suit required the team members to extend their arms and legs in a spread-eagle position. The arms formed the camber of the wing while the legs formed the body and vertical stabilization. On their boots were fins that extended when the air channels were activated which gave some horizontal stabilization like the rudder of an airplane. Together it made for an incredibly stable platform and resulted in less fatigue to the flyer.

Kirkorian adjusted the camber of the suit using the controller in her left hand and felt the miniature actuators move arched bars on the front of her arms to regulate lift. They were a minute and half into their flight when Kirkorian's head up display flashed red with a suit malfunction.

"Lead, two, suit malfunction. I've lost half my compressed air channels and HUD shows I'm losing altitude. Adjusting camber but my glide ratio has dropped to just over 4.5," Kirkorian reported.

"Roger, Diamond formation, Moose, Hammer tighten up on me. Kirkorian, park in the pocket behind and above us, Naz position behind and below Kirkorian. Altering course to alternate LZ," ordered Jericho.

Each team member repositioned as commanded while Kirkorian struggled to get above the front three. Her movements had to be extremely precise. If she elevated too much, she would bleed off too much energy and drop like a rock. Once she was in position, she immediately felt the additional lift from the air coming off the leading group, but they were still losing altitude faster than they wanted. After a few seconds, the glide ratio stabilized to around 4.7, which wasn't great but should get them to the alternate LZ.

Minutes of flight felt like hours as everyone worked their suit controls to get the absolute best flight pattern they could. The most dangerous part of the flight was coming up fast, crossing a ridgeline before dropping into a canyon for landing. Kirkorian knew it would be challenging but as long as she had half her compressed air channels full, she could make it.

"Ridgeline in thirty," came Jericho's voice through the secure comms in the helmet.

Just then, Kirkorian's warning alarm sounded again. "Lead, just lost the secondary air, can't hold position," she announced.

"Okay, heading for that slight gap to our right. Kirkorian, keep me appraised of your sink rate," instructed Jericho.

"Lead, ratio now 3.9. That ridge is going to be tight," she answered.

"Lead, I'm in position. Kirkorian, I'm moving below you. Just before the ridge, I'm going to flare up. When I say, cup your hands and catch my leading edge and we'll pop right over the ridge," stated Naz as he adjusted his camber to match Kirkorian's.

"Roger," was the short reply as Kirkorian focused all her energy trying to get every ounce of lift from her suit.

"Three, two, one, now," called Naz.

He pushed his legs down and pulled his arms up at the same time catching more air and zooming up into Kirkorian. At the same time, she cupped her hands and just caught his arms as he hit her from below. They cleared a set of boulders by less than a foot. The ridge sloped steeply down the other side, Naz dove for the ground to get more airspeed. Kirkorian's suit suddenly grabbed air as Naz dove. She flew about 100 feet off the ground as the thermals from the floor of the canyon gave her a little lift.

Three hundred meters later she pulled her chute that jolted her backward. She swung her legs into landing position seconds before hitting the ground. Jericho, Moose, and Hammer landed a couple hundred meters ahead of her, but she didn't see Naz.

"On the ground, where's Naz?" Kirkorian asked.

"Right behind you, nice flying Kirkorian," Naz replied.

"Thanks, you too. I'd have never made it over that ridge without it," she answered giving Naz a fist bump.

They took off their wing suits and unpacked their guns and gear. They folded their suits and moved to meet up with the rest of the team.

"Nice work you two. Hammer's got a hole over there by those boulders for the suits," ordered Jericho.

Naz and Kirkorian threw their suits in the hole then Hammer threw in a thermite grenade and covered them over with the sandy dirt. The intense heat of the oxygen rich thermite made the sand glow a dull red as it destroyed the suits in minutes.

"Alright, 13 minutes to the first scheduled contact. We're about four and a half clicks out so we have some humping to do. Moose you're on point; we move in diamond formation, Kirkorian in the middle, Hammer left, Naz right, and I'll trail. Keep those night scopes scanning your sectors. Don't rush, we have time to make the RZ. Barring any other contact, it should take us under two hours. Move out!" ordered Jericho.

The team entered the main valley following the dry creek bed they saw during their prebrief. Jagged shadows from the full moon behind the steep eastern ridge of the valley nearly covered the valley floor. They moved as one in a steady walk across the rocky, scrub brush covered terrain as each person scanned their designated zone for anything that looked out of place. Their black uniforms made them virtually invisible in the dark shadows. After about an hour Kirkorian whispered over the secure comms.

"Movement one o'clock."

The whole formation immediately stopped and instinctively squatted down. It was only a few seconds but seemed much longer before Kirkorian reported, "Mountain goat, we're clear."

The remaining hour was uneventful as they approached the rendezvous point. Moose raised a fist and again, they stopped and squatted, weapons scanning for threats.

"All clear," reported Moose.

"Kirkorian, drop your pack and get on overwatch, report in position," ordered Jericho.

She immediately complied and sprinted up the slope. A couple minutes later, "Overwatch in position, clear."

"Move," ordered Jericho.

The rest of the team moved to their preplanned positions and settled in to wait.

Twelve minutes later: "Lights; one green, two red, one green," reported Moose.

Everyone's senses were instantly piqued as adrenaline flooded their systems in anticipation of action. Every movement, every smell, every sound, no matter how small or how faint was a potential threat that needed attention.

"Send the reply," ordered Jericho coolly.

Moose complied with his infrared light. Invisible to the naked eye, the light could only be seen by someone with night vision glasses. A truck pulled out from the area of the RZ.

"Truck," reported Kirkorian. "Two targets, distance 100 meters. Passenger door opening and one target exiting."

"Got target one," reported Naz.

"Driver," reported Hammer.

"Target one flashing lights; one green, two red, one green," reported Kirkorian.

"Naz, Hammer, stay on target. Kirkorian scan behind the truck and hold until I signal. Remember, raised fist you take them all out. Okay Moose let's move," ordered Jericho.

Jericho and Moose stood and walked toward the truck. Kirkorian scanned the ridge to their left and swung down, left to right behind the truck. As she scanned about 100 meters behind the truck, she saw the nose of another behind some rocks.

"Another truck, 200 meters, eleven o'clock, partially hidden," Kirkorian reported.

There was a single click of the radio to acknowledge from Jericho. Once spotted, she had the new target in her sights and would deal with that threat if necessary. If this were an ambush, no sense telling the enemy there were others ready to engage. He and Moose never hesitated or broke stride despite the danger.

The man who flashed the light from the truck stood perfectly still as Jericho and Moose walked up to him. Nearly a foot shorter than Jericho, the man looked to be in his mid-thirties with a short beard and mustache and a tan uniform. He had a red, green, and yellow plaid fabric wrapped like a turban around his head and a military web belt with a pistol, and radio attached.

"As-Salam-u-Alaikum, welcome to Iran. I am Commander Chiya of the Kurdish militia," stated the man as he extended his hand to Jericho.

"Wa 'alaykum salaam, thank you for your kind hospitality. I've brought the gift of tea to celebrate morning prayers," replied Jericho in perfect Kurdish, shaking the other man's hand firmly.

"Thank you, my friend, here is a gift of coffee for you," answered Chiya.

"Ah yes, that is a fine gift indeed. If only we had something special to spice these up for both of us," replied Jericho handing the coffee to Moose.

With that Chiya pulled out a small bottle of Kentucky Bourbon.

"I understand you like your coffee with a little bite," Chiya replied with a smile on his face.

Jericho let out a good laugh, slapped Chiya on the shoulder and nodded to Moose who waved for the others to come in. The preset challenge and reply verification of identities was complete.

Chapter 24

Gut Check

This was the second major crisis for the Southwest Asia section in just a few months. The mass of data flowing into it had to be parsed, divided, and analyzed. Sifting through the overlapping and duplicative material from various sources was like trying to find tiny useful bits of information in piles of confetti. Then once extracted, piecing them together into a coherent picture.

They sifted and traced every lead as the Iranian response was plotted on a big screen overlooking the section. Given the size and scope of the response, the Iranians weren't being very careful with their communications. That made identifying and confirming certain movements relatively straight forward.

As Mo read through the latest intercepts, she noticed something odd.

"Hey KZ, can you come take a look at this? Something's off to me," she inquired.

Karim peered over Mo's shoulder at her computer monitor.

"Scroll back. I want to see what NSA captured say...within the past three to four hours," he requested.

Not only did Karim have a photographic memory, but he could read and parse information faster than anyone else in the CIA. As Mo was scrolling, Karim suddenly reached down and took control of the mouse. The words on the screen were flying by as Mo desperately tried to keep up. But Karim had found something, and he was like a bloodhound on the scent.

"Dammit," he exclaimed as he reached over to Mo's phone and punched the intercom for Gerlacher. "Zack, come over to Mo's station, I need to show you something right away."

The section chief was there in less than 30 seconds.

"What have you found?"

"Look here," Karim began pointing at an intercept on the screen. "A police checkpoint reports an IRGC team, a man and a woman, passing through on their way to Ghods. The two claimed reports of the suspects moving west, and they were sent to Ghods to coordinate. These are other reports of the suspects moving in different directions with one coming less than 10 minutes before the checkpoint encounter of them moving south. No other reports show them moving west.

"Then a phone call was made nearly two hours later from a location not too far from the facility to Vahdati Air Base to mobilize a company of soldiers to head to Ghods. Shortly after that an encrypted radio signal was intercepted near Dezful and a reply from that location near the facility. NSA says the encryption is consistent with the new Russian tactical radios we've seen in Syria.

"This indicates someone is moving a lot of firepower in a direction we haven't seen before," Karim continued with a sense of urgency. "And the use of the new radios suggests they think their comms are compromised. Zack, given what we know from intercepts about the two suspects, especially the woman, these two are smart and dangerous. If I were the on-scene commander, I'd be moving as many troops toward them as possible without causing too much suspicion. That's what we're seeing, and they're headed straight towards our team."

"Okay, so assuming the pair is moving west, what are the possible exfil options for them?" asked Gerlacher.

Karim paused to organize his thoughts.

"Well, it would make sense to move toward the Iraqi border, easier to make a quick jump for extraction. Some place like the vicinity of Mehran. But what bothers me is, why tell them they're moving west. I mean, it makes sense to say it to get past the checkpoint but I sure as hell wouldn't keep going that way. And these two are smart, they've already avoided the net slung around Dezful.

"If it were me, I'd go north toward Ilam or Eslamabad-e-Gharb," Karim stated confidently as he pointed to the screen. "Puts me in the area of the Kurds and makes IRGC problems significantly harder. That way I have multiple ways to get to the Iraqi border and way too much territory for the IRGC to cover adequately. Zack, my money's on them heading north. We need to flash the team to head to Ilam. Given the road structure, my educated guess is that is where they're headed using the road to Ghods so as to avoid the main highways.

"Give me probabilities Karim, how confident are you?" asked Gerlacher.

"70/30, it just makes sense," he answered. "They've been deliberate to this point and haven't shown a penchant for careless mistakes. They've almost gone ghost and you can see the frustration of the Iranians in their open transmissions. Potentially they could go east to Afghanistan but that's more open terrain and more risk. No, they'll try to get to Iraq, then make their way south to Saudi," Karim answered.

Gerlacher stared at the screen deep in thought.

"That makes sense. We know he's former EOD so he knows how to control his emotions. The girl is one of their suppliers which means she likely has contacts in the black-market world. If so, she would also need a bit of guile to work with those people I'd imagine," Gerlacher said mostly talking to himself.

With that he punched the speed dial to the DDI.

"Janelle, we need to move the team toward Ilam asap. We believe the suspects are headed that direction from Ghods along country roads."

"How sure is Karim about this intel?" she asked.

"70%. We found something in the recent NSA intercepts, and he feels their actions to date make it likely they're using a diversion to the west, but they'll head to Kurd territory," Gerlacher answered.

"Is he there with you?" DDI Hayes asked.

"Yes ma'am, with James as well," he replied.

"Put me on speaker," Hayes ordered.

Gerlacher complied. "You're on."

"Karim, what route do you think they are taking and how long before they get there?" Hayes queried.

"Ma'am, I can't be sure because it will depend on whether they follow through with their feint. They told a checkpoint they were headed to Ghods to coordinate a search in that area and the information was relayed by radio to the police there. These two are pretty cool characters so I wouldn't put it past them to keep the charade up to delay the IRGC response.

"There are reports of sightings all around Dezful but this one feels...different. It's just a hunch but it's what I'd do. Take advantage of the chaos, send a report just before moving through the checkpoint to shift the focus in another direction, then use their knowledge of IRGC procedure to get through the checkpoint. It all makes sense ma'am," Karim finished.

"I'm not seeing any roads north out of Ghods," Hayes responded.

"No ma'am, either Highway 64 east-west or country roads south. I suspect they chose Ghods because of that. Anyone chasing them would have to assume a run to the border and the fastest is west or south. But they have no protection in either of those directions. So, the likely route would be north out of Dasht Abbas," Karim replied.

"That's a hell of a lot of supposition Karim," Hayes answered.

"Yes ma'am, but an educated guess. If I'm in the mind of our target, I don't just want a way out, I want a real threat to my pursuers. Two individuals may not get the attention of the Kurds, but an armed force most definitely would. North ma'am, that's our best shot," Karim stated confidently.

"Okay then, we go on Karim's gut. James, put in keywords for every town and village along a route that Karim thinks is most likely; we need NSA sucking up everything about these. You work with one other person, but the rest of the team keep looking at other leads in the event they are moving west or south. Karim, until this is confirmed, I need that big brain of yours to be open to other options but if we get more nuggets that reinforce your theory, you go full KZ on it. Thanks Zack, I'll let the DDO know."

DDI Hayes killed the connection.

Chapter 25

Action in the Gulf

Commander Gasem sat in the Command Information Center, CIC, of the HMS Tabuk drinking his coffee, a habit he picked up training with the Americans. He cut quite a commanding figure in his crisply pressed blue camouflage uniform for a man in his early forties and strong, square face. The CIC was eerily quiet for a small room with nearly a dozen sailors focused on a variety of electronic systems. It was the heart and brain of the ship. The sullen green and red glow coming from the radar and weapons control screens cast odd shadows along the walls stacked with electronic cabinets.

The Tabuk was the newest Corvette class ship in the Royal Saudi Navy and Gasem had captained her for the past 3 years. They protected Saudi ports and the vital shipping lanes that carried oil, the lifeblood of the kingdom. Their current mission was escorting a convoy of four supertankers through the Straits of Hormuz; two Saudi, one Bahraini, and one UAE flagged ship. Gasem positioned the escorts between the tankers and Iranian waters. The Tabuk on the port side of the convoy between the first and second tankers and the HMS Faisal, an older Al-Sadiq patrol boat between the third and fourth tankers.

The convoy was 15 miles off the Emirates coast moving through a narrow passage between it and the Iranian controlled island of Abu Musa, a distance of only 35 miles. Suddenly the radar operator sat up and leaned into his screen.

"Captain, four targets from Abu Musa on direct bearing three-zero-zero degrees moving at 40 knots. Appear to be Fast Attack boats sir," the controller said with excitement in his voice.

"General quarters, communications hail them and warn them off or they will be fired upon," ordered Gasem.

The communications officer's radio calls were met with silence.

"Sir, 16 miles and closing fast. Four boats in a diamond formation. Now four more just appeared, two bearing two-seven-zero moving at 40 knots and two bearing three-two-zero at 40 knots." The controller reported.

"Weapons get a fix on those first four and the two northern ones," Gasem ordered. "HMS Faisal this is Tabuk, eight targets inbound. Prepare to engage northern targets, they are trying to encircle us," he radioed to the trailing escort patrol boat. "Communications, tell them they have ten seconds to break off or be fired upon."

"Yes Sir!"

"Three incoming anti-ship missiles!" the defensive systems operator announced.

"Phalanx on full auto, weapons fix two targets in center attack force," Gasem ordered in a calm but commanding voice.

"Targets locked."

"Fire!" Gasem ordered.

Two Harpoon missiles roared out of their launchers and arced toward the oncoming attackers.

"Incoming missiles are headed for first tanker sir!" the radar operator announced.

"Flank speed, now. We need to get in front of them," he said more urgently.

Though most hadn't seen combat before, the voices of the crew quickly became calmer as they mirrored the demeanor of their skipper. Moments later the Phalanx gatling gun system erupted in a thundering roar of fire and bullets that sounded like they were being spit out of a hurricane. A huge explosion lit up the night sky as the first missile exploded, the Phalanx pivoted, and a second explosion, closer. Then it pivoted once more and another explosion just off the aft quarter deck spewing shrapnel into one of the aft deck gun mounts.

On the horizon, two explosions lit up the sky as the Harpoon missiles met their targets, incinerating two attack boats almost instantly. To the north, the crewmen manning the other aft deck gun saw an eruption of fire and light from the Faisal's Phalanx system with the sound reaching them seconds later followed by two flashes from exploding incoming anti-ship missiles. Another explosion lit up the night sky to the north indicating one of the northern attack boats had been eliminated.

"One of the southern pair breaking off heading toward us, closing speed is nearly 80 knots," reported the radar operator.

"Two torpedoes in the water, forward. Started pinging almost immediately," announced the sonar operator.

"Hard to port, deploy countermeasures," ordered Gasem.

The whole crew held their breath for what seemed like an eternity until Gasem called out, "hard to starboard!"

The crew had to hold onto whatever they could grab as the big ship dug into the water. Its two huge diesel engines growling like angry bears driving the twin screw propellers and churning the water into a boiling cauldron behind the ship. One of the torpedoes exploded against a decoy and the other zipped past the aft corner of the ship, missing by mere feet.

"Deck battery's, engage targets!" Gasem commanded.

The big three-inch gun on the forward deck roared to life firing high explosive shells that arced bright red in the darkness like a finger of death reaching out. The remaining 20mm cannon on the aft deck engaged the attackers in the center as tracer rounds lit the sky from both sides. South of them a barrage of rockets arced through the air from the attacking force, some getting knocked down by Faisal's Phalanx system, but not all. Three rockets hit the patrol boat midships with huge explosions, but the ship was still fighting and returning fire. Another explosion on the northern attackers as the big three-inch gun found another target. There were two more to the south.

"Sir, two UAE F-16's inbound, the surviving three attack boats are breaking off."

"Copy, secure weapons. Senior Chief, damage report," ordered Gasem.

"Port side aft deck gun damaged, damage on port quarter deck from shrapnel, two radar nodes out but full coverage, one dead, two wounded sir," replied the Senior Chief.

"And the Faisal?" asked Gasem.

"Faisal reports major damage amidships. Radar and weapons management systems have been seriously damaged. Seven dead and thirteen injured. She needs to head to port. Tankers report no serious damage, mostly some bullet holes but nothing major and no casualties," replied the Senior Chief.

"Comms, contact US 5th fleet, let them know the situation and get some help out here. We need search and rescue to pick up survivors and medevac for injured crew. Ask those fighters to stay overhead as long as they can. Chief, make sure the helipad is operational, that's the priority right now. Let the convoy know we're still with them and will continue the mission," Gasem instructed.

He then picked up the intercom, "Attention crew of the Tabuk this is the Captain. I'm proud of every one of you, everyone performed brilliantly. While the attackers have withdrawn for now, we will maintain battle stations, weapons tight, but be ready for another attack."

"Sir, we're being hailed by the USS Gravely. They're launching their Seahawks for search and rescue, they will rendezvous with us in less than an hour," reported the communications officer.

The Gravely was one of the newest Arleigh Burke class destroyers and significantly upgraded the firepower of the convoy. Its Tomahawk missile system now gave the convoy a powerful offensive punch to strike at the Iranian facilities on Abu Musa itself if necessary.

"Sir, the Captain of the Gravely would like to speak with you," reported the communications officer.

"USS Gravely, this is Captain Gasem of the HMS Tabuk, go ahead."

"Captain Gasem, this is Captain Chesterton. Search and rescue headed your way. How many casualties do you estimate in the water, over?"

"Captain Chesterton, thank you for the assist. Four Iranian fast attack boats and crew neutralized. Radar and sonar signatures suggest six Peykaap class, one MIG-S-2600 Class, and one Azarakhsh class attack boats attacked the convoy. The 2600 and Azarakhsh both retreated back to Abu Musa with two Peykaap. That would put a possible twenty souls in the water. We're deploying four zodiacs now to help with the recovery," Gasem answered.

"We'll follow your lead on the recovery effort. We've got a Corpsman onboard to help with the wounded, there's a UAE SAR chopper headed to you from Abu Dhabi, we'll be there in less than an hour. Gravely out!"

"Sir, the Emirates vessel Ganthoot is steaming to us. They were off the coast of Dubai and should also be here within the hour," the communications officer stated.

"Good, that should keep those Iranian animals away for a while. Radar, direct Gravely's helicopters and our zodiacs to the last known positions of the enemy fast attack boats when we engaged them. Now it's time to do Allah's work and recover the fallen," Gasem instructed.

Chapter 26

Change of Plan

The Kurdish safe house was a small building with concrete block walls and a worn wood floor. It had a kitchen, living room, and a small bedroom with colorful Persian rugs strewn around. The rugs, though colorful, were worn showing their age and the hard life in the countryside.

The ops team concealed their weapons in two vehicles and changed clothes. Jericho, Moose, and Hammer were dressed like construction workers and loaded a white Renault SUV with German power-tools. The heavy, dust covered tools would inhibit a checkpoint from unloading the SUV to find the hidden compartments below them. Naz and Kirkorian dressed as a merchant and his wife and loaded a grey Mercedes Sprinter van with cosmetics full of glycerin. The glycerin would hide the odor of the explosives hidden in the side panels. Since glycerin is a common component not only in cosmetics and lotions, but also explosives, bomb dogs would alert on virtually everything in the van.

With the gear secured, Jericho checked in with Ops on the satellite phone. The sat phone was Russian, bought in one of the arms markets in Pakistan. The call linked to a number in Baghdad, routed through Kuwait, then to CIA headquarters. If the Russians were scanning, they'd only find one of their own.

"Ops, Jericho, we're loaded and ready to go. Updates?" he said into the phone.

Jericho stood listening for a minute or two. "Casualties? ...Okay...How long ago did they leave Ghods?...Uh hm...what kind of force are we looking at?"

"Well, that can't be good news," Naz whispered to Kirkorian.

"Nope," she answered.

"They're being deliberate, you think that's the route they'll be taking?" Jericho continued.

"Copy all. Will check back in three hours. Jericho out," he said as he punched off the phone and folded the antenna back down.

"Alright people, you heard our plan has changed. Hammer, the map," Jericho began. "The Iranian LEOs reported our suspects in Ghods seven hours ago and possibly heading our way. Langley thinks they will make their way to Ilam to get into Kurd territory and make pursuit more difficult. They think this route from Dasht Abbas to Ilam is the most likely. Lots of small towns and villages along the way and lots of false routes they can take.

"The Iranians have sealed the border areas to the south, but these two are smart. Intercepts show that the IRGC Commander may think they're headed toward us as well. He sent a company sized force to chase them. Fortunately for us, they had to split up, but at least two of the groups will converge here, just northwest of Jafar Abad, the third here just southeast of Cheshmah Kabod. That's just shy of 100 men," Jericho stated pointing to the locations on the map.

"We're going down this route in the opposite direction and check out the towns along the way. I want everyone to understand, we're in no hurry. We think the suspects are headed this way, so we don't want to miss them. They're in a white SUV like every IRGC shithead drives so we do what the cops are doing and pay attention. These two are reported to have a lot of firepower so while extraction is the mission, we need to be very careful.

"Lastly, there's been an incident in the Gulf. A Saudi navy escort just tangled with a coordinated surface attack by Iranian naval forces near a disputed island. Iranian naval fast attack boats hit an escorted tanker convoy 15 miles off the Emirates coast. Looks like four Iranian fast attack boats and crew neutralized and one Saudi ship was heavily damaged. Eight dead and fifteen wounded on the Saudi side; Iranian casualties are unknown. Search and rescue is ongoing; they've found three alive but are still pulling bodies out of the gulf. Things just got a little hotter people. Let's move out."

Jericho shook hands with the Kurd Commander and climbed into the SUV with Moose and Hammer. Kirkorian and Naz got into the trailing van and followed them. The top-heavy van swayed back and forth as they maneuvered down the rutted dirt road in the dark. Kirkorian had to hold onto the nylon strap riveted to the van above her right shoulder to keep from getting thrown out of her seat.

Fifteen minutes later they pulled onto the paved road and the two vehicles moved southwest toward Ilam, just under an hour away.

Panic in the Pipes

The scientist awoke with a pounding headache. He was completely disoriented. Wherever he was, it was pitch black, so he crawled to find a wall. The floor was cold and felt like concrete. As his eyes began to get some semblance of focus, he saw a very dim, thin line of light coming from what he guessed was the bottom of a doorway.

He crawled to the wall on the same side as the little slice of light and slowly felt his way toward it. The wall was concrete block, so he counted blocks as he moved to get a sense of size. He moved his hands slowly in an arc as he moved to his left. He had no idea what he'd encounter and didn't want to slice his hand open on some sharp object.

His left hand felt metal, and as he slid it down, he felt what he suspected was a hinge. He had no sense of time but figured it had taken a good ten minutes to get to this point. From the hinge, he moved up and down along the door edge to find the other two hinges. He moved his hand back to the center hinge, then slowly slid to the left on the steel door until he found the doorknob.

He slowly turned the knob and pulled carefully. To his surprise, it was unlocked and moved easily and silently. As the door opened, a dim grey light began flooding part of the room showing it to be empty. He pulled the door open and stood in the doorway looking onto an unfamiliar street. It was nighttime with a bright full moon illuminating the area.

The light of the full moon stung his eyes as his head pounded with every beat of his heart. And that heartbeat now accelerated with the understanding that he had no idea where he was. He looked down and realized he was still dressed in the casual clothes he had on the boat. He shoved his right hand into his pocket looking for his cellphone, but it wasn't there. He checked his left pocket and found it. When he pulled it out, it was turned off. He turned it on and went to unlock it with his code, but there was no lock on the screen. He realized it wasn't his.

He looked at the phone in his hand and opened the call list. There were just two calls to a number he didn't recognize. He looked up and down the street, but nothing looked familiar. He found a flashlight app on the phone, turned it on and looked in the room, but it was completely empty. The smell of diesel fumes, seawater, and decaying seaweed along with the distinctive sound of seagulls meant he was near a port.

"What the hell happened to me?" he thought as he struggled to get his bearings, but nothing was making sense.

All he could think of was to call his security team. Hopefully they could track the phone and come get him. He looked at the screen of the smartphone and a shiver went down his back.

"Ahvaz, Iran. This is impossible! How did I get here?" the scientist mumbled.

He wracked his brain to remember anything that could tell him what had happened to him as panic and fear began to set in. The last thing he remembered was getting on the excursion boat for a short trip in the gulf with a hooker.

"Oh my god, the drink. What a damn fool, I was drugged!" he said as the shock of what happened, and the realization of the danger began to sink in.

The last thing he remembered was the woman bringing him a glass of Scotch to "relax" before the festivities began. It was a good single malt with a strong smoky taste. Just the type of liquor that can hide the taste of pretty much any drug they gave him. He just knew he had to get out of here, and fast. So, he dialed his head of security.

From the scientist's description, his security chief suspected he was near the large seaport industrial zone in the main city port. He was instructed to shut off the phone and find someplace to hide in the zone close to the highway. Then, two hours from his first contact he was to make one last call from the phone for pickup instructions, then wipe it clean and get rid of it. But getting to the industrial zone was excruciatingly slow going and took the scientist over an hour.

The smells coming from the dumpsters there nearly made the scientist gag. He tried to stay in the shadows of the buildings and occasionally ran into a barrel of something gooey and sticky. He could only imagine the chemicals he was being exposed to, but he had to keep moving. His one satisfying thought was that to destroy the electronic threat in his possession, he could think of no better place than one of these barrels of caustic toxic goo he was passing.

He crouched at the corner of a building and looked at a sea of steel and concrete pipes. Some were big enough to crawl in. He guessed it was a few hours to sunrise based on the position of the moon and then the place would become a beehive of activity. He looked up and down the pathway then dashed across and ducked in between two stacks of iron pipe. He moved along the path between the stacks and darted between the rows.

The scientist was two rows away from the large diameter pipes when he saw flashing lights illuminating the storage yard. Panic rose in him like waves crashing against rocks. He struggled to control his breathing, but his heart was racing.

He heard shouting behind him and people running in the gravel pathways between the pipes. He had to move. He looked up and down the next row and dashed across to another bundle of pipe. The scientist was one row away now. He made another dash to the larger steel pipes and scurried into one on the bottom, crawling about two meters in.

Light strobed from both ends of the pipe as people ran with flashlights in their hands. The sounds of running and shouting got closer. Suddenly a man was tackled at the far end of the pipe. Lights illuminated the scuffle as the man was subdued. As police put handcuffs on him, his head was directly in line with the pipe.

The scientist broke into a cold sweat when the man turned his head and seemed to stare right at him. With no backlight to illuminate inside the pipe, the man was looking into a pitch-black void and the scientist was safe from detection. But panic makes even the most logical person think and act illogically.

Wracked with fear the scientist shimmied backwards and was betrayed by the very physics he spent his life studying. The cell phone slipped out of his pocket and hit the metal pipe with a subtle clink. The solid metal pipe amplified the noise. Almost immediately police appeared on both ends as flashlights illuminated him from two directions.

"Out, out," the police shouted at him in Farsi.

"Egyptian, Egyptian. I was robbed!" the scientist pleaded in Arabic as they pulled him out and to his feet.

A policeman stepped forward and spoke to him in Arabic. "What are you doing here?"

"I was robbed earlier. They took everything; wallet, passport, money, everything. I had no documents and was disoriented so I was trying to find somewhere safe until I could contact my diplomatic mission."

Though mostly true, the scientist lied through omission as convincingly as he could.

"Why didn't you come to us?" asked the policeman.

"I'm sorry, I'm sorry, I was afraid. I was working in Basra and just wanted to do a little shopping. Then I got robbed and had no money or identification. I heard the running and shouting and just tried to hide not knowing who it was," the scientist responded.

"What's your name?" the policeman asked sternly.

"Mohammed El Masry," the scientist answered using his maternal grandfather's name.

"Bring him with us until we confirm his identity," ordered the policeman.

As the scientist was searched, he realized the phone was still in the pipe. Finally, he was handcuffed and led to a police car for the short drive to a small district station. Along the way, he prayed they wouldn't be so eager to find out about a vagrant with no papers. He was pulled from the back seat and led up the stairs to the front desk with the man they caught in the storage yard.

The desk Sergeant looked up.

"Who are these two?" the Sergeant asked.

"This guy is the drug dealer," the patrolman said pointing to a young man in jeans and a torn sweatshirt. "We found this other guy in the pipe yard during the capture. He claims to be an Egyptian who got robbed of his papers and wallet. But he's pretty grubby and smells, so he might just be another illegal from Iraq trying to find work," a patrolman reported.

"Okay, take the drug dealer to interrogation. Are you sure they weren't working together?" the Sergeant asked.

"Positive. We chased the dealer for several blocks, and he was alone. This other guy, I just think he was in the wrong place at the wrong time," answered the patrolman.

"But no papers you said," inquired the Sergeant.

"No, nothing. No wallet, passport, keys, cell phone, nothing," answered the patrolman.

"Alright, put him in holding until we have time to figure out his real story," ordered the Sergeant.

Chapter 28

Close Call

It was quiet in the car as Ebrahim moved steadily along their escape route as Azar monitored the radio. There were multiple reports of units moving in all directions.

"Well, sounds like they aren't sure what direction to take, but they may only be about an hour and a half behind us now. What do you want to do?" asked Azar.

"We just got through Abdanan so we keep going and minimize our time in any town. The next good-sized town will be Darreh Shahr; we'll be going through at night so fewer people to encounter. We need to make a plan. I'll pull over at the next turn off," Ebrahim answered.

Two minutes later Ebrahim turned right onto a dirt path that led down between two small ridges. The path curved around to the left hiding the SUV from the road. He shut off the engine and turned to Azar.

"So, if the IRGC is moving in all these directions they might suspect we're heading to Kurd territory. That means we could encounter soldiers who may not be in a generous mood when it comes to capturing us," he began calmly.

His voice was that of cool logic looking at the options before them. It was clear he had been weighing the odds of their escape without violence for some time.

"Now, we can escape and evade in the hills for some time; we have the food, but water will be the limiting factor. That would give the government more time to flood the region with troops and we'd be surrounded. They'd use the Russian satellites to do thermal searches and would tighten the circle until they found us," he continued.

"But they are disorganized right now, and that's our advantage. It means we might have to fight and kill some of our countrymen. The only other option is to turn ourselves in and I tell them I forced you to help me by threatening your friends and associates. After all, they believe I blew up my facility and killed hundreds of my colleagues already so why not threaten you. I'm a dead man no matter what and all I can try to do is save you."

Azar looked at Ebrahim and put her hand on his cheek.

"Darling, we've already been through this. I know you want to protect me, but trust me, wherever you are, I'll be by your side."

"I don't think you understand Azar. You are the most important thing in my life and if it comes down to sacrificing myself to allow you to escape, I do it willingly. Promise me you won't hesitate if I tell you to go. Promise," he said, almost pleadingly.

Azar leaned over and kissed him gently.

"I promise," she whispered. "Now, no more talk of dying, we are not going to die."

They were ten minutes beyond Abdanan when the APB call went out meaning they would have to avoid local police along their route. The small villages wouldn't have the professional police like larger towns, but they were still a threat. Periodically they'd go off-road on navigable paths to get around either a police car or an entire village. All this cloak and dagger slowed them down to nearly a third of the speed they could be traveling.

The road climbed into the hills and wound around with multiple switchbacks. Several curves were dangerously close to steep drop-offs with virtually no apron. The road itself narrowed to barely allow two cars to pass each other as Ebrahim carefully navigated the sharp curves. He felt lucky there was a full moon to give some light, but where the hills created shadows, the drive was extremely tense.

They finally started downhill, and the next big obstacle was Darreh Shahr where two main roads merged. It was a small city but had a full-time police force. Azar's face was lit up by the dull green glow of the GPS.

"In two kilometers we'll cross over the Darreh Shahr river. Ebrahim, we need to stay on this side of the river," she said.

"Okay," he replied.

The road would cross the river then wouldn't loop back across until two bridges on the north side of the city. If they tried to cross there, the police would have roadblocks covering those bridges.

"There's a turnoff in about 500 meters; take a left into the parking lot so you can look at the satellite map. The road will curve to the right and then it's fifty meters on the left," she reported.

Ebrahim was looking hard for the turn and just missed it in the dark. "Shit," he growled, frustrated with himself as he backed up and turned into the small lot.

Azar spoke as she traced the route on the GPS.

"Okay, there's a farm just ahead on the left. Looks like less than a kilometer after that the road crosses the river and we can't get back to the other side until one of these bridges here. If we turn at the farm, we can maneuver around it and follow this dirt path through these fields. We pick up roads again in Rashnoo Abad and can stay on outer roads to rejoin the main road here, just south of the stadium on the edge of Darreh Shahr," Azar said tracing the route on the GPS.

"So, a few kilometers of backcountry and back on the road. And we miss the most likely checkpoint. Okay," he answered.

With a nod of her head, Ebrahim threw the SUV back into drive and headed back down the hill. The shadows from the hills under the bright moonlight made it feel like they were traveling through a series of tunnels; light where the moon shown through gaps in the hills, and pitch black where they could only see as far as the next curve with their headlights. A few minutes later they came up on the turn-off.

"Two hundred meters," Azar announced.

Ebrahim checked his mirrors and slowed down to a crawl trying desperately not to miss the poorly marked turn. He made a sharp left onto what was barely a road. It looped around a small industrial site full of agricultural equipment, past some concrete block houses, and dead-ended near a field. Just to the right were two well-worn ruts that constituted a drivable path through the fields used by the farm machines that maintained them.

The drive through the fields was agonizingly slow as the big SUV jerked and swayed with every rut and pothole. Ebrahim tried to avoid the bigger ones but every so often they ran into a bone jarring pothole throwing the two of them violently about. Half an hour later, they emerged from the fields and back onto paved roads. But they lost valuable time.

Entering the southwest corner of Darreh Shahr they stayed on outer roads. They slowly made their way around the city streets to avoid the main thoroughfares. They had to maneuver around a traffic circle then follow a main road for a short time. Sirens rang out behind them sending an immediate surge of adrenaline flooding their bodies. Ebrahim's hands tightened on the steering wheel as Azar's right hand went down to the gun at her side.

"Lights behind us," Ebrahim said.

He pulled to the side of the road and turned off the lights as they both slouched down in their seats. Ebrahim watched the mirrors as a police cruiser and ambulance zoomed past.

Azar looked at the GPS. "Hospital just ahead."

"Right," he replied and pulled back out onto the street.

It took another 15-20 minutes to navigate the side streets until they could emerge onto the main road again northeast of the city.

"Well, that took a lot longer than expected. Hopefully the rest of these towns aren't as challenging. Where are our pursuers?" he asked.

"There's just some local law enforcement chatter, none on the military channels. They must realize we're monitoring them and are using something else. I've been scanning for the past hour, but nothing," Azar replied.

"They must be using an encrypted system we don't have. I saw some radios with the security personnel who came to the facility for the test I'd never seen before. I assume they're Russian or Chinese," Ebrahim pondered. "We'll need to just monitor the police channels then. They won't be so good at hiding information, but it also won't be as current or complete."

"Agreed. After the APB call came in, there were some calls from towns south of us. I suspect they've split their force to run possible routes. That means fewer soldiers along our route to deal with and they'll likely stop at each town to check them out. Still, it will come down who can navigate this route the fastest. Do you think they've sent soldiers to Ilam?" she asked.

"I would if I were running this search. We have to expect it and plan for it. I'm assuming you know some alternate routes once we get there?" Ebrahim inquired.

Azar looked at him and smiled.

"Yes, I think I do."

They continued north and had to maneuver a little bit around Abbas Abad and Bedreh. In Vali-e-Asr they saw a police cruiser, but the officer was sleeping, and they slid past him quickly. The fact that it was the middle of the night proved an advantage with these smaller towns and villages. Even if they had a full-time police force, their night crews were extremely small to virtually non-existent and allowed them to move a little faster than before.

After an hour, Ebrahim looked at the gas gauge.

"We need to stop for gas somewhere. Can you find something, preferably out of the way?"

"There's one in about six minutes on the right. We go through some hills and there'll be a sharp switchback then only two kilometers after that. It's by itself with a restaurant across a parking lot," Azar answered.

"Let's hope it's open. Otherwise, we'll be looking for one in a larger town," he replied.

Five minutes later the road made a shallow curve to the left and there was the flickering sign for the station. Ebrahim pulled off the road and up to a pump. The station looked open but run down, the metal siding streaked with rust under a dim fluorescent light. As he stepped out of the SUV there was a handwritten sign taped on the pump indicating they had to prepay inside. Ebrahim looked through the window at Azar and did a head nod toward the station, then turned to go in and pay.

He opened the door. Little bells on a spring bracket mounted above the door jingled as it hit them on the way by. A boy, no more than sixteen, pushed through a curtain covering the doorway from a small office behind the counter. He looked at Ebrahim, then out the window at the pumps, then back at Ebrahim.

"Sixty liters," Ebrahim said as he tossed money on the counter to pay for it.

Just then, the bells jingled again. A policeman walked through the door and Ebrahim struggled to remain calm. He felt his heart pounding in his ears. He quickly sized up the man, shorter by several inches, thin and wiry, and walked with a slight limp on the left side.

"Peroz, I see your father has you working again tonight. What have you done this time boy?" the policeman asked.

"Nothing important, sir," the boy replied, looking ashamed.

"Nothing important! You call being caught alone with the mayor's daughter nothing important?" the policeman bellowed with a hearty laugh. "You're lucky he didn't have me arrest you! Don't worry, I talked him out of cutting off that dick of yours."

The boy's face turned white as he looked at the policeman, then at Ebrahim, and back.

"I'm just joking. You should keep a low profile for a while though," the policeman said with a wink and a smile.

He looked at Ebrahim and his smile vanished.

"So, what's your story? We don't see many travelers here at this time of night. Where are you headed?" the policeman asked in a stern voice.

"Just headed to Ilam for a friend's wedding tomorrow," Ebrahim responded.

"Seems you got a late start, where are you coming from?" the policeman queried in more of an interrogating tone.

"Dasht Abbas. I had to work late so I couldn't leave," Ebrahim answered, forcing himself to smile.

"And what do you do there...what's your name?" the policeman asked.

"Hasan. I'm a maintenance technician for the power plant there. I work the mid-shift and I only have two days off, so I had to drive up tonight," Ebrahim said as he used every bit of his EOD training to remain calm.

"I see Hasan, so..." the policeman was interrupted by a radio call.

There was a suspicious person seen possibly breaking into a local market and he had to check it out immediately.

"Have a safe trip, Hasan. Peroz, a bottle of water," the policeman ordered.

The boy threw a bottle of water to him, and the policemen threw some money on the counter and rushed out the door. Once he was gone, the boy gave Ebrahim his change and he walked quickly to the car to fill up.

It took an agonizing five minutes; despite the rundown appearance of the gas station, the pumps were new and pumped quickly. Ebrahim jumped in and started the engine to leave as quickly as possible.

"Did you see the policeman?" he asked.

"Yes," Azar answered. "I slouched down in the seat so he wouldn't see me. Thankfully the lighting sucked at the pump, but when I saw him questioning you, I made an anonymous call to the station to report a break-in. I guess it worked. I really didn't want to leave any bodies here."

"Yes, I told him I was headed to a friend's wedding in Ilam. Seemed plausible enough but he wasn't so easily brushed aside. Thanks," Ebrahim replied with a small smile. "But now we need to put some distance between us and him."

Chapter 29

Moving Chess Pieces

Within the King's secure bunker, the circular conference room had large monitors along the outside walls between six large marble columns. The conference table was shaped like a capital C with the Saudi King seated at the apex. A small pot of spiced tea sat on a shiny brass trivet that protected the Brazilian maple tabletop with its warm, intricate grain contrasted in the darkly stained finish.

The King wore a simple cream-colored linen shirt, pants and sandals. Only under the direst circumstances would he be awakened in the middle of the night. But a major naval incident in the Gulf after a nuclear event in Iran certainly qualified. Smoking one of his favorite cigarettes from Turkey, the King sipped his tea and listened to his Chief of Naval Operations brief the incident in the Gulf. The blend of tobacco smoke and spices from the tea left a sweet aroma hanging in the air.

Bandar sat to his right as the Admiral finished the detailed report when the secure phone at his elbow rang.

"Bandar."

"Sir, we've received a call from the scientist's security chief. The scientist called in and claims he was kidnapped and is in Ahvaz Iran. He says he doesn't know where; he just woke up in an empty warehouse with a phone in his pocket," the Deputy Director of Intelligence reported.

"When did he call?" Bandar asked.

"Twenty minutes ago. I put a call in to the Americans for location assistance and they've narrowed it down to a four-block area," the Deputy Director answered.

"Do we have any assets close?" Bandar asked.

"We have a few but the ones who are closest have gone dark according to protocol," he answered.

"I see," Bandar said in thought.

He wasn't sure how much he trusted the man since his reaction yesterday, but he would be the one to know what assets they had in-country.

"We need our closest asset to make contact so have state television run the coded story for him. Whatever information this scientist has, we need to recover him and verify it before the Iranians," Bandar instructed.

"Yes sir," was the reply and the line went dead.

"Your Majesty, sorry for the interruption, we might have a location on the scientist. He claims he was kidnapped and is in Ahvaz. We're working to secure him," Bandar relayed to the King.

"That's concerning that he's in Iran. Do you think he's involved?" the King asked.

"It's certainly possible given his background. It's also plausible that if you wanted to set up the Kingdom for blame, he would be a perfect mark. It would be a propaganda coup if the Iranians captured him and marched him in front of the world. If it were me, that's what I'd do," Bandar answered.

The secure phone rang again, "Bandar...standby. Sir, the American CIA Director and Secretary of Defense are requesting a video conference with you and our Chief of Military operations."

"Is General Aziz on the line?" asked the King.

"Yes, sir. The command center has already brought him on," Bandar answered.

"Conference them in," the King ordered.

"Good evening your Majesty, this is Director Anderson and I'm here with Secretary Jackson. we apologize for contacting you at such an hour but events in Iran are happening very fast that require our coordination," Anderson began.

"We have a team on the ground searching for the suspects in the attack on the nuclear facility. Our intel shows they are not the ones who executed the attack but would provide valuable intelligence if we secure them first."

"Why don't you think they did the attack on the facility Director?" the King inquired.

"Sir, a Caliphate operative inside the facility timed the explosion to correspond with the nuclear test. We didn't know the details of the facility, just a general area. But our sources indicate the asset was in place long before the Iranian suspect arrived there," Anderson answered.

"Where did this intel come from and why weren't we informed ahead of time?" the King asked with a hint of frustration.

"Sir, I'm afraid I cannot divulge where the intel came from, and we had no operational details just a coded location. As for informing you ahead of time, you know the relations between our intelligence agencies is a delicate balancing act that we perform every day," Anderson deftly deflected.

The King shot a glance at Bandar who just shook his head yes.

"Yes, I understand. You still do not trust us," the King replied.

"Sir, trust goes two ways," Anderson stated bluntly. "But this call isn't to rehash those issues, it's to respond to the real threat we both face today. We know neither you nor the Israelis were behind this incident. But that's what Tehran believes and it's dangerously close to escalating. As I mentioned at the start, we have a team on the ground working to locate the suspects. We need to solidify their extraction plan, and we'd like your help sir."

"How can we help?" asked the King taking a long sip of his tea.

"We believe the suspects are headed to the Ilam region to take advantage of the Kurdish insurgency forces there. If our team makes contact, we'll have to move quickly to get them out. Right now, the preferred extraction is through Kurdish territory and across the Iraqi border. When that happens, we may need a diversion and given the incident in the Gulf, they may have unwittingly given us the perfect cover for that," Anderson began.

"Sir, this is Secretary Jackson. We only need to shift their attention briefly for a border crossing in the north; we would draw their forces south with a buildup of our offensive forces in the area. We already have fighters headed to Kuwait but would prefer to land them at King Abdulaziz and Prince Sultan Air Bases.

"The USS Ronald Reagan strike group is steaming to the mouth of the Strait of Hormuz to give overflight of shipping. This will force the Iranians to pay attention to their southern areas. Sir, we would like you to make a very public buildup of land, naval, and air forces on your eastern coast. Kuwait, Bahrain, the UAE, and Oman have all agreed to do the same; this will give the Iranians pause if we are there as well.

"More importantly it will force them to move troops and intel resources south, away from our team on the ground," Jackson continued. "We have prepositioned a quick reaction team in Kuwait should we be forced to do a hot extraction. But if we do that, we may need to provide a real threat for the Iranians to deal with. We know your military wants to strike back at the Iranians for the attack on your shipping.

"So, we propose that if we need to do a hot extraction, we do a limited attack on the naval facilities on Abu Musa with large scale radar jamming all along the Iranian coast. This will require multiple fighter caps to make sure there's no enemy response. Are you and your forces willing to take the risk of an Iranian response?" Jackson finished.

"When will your fighters enter our airspace?" the King asked.

"Sir, they are thirty minutes from entering now and we can reroute them immediately," Jackson answered.

"Permission granted. General Aziz, what are your thoughts on this plan?" the King asked his military chief.

"Your Majesty, the most immediate risk is to our oil facilities from cruise missile attacks. We've already moved additional anti-missile and anti-air batteries to guard them. We have 24-hour AWACS coverage between our airplanes and the American E-3s. They have linked their satellite coverage to our central command center and our forces are already on alert after the nuclear incident so making the public pronouncements won't change anything we haven't already started.

"I'm certain the Admiralty would love to put some missiles into Abu Musa; that is a thorn in the strait and would make our response to their attack proportional. It's the least risk of escalation. The plan for large scale activity during a hot extraction carries more risk, but no more than if the Iranians truly believed we sabotaged their facility in my opinion," the General finished.

"What about the border with Yemen? Do you think the Houthi rebels will take advantage?" asked the King.

"Yes sir, that will happen. But with the coastal allies also showing a buildup, and the Americans landing, we can reinforce the southern border and make our play with air and naval power," the General answered.

"Your Majesty," interjected Jackson. "The Iranians will face a very difficult situation. A unified Arab peninsula backed up by American forces. They will undoubtedly ask for help from the Russians, but it will take time to position as they are tied up in Syria. The threat there from Turkey and Israel means they can't just simply move from there to Iran but most likely would seek to threaten northern Iraq. The other main danger is the Iraqi Shiite militias so I would advise splitting your ground forces to reinforce both northern and southern borders. Kuwait has mobilized and we are moving more troops to Kuwait and the Kurdish region in northern Iraq."

"Secretary Jackson, what is the scenario if this escalates beyond our control?" the King inquired.

Jackson paused briefly before answering.

"Sir, Iran would most likely start with asymmetric warfare using their militia allies in the region; Houthis, Iraqi militias, Hezbollah, Syria, and the Palestinians who feel betrayed by the Sunni Islamic powers. This could explode worse than the Caliphate operations which are also still a threat. Egypt would strike at the Muslim Brotherhood protected by the Palestinians in Gaza crushing them between Egypt and Israel. Israel would attack the West Bank, Lebanon, and Syria undoubtedly engaging Russians supporting the Syrian regime.

"Once Egypt enters, the Caliphate and Muslim Brotherhood aligned groups in Africa would turn against them as well as the Shiite aligned groups on that continent. Civil wars in Libya, Tunisia, and Morocco would soon follow making the Arab Spring look like playtime. The Russians will enter full force aligned with Syria and Iran drawing the Turks into battle in northern Syria. If that happens, NATO will reinforce Turkey according to Article 5 of the NATO charter.

"Iran will attack American forces in Afghanistan and Turkmenistan drawing the Afghans into the conflict and possibly the Turkomen. India will support Afghanistan to keep Pakistan out after the recent flareup there. The Kurds in norther Iraq, Syria, and Iran will revolt thereby exploding tribal conflicts from the west coast of Africa to India and could very well expand from there. That's just what I would expect sir, and it's not even the worst-case scenario," Jackson answered unemotionally.

"Your Majesty," Anderson added. "My senior intelligence analyst who's been tracking the Caliphate and its operations believes this is the scenario they are trying to ignite. They want a Sunni, Shiite war to break out which is why they've taken elaborate steps to implicate your country and have not taken credit themselves. He thinks that if the Islamic nations are devastated and brought to their knees, the new Caliph will rise up to unify those who remain. He doesn't know who or how, but he strongly believes that is their ultimate goal. But to do that, all the governments of the Islamic nations must be overthrown or weakened to the point that they cannot resist the new Caliphate."

The King looked up at the ceiling and took a long drag on his cigarette then slowly exhaled the smoke. He closed his eyes and said a prayer. When he opened them, he crushed his cigarette out in a gold and marble ashtray.

"Do I have your President's assurance that the United States will fight side-by-side with my country?"

"Yes, your Majesty," answered Jackson.

"General, make it so. Thank you, gentlemen," the King ordered.

Chapter 30

Captured

E brahim pulled away from the gas station quickly but had to slowed down near Chenar Bashi. The road passed just outside of the village, and with no full-time police, they guessed correctly there wouldn't be anyone watching. They passed through a couple of small villages that barely even registered on a map. About a half hour later they approached the next big obstacle, Jafar Abad. Though not a big town, it was large enough for a professional police force.

"Have we heard anything from Jafar Abad?" asked Ebrahim.

"No, nothing," Azar replied.

"Hmmm," he grunted.

Ebrahim always seemed to have a sixth sense during his time in the Army. He could look at a road, or a situation and sense something was wrong. It saved him and his fellow soldiers multiple times. He had that same feeling and slowed down a bit.

"What is it?" asked Azar.

"Nothing, just a feeling. I'm sure it's nothing," Ebrahim answered.

They passed a long industrial building on the right side of the road and Ebrahim slowed down some more. There was another industrial building coming up on the left with bright lights illuminating the outside. As they approached, a car pulled out from the side of the building and blocked the road. Ebrahim slammed on the brakes and looked in the rearview mirror as another car came up behind them.

"Dammit," he grumbled.

"Okay, stay calm and remember our story," Azar said.

Azar moved her right hand to her gun as a man stepped out of the car in front of them. He was wearing a policeman's uniform and walked slowly up to the driver's side window. Ebrahim rolled it down.

"Good evening. May I ask where you are heading, please?" the policeman asked.

Ebrahim looked at the uniform. "Good evening commander. We're headed to Ilam for a wedding. I'm afraid I got off work late and the ceremony is early, so we wanted to get there tonight."

"I see, I love weddings myself. Are you in the wedding young lady?" the policeman asked Azar as he shined his flashlight at her.

"No sir, it's my husband's friend," she replied.

"Husband, well congratulations, I wasn't aware you two were married!" the policeman replied.

Ebrahim's blood ran cold.

"We were led to believe your...husband was traveling alone. And you," the policemen said turning his gaze on Ebrahim. "You seem to know quite a lot about police uniforms. Thank you for recognizing my rank."

"Former military; I guess you never forget some things, sir," Ebrahim replied.

"Oh, yes, yes. Some things you never forget. I suppose you're right Sergeant, the more things change, the more they stay the same. For instance, you have three sniper rifles trained on you and are surrounded by four patrol cars. Now you're rightfully thinking, is he telling the truth or just bluffing until backup gets here. Well, that's what I would be thinking of course.

"I suspect Miss Barghani over there is calculating how many people she can shoot to create enough chaos to allow you to make an escape. Well, yes, you could probably kill me, but if you make the slightest move, in less than a third of a second two bullets will come through the windshield. The first to make a hole in case the windshield deflects its trajectory, and the second into that flawless forehead of yours. Then another into your head Sergeant before you can get your hands off the steering wheel. And if you kill me, well that will make some very powerful people very, very sad.

"So, miss, I'd prefer you remove your hand from your weapon and put them on the dash, I'd hate for that pretty head to get a big hole in it. Or have that HMX you're carrying in the back accidently go off. But you know that won't happen, right Sergeant? After all you were EOD, correct?"

Ebrahim looked at Azar, shook his head no and closed his eyes. He slowly put his hands on the dashboard.

"She is innocent. I threatened her family so let her go," Ebrahim pleaded.

"Well Sergeant, if that is true then we will find out. Now I suggest you don't say anything to anyone until the IRGC Commander gets here. Please exit the vehicle with your hands up," the Police Commander instructed as he opened Ebrahim's door, and a female officer appeared at Azar's and did the same.

They put them both against the car, searched them, handcuffed them, and put one in the trailing car and one in the other. The Commander whispered to one of his men who got into the SUV and drove off. The small convoy moved quickly into town and maneuvered through the narrow streets to the police station.

***

Mokhtari laid on a sofa in his office. Over the years he developed the ability to rest but remain alert. He could think through complex issues while drawing his heart rate down; in essence, recharge his body while his mind was still active. The evidence was almost overwhelming but had elements that seemed oddly out of place. The timing of the phone calls, the almost pristine laptop in the dumpster at Hamadani's apartment, the cell phone link to the Saudis. All reasonable, but sloppy for an operative who was able to not only get access to the facility without being discovered but bring in explosives and rig it all in the time Hamadani was employed there.

Then there was the tenuous link to the Zionists; the burst message, the emails on the laptop which conveniently used an older crypto. Again, seemed sloppy for a current Mossad operative but possible for a mole. Just another oddity that was reasonable but implied mistakes by experienced operatives. Though it could have been due to the short notice about the test which caused them to move up their plans.

The explosive assessment team said the placement of the bomb was virtually perfect. It was in a concrete depression under the master control panel that created a directional blast. Given the radius and the char pattern on the walls the bomb team figured 200-250 kilos of high explosive. The results from the recovered chemical residue samples indicated RDX, and there was plenty of that in the girlfriend's storage area.

The explosion ensured whoever was at the control console was incinerated. The directional blast inside a room with reinforced concrete walls, caused an overpressure that killed everyone instantly and blew the security door completely off. It was a very professional job and fit the skill set of an ex-EOD like Hamadani. But over the years Mokhtari had learned to listen to his inner voice. And that was telling him he didn't have all the answers.

He had a lot of implications of who, but the why was still a mystery. No group or country had taken credit. As a matter of fact, just the opposite. Both Israel and Saudi claimed neither had attacked the facility. Unfortunately, it didn't stop the regime leaders from striking back before the full information was known. The incident in the Gulf proved that. But that was someone else's problem.

There was a knock at the door. "Enter," Mokhtari called out.

A Corporal entered the room. "Sir, we just got a call from the Police Commander in Jafar Abad. They've stopped an SUV with a male and female matching the description of our suspects. He's asking for orders on how to proceed."

Mokhtari sat up immediately. "Tell them to guard them carefully and not let them out of their sight. And no one questions them but me, understand?"

"Yes, sir."

"Get my chopper fired up, I need to get there immediately. Where is Captain Al Madani now?" Mokhtari asked as he quickly stood up and in three steps was at his desk grabbing the suspect file.

"They're in Darreh Shahr."

"Call and let him know about the suspects. Tell him I'll meet him in Jafar Abad," Mokhtari ordered as he followed the soldier into the command center. "Anything on the missing clerk yet?"

"No sir. Friends and family don't know her whereabouts," answered the soldier.

In less than ten minutes, Mokhtari was lifting off the helipad outside the Operations bunker.

***

The police Commander escorted the group into the station and walked up to the desk Sergeant.

"We have two people that match the description of the suspects identified in the APB. Tell the Commander they're here and that his men did a great job. I'm glad my officers and I could help," the Commander said.

"Well, we are fortunate you showed up when you did, thanks for the assist," the desk Sergeant replied.

"We were simply tasked to help in the response to the incident and helping local units along the way. When your Commander got that phone call, he certainly had to act on that hunch. We were just in the right place at the right time I guess," answered the Police Commander. "I know you're shorthanded tonight so tell your Commander we'll handle the patrol, so he doesn't need to call anyone in."

"Yes, sir. You two," the Sergeant said pointing at two of his officers. "take the suspects to separate interrogation rooms. I'll notify the Commander they're here."

"Good luck," the police Commander said then waved his men back out to their patrol cars and headed off into the night.

As Ebrahim and Azar were escorted to interrogation rooms the Jafar Abad police commander, Commander Ahkazmanesh, came bounding out of his office. His slightly wrinkled green commander's uniform hung a bit loosely off of his thin middle-aged frame but his eyes gleamed with pride at capturing the country's most dangerous fugitives in his precinct.

"Sergeant, Colonel Mokhtari of the IRGC is on his way by helicopter and should be here in about forty minutes," Ahkazmanesh announced. "Separate these two across the hall from each other. He wants to interrogate the suspects and I want guards in both rooms, he says these two are extremely dangerous."

"Yes sir. Do you want to question them before he gets here?" the Sergeant asked.

"No, he specifically said nobody questions them but him and I have no desire to get on the wrong side of the IRGC," Ahkazmanesh replied. "How many men do we have in the station?"

"Six, sir, including us. Commander Gazsian said he and his officers would take the patrol tonight, so we didn't need to call anyone in," said the Sergeant.

"Excellent!" Ahkazmanesh answered. "Remind me to thank him, not only for handling the roadblock but for the patrol."

Chapter 31

Through the Front Door

Jericho pulled onto a dirt path two miles from Jafar Abad. He opened a small computer and established a satellite link.

"Okay, so we don't know a lot about the layout, but these are the suspects the IRGC is looking for so expect extra security. Thoughts?" he asked the team.

"The intercepts indicate they have a similar look as Naz and I. If Hammer and Moose pose as officers, they can bring us right through the front door. Once inside we neutralize the officers in the front and work our way to the interrogation rooms. It will cause some confusion having two sets of suspects because these are local LEOs not IRGC. Jericho can give false calls to any patrols. They would have, what, 10-12 officers, tops? I like those odds with the element of surprise," Kirkorian suggested.

"Chief, it fits with the covers. Hammer and I say we're from one of the villages we just came through and needed to bring the suspects to a station with higher security. It could work," Moose added.

"I agree Chief. Expect the inside to be just like every small-town police station," started Naz. "They'll have a front entrance with a desk Sergeant. Given the size of the town, maybe a ready room, a couple interrogation rooms, and some desks for officers to write reports with a few offices for dispatch and Commander. In the back will be the cells. Satellite shows a single-story block structure with a fenced parking area behind the station accessed by this alley. Chief, there's not enough of us to do a multi-point entrance. Front door is best option."

"Okay, so we're all agreed, we walk through the front door and say hello. Naz and Kirkorian, take the SUV and case the front. We'll come in from the back. Moose and Hammer will walk around it and meet you at this intersection. We don't know where the other officers are patrolling so we need any information we can gather before we make entrance.

"When I give you the signal, take the SUV and park by this intersection. I'll take the van to the parking area and if it's guarded, I'll neutralize them; pull in and park near the closest exit in the back. Clear the front as quickly and quietly as you can then work your way back. Let's go," Jericho ordered.

Naz and Kirkorian climbed into the SUV and led the group back onto the highway. Jericho held back in the van several hundred meters as they entered the darkened city. Residential neighborhoods appeared on the left side of the road with only a light or two visible. Otherwise, the only light came from the full moon.

"Left turn in 500 feet," Kirkorian instructed. "The station is a quarter mile on the right."

Naz drove past the front of the police station then turned down an alley. He pulled up to the back of a building and parked. He and Kirkorian got out and walked around the corner. They walked down the dark street, staying in the shadows of the closed markets. They went about half a block when a man in uniform stepped out at the corner they were heading for and just stood there looking at them. They slowed their pace and Kirkorian pulled out her phone as if to make a call but had her backwards facing camera on. There was someone following them.

Naz leaned over as if to kiss Kirkorian's neck and whispered into his comms, "Jericho we have a problem."

The man in front of them started walking towards them. Kirkorian saw an alley coming up on the left and hooked Naz's arm; when they got close, she started laughing as if he'd told her something funny and pulled gently turning into the alley. They got about 15 paces down when another man in a uniform stepped out from a doorway. Naz and Kirkorian stopped dead.

"Hello, Sheir zan. Or should I call you Zmarei, the Lioness, like the Afghans," the man said.

His voice sounded familiar to Kirkorian but she was wracked with confusion. In Farsi, the term Sheir zan roughly translates to *a woman like a lion that is not afraid of anything*. It was the nickname her uncle Grigor called her when he took her on their hunting trips. He taught her how to be a sniper, to stalk her prey and make a long-range kill. How the hell would this man know either of those nicknames?

She felt Naz tighten getting ready to strike as his right hand started slipping behind him to get his knife. His hand grasped the handle as the man stepped forward into a dim, overhead light.

Kirkorian gasped. "Oh my god! Uncle Darius?"

Naz's head snapped to look at Kirkorian. "Wait, Uncle?"

"Hello Chief Petty Officer. Yes, Uncle. Otherwise known as Police Commander Darius Gazsian and you can remove your hand from your K-bar now," Gazsian said extending his hand to shake with Naz. "Her father is my brother-in-law and runs that special op training center in Texas you like so much. My sweet Shirin, it's so nice to meet you in person. It's been so long since I've seen your mother and father, but you are the spitting image of her," Gazsian said as he stepped in to give her a hug.

"Naz, status report?" Jericho urgently called over the comms.

"Everything is fine here boss. Just ran into some friends that HQ sent us; will tell you more in a bit," Kirkorian reported.

"Your family runs SA2?" Naz asked with the look of shock on his face.

Just then a helicopter flew low overhead. "That will be the IRGC commander. There's a field behind the police station, he'll land there," Gazsian said.

"Jericho, chopper headed your way carrying the IRGC commander," Naz began.

"I know, he almost landed on our goddamned heads. Two people getting out and heading to the station," Jericho whispered.

If the situation wasn't so tense, it would have been funny, but they had deadly serious business to finish, and this was just one of many surprises.

"To answer your question Chief, yes, they do. But right now, we have other things to discuss," Gazsian said. "The two suspects are in the station. My men and I did the capture, so they are unhurt. They will be located in the interrogation rooms, ten meters down the hallway to the left as you enter the front. I assume that's your planned entrance, correct?"

"Yes, we're to be taken in as a set of suspects by two of our team posing as officers from a village we passed on the way here," Kirkorian replied.

Just then Gazsian's radio came to life calling him back to the station.

"I suspect the IRGC commander wants a debrief of the capture. Give me ten minutes before you enter. My men and I cannot help in the snatch and grab, but we can make sure no civilians get in the way. There are only six officers in the building right now so get your team ready to move. There's a platoon sized force coming from Darreh Shahr, maybe forty-five minutes out so you need to move quickly. Shirin, I wish we could have more time to talk, but you must go. Now!" Gazsian explained.

"Jericho, eight hostiles in the station, six LEOs and two IRGC including their incident commander," reported Naz. "The targets are located in interrogation rooms about ten meters down the hallway to the left of the entrance."

"Okay, get in position, Moose and Hammer headed to you," Jericho ordered.

"Uncle, be careful," Kirkorian said as she gave Gazsian a quick hug then got her game face back on.

"You too Sheir zan. Now go!" Gazsian answered then turned, headed back down the alley.

Kirkorian and Naz moved back up the street and stood in the shadows of a shop entrance across from the police station.

***

Director Anderson dropped a capsule into the single serve coffee maker on the credenza behind his desk and pushed the button. He closed his eyes, ran his hands through his gray-streaked hair, and leaned back as the dark brown liquid filled his cup. The deep, nutty aroma of the premium Panamanian dark roast coffee was strangely relaxing. It enveloped him in anticipation of its warm, zesty tang and earthy undertones born of the nutrient rich volcanic soil it was grown in. Just the thing to help ease the strain he'd been under these past several months.

A major battle in Afghanistan, a nuclear Iran, the battle in the Gulf, all within such a short time of each other stressed American national defense assets to heights not seen since the first Gulf War. Made even more stressful as the option for a hot extraction was a plan only between Jackson and himself. The quick reaction team wasn't military; Anderson personally set it up. The President had balked on the infiltration plan; he'd be apoplectic if he knew what they planned if the extraction went sideways.

The fact the US was there would be the big stick that backed up their Arab allies. If Iran attacked again, the President was on a tightrope and would have to respond. The wrong step in any direction meant disaster and only two ways off, forward or backward. Anderson and Jackson were betting the President would only move forward.

Anderson pulled the coffee cup from the machine and took a sip. He relished the hot liquid as it slid down his throat. The combination of the rich bodied, slightly bitter taste and the aroma let his mind drift. In the past he would have lit a cigarette with the coffee. The combination just seemed perfect together. But after years of his wife's insistence, and the government going smoke free in its buildings, he finally quit. Though at times like these, those cravings came back stronger than ever.

The warble of his secure phone yanked him back to reality as he punched the button to answer the DDI's direct line, "Anderson."

"David, we've confirmed the targets have been arrested and the team is headed their way. The main IRGC force is less than an hour and a half away, so things need to happen fast. Timing is tight so it'll be dicey," Hayes briefed.

Anderson looked at the clock; 17:00 DC time, that was 01:30 Tehran time.

"Call Silas and Secretary Jackson. Contact the Joint Ops center and tell them to start the clock on Operation Copperfield and loop in the Situation Room. Tell the White House I'm on my way over. Lastly Janelle, initiate Joint Protocol 4. We don't know if this thing will spiral out of control, but I want to be ready if it does. Secretary Jackson is already onboard, and I need this activated before I get to the White House," Anderson ordered.

He punched off the line, poured his coffee into a travel cup, and shoved the operational planning documents into a locked briefcase. Lastly, he opened the top right-hand drawer of his desk and pulled out an encrypted cell phone then quickly exited his office for the White House.

Chapter 32

Dangerous Prey

The helicopter landed in a field a short distance behind the police station and Mohktari stepped off with another soldier. Once they were clear, it took off and headed back to Dezful. As they walked toward the station, his cell phone rang.

"Mohktari," he answered.

"Sir, Major Shavani. Our friends tell us that cell phone number used to call the phones at the facility briefly came online a few hours ago."

"Where was the signal picked up?" asked Mohktari.

"Ahvaz, but it was only on for a short time. Not enough to get a full triangulation," the Major answered.

"I see. So why the hell am I just being notified of this now?" Mokhtari asked angrily.

"Sir, our friends reported it to Tehran rather than us," the Major replied.

"Of course," Mokhtari said disgustedly. "And have our friends been able to narrow it down?"

"They got about a ten-block area based on analysis of the cell tower pings," the Major answered. "We've already started moving assets to intercept."

"Okay, I want two full companies of soldiers there immediately. Pull them from the border if you must but seal off that city. And make sure it's done a hell of a lot better than they did in Dezful," Mokhtari ordered.

"Yes sir. Captain Al Madani reported he's about 40-50 minutes from your location," stated the Major as Mokhtari ended the call.

He moved quickly to the front of the station. As Mokhtari pushed through the front doors, the Desk Sergeant instinctively came to attention at the sight of the IRGC Commander.

"Colonel, welcome, my Commander is expecting you. He's down the hall, I can have someone get him," the Sergeant replied nervously.

"Is he interrogating them? I said no one interrogates the suspects but me," Mokhtari said in his calm but threatening way.

The Sergeant swallowed hard; his mouth suddenly very dry.

"No, no sir. Nobody has interrogated the suspects in compliance with your orders."

The Sergeant nervously picked up the phone and fumbled it just a little and dialed an extension.

"Tell the Commander Colonel Mokhtari is here."

Mokhtari stood straight, staring at the Sergeant who found it extremely hard to concentrate. The Sergeant tried to go back to working through the night's paperwork but increasingly felt like he just wanted to melt into the woodwork. The police Commander bounded down the hallway with a smile on his face.

"Welcome Colonel, I'm Commander Ahkazmanesh. We have your suspects down the hall in the interrogation rooms. They're all ready for you."

Mokhtari turned his head to look at the Commander. His look stopped the Commander in his tracks as he looked between Mokhtari and the desk Sergeant.

"Do we have a problem?" he asked.

"Did you question the suspects?" Mokhtari asked.

The calm, commanding tone sent a cold shiver down the Commander's spine.

"No sir. We followed your instructions exactly. We've had guards in each room and both suspects are secured. Did someone say we interrogated them?" asked the Commander.

He looked at the Sergeant who shook his head no.

"Good. So, commander, tell me how you captured these two individuals. Don't leave any details out," commanded Mohktari.

"I got a call from a police sergeant in a village 30-40 minutes from here. He said he spotted a large white SUV at a gas station late at night that matched the BOLO. A man was in the station paying for gas when he went in to investigate. He was the only officer on duty with no backup, so he just asked some questions. He said he got a weird feeling from the man, so he went back and checked the BOLO and figured the man's description was close enough to your suspect that we should check him out when he came our way.

"We had a team of officers from Kermanshah who arrived about an hour before that," Ahkazmanesh answered. "They were on their way to support your security efforts around

Dezful and their commander offered to help with the roadblock. Since mine had worked all day, I accepted. Between his team and a few of my men, the stop went flawlessly. He set up a four-car box with snipers and arrested the suspects without incident."

"Sounds like a textbook takedown. I need to speak with this police commander. Where is he?" Mokhtari asked.

"Commander Gazsian and his men took over city patrols so we could secure the suspects for your arrival. We'll give him a call." Ahkazmanesh pointed at the desk Sergeant who picked up the phone.

"Come get me when he arrives. I'm going to talk to the woman first," Mokhtari instructed.

"Yes, sir," Ahkazmanesh replied.

The Police Commander turned and escorted the IRGC soldiers down the hall.

"The woman is here on the right, the man on the left," Ahkazmanesh said pointing to the interrogation room doors.

Mokhtari pointed for the solider to guard the man while he questioned the woman. As he entered the interrogation room, he motioned the policeman to leave. Azar looked up with a blank expressionless face as Mokhtari sat down across the table from her and just stared.

"Miss Barghani, I'm Colonel Mokhtari of the IRGC Security Directorate. I have some questions for you, and I expect truthful answers, do you understand?" he said in that same calm, threatening voice.

Azar's eyes burned with hatred, but she said nothing.

"What, no convenient lies like those you told the guards at the storage facility? We know you took supplies from that facility including explosives. So, either you were part of the attack on our research facility, or you are helping the man who did it escape. Either way, we know who you are and what you're capable of. Well, we can either have a polite conversation and you tell me everything, or a less polite discussion, where you will tell me everything anyway," Mokhtari stated as his eyes burrowed into Azar.

There was a knock on the door and a policeman opened it.

"He's here sir."

"Still nothing to say to me? No? Well let's see what your boyfriend has to say then."

With that Mokhtari stood and walked out of the room as Azar struggled against the handcuffs with rage.

In the hallway, the two Police Commanders walked down the hall. Commander Gazsian extended his hand to Mokhtari.

"Commander Gazsian, Colonel, at your service." Gazsian said as he shook Mokhtari's hand.

"Commander, Ahkazmanesh here tells me you supervised the capture of the suspects. I must say, from his description it was virtually perfect. Where did you learn that tactic?" Mokhtari asked.

"Thank you, sir, but I've found success comes with leverage to minimize loss of life. And a mass advantage of firepower applied carefully ensures a simple choice, surrender or death," Gazsian answered.

"Hmm. Have we met before? You look very familiar," Mokhtari asked quizzically.

"Yes, Colonel. My wife did your general's heart surgery, as she has also done on two Supreme Leaders and the previous President. She has quite literally kept the regime alive since the revolution. You were head of security for the General's surgery in Kermanshah. You see, she's the best cardio-thoracic surgeon in Iran. We do the surgeries in her hospital because it's easier to hide the patient, the procedure, and the surgeon. It's all about...discretion," Gazsian said.

"Ah yes, I remember. Your security team was highly professional. Given the level of visitors you have at your hospital I can see where your skills come from. Thank you for your help; we are truly lucky you and your men were here," Mokhtari said. "Excuse me, time for me to get to work."

He turned and entered the room holding Ebrahim while the two commanders walked back to the front.

***

As the two commanders passed the ready room, Gazsian noticed two officers sitting drinking coffee. When they got to the front desk, another officer was talking with the Desk Sergeant.

"I'm off to continue patrols. I'll see you in the morning," Gazsian said as he shook hands with Ahkazmanesh.

As he turned, two officers came through escorting a man and a woman. Gazsian turned his head and called out, "Hey Sergeant, tell those two in the ready room to get off their asses. IRGC is going to be here in less than a half hour and they won't suffer individuals being lazy with their prime suspects."

"Yes sir, I'll get right on it," the Sergeant replied.

Gazsian walked past the four without a word and exited the station.

Chapter 33

Securing the Packages

In the interrogation room, the IRGC soldier stood scowling at Azar. When he entered, he growled at the policeman to "get out" as he put his hand on his combat knife. The soldier relished the fact he was an untouchable IRGC soldier. Having the power to kill without consequence, even a policeman if he chose to, gave him a satisfying sense of superiority.

Azar looked at him with contempt.

"So, I see the Colonel brought his lapdog with him. I'm guessing he doesn't trust you," she said defiantly.

He just smirked.

Azar laughed.

"How funny, you're nothing but a stupid asshole with a gun. He said he's the only one who can get answers correct?"

The soldier's smile disappeared as he tried to keep a neutral face. But how dare this…woman speak to him in such a manner.

"Do you hold his dick while he takes a piss to?" she goaded him. "No, no, he wouldn't trust you to do that either. Maybe to wipe his ass after a shit!" she taunted.

The soldier stepped forward and gave Azar a backhand across the face.

"Shut up bitch. You'll get yours soon enough and I'll take pleasure in watching you suffer!" he raged.

Azar smiled with bloodied teeth and a red welt on her right cheek.

"Of course, you'll watch. They wouldn't trust you to get information from me because you can't get it up for a woman." Azar laughed again. "Yes, that's it. You only get hard for another man! I should have known why they sent you to guard me!"

This threw the guard into a rage.

"I'll show you what a real man can do you bitch."

The soldier moved to Azar and grabbed her, throwing her on the table. She pulled her knees up and kicked at him as he struggled to pull off her pants. The soldier pulled her to the edge of the table and slapped her again. They struggled as she maneuvered her body slightly backwards and to the right on the table.

The guard grunted, slapping her again trying desperately to control her and finally show her who truly had the power. He reached back for a hard backhand and this was the opening Azar was waiting for. As his hand came around, she turned and ducked her head making him miss but leaving him completely open and off balance.

Azar quickly swung her legs up around the neck of the soldier in a leg lock, squeezing as hard as she could. At the same time, she swung her body to the left driving the soldier's right shoulder into the table stopping his momentum, and his ability to roll with her. As she continued to roll, the soldier's body went limp with a sickening popping sound. Death came swiftly to him.

She released him and quickly moved to his pocket, found the handcuff keys and had them off in seconds. She grabbed the soldier's handgun and knife and moved to the door.

***

The four operatives walked through the front door of the police station and gave way to Gazsian, who was leaving. They moved to the front desk.

"What can I do for you two?" asked the desk Sergeant.

"We're from up the road and stopped these two fitting the BOLO for the Dezful suspects. We don't have facilities to hold them, so we brought them to you guys. So, what do you want us to do with them?" Moose asked.

"I'm Commander Ahkazmanesh; we already have suspects in custody, but I guess until their identities are confirmed we can manage a couple more. Officer, take these two to the ready room and tell those two idiots to guard them," the Commander said.

"Yes, sir," came the reply.

As the officer turned towards Hammer, he stopped. The three policemen came face to face with guns pointed at their heads. Naz put a finger to his lips for them to remain silent. Kirkorian looked down the hallway as Moose zip tied the officers' hands and gagged them.

He leaned into the group sitting on the floor.

"We don't want to hurt you but if you move or make a single sound, the next sound you hear will be my bullet hitting your head. So, sit back and have a nice nap."

Moose pulled out three auto-injectors of a fast-acting sedative, selected a setting and pressed them against the neck of each man.

"Let's go," Kirkorian whispered.

Naz, Kirkorian, and Hammer got back into position with Hammer acting as an officer again escorting the others down the hallway. Moose took a position at the front as a lookout. The three operatives turned to the right into the ready room causing the two officers seated there to look up.

"Your Commander told me to bring these two suspects here. He said you two should guard them as suspects in the terror attack," Hammer stated as the group kept walking closer to the policemen.

The two officers stood up and walked over to the three operatives. When they got a couple of feet away, Naz and Kirkorian pulled out their weapons and pointed them at the officers' heads. Again, Naz put a finger to his mouth as Hammer quickly zip tied their hands and gagged them. They moved them to the corner of the room and sedated them.

"Five hostiles neutralized," reported Hammer over comms.

"One hostile neutralized in the motor pool," reported Jericho.

That meant only the two IRGC soldiers were left to be dealt with. Just then the team heard a man cry out in pain from down the hall.

***

Mokhtari entered the room and stood across from Ebrahim. His blue eyes pierced Ebrahim's heart at the thought of this man torturing Azar because of him.

"So, tell me Sergeant. Why did you sabotage the facility?" asked Mohktari.

Ebrahim looked up. His eyes sad and his body reflecting total defeat.

"The girl had nothing to do with this, don't hurt her," he pleaded.

"I see, so you admit you're the saboteur then. That was easier than I expected. As for your girlfriend's guilt or innocence, well she helped you escape so she is not innocent here," Mokhtari said calmly.

"I don't expect you to understand that we love each other. She helped me because I didn't do the bombing and you would have killed her anyway just for sport even if she hadn't helped me. I'm sure a man like you would torture his own wife to get information. Tell me I'm wrong," Ebrahim said angrily.

"Well, you speak as if we had a choice. You killed over a hundred people and put our nation in grave danger. You're the single biggest threat we have. You sealed your fate the moment you ran, and you endangered Miss Barghani. So, you will tell me everything," Mokhtari said in a quiet, but firm voice.

Ebrahim sighed and looked down at the table. When diffusing bombs, he always understood his life rested on a razors edge. He always resigned himself to being a dead man, so Mokhtari was right, no matter what happened, his fate was sealed. When he looked up, his face took on his neutral EOD look.

"I'm the single biggest threat? Now who's lying? Let me ask you Colonel, how much explosive was used in the attack on the facility? Given the force that I felt, I would have to guess two to three hundred kilos?" Ebrahim asked.

"Hmmm, what a good guess. Almost like you knew the answer. But then again, you are the explosives expert here are you not?" Mokhtari answered coolly.

Ebrahim continued his arguments with surprising calmness.

"You personally set up the security protocols I would imagine, so you know them inside and out. Tell me, how long would it take to smuggle that much explosive into the facility under those protocols? And not just the explosives, from the radio traffic we know there was nuclear material vented into the facility and that couldn't come from the explosive. I'm guessing your assessment team already figured out it wasn't a dirty bomb which means someone had to sabotage the conduit system connecting the blast chamber to the facility. How long would that take?

"And I've been wondering why a cell phone module with steel screws instead of brass like I used was there at the entrance that rang a phone I had never seen in my bag. Certainly, it's occurred to you that if I were the bomber, I could just initiate it from where I was, no reason to use a cell phone trigger. I'm a dead man and we both know it, so I've no reason to lie. But you're a smart man Colonel. It wasn't me, or at least there was someone else who had the means and opportunity to commit this act. Don't you think?"

"Ah, well now we're getting somewhere. You know so much of what happened and yet claim you weren't involved. But then you admit you had an accomplice inside the facility. And who would that be?" Mokhtari asked inquiringly.

"Colonel, I'm sure you've run the timeline in your head. Even if I was involved, this plan was in motion long before I was even brought into the facility." Ebrahim paused and looked at him.

He recognized slight facial changes in Mohktari.

"And that's what's been bothering you, isn't it?" Ebrahim asked.

Mokhtari walked over to the table and leaned into Ebrahim as his face took on a more dangerous look.

"And who did this?" he said softly, almost hissing.

Just then the door opened. Ebrahim's eyes went wide. Before Mokhtari could fully turn around he took a hard kick in the kidney. Instinctively he turned toward the threat bringing his arms up to try and block the next attack when a fist came slamming into his midsection. He was still trying to catch his breath and his bearings when his legs were swept from under him as his left arm was pulled behind him dislocating his shoulder. His head hit the table, stunning him as he went down. He felt someone grab his right arm and snap it like a twig letting out a scream of pain.

As he lay there stunned and in pain, he saw Azar kneeling on his diaphragm making it extremely hard to breathe.

"You son of a bitch. I bet you don't remember me, but I remember you. I remember your voice and your face ever since you led those Hezbollah animals into my kibbutz and killed my family. You killed my brother on top of me. He was eleven and was just trying to protect me. Now you can feel what I felt that day when your missiles ripped open the body of a scared eight-year-old girl."

Azar took the dead guard's knife and sliced Mokhtari from his abdomen to groin as he screamed again.

"Now, I've nicked your femoral artery, just a little bit. If you're lucky someone will find you in the next ten minutes before you bleed out. Too bad you can't use your arms to stop the bleeding. Neither could I," Azar hissed as her whole body shook with rage.

She got up and took the handcuff keys to unlock Ebrahim's handcuffs. He just stared at her with his mouth open. Just then the door opened again, and a woman stepped inside. Azar swung around with the knife and moved quickly at the woman who blocked the attack in a single fluid motion, knocking the knife out of Azar's hand.

Azar spun with a flying kick that the woman skillfully deflected; clearly this woman had training. She finally performed a maneuver that no one in the world could block, learned long ago and drilled into her head by a Nepalese Master. As Azar moved through the air, it was like moving in slow motion in her mind; she saw her target, positioned her fists and feet, and...went tumbling into the wall.

"Udhdaredātmanātmānam" the woman shouted in an ancient dead language.

Somehow, she had blocked Azar's attack. Azar recovered in a crouched position ready for another attack, but the woman's word made her stop.

"Where did you hear that phrase?" asked Azar panting, from the exertion.

The woman just stood there, as though there was no exertion at all on her part, then extended her right hand to Azar.

Kirkorian responded in perfect Hebrew.

"Because Master Prabhjote taught that Sanskrit phrase to me as a little girl too so his students could identify each other. My name is Shirin and we're here to get you out of here."

"Who the hell are you?" Azar answered in Hebrew.

"We're Americans and we were sent in to find you two. We don't have much time but when you made your attack, I recognized the fighting style immediately. Sorry but I didn't want to hurt you, and I knew the only way you could have learned that was from my father's martial arts master. I'm guessing you're Mossad?" Kirkorian asked.

Azar looked at Ebrahim who still had one hand cuffed to the table. His face couldn't hide the confusion, but he recognized the word for Mossad.

"Azar! You're Mossad? So, I was just your mark? You're a spy?" Ebrahim sputtered.

Naz came through the door. "What the hell happened?"

"Naz, put a tourniquet on the Colonel's leg here and dose him; we need to get these two out of here," she said in English. "Time to move. Now! There's a platoon sized force minutes away. You, what's your name?" Kirkorian asked Ebrahim in Farsi.

He was still in shock at what just happened and didn't answer.

Kirkorian unlocked his hand, and he brought it up to fight her off. She grabbed his arm with an arm-bar maneuver pulling it straight up and bending it backwards, putting tremendous pressure on the elbow and shoulder. It caused searing pain, and she could snap it if she wanted.

"We're here to help you escape so stop fighting me," she whispered in his ear. "If you want to walk out of here, you'll do what I say because we don't want to carry you. If you stay here these people will kill you. Are you going to stop fighting me and come quietly?"

"Yes!" Ebrahim gasped.

"Kirkorian we've got to go. That main force is only about 5 minutes out," Hammer reported.

"His name is Ebrahim. Please don't hurt him," Azar pleaded.

Kirkorian let his arm go. "Both of you, shut up and follow instructions."

"Who the hell are you people?" asked Ebrahim as he stood up.

"We're American. Now stop talking and move. We'll explain everything later. Jericho, we've got the packages and coming out," Kirkorian reported into her comms.

"Come out the back. Their vehicle is here with a ton of good stuff we can use. Leave the other," Jericho instructed.

Moose joined the other team members in the hallway. Together they moved to the back of the station. They passed through a steel door to a garage area where Jericho had the van parked, next to the white SUV of Ebrahim and Azar.

"Moose, Hammer, take the SUV. Naz, Kirkorian with me. Put these two in the van, I've moved some of the stuff from their SUV to us. Nice work on the equipment by the way," Jericho said to Ebrahim and Azar. "Having their radios will be handy."

The team moved out of the facility, up the alley, and pulled onto the main highway. A string of headlights was visible coming from the south in the darkness. As the van accelerated Ebrahim did his best to avoid looking at Azar.

"Azar, did you ever truly love me or was I just your…mission?" he asked.

"Ebrahim, of course I love you. Yes, it started out as a mission to get close enough for information, but I was already gathering it from my work with the company. But I really did fall in love with you," she answered quietly, almost imploring him to believe her.

"Why should I believe anything you say to me? You've been lying to me the whole time we've been together. Why did you bother trying to save me anyway? You should have just left me and saved yourself. Or maybe you were just trying to get me out to turn me over to your Mossad handlers once we were safe. How could I have been such a fool," he said bitterly.

"I could have left you at any time. Yes, I had an escape plan. But I stayed for *you*! I saved *you*!" Azar replied with tears streaming down her face. "I stayed for you and for our family!" she said, crying.

"Family, what family?" he said angrily.

"I'm pregnant you idiot!" she screamed. "I'm going to have a baby, your baby Ebrahim."

She buried her face in her hands sobbing. Her shoulders heaved up and down with the gasps of her pained cries. Ebrahim sat speechless. Kirkorian put her arms around the distraught woman and gave Ebrahim a look that sent a chill down his spine.

"Is, is this true?" Ebrahim asked stuttering.

"Look at her. What do you think asshole?" Kirkorian hissed at him.

Ebrahim was conflicted. This woman turned out to be a Zionist spy and yet he loved her still. He looked down and ran his fingers through his hair.

Azar looked at him. "I'm so sorry. I was going to tell you on our trip before all this happened. Please forgive me."

After a few moments Ebrahim found the courage to speak.

"Were you happy when you found out?" he asked.

The question brought a slight smile to Azar's tear-stained face.

"Ebrahim, I love you and I've never been happier in all my life! I couldn't wait to tell you."

Ebrahim moved to the other side of the van and took Azar into his arms. He put his hand on her face to wipe away some tears and kissed her forehead.

"Then we'll figure this out...together."

***

The tension in the Situation Room among the President and his national security team could be cut with a knife. For the second time in months, there was a significant threat to US interests and the possibility of a major military escalation. President Saldana paced as events unfolded, completely helpless to influence the course of any of them.

"How long before the team makes contact?" asked Saldana.

"Right now sir," replied the senior operations specialist at CIA.

"No video of this?" asked the President.

"No sir. The team is under cover, so we'll only get verbal reports. Ops just has satellite overwatch," Jackson replied.

"Colt, tell me again, what are the risks?" Saldana asked nervously.

"Sir, the Gulf states are taking the greatest risk. The Saudis have every reason to strike the facility that launched the attack on their convoy and should be seen as a measured response. But yes, there's a chance Iran could escalate. If that happens, we are ready for it. But remember sir, this creates a situation to get our people out of there with two very important assets," Jackson briefed for the second time.

"Goddammit I don't like this. I came into office promising to get us out of wars, not start them. So, what happens in my last year? We nearly start World War three, twice!" Saldana growled.

"Sir, we didn't start the engagement between Pakistan and Afghanistan, and we didn't start this one. The Iranians violated the treaty by detonating a nuclear trigger. The fact they were also targeted by the Caliphate also isn't on us. But we have to respond to the facts on the ground Mr. President," Anderson reminded him.

"And the opportunity to secure someone who can give details on their progress, is worth every effort expended to get them out," Jackson added.

"You mean every life lost, isn't that right Colt?" Saldana asked.

"Sir, every person you send into harm's way does so voluntarily. They all believe their leaders use their skills only when absolutely necessary," Jackson answered.

And that was the problem for Saldana. The fact others would sacrifice so much on his authority was a constant struggle for him. Did he send them as the last option? Was there a better one? He was always gripped with indecision, especially in life and death decisions. Because when he said yes, people died.

It all felt surreal, like a video game, ordering the death of an enemy. But the deaths of Americans weighed on him like an anchor. And he had the souls of over a thousand American soldiers and operatives hung around his neck. It was the part of this job he would never miss.

It was deathly silent in the Situation Room as the President became increasingly nervous.

"Platoon sized force moving northeast currently near Ilam Lake. Another larger force moving north about ten to fifteen minutes from Jafar Abad," reported the Ops center.

Jackson looked at Anderson who excused himself and left the room. When he returned, he caught Jackson's eye and calmly returned to his seat. Minute after agonizing minute passed.

"Son of a bitch, what the hell is going on in there?" asked the President with a hint of desperation.

"Two packages secured, southern force three minutes out."

Chapter 34

Operation Copperfield

A minute after the American team exited the police station, the IRGC convoy arrived. As Captain Al Madani pulled up in front of the station, he saw a white SUV parked a short distance down the street.

"Sergeant, have someone check out that vehicle. Squad one, with me," he ordered.

The group of soldiers entered the station and found the entrance empty and the front desk phone ringing. As he approached the desk, he saw the three officers tied and gagged on the floor. He drew his sidearm and the squad immediately brought their weapons up ready for action.

"Check on these men. You four check down that hallway, the rest with me," Al Madani ordered as the squad split to clear both hallways of the station.

"Get me a medic in here, squad two check the perimeter, squad three the motor pool," he ordered on his radio.

Al Madani's team got to the ready room; a soldier did a quick peek around the corner. He gave a hand signal with two fingers pointing down. Two soldiers popped around the door frame pointing their weapons in different corners of the room and sweeping in an arc to clear any hostiles.

"Clear. Two down like the ones in front."

A medic and another fire team came down the hallway to the ready room as Al Madani and the squad moved to the interrogation rooms. They opened the door on the right and found the dead guard. They then opened the one on the left.

"Clear, but the Colonel's down," the soldier reported.

"Medic!" Al Madani shouted.

"Move!" the medic exclaimed as he entered the room. "Sir, we need a surgical hospital right now or the Colonel could bleed out. Whoever did this used a military tourniquet and probably saved his life but he's been sedated like the rest!"

Al Madani turned to one of his Platoon Sergeants.

"Get on the radio and find out if there are any other officers in the town. Whoever did this can't be far; it looks like this just happened," Al Madani ordered.

The Sergeant went to the dispatch office and made the urgent call.

"Command, this is Viper. Colonel Mokhtari is seriously injured, and the prisoners have escaped. What are the locations of the unit from Ilam and Second Platoon right now? Over," Al Madani asked over his secure radio.

"Viper, Command. Second Platoon is about ten kilometers west of Balyen, the Ilam team is just south of the city and will set up a roadblock at Balyen. Second Platoon is prepared to join them there. Over."

"Copy all. We don't know who is helping them, but we have to prevent them from getting to Kurdish territory, so I suggest getting some gunships overhead. Be advised, Colonel Mokhtari is being medevac'd to Ilam for surgery. Over," Al Madani reported.

"Roger. Command out!"

A minute later Gazsian was escorted to Al Madani.

"Hello Captain, Commander Gazsian. Ilam is sending a chopper; it will be here in a few minutes. I've asked for a surgeon from Kermanshah to fly in for the surgery. I know the surgeon our nation's leaders trust; she's the best in the country. Trust me, the Colonel will be in excellent hands."

"She?" asked Al Madani.

"Yes, Captain. *She* is my wife. She's performed surgery on our top leaders and there's no one better. We need the best to ensure your Commander survives, right?" Gazsian said. "Now is anyone else injured?"

"The policemen were drugged and cuffed, they'll be alright. One of our soldiers is dead. Very strange, why didn't they just kill everyone?" asked Al Madani.

"Perhaps that wasn't the objective Captain. But let me and my men handle the cleanup," Gazsian said.

Gazsian barked orders to his men to secure the civilians and keep them out of the way of the soldiers. With Mokhtari loaded onto the helicopter, Al Madani left the station and got his platoon moving again.

***

The President clapped his hands at the news the team was successful, but the situation was still precarious and the political appointees in the Situation Room shifted nervously.

Jackson picked up the phone. "General, commence Operation Copperfield."

US aircraft flying just off the coast of the United Arab Emirates and Saudi Arabia turned on their radar jammers at the same time and Iranian long-range radars were blasted with millions of watts of electronic noise. Saudi F-15E Strike Eagles launched a salvo of air launched cruise missiles against the airfield and port facilities on Abu Musa Island. They were supersonic German missiles with large warheads and ground hugging radars. Once launched, they were autonomous, flying a preprogrammed route, and could not be stopped.

"Eight Iranian fighters are launching and moving towards the border but are still blind. Expect burn through in three minutes," reported the Central Command operations center in Tampa.

"What's burn through?" asked Saldana.

"Sir, we are brute force jamming their long-range radars, meaning we are jamming over a broad range of frequencies at high power. Once the fighters get to their own radar range, it will be a more focused beam allowing some ability to reduce the noise, therefore they will burn through that noise wall. But we expected that," Jackson answered like a professor in a classroom.

"Time on target, one minute," reported CENTCOM.

The center monitor of the situation room switched to an image of Abu Musa. There were two bright flashes over the port facilities and as the bright flashes subsided, the image showed multiple boats on fire and several secondary explosions as the fuel and ammunition depots were both ignited by the blast. About three seconds later two flashes hit the airfield. The image stabilized and a hangar and a building next to the parking ramp were both in flames as several aircraft and helicopters were now ablaze.

Moments later, "Primary targets destroyed. CAP has all enemy aircraft locked on," CENTCOM said. "Iranian gunboats in the Gulf have begun to sortie. RSN and Fifth Fleet moving to intercept."

"Mr. President, it's time for you to make the call to the Iranian President," Jackson said calmly.

Less than a minute later the President's Chief of Staff handed Saldana a phone.

"President Rahimi a few moments ago forces from the Gulf states executed an operation on the island installations on Abu Musa. This is in response to Iranian naval attacks on a tanker convoy in international waters earlier this evening. We know of your military's response to this operation but let me be clear," Saldana said sternly.

"If your military assets cross the internationally recognized demarcation line of your airspace and waters, they will be engaged by a coalition of international forces. Mr. President, I would urge you to recall those forces now or risk an escalation that your country cannot afford. We already have assets in place to defend any aggression by your country, and there is no more need for loss of life."

"President Saldana, you dare insult me when it was you who attacked Iran?" Rahimi responded indignantly.

"In response to your attack sir, in international waters in violation of international law," Saldana interrupted.

"I never authorized any attack in the Gulf. How can I trust anything you say? This is preposterous and just some manufactured information to justify your strike on us. You were probably behind the terror attack on us as well," Rahimi shouted.

The images on the front screen changed to show the Presidential palace in Tehran. Two men could be seen on the rooftop patio, one on a cell phone.

"Mr. President do not make a fool of yourself. Of course you know about the engagement in the Gulf, the commander of the Revolutionary Guard is standing next to you, briefing you right now. We will be happy to turn over the survivors from that engagement after you recall your forces and they have been fully debriefed. This facility that was apparently sabotaged conducted a nuclear test which means you violated our nuclear agreement, attacked noncombatants, and we both know it. So *do not* lecture me about trust.

"Recall your forces or suffer the consequences. You have," the President looked at the Chairman of the Joint Chiefs of Staff who put up three fingers, "three minutes to comply before your forces are engaged by the combined forces of the United States and four other nations. That will be followed by attacks on all your refineries and oil production facilities.

"And finally, Mr. President, there's a B-2 overhead targeting you right now. Thirty seconds after the attacks start a 2000-pound warhead will hit your villa. You will try to make it to your underground bunker, but you are on the fourth floor, and it is 100 feet below the surface. Thirty seconds after the first warhead hits your villa, a ground penetrating warhead will hit, destroying everything, and everyone in your villa and bunker. Recall your forces ***now***! You can trust that!" President Saldana hung up abruptly, his hands slightly shaking.

He closed his eyes and rubbed his face. Saldana was rarely aggressive when talking to other leaders, so this was uncomfortable for him. As he looked at the men and women around the situation room table, they sat silently. Most had a look of affirmation for the tone and action he took, some the look of concern. But Saldana oddly felt, satisfaction.

"Sir, we don't have a B-2 overhead," the Chairman commented.

"Admiral, you know that, and I know that, but President Rahimi doesn't. I figured he needed a little firmer...nudge," the President remarked quietly.

"Sir, anti-air systems coming online all over Iran. CENTCOM, fix and target as many as we can along possible ingress routes," Jackson ordered.

"Well played Mr. President. Didn't know you were such a good poker player," Anderson said quietly.

"Well don't congratulate me yet David, they haven't recalled their forces," Saldana replied.

He thought he'd feel remorse over the lives lost, and more that could be lost if the Iranians didn't back down...he didn't. The Iranians had screwed him. They lied and continued their nuclear program despite their promises not to. The sabotage on the facility was proof of their deceit and the total embarrassment he felt over being duped. That pissed him off the most.

"Sir, fighter aircraft are turning back and several entering combat air patrol maneuvers. Naval assets are also slowing and forming picket lines, but all remain in Iranian territorial waters. Iranians are requesting helicopters and ships to evacuate the wounded from Abu Musa," the Commander of CENTCOM stated.

Jackson looked at the President who nodded his approval.

"General, three helicopters and two ships but they will be escorted. Offer medical assistance for their wounded and be prepared to hand over the prisoners from the previous engagement," Jackson ordered.

Chapter 35

Tightening the Noose

Events were moving fast, and Jericho figured their pursuers would have to clear the police station before following them. That meant a narrow window to reach the extraction point. Headquarters reported three sizable forces moving in their direction so if their timing was correct, that window was paper thin.

Just then he got a call on the satellite phone. "Jericho."

"A group has split from the southwest moving fast toward Balyen; estimate two full squads. They'll arrive before you," operations reported.

"Upload the latest imagery; we'll make a plan. Is extraction still on track?" Jericho asked.

"Infil in five," was the reply.

"Copy, prepare for a hot extraction. Datalink to the CST," Jericho instructed as he pulled out a portable satellite terminal.

"Okay folks, you heard this will be a hot extraction. We won't get to Balyen before reinforcements, so we need to come up with another plan. We need to slow down these guys chasing us then find a way around the ones in front," Jericho announced.

"I can help with that," Ebrahim said.

The American operators looked at him.

"I'm an explosives expert who spent my career diffusing IEDs. We have everything we need," he added.

Azar wiped tears from her face as her Mossad training kicked in.

"Ebrahim's right. Setting an IED will force them to stop and clear the road. Could give us an extra five to ten minutes."

"Alright, go," Jericho ordered.

"Azar, grab two of those IR sensors, two batteries, two rolls of wire, tape, and two detonators. You, what's your name?" Ebrahim asked.

"Call me Shirin," Kirkorian replied.

"Shirin, grab two blocks of HMX from that box, two boxes of ammunition, four grenades, and that primacord," Ebrahim instructed. "When we pull over, Azar wire the IR sensors as our trigger switch, and use the batteries to power the detonators. Shirin, run wire back twenty meters. Get some larger rocks and dig out a small depression in the dirt and gravel on the side of the road, put the HMX in the hole with the box of ammo pointing towards the road with the two grenades. Then push the detonator through a piece of primacord and into the HMX and connect the wire.

"Put the larger rocks behind the HMX and pack some dirt behind them then throw some loose dirt on the ammo side to cover it. String some primacord across the road and throw some dirt over it. I'll be doing the same on the other side. Azar, once we're clear, activate the sensors and get the hell out of there. When the lead vehicle passes the sensor, it will break the beam and initiate the IEDs hitting the front and middle of the column. Trust me, it will definitely slow them down," Ebrahim finished.

"Okay, everyone ready?" asked Jericho. "Pull over Naz."

As the van pulled off the road, so did Hammer and Moose. Kirkorian yanked open the door and she, Azar, and Ebrahim jumped out. Kirkorian raced to her location on the van side of the road and quickly but methodically set her trap. As she strung the primacord across the road she grabbed a bunch of dirt to throw on it.

She was about halfway across the road when Jericho called out, "Headlights!"

She sprinted back to the van with Ebrahim right behind her. As they passed the IR sensors, Azar activated them and followed the two, jumping into the van. Jericho slammed the sliding door behind them.

"Go, go, go!" Jericho shouted as Naz gunned the accelerator spraying dirt and gravel behind them.

Thirty seconds later two huge explosions ripped through the night sky. Naz glanced back in his mirrors and saw two fireballs rising from the roadway as flames danced in the shadows of the smoke billowing from the wreckage.

Jericho scanned the satellite picture. "Okay people, there's a turn off a mile up on the left. There's a dirt road and a dry riverbed just beyond it. We'll take a left there, follow the riverbed and try to move after the southwest force gets closer to Balyen. Then we can slide in behind them for extraction.

***

Al Madani's excitement grew by the second. They were so close he could feel the saboteurs as his column raced north. He ordered two squads from second platoon to sprint ahead to reinforce the team from Ilam and had two attack helicopters inbound. It eliminated any chance of escape as he tightened the noose.

The great Mokhtari had them and lost them. What a boost to his career if he was the one to bring in the suspects that Mokhtari lost. His self-congratulations exploded like a fiery hurricane right behind his vehicle. The twin IED blasts lifted his truck off the road and spun it around, turning the second and fifth vehicles into flaming skeletons. Gravel became supersonic shards of destruction as the bullets and shrapnel ripped gaping holes into the non-armored vehicles around them. Over a dozen men lay dead or dying as the column came to a halt.

Al Madani's ears were ringing as he stumbled out of his vehicle and looked at the blazing carnage. His head felt like someone was pounding it with a hammer, but he had to get his senses back quickly. Lives depended on it. The acrid smoke from the flaming tires and melting metal stung his eyes and gave his throat a burning sensation.

"Command, this is Viper," Al Madani reported, coughing. "We need medivac immediately. Two IEDs hit our convoy and we have multiple casualties. Will treat the wounded and leave a medic until it arrives; the rest will continue the pursuit. Where the hell are those helicopters?"

"Viper, Command. Medivac on the way, moving another rifle platoon from Kermanshah to Balyen."

"Sergeant," Al Madani shouted to his Command Sergeant. "Consolidate the wounded and give me an accounting of our remaining combat capability!"

"Yes sir!" came the reply as he sprinted past the wreckage of at least six vehicles.

"Get EOD up here now! We need to clear the road ahead. Tell them to run the road with the dogs so we can get moving," Al Madani ordered.

The bomb sniffing dogs came up from the back of the convoy. The IRGC had learned some hard lessons against the Kurds. They always had EOD and bomb dogs accompany any units in Kurdish territory. It meant Al Madani had to be extra careful now which would slow him down.

He got on the radio. "Fox 2, where are you?"

"Sir, we're two clicks west of Balyen at most direct route. Have a dozen men moving ahead of our main column likely less than a kilometer out. I heard the medivac call. What are your orders?" the Second Platoon commander asked.

"Proceed most direct route but lookout for any routes they could take to avoid us. I suspect they'll go off road now so flank both sides of the highway. We'll get satellite help from our friends," Al Madani ordered. "Command, Viper. Requesting a thermal satellite scan immediately, ten kilometers either side of the highway between Jafar Abad and Balyen. Over."

"Viper, command, request has been submitted."

The Sergeant in command of the EOD team reported to Al Madani.

"Sir, dogs have run the sides and there's no more explosives. We found two infrared posts with wires attached; they must have used them as the trigger. As soon as the beam was cut, the IEDs detonated. They didn't have time to really make them directional, but it was effective enough. Had they put more rock and dirt behind them, things could have been much worse. Nine dead, five in extremely bad shape, another seven wounded, six vehicles out of commission."

"Medivac is ten minutes out. Leave some men to care for the wounded. Let's get everyone else mounted up and ready to move," ordered Al Madani.

Chapter 36

Last Stand

Jericho stared at the satellite picture on the small electronic screen. The video gave off an eerie grey glow that lit up his grizzled features.

"Okay, the IEDs have stopped the southern force for now. The one north of us should be clear in a bit. Let's get moving slowly," he instructed.

The team followed a side road leading to a large warehouse and maneuvered around its south side. They found the dry stream bed and navigated to a point where it opened into a larger valley. They moved another 300 meters.

"Hold it, all stop!" exclaimed Jericho over the team comms. "The northern force has stopped near two long warehouse structures about a kilometer northwest."

"Okay you bastards, what the hell are you doing?" he said half under his breath. "Dammit, they must be getting satellite imagery. Thermal imaging shows movement from Balyen directly toward us and the northern force has turned and looks like they may be trying to flank us. The southern group has slowed and looks like they are about to take the same route we did.

Jericho continued in Farsi so everyone could understand the instructions.

"Okay people, time to earn our pay. Ebrahim, are you ready to use that explosive brain of yours again? We need to block this southern group to keep them from encircling us."

"Yes, sir. I just need one other person," he replied.

"Hammer, go with Ebrahim and make that gully a death trap. Moose, Kirkorian, get on overwatch and keep them in a 120-degree fan in front of us. If they flank us, we're dead. Naz, Azar with me. I take it young lady you're skilled with weapons, so let's go," Jericho ordered.

Ebrahim threw a duffle bag to Hammer, tossed another over his shoulder, then the two grabbed the box of HMX and took off running back down the dry stream bed. Moose grabbed a modified M224 lightweight mortar tube that could be fired in a handheld mode. He picked up a pack with 60mm high explosive mortar rounds and his rifle. Kirkorian grabbed her Remington sniper rifle, another rifle with a grenade launcher, and a duffle bag with additional grenades and ammunition.

The two of them raced up the hill in front of them which gave them a 360-degree view of the battlefield. Jericho, Naz, and Azar turned where the creek bed branched off in a Y and raced to a grove of trees at the mouth of the small cutout. They hid the vehicles and positioned themselves in an arc providing overlapping fire for each other that covered the approach from Balyen.

Ebrahim and Hammer set up another IR trigger with HMX buried along both sides of the gulley. They placed half a dozen anti-personnel mines up the slopes to prevent anyone going around their traps and force them into a kill box along the creek bed. With their traps set, they quickly retreated to the point where the creek bed branched into the Y and set up with automatic rifles.

With the positioning of the three groups, they had both axes of approach covered with at least three to four guns and heavy weapons. It didn't take long. Ebrahim and Hammer had just taken positions when gunfire rang out behind them. Kirkorian had targets, and she was hunting.

"Two vehicles, making a dash," Moose reported, looking through the view finder of the binoculars. "Eight hundred meters. They're about to make the turn onto the southwest highway."

"Got 'em," Kirkorian replied as she clicked an adjustment into her scope using a little dust blowing across the road as a windage guide.

She took a breath, let it out about halfway, and slowly squeezed the trigger. The rifle rocked backwards with the power of the bullet being expelled from the barrel at supersonic speed. The head of the driver of the lead vehicle jerked violently backwards as a red spray covered the inside of the truck. The weight of the man's hands made it turn suddenly at high-speed causing the top-heavy truck to roll wildly. Parts of glass, metal, and fuel sprayed all along its path as the exterior of the vehicle disintegrated until it came to a stop on its roof and ignited into a fireball.

The truck was still rolling violently as the trailing vehicle tried to stop. Kirkorian had already chambered another round and fired a shot that caught the driver of the second truck in the head as well. As his muscles went limp, the weight on the brake was released and the truck kept rolling toward the burning wreckage of the first. Three other men were lucky enough to bail out of the truck. Kirkorian killed a third, pinning the surviving two behind the wreckage of both trucks.

A minute after the trucks were neutralized, mortar shells started landing on the slope just below their position. Initially they were smoke rounds to obscure the vision of Moose and Kirkorian. Then the high explosive mortars started landing.

"Time to move," Moose said as he tapped Kirkorian's shoulder.

The two of them moved up the slope another 50 meters and reset. Suddenly the roar of machine gun fire erupted from a tree line about 300 meters from Jericho's position.

"Covering fire on the right, watch for a flanking maneuver," he announced over comms.

Moose looked through the binoculars and spotted a mortar position near some buildings. He loaded the M224, positioned the base on the ground wedged against a rock and pulled the trigger. The 60mm high explosive round came out with a loud thud; seconds later the corner of a building exploded in a shower of wood shards and metal. He loaded another round, aimed slightly left, brought the tube up about half an inch, and pulled the trigger. The mortar round landed fifteen feet from the IRGC mortar team killing two instantly and knocking the mortar out.

The distinct sound of heavy machine guns rang out across the flat scrub bush covered plain. The red glow of the tracer rounds reached out like fingers of fire seeking to destroy whatever they touched. Soldiers moved across the ground in rows with each row alternating between moving and then laying down covering fire for the next row.

"Hold fire; pick your targets people, let them come a little closer," ordered Jericho as the din of battle grew louder with every movement of the enemy.

The front row of the advancing enemy was 100 meters from Jericho's position. "Fire!" he commanded as a roar of return fire erupted from the three operatives. Six soldiers fell in less than three seconds as the advancing enemy dove for cover. Naz racked a grenade in the launcher attached to his rifle. It made a loud pop as it exited the tube and seconds later exploded in the middle of a group of soldiers.

Two rocket propelled grenades came streaking through the air toward Naz's position. One landed short in a pile of rocks and the other went over their heads exploding in the dry creek bed throwing gravel in all directions, ringing off the side of the camouflaged van.

The attackers in front of Jericho retreated as the sounds of screaming wounded rippled through the air between volleys of covering gunfire.

***

On the highway from Jafar Abad, Al Madani's convoy was almost to the turn off that command reported led straight to whoever was helping his targets escape. Suddenly his radio was bursting with chatter of a major engagement happening. A sniper had taken out two vehicles moving to encircle the force of unknown size that now appeared to have the high ground. The platoon commander, a fairly new lieutenant, ordered mortar fire on the hill.

"Good idea," Al Madani thought.

But before he could check satellite imagery, the platoon commander ordered the men on his left flank to attack in line formation. Al Madani desperately worked to pull up the satellite image of the location of the battle. As the image came into focus, he immediately saw the danger. They were attacking over several hundred meters of open ground. He grabbed the radio microphone to the sounds of that attack force taking heavy fire and casualties from another group in a tree line at the bottom of the creek bed.

And someone was returning mortar fire, hitting the first mortar crew and disabling it. The Lieutenant was beginning to panic. Al Madani could sense it before he heard the cries for orders from the men dying in the open field of fire. There were none coming.

"Fox 2, this is Viper, pull back now!" Al Madani ordered. "Fox 1, move a squad forward, leave extended space and watch for IEDs if possible. We need to catch them from behind," he ordered the platoon commander in his convoy. "Fox 2, reset your mortars under cover and target that hill. They have overwatch and likely a mortar crew up there. Keep your heavy weapons team firing on that tree line. Reposition your troops to make a coordinated attack on both flanks, we'll be there in 30 seconds," Al Madani instructed the Second Platoon commander.

Three vehicles sped ahead of the main force down the gulley the ops team took ten minutes earlier. Suddenly two huge explosions erupted like a volcano engulfing the two lead vehicles. Two light armored vehicles were on fire, their sides collapsed from the force of the opposing pressure waves from the HMX explosives. Being buried into sides of the narrow gulley, the focused explosive force was amplified tenfold. As the fireball rose above the gulley, Al Madani could see the crushed wreckage of the two vehicles. Men jumped out of the third trailing vehicle and scurried up the right slope, only to have it explode beneath them. Just like that, a dozen men were gone.

"Fox 1, move on both slopes and the center. We need to pressure them now!" Al Madani ordered. Men dismounted from their vehicles and moved on foot along both slopes and past the burning wreckage of the first two vehicles. The ground on the right slope erupted.

"Fox 2, attack, now!" shouted Al Madani in the radio over the roar of battle unleashed around him.

***

The dry gulley was now a roaring inferno.

"Infantry movement on the left," shouted Hammer.

Ebrahim counted to three and turned the handle on the detonator. The left slope of the gulley erupted in a flash of orange-yellow fire. The cries of wounded and dying men immediately rang out. Suddenly a barrage of gunfire dug into the dirt and rocks all around him and Hammer.

"It's getting pretty hot down here chief. We're going to have to move soon," reported Hammer as he rose to return fire.

"Large group moving on the left flank," reported Kirkorian who took out two more soldiers and Moose let loose with another set of mortars.

One of the mortars hit in front of an armored vehicle forcing it to turn away violently, but still intact. Suddenly another set of mortar rounds landed on the hill forcing Kirkorian and Moose to duck for cover, spraying dirt and gravel all over them. They responded with another volley from the hill along with Jericho's team forcing the attackers to retreat.

"Chief, looks like they're pulling back. I suspect they'll throw everything at us next, You need to get those assets out of here and get them to the extraction point," Kirkorian said.

She looked at Moose who gave her an affirmative nod.

"Chief, Moose and I will blow a hole in the left flank and cover your movement. We'll follow when we can, but you need to move now before they get their shit together!" she added.

Jericho understood immediately the implication of Kirkorian's plan.

So did Naz. "Chief, no. We can get everyone out, we'll just shoot our way through them."

"They'll have everything trained on that van unless we put something on their heads. We both know it," Jericho replied.

"Chief, no man left behind," Naz said almost pleadingly.

"Hammer, blow the remaining charges in the gulley, get Ebrahim back to the van and come get us," Jericho ordered.

Ebrahim twisted the trigger on the last two sets of explosives bringing rock and dirt collapsing into the gulley.

Hammer tapped him on his shoulder. "Time to go, get back to the van."

Ebrahim started moving to the van. Hammer took three strides toward it when gunfire erupted from his right, twisting him to the ground from the impact of the bullets tearing into him. Ebrahim turned, dropped to a knee and returned fire, cutting down a soldier who was running toward them.

"Can you move?" he asked.

Blood was coming from Hammer's mouth as he coughed, "Yes."

Ebrahim swung Hammer's left arm over his shoulder and dragged the big man back to the van. He yanked open the side door as three more shots rang out behind him, three more kills for Kirkorian. He lifted Hammer into the van, jumped into the driver's seat and gunned it toward Jericho.

Moose and Kirkorian launched a barrage of grenades into the gulley then turned their attention toward the front.

"Move, move, move," ordered Jericho to Naz and Azar as he laid down a barrage of covering fire across the open plain.

The ground erupted with a wall of gunfire in return. Jericho was hit in the side and left arm forcing him to wrap the strap of his rifle around his injured arm to keep control as he fired. Each burst put tremendous pressure on the injured arm causing agonizing pain. Azar was hit in the shoulder and the side, spinning her to the ground. As she struggled to get to her feet, someone appeared and kneeled beside her with a roar of machine gun fire then reached over with one arm and lifted her off the ground. It was Ebrahim.

He moved her to the van as Naz and Jericho moved, each providing covering fire for the other until they were at the van.

Ebrahim shouted to Naz, "Drive, I'll treat the wounded!"

"Kirkorian, coming out!" Naz called.

Moose and Kirkorian launched a half dozen smoke rounds from the grenade launcher and mortar toward the front and down the gulley.

"Go, go, go!" she yelled on the comms.

Naz floored the accelerator of the van; and headed northwest. There was an airfield at Cheshmeh Kabod just four and half kilometers away and they had to make the highway less than a kilometer from them. Gunfire hit the side of the van as it careened over the rock and gravel. In less than 30 seconds they made the pavement and accelerated.

Kirkorian took out two more drivers as Moose dropped mortars on their lines forcing the enemy to take cover. Four vehicles dashed north from behind the warehouse buildings. Moose dropped a mortar that hit the last one but three got away in pursuit of the rest of the team. Suddenly the ground exploded all around Moose and Kirkorian. The concussion from the blasts threw them both high into the air and dropped them back to the ground like rag dolls.

Kirkorian was dazed and couldn't move. Her ears were ringing, and everything was a blur. Pain racked her entire body. She could feel bullets hitting nearby spraying dirt and gravel in her face. It was like she was watching a movie in slow motion through a fish tank. There were bright red orange explosions above her. She thought she heard a million mad hornets fly by followed by the screams of dying men. Her world was exploding, and then went black.

***

Al-Madani's fire team on the left slope of the gulley above where the mines were detonated opened fire in the direction where enemy rifle fire came from, hitting a target. The enemy returned fire, striking a soldier who fell to the ground with blood gushing from his belly. Suddenly the three others in his fire team went down with rifle shots to the head.

More explosions erupted in the center pinning the attackers in a confined space, preventing them from moving forward. They desperately fired in the direction of the enemy, but their vision was obscured by the thick black smoke and bright yellow-orange fire raging in the narrow gulley. The enemy then launched smoke grenades into it adding to the confusion.

"Command, Viper, where the hell are those choppers? We are engaged with an armed force with heavy weapons and taking casualties," Al Madani called with increasing urgency and frustration.

"Viper, Blade two-two, thirty seconds out," called the attack helicopter flight leader.

"Blade two-two, top of the hill located approximately two-seven-zero, 300 meters from our position. Will mark our location with a beacon," responded Al Madani.

"Beacon acquired, coming in hot," the flight leader reported.

"Viper, Fox 2. Taking heavy mortar fire. Van making a run, in pursuit."

"This is Viper, everyone advance, now!" Al Madani ordered as his troops started moving forward quickly.

He heard the helicopter's approach. Then the distinctive sound of rockets coming off the rails impacting the top of the hill seconds later with a mighty roar. His entire troop opened fire and moved up the hill. His anticipation rose with each stride. As he neared the crest, he saw a man and woman on the ground.

Both helicopters suddenly exploded into flaming hulks plummeting to the ground like falling meteors. They hit the ground with mighty explosions that shook the earth beneath Al Madani's feet. Rocket flashes and the sound of a million buzzing hornets lit up the night sky on the plain below him. Red fingers of death spewed out of something ripping man and machines apart as concussions from explosions coming from second platoon reached the ridge. Someone had joined the battle and was chewing up his men by the dozens.

"Command, Viper. Large attack force engaging from the north. We need immediate reinforcements!" Al Madani screamed

The buzzing suddenly got louder. Men on his left and right screamed in agony as the white-hot supersonic bullets tore into their bodies and shattered bones. Al Madani recognized he was facing a much larger attack force and his position was lost. He had to call a retreat before his entire company was wiped out.

"Fox 1 and Fox 2, re...," but his radio call was cut short.

Chapter 37

Extraction

Three modified Kawasaki C-2 transports flew at low level and performed perfect combat landings on the Cheshmeh Kabod Airport runway in total darkness. After landing they taxied to the south end of the runway and the rear ramps were lowered before the aircraft even stopped. When they did stop, four combat vehicles drove out of each aircraft.

The vehicles were built by Ruggud Corporation called Advanced Tactical Attack and Control Systems, or ATAACS for short. They were experimental advanced hybrid electrics that ran entirely on electric motors both from onboard batteries and a miniature rotary engine driving two permanent parallel electric generators. Combined with special open cell wall tires, they were completely silent on their approach.

They were covered with special tiles that produced reflections of their environment making them virtually disappear from a distance. The outer skin was a special composite made of a carbon graphene aerogel with embedded industrial diamonds covering a ceramic/steel composite armor inner skin. Not only was it ultra-lightweight, but it literally ground down anything passing through it. It also protected from armor piercing rounds by absorbing the extreme heat generated that would melt normal armor. It also meant the vehicle had no thermal footprint.

The interior was protected by a specialized lightweight armor material that contained advanced ceramic particles suspended in curtains of liquid gel. They hardened to five times harder than carbon steel when struck by the force of high-speed projectiles. The flexible backing was like a catcher's mitt, absorbing the force of the impact of anything that penetrated the outer armor and deflected that force through ripples of the material like the ripples in water.

There were two ATAACS variants: squad transport and force protection. The squad transport carried a full squad of eight: one driver and seven riflemen. The force protection configuration had a driver, a gunner, and carried four riflemen.

The vehicle had camera and sound sensors on all sides. In force protection mode, the gunner controlled a complete sensor system that gave him a 360-degree view around the vehicle. Combined with indicators that showed the direction of gunfire, he used a joystick to slew a mounted 20mm gatling gun to any sector around the vehicle.

Once in a sector, he had an integrated virtual reality helmet that aimed the gun automatically. So, wherever he looked, that's where the gun aimed. Then all he had to do was pull the trigger and unload a torrent of fire that could put a bullet in every inch of anything it was aimed at.

Each aircraft carried two of each vehicle. They raced into the night at nearly 60 miles per hour over the rough terrain in complete silence. Two vehicles headed to the terminal building to secure it and eliminate anyone from radioing for air support. The remaining ten raced toward the emerging battle going on just to their south.

Along the Iraq/Iran border, another C-2 orbited just inside Iraqi airspace with the operational commander and two drone operators. The Quick Reaction Force had launched six small stealth drones shaped like an unmanned B-2. Three drones had air to air missiles and three drones carried advanced Brimstone missiles. The Brimstone was an upgrade to the Hellfire anti-armor missile with a millimeter wave seeker head.

"Sir, two attack helicopters inbound to Little Roundtop," reported the air surveillance operator.

"Okay people let's give them some air cover," the commander instructed.

"Hotel one-one, Jackknife, over," he radioed.

"Jackknife, Hotel one-one go ahead."

"Two attack helicopters inbound to Little Round Top, sending air cover. Enemy is almost on top of them so get the lead out," Jackknife stated.

"Roger, twenty seconds out," came the reply.

"Be advised, van with friendlies on the move at high-speed heading your direction. Tagging it for you on the TCDL," Jackknife reported.

The TCDL was the Tactical Common Data Link. A secure data link system used to send data and streaming video from airborne platforms to ground stations.

"Got it Jackknife, ten seconds to contact," Hotel one-one reported.

"Sir weapons hot, three seconds," the senior drone operator said as four advanced Peregrine radar missiles rocketed from the drones. "Splash two bogeys," came the reply a few seconds later.

"Red 2 and Red 3, swing to the left and come in behind the enemy force behind those buildings. Red 4 and Red 5 hit that gulley, Red 1 will move up the hill from the north," the attack leader commanded.

Each team included a force protection vehicle and a squad carrier. The four vehicles moved silently into position behind the IRGC's second platoon, the squads dismounted, and then the mini guns opened fire. As the mini guns devastated the troops from behind, the advancing infantry took advantage of the complete confusion and cut down the disoriented soldiers at will.

"Red 1, Red 4. Contact with the van, three wounded. Switching men to get them to extraction. They'll need medical on arrival, and we will advance in twenty seconds."

"Roger. Red 5 Tighten on my left and swing close to the base of Little Round Top. We'll make our approach from the north. Hotel one-one, packages headed your way, get medical ready," Red 1 ordered.

"Roger," came the reply as the four vehicles pivoted slightly to the right to line up on the new axis of attack.

Moments later, the mini guns opened up and a few seconds after that the vehicles stopped and the rifle teams jumped out to engage the surprised enemy. Red 4 crested the top of the hill and Naz jumped out as the vehicle skidded to a stop. There was a group of soldiers in front of them, just a few feet from Kirkorian as he dropped to a knee and shot an IRGC Captain in the head then pivoted and took down two more soldiers. He sprinted to Kirkorian's side.

"Kirkorian, Shirin," he shouted then checking for a pulse. "Medic!"

Two medics rushed to where Kirkorian and Moose lay motionless. They worked feverishly on the fallen soldiers, got IVs into them to pump fluids, then picked them up and carried them to separate vehicles.

"Hotel one-one, team recovered, heading to extraction," reported Red 1.

The advance teams spun around and headed back to the airport. As the convoy hurtled past the road leading to the devastated IRGC second platoon, Red 2 and 3 joined them leaving the shattered wreckage of nearly a company of IRGC soldiers in its wake.

All vehicles returned to the aircraft, the ramps were closed, they took off, and turned west along their egress route. Onboard two of the transports were combat surgeons to treat the wounded in the air to make sure they were stabilized.

***

Several of the political appointees in the Situation Room began pacing. The action in the Gulf from Operation Copperfield, a twist on the famous illusionist, gave the extraction force the cover it needed. While the President knew there was a quick reaction force going in to make the extraction; he just didn't know its composition.

As the attack on Abu Musa ended, the screens switched to the satellite imagery of the extraction. There was a graphic of an aircraft moving across the screen.

"Sir, the QRF will land at this airport here, Cheshmeh Kabod. We're hoping the team can slip past the pursuers but if not, we've prepared a contingency for a hot extraction," briefed Anderson.

"What do you mean a 'hot extraction' David?" asked President Saldana.

"Sir, the QRF is an armed force to cover the extraction," he replied casually.

"Are you telling me we will have soldiers on the ground inside Iran? I never authorized that!" Saldana said angrily.

"Sir, you allowed for the mission to be accomplished 'by all means necessary.' We need this QRF on the ground to ensure we recover our team. They're highly skilled operatives with advanced equipment. The Iranians are tied up with the attack on Abu Musa; they will never see these guys coming. It's what they do," Anderson answered calmly.

Saldana was steaming. He glared at Anderson then turned to glare at Jackson.

"Touchdown in two minutes," CIA operations reported.

The satellite picture zoomed into the airport. The electronic airplane graphic was making a right-hand turn to land to the south-southeast. Saldana couldn't see the aircraft, but the electronic image showed their location.

"Explosions at Little Round Top, readjusting satellite image," stated the disconnected voice from the operations center.

"What's Little Round Top?" asked Saldana.

"The location of our ops team, sir. The extraction force is Big Round Top," answered Jackson.

The picture on the screen zoomed out and shifted to center on the location of the team. Flashes of gunfire were clearly visible as intermittent bright blooms showed up on the screen eliciting gasps from the people in the situation room.

"What the hell's happening?" asked Saldana anxiously.

"The team is under attack from a platoon sized force in front of it, here. And another platoon size force behind it here," answered the Chairman of the Joint Chiefs who pointed out the positions of the opposing fighters.

Suddenly a brilliant flash caused the screen to nearly white out completely with its intensity in the creek bed behind the team's location.

"Oh my god!" Saldana said startled. "What the hell was that?"

"Sir, seems the team set a trap for anyone coming from that direction," answered the Admiral.

There were more gasps as the secondary explosions came from the wreckage and the mines exploding on the hillside. The image became a confusing, jumbled mess of gun flashes and explosions. First on the right toward the gulley then the left.

"Heavy mortar fire on the left; there's movement from the creek bed. Looks like a van is making a run for the extraction point. Someone is providing covering fire from the hill," narrated the Admiral.

The rate of fire all around the team increased when the distinct shape of two attack helicopters came into view.

"Oh no!" exclaimed Jackson.

The red streaks of missiles coming off the rails of the helicopters followed by the tremendous explosions on a spot indicating the friendlies on the hill shocked people into silence. A few put their hands to their open mouths as the President's Communications Director turned away crying. Seconds later, there were two brilliant flashes from the helicopters as they were hit with air-to-air missiles. Then two more as their flaming carcasses smashed into the Iranian countryside. Streams of red orange appeared to the north of the friendly force like two dragons spewing fire, igniting flaming destruction on everything they touched. Two more streams of death appeared around the hillside reaching into the creek bed and along the ridgelines.

Minutes seemed like hours as the small group of politicians and political appointees sat, aghast at what they witnessed. As the firing stopped, the carnage remained. But the friendly forces were headed back, and the next challenge was getting out of Iran. Jackson knew the question before the President could ask it.

"Sir, their radars are looking out, not inside right now. We have fighters in the area should they need cover," he said quietly.

The reference to the battle of Gettysburg now seemed aptly appropriate to Jackson. Little Round Top was where the Union had repulsed wave after wave of Confederate attacks by larger forces. And defeated them with stubbornness, guile, and tremendous heroism.

"Jackknife reports border in one minute," CIA operations reported. "Two dead, six wounded, three seriously."

Saldana looked down and rubbed his eyes.

"All clear. Jackknife is requesting to go direct to Ramstein for the wounded. Onboard docs have them stabilized but they need surgery and they're saying Landstuhl is best for this type," the Senior Operations Commander requested.

"Chief, do they need air refueling?" asked Jackson.

"Jackknife says they've coordinated that internally sir," he replied.

"Do it. I'll coordinate with Ramstein and have them prepared to receive them," answered Jackson as the link was closed.

"They've coordinated internally? I thought you said they weren't military?" asked Saldana.

"They aren't sir," replied Anderson.

"Then who the hell are these guys?" Saldana demanded.

"Sir, let's just say they have extensive resources for missions like this and leave it at that," Anderson answered.

Chapter 38

Debrief

The flight to Ramstein Germany took about four hours. They landed as the first glint of dawn approached and taxied to the northwest corner of the ramp. Ambulances met them as men carried the wounded to the waiting vehicles. Once loaded, they sped off, headed to Landstuhl Regional Medical Center, the largest Army medical center outside the U.S. specially equipped to handle severe combat injuries.

Naz watched helplessly as his friends were loaded into the waiting ambulances, but Moose was dead. Naz guarded Ebrahim and Azar, and since Ebrahim wouldn't leave her side, Naz rode with them. She'd lost a lot of blood and the medics worked tirelessly to keep her blood pressure up during the flight.

The ride took just a few minutes but to Naz, time stood still. He'd been in firefights, been wounded, and had team members wounded or killed, but this felt different. He'd nearly lost his whole team and hoped these two were worth it.

The ambulances pulled up to the Emergency entrance and the wounded were quickly moved to the ER. The most severely wounded were met by separate teams of doctors and nurses who rushed them straight to imaging then the OR. Lastly the dead were brought in and taken to the morgue for processing.

Naz and Ebrahim ran beside Azar until they got to a set of large double doors when the doctor turned and put his hand on Ebrahim's chest.

"This is as far as you go. There's a waiting room to your right, we'll come get you when we have more information," the doctor said.

"Doc, be advised she's pregnant," Naz offered.

"They radioed ahead with that so we'll do the best we can for both of them," the doctor answered then turned and ran to catch up as the automatic doors closed behind him.

"Where are they taking her?" Ebrahim asked Naz in Farsi as they stood watching Azar disappear.

"She's in good hands, trust me. There's no better place for her than right here," Naz replied. "Let's go; the doc said there's a waiting room this way."

"Do they know she's pregnant?" Ebrahim asked, panicked.

"Yes, they'll be fine. They both will. Let's go," Naz answered as confidently as he could though his thoughts were on his unconscious partner.

Naz directed Ebrahim to a chair in the waiting room and the two sat down. After a few minutes three men walked up to them. They were dressed in black fatigues, black boots and no other markings. Naz instinctively profiled the group and determined the one in the middle was in charge.

He was slightly taller than the other two with short salt and pepper hair. Even though he looked to be in his sixties, the man was in great shape. The neatly pressed shirt made a perfect V from his broad shoulders to his belt. His face had the distinct lines of someone who dealt with stress his entire life. His eyes were dark brown with an intensity that only comes from someone who commanded any room he walked into.

"Morning Chief Petty Officer Nasseri, my name is Grigor Sabah, call sign is Jackknife. I'm the commander of the extraction crew. Sorry for the loss of one of your team; you all did a spectacular job. Is this the package?" he asked.

"Yes sir, at least one of them. They just took the woman back for imaging and surgery," Naz replied.

The man looked directly at Ebrahim and spoke in Farsi.

"Sergeant Hamadani, my name is Grigor; we need to talk. We will speak with Miss Barghani later, but this cannot wait. We can do this here or somewhere more private if you'd like."

Ebrahim shook his head no.

"I will tell you everything you want to know. Please call me Ebrahim. I would like to stay here until I know Azar is out of danger, please," he replied.

"I understand Ebrahim," Grigor answered.

The commander nodded to the man on the right who called for the camera crew to come to the lounge then posted a security team to prevent others from entering. As the team set up, Grigor turned to Naz.

"Chief, your team leader got lucky. The bullet hit the bone, so his arm needs some rebuilding but he's otherwise in good shape. The other team member, Hammer is it? He is in surgery as well but seems he owes his life to the Sergeant here. Without his quick action with the field kit, I'm told he might not have made it off the battlefield.

"My niece has gone to surgery with a TBI and some broken bones. Her position was hit with an AGM and that's what killed your teammate. He actually saved Shirin's life. He was positioned between her and the strike, so her injuries are more concussive than shrapnel related. Not great news but better than the alternative. So, settle in for the long haul as it's going to be touch and go for a while," Grigor said more calmly than Naz would have.

"Wait, niece? Are you Shirin's uncle?" Naz asked, a bit shocked.

That's when he saw the family resemblance with the head of the training center in San Antonio.

"Yes Chief. My brother and I run SA2, and I remember you training there with your Seal team. I'd love to catch up, but we've got business to take care of right now," Grigor replied in a calm and professional manner, then looked to the camera team. "Are you ready Charlie?"

The man nodded and turned on the digital recorder. The setup was connected to an encrypted cell phone and was live streamed back to CIA headquarters. Naz was amazed at how Grigor could compartmentalize the needs of his job and his concern for Shirin. Something Naz was struggling with much more than he expected.

"This is Grigor Sabah conducting a post extraction debrief with Ebrahim Hamadani, Iranian national, at Landstuhl Medical Center Germany." Grigor continued his questioning in Farsi.

Grigor questioned Ebrahim about the research facility and everything from the past 48 hours. He got very interested when Ebrahim talked about the special visitor to the facility.

"Did you know who the visitor was?" asked Grigor.

"No sir, just that he was some VIP," Ebrahim answered.

"What did this VIP look like?" asked Grigor.

"Asian, maybe Chinese or Korean? I'm not sure," Ebrahim replied.

Grigor looked at the camera then back at Ebrahim and had him continue with his activities. He talked about stopping at the Electrician's house and Grigor got very interested again.

"Tell me more about this Massoud. Who is he and what do you know about him?" he asked.

Ebrahim described Massoud, his modules, the fake log entries, and what he and Azar found at the apartment. Then discussed all the issues that pointed at Massoud as the operative who executed the bombing.

Just then a surgeon came into the waiting area. "Sir, I've got updates for you."

"Charlie, pause please. Go ahead doc," replied Grigor.

"The Iranian woman is in critical but stable condition. The shoulder wound was a through and through, but the abdominal wound was more severe. The bullet caused a tear in the liver, but we got it out and repaired the damage. She received a transfusion and I expect she'll make a full recovery," the surgeon stated.

"What about the baby?" Ebrahim asked Grigor anxiously in Farsi.

"Sorry doc, what's the status of the baby?" asked Grigor.

"It has a strong fetal heartbeat. There was some distress due to the mother's injuries, but it's been checked by the OB, and everything appears normal. We'll monitor mom and baby closely for the next 48 hours," the surgeon answered as Grigor translated.

"And the others?" asked Naz.

"Mr. Hammersmith is stable. The cardio-thoracic surgeon repaired the chest wound and stabilized the shoulder, but he has a couple more surgeries to go through to repair the damage to the shoulder and right leg," the surgeon replied.

"And Kirkorian?" asked Naz.

"Sorry, I don't have much information. They are repairing the damage but the most critical is the traumatic brain injury. They are working to relieve pressure on the brain so she will be in the OR for several more hours I'm afraid," answered the doctor.

"And my other wounded man?" asked Grigor.

"I'm sorry sir, he died on the table. A fragment lodged in his aorta causing an aortic dissection; there was nothing we could do. To be honest, the team was surprised he made it off the battlefield," the surgeon stated.

"Thank you, doctor."

With that, the surgeon gave a little nod and left. Grigor continued the debrief through the whole escape and extraction. When he finished, he made a motion to cutoff the video and turned to Ebrahim.

"So, this is what happens next. You will have a short visit with Azar, but you must be escorted at all times. I know you understand that we need to verify everything you've told us, and you both will be held separately for a brief time until that's done. You will be transferred to a secure location for a more thorough debrief. Do you understand?" Grigor asked.

"Yes sir. Please, Azar had nothing to do with this, she was just helping me," Ebrahim answered, almost pleading.

"I know, we'll talk more later. You can have a few minutes with Azar then she must be debriefed. Are you ready?" Grigor asked.

"Yes sir."

And with that Grigor nodded to one of the men guarding the waiting area.

"Chief, we'll debrief with you in a bit. Stay with the Sergeant until then," Grigor ordered.

"Yes sir," Naz replied as the three stood up.

Grigor reached out and shook Ebrahim's hand, then Naz's. Then walked out with the video team trailing. Naz took Ebrahim by the arm and escorted him to the recovery room. As they entered, Azar was hooked to several machines monitoring her vitals and delivering medications through the IV placed in her wrist. A man stood next to her speaking in a low voice in a language Naz recognized immediately. When the three walked up to the bed, the man stopped talking.

"Who are you?" asked Naz.

"The name is Eitan. I'm here to assist in the debrief of this woman," he responded.

"Mossad?" asked Ebrahim.

"I'm here to represent the Israeli government, Sergeant Hamadani," answered Eitan in Farsi. "Your government falsely implicated my country, so we need to make sure we fully understand what was going on and what happened."

"I know Azar is Mossad, if that is her real name, but I don't care. She's carrying my child, so I'll do whatever is necessary to protect them both," Ebrahim replied.

"I'll let you have a little time with her," Eitan said as he stepped back from the bed and left the room.

Ebrahim pulled a chair to the side of Azar's bed and carefully cupped her hand in his. She turned her head and smiled.

"The doctors say that you and the baby are doing well," he said quietly. "I guess now you'll have another scar I can tease you with."

Her eyes welled up with tears. "Ebrahim, I'm so sorry."

"No, no tears. You're alive, you're safe, the baby is safe, that's all that matters now," he said in a calm, soothing voice.

"But I lied to you, betrayed your trust, and you still saved me," she replied with her tears streaming down her face.

Ebrahim leaned in and softly wiped the tears from her face.

"It wouldn't matter whether or not you were carrying my child. I love you with all my heart. I would do anything for you, to protect you, to make you happy. You are my life, and I can't imagine living it without you. And if that means sacrificing myself so that you survive, I'd do it again without hesitation."

Azar pulled his head to hers and kissed him deeply through her tears.

"I love you too. No more secrets between us, so I need to tell you the truth about me," she began.

"My birth name is Azaria Mizrahi, and I was born in Qiryat Shemona. It was the largest city near our village on the border of Lebanon. When I was eight years old, we were attacked by Hezbollah fighters led by that Iranian Colonel. They killed dozens of people with a barrage of rockets and then came in and killed any wounded they found.

"One of their rockets hit my family home killing my parents, but my brother and I were playing outside. The scar came from a piece of shrapnel from that attack. My brother was eleven and wounded, but he saw the gunmen coming and laid on top of me hoping they would think us both dead. He shushed me and told me not to cry no matter how much it hurt.

"The Colonel walked up and shot him in the head while the others laughed. I could see his face from under my brother's arm as I gritted my teeth and tried not to make any sound. It was my fault my brother died. I made a noise that the Colonel heard, and he assumed it came from my brother.

"Moments later the IDF showed up and those pigs ran back to their holes. A soldier found me, and rushed me to the hospital, but I nearly died. I wished I had for a long time but after I was healed, they offered me the chance to get revenge and I took it. Yes, I was Mossad. But I'm done with that. You and our child are what's most important to me now," Azar finished putting her hand on his face.

"Well, hello Azaria. My name is Ebrahim," he said as he leaned over to kiss her. "No more secrets."

Grigor appeared at the door.

"Time to go, gentlemen. Azar, they'll be moving you to a private room now; we'll have our discussion there with your country's representative in attendance. Sergeant Hamadani, you'll be taken to a facility on base for a more detailed debrief tomorrow.

Unfortunately, we must detain you for now, but I assure you, you will be comfortable. I'm sure you understand," Grigor stated in Farsi calmly but in a commanding way.

"Chief Petty Officer, I'm told my niece may be coming out of surgery in about an hour. I suspect you'll want to be here when she does. So, I will debrief with you and your team chief in his hospital room this afternoon," he finished in English and motioned for two of his men to escort Ebrahim.

Ebrahim kissed Azar again.

"I'll see you as soon as I can. Rest, heal, and take good care of our baby."

He smiled at her, squeezed her hand and brushed some hair from her face. Then turned and nodded at the two men and left the recovery room.

Naz walked over to Azar's bed.

"I think Mossad is going to be challenged to replace you. And I'd fight by your side again, any time. Don't worry about Ebrahim, he'll be fine, and if I haven't said this before, congratulations on your pregnancy."

"Thank you," Azar replied taking a tissue to wipe the tears from her face. "Just make sure they know, he was set up. I saw his boss' apartment and his bitch of a wife; something was just off with those two. And just so you know, I could have executed my exfil plan at any time, but I believe him. I couldn't leave him there to be executed by those animals."

"Well, I'm not sure I have much influence, but I think everything will work itself out," Naz replied.

"How is the woman operative? I see you care for her," Azar asked.

"It's touch and go from what I'm told. I've only known Shirin a short time, but she's one of the best," Naz replied.

Azar looked at him and smiled. "You know there's a critical skill that's kept me alive for so long in deep cover, and that's the ability to read people. You have feelings for her. It's written all over your face in the way to talk about her. It's okay you know. Look at me, I fell in love with my mark and am going to have his child. But I wouldn't have it any other way. He's a good man who worked for bad people."

Naz looked down, a little embarrassed. She was right of course. He had feelings for Shirin from the first time he saw her.

"Well perhaps you're right but nothing will come of it; I doubt she feels the same. I hope you recover quickly. And from a man's perspective, Ebrahim would die for you no matter what," Naz replied.

"I will say a prayer for Shirin," Azar said grabbing Naz's hand

"Thank you. Take care Azar," he answered.

A nurse and an orderly entered and prepared Azar's hospital bed for transfer to her room.

Chapter 39

The Reckoning

In Ilam, Mokhtari laid in his hospital bed thankful for the IV morphine flowing into his arm. Clearly the woman who put him here was Mossad which made sense; the leadership thought the Zionists were involved. He didn't remember her of course. He'd led many raids on Jewish settlements during his time in Lebanon. But turning her hatred into a deep cover agent was genius. There is nothing more motivating than revenge.

A person will endure whatever pain is required to carry out that revenge. Though some will be unable to harness and control their rage, this woman did up until the end. Who knows how long she could have been embedded if not for the bombing? That one stroke crippled his nation's nuclear ambitions. The loss of so much knowledge and equipment would take time to rebuild, but at least they saved some of the information.

A woman wearing a long white lab coat, green scrubs, and a bright floral head scarf loosely wrapped around her head led two men similarly dressed into his room. She was older with streaks of black running through gray hair pulled back into a tight bun that bulged a little under the scarf. Shorter than the two men, she was about five-foot-three with an athletic build that was visible even under the baggy scrubs.

Despite her age, the cream-colored skin on her face was smooth as silk and her hazel eyes burned with a fire Mokhtari immediately recognized.

"Colonel Mohktari, I'm Doctor Gazsian. I'm in charge of your surgical care. These are the surgeons who helped put you back together," the woman began as she pointed to the men standing next to her.

Mokhtari had never seen a woman command a room like this inside his male dominated country. The two male surgeons were both medium height, one a bit heavier set than the other but they both seemed...afraid of her. It surprised him that he found this demeanor oddly attractive. Even more surprising, he recognized the name.

"This is Doctor Pahlavi;" she said pointing to the man on her right. "He's the orthopedic surgeon who repaired your broken arm and reset your dislocated shoulder. Both of those injuries should heal quite well, though there will be some discomfort for a while. Your shoulder has several nerves that run near the socket. Your radial and ulnar nerves were impinged by the dislocation for a bit so you might have some tingling or a burning sensation in that arm. You will still have full function, though it's unknown if there will be any permanent nerve damage; only time will tell.

"This is Doctor Adinejah;" pointing to her left. "He's a vascular surgeon and he repaired your femoral artery and a couple veins in your arm that got cut by the broken bone. Fortunately, the break was relatively clean, so it missed the radial artery; you got lucky. The two of us also corrected the knife wound from your belly to your thigh.

"This was the most dangerous wound. If not for the quick action of someone at the police station who put that tourniquet on you, you'd have bled out before you got to us. We repaired several meters of intestinal tract, your colon, and your liver. Unfortunately, you'll be having a liquid diet for a bit. Needless to say, there was a lot of damage, but we were meticulous and repaired it all. Do you have any questions, Colonel?" Gazsian asked as more a directive than a question.

"Doctor Gazsian, you say. Are you that police commander's wife? Am I in Kermanshah?" he asked.

"Yes Colonel, Commander Gazsian is my husband, and no you are in Ilam. He had me flown in to manage your surgery under orders from your commander. He's in the hospital leading security; seems you have some important visitors waiting to speak with you. I can have him paged if you'd like," she answered nonchalantly.

"Yes," he replied.

"If you need anything, just let your duty nurse know. I'll check back tomorrow morning. The physical therapist will be in later to talk about your rehabilitation plan. You will follow that plan in detail. If you ruin my good work, I'll have you thrown into Evin Prison for your recovery," Gazsian said with a perfectly straight face.

Mokhtari sat for a moment looking at her. She stared back with an expressionless appearance. Evin was the most brutal prison in the world and definitely not a place to get healthy after surgery. Mohktari was normally very good at reading people, but he couldn't tell if this woman was joking or serious. She certainly had the contacts to do it.

She broke into a smile.

"Don't worry Colonel. That's not a very good place to recover from your wounds. But I do caution you, do not try to go faster than the plan. You might just end up worse off."

She turned without another word and walked out of the room. The other surgeons followed like ducklings. Mokhtari had a unique sensation. Normally people were deathly afraid of him. Even generals would stand in fear of him, but this woman didn't. She acted as an equal. No, not an equal, a superior.

He pondered this for several minutes. It wasn't simply that she was connected; women don't have the same stature in his country that men do. And it was more than the confidence of a surgeon, though she exuded that. No, it was something else.

The woman had to have nerves of steel if she was operating on the leadership of the country. One slip and she would be blamed and executed. And maybe that was it. She knew she lived quite literally on a knife's edge but didn't seem to care. Not even the country's generals dealt with that kind of pressure. Where every decision and every move of every day truly meant life or death. And she had done it since the revolution. He could only admire her.

There was a knock at the door and Commander Gazsian entered the room.

"Nice to see you awake Colonel. We thought we'd lost you there for a bit," Gazsian said.

"Thank you, Commander," Mokhtari answered. "So, what happened back there? The last thing I remember was that woman coming into the interrogation room, smashing my arms then slicing me open. Apparently, she was Mossad. I thought she was going to kill me but clearly wanted me to suffer. Then someone came in and a fight broke out. I'm a bit cloudy on what happened after that. But I thought I heard someone speaking Hebrew then English."

"Yes, there was an operations team that attacked the station and rescued the suspects," Gazsian replied. "They didn't seem to want to cause casualties because they incapacitated the officers with sedatives. They apparently even saved your life by putting a tourniquet on your leg. Unfortunately, your man was killed, we believe by the woman.

"Your men chased them and engaged in a battle near Balyen. But an armed force crossed the Iraq border and attacked, all the suspects escaped, and our forces took very heavy casualties. The surgical teams here worked through the night on the wounded," Gazsian answered.

"Was it the Americans?" Mokhtari asked.

"Most likely but your people will have to tell you that. I'd say that's a good bet from the wounds my wife treated," Gazsian replied.

"Your wife is impressive. I hope her work is as impressive as her demeanor," Mokhtari said.

"It's better, trust me," Gazsian answered with a chuckle.

"I'll bet it's hard for her to be in the women's section of the mosque. She must give your Mullah a run for his money," Mokhtari said with a pained laugh.

"No, in fact she sits with me...in our church. You see we are Orthodox Christian," Gazsian replied bluntly.

Mokhtari sat in stunned for a moment.

"And the Ayatollah allows her to conduct surgeries on him?"

It was Gazsian's turn to laugh.

"I told you; she is the best. We have a special relationship with the leadership. She was a surgical resident in Tehran when the revolution started, and I was a junior officer in the police. She worked over 36 hours straight performing surgery after surgery on the civilian wounded from the battles with the Shah's guard, including some who would rise to leadership roles.

"As for me," Gazsian continued. "They executed the senior members of most of the police forces which made me the sector's senior officer which included our Christian enclave. They figured they needed me and my officers to keep the Christian population in check while they consolidated power and not fight on multiple fronts. I agreed. My wife and I are Iranian and neither of us will abandon our people regardless of their religion.

"So, here we are forty years later. Still taking care of all kinds of people. We know that if either of us makes a mistake our lives are in danger. But through our faith we deal with it, and it has reaped benefits for our community. The government leaves us alone without interference," Gazsian answered calmly.

And there it was. Mokhtari was right but not in any way he expected. Not only a woman but a Christian woman that had the undeniable trust of the highest leadership of the country. She was even more impressive than he imagined.

And so was her husband. A police commander responsible for the safety and security of those same leaders at their most vulnerable moments. For these two to rise to such prominence and importance from one of the most repressed segments of Iranian society was more than just remarkable, it was miraculous.

"Well Commander, it seems Allah has a sense of humor. You and your wife surprise me at every turn. I was told there were people who wanted to see me; can you tell me who it is?" asked Mohktari.

"General Soleiman and General Rasfashani. I've already spoken with them about the incident at the station, so I expect they'll want your side and whatever you got from Hamadani and Barghani. And one last thing Colonel. I'm told your man, Captain Al Madani, was killed in the engagement. I'm sorry, he seemed like a highly competent officer. I'll get the generals for you now," Gazsian said.

"Thank you, Commander. I hope we can talk more," Mokhtari replied.

Several hours later Mokhtari woke as the late afternoon sun streamed through his window. He had to blink his eyes to adjust to the bright light. For a man of his age who was more fit than some Olympic athletes, he was totally drained after just a couple hours of debrief.

In addition to the generals, a team from the operations center flew in to brief him on the investigation and the engagement during the escape. The losses from the American rescue mission were worse than expected. Nearly a whole company of soldiers was shattered. Most everyone was convinced that with the entrance of the Americans, it proved Israel and Saudi Arabia were behind the attack on the facility.

But things Hamadani said still gnawed at Mohktari. The evidence *was* too good, and the time frame *did not* line up. But the woman was definitely Mossad, so things were a bit confusing. If the attack was a Zionist mission, then why set up the very person linked to the Mossad asset? And if it was someone else, did they know the woman was Mossad? Too many loose ends for Mokhtari to just accept the event as solved.

The pain medications made his mind a little foggy which made him slow to recognize things around him. But he heard a noise to his left and as he turned his head, a smile came over his face.

"Hello little princess," Mokhtari said quietly.

"Hi Poppa," the little five-year-old girl answered.

She was standing on a chair with her elbows on the bed and her chin resting in her hands. Her curly black hair was pulled back in a ponytail and she had a big smile on her cherubic round face with a small nose.

"Daddy told me to watch you while he went for some tea. You sleep funny," she said with a little giggle.

"I sleep funny? How so little one?" he asked.

"When you moved your face scrunched up like this," she said as she squinted her eyes, pursed her lips, crinkled her nose, and let out a little groan.

It made Mokhtari laugh which caused pain to shoot through his body from the extensive stiches holding him together. The pain caused his face to crinkle in a grimace and his granddaughter to giggle.

"Just like that, Poppa!" she said gleefully.

"Well little one, Poppa was hurt very badly, and the doctors had to sew me back together like your mom sews your clothes. Moving makes it hurt, but they fixed it. I'll show you when it heals, but it looks pretty scary right now. But I promise, I'll show you," he replied reaching up to tweak her little button of a nose.

A man walked into the room carrying a foam cup. Tall and slender like Mokhtari with a closely cropped beard and short black hair.

"Leyla, stop pestering your grandfather. He needs his rest," the man said.

"Naveed, she's not pestering me. Leyla's been cheering me up. She said you asked her to watch over me and I can report she's done an excellent job!" Mokhtari said with a smile.

"How are you feeling? The surgeon said the wound was extensive. Who did this to you?" Naveed asked.

"I'm feeling better, son. Unfortunately, who did this I can't tell you," Mokhtari replied.

"I assume it has to do with the terror attack on the nuclear power plant? Those Zionist bastards. And to think they were helped by those Saudi dogs," Naveed said with disdain.

"Well, that's what I'm trying to find out, son. How is your mother?" Mokhtari asked.

"Worried as you'd expect. We got here while you were asleep, and she went to speak with the surgeon and get something to eat. So, they let a woman operate on you? That was a big surprise," Naveed said as more of a question than a comment.

Mokhtari chuckled again and winced. "And a Christian as well!"

"What the hell kind of hospital is this? And how could the leadership allow this?" Naveed asked indignantly.

"On the contrary, the Commander of the IRGC ordered it. She's treated multiple government officials and they have a whole damn wing set up in her hospital in Kermanshah for them. I guess I should be honored the leadership thought so highly of me," Mokhtari replied.

"It seems like an abomination to me. You would think we had enough surgeons in this country we didn't have to rely on a Christian woman. I think I'd rather die than have her operate on me," Naveed said disdainfully.

Mohktari's face changed, and his smile disappeared. It became that dark, neutral look with fiery eyes that immediately indicated a threat.

"I'll hear nothing from you about death," Mokhtari quietly hissed at his son. "You've not seen combat, seen men mortally wounded, crying for their mothers or a miracle from Allah to help them, or watched men die. So, when the pain sears you to your soul, and you are begging for help, from anyone, then you can talk to me about who you will let treat you. Until that time, you will keep your mouth shut about it."

Naveed looked down at his feet. Mokhtari was always strict, and Naveed knew that many feared him. He'd heard this tone before, and strong, brave men wilted in front of his father when Mokhtari spoke to them that way. Mokhtari rarely used it on his sons, but on the few occasions he had, his sons knew their father could, and likely would, kill them if they disobeyed.

"Yes, father. I'm sorry I spoke out of ignorance," Naveed demurred.

Just then Mokhtari's wife walked into the room. She was short and plump with bright floral dress and white hijab covering her head.

"Praise Allah, you're awake. Jahan, we thought we would lose you," she said as she quickly shuffled over to his side and grasped hold of his hand.

Mokhtari smiled. "I'm still here Afsaneh. You know me, I'm too stubborn to die just yet," he said softly.

"I spoke to your surgeon. I must say I was surprised it was a woman, and she was very impressive. She reminded me of you when she spoke. I don't think I've seen anyone like her. Did the government approve of her doing your surgery?" she asked.

"They flew her in for it," Mokhtari replied as he glanced at Naveed who looked down at his feet.

"Well, it looks like it will be a long recovery. She told me they'll let you go back to Dezful in a day or two. I'll have Naveed call your aide to prepare the house for you. No stairs for a while so we'll convert the sitting room to a bedroom and set up your office in the study. They're already running communication lines to the house. General Kamaliazad has been very helpful with that," Mokhtari's wife stated like an operational report.

"Naveed, take Leyla to get something to eat then back to the hotel. Your wife is there alone with the baby. I'll be there in a few hours," she ordered.

"Yes Mother," Naveed answered.

While Mokhtari was strict with his children, his wife ran the household with an iron fist and gave the impression she could be just as ruthless as her husband. While she rarely gave orders to outsiders, when she did it was understood that it was backed up by the Colonel without question. If you crossed her, you crossed him. And that was very dangerous indeed.

"Father, your cell phone has been ringing every fifteen minutes for the past hour. I've put it on the table beside you," Naveed said. "Come along Leyla, say goodbye to your grandfather and let's go."

Naveed lifted her up to be face to face with Mokhtari.

"I'll see you later Poppa. I love you!" she said as she leaned in, put her little hands on both sides of his face, and kissed his cheek.

"I love you too little princess," he replied with a smile.

For a man notorious for the brutality he inflicted on others, this little girl turned Mokhtari's heart to jelly and filled him with such joy. Her bubbly excitement for life was infectious. She gleefully found joy and happiness in every little thing around her. So much so that people could almost get lost in the innocent ignorance of it.

As Leyla left with her father, she turned and gave one last wave. Once she was gone, the adult reality of the situation slowly returned. Mokhtari nearly died, should have died, and yet here he was. Given the devastation during the American rescue mission, why did their operatives save his life instead of letting him bleed out? That's what he would have done; there was no need for survivors.

It wasn't weakness or cowardice as some of his leaders thought. No, they walked in the front door and engaged the officers directly. They deliberately drugged the police to avoid casualties. But he was IRGC, a soldier; he never expected mercy from an enemy. Not just mercy, but they saved his life.

Obviously killing was a choice for them not an expectation. They had the opportunity and skills to kill quite effectively as the engagement near Balyen proved. And the thought crossed his mind that had the team not been cornered, there wouldn't have been such a loss of life. Clearly, he had to rethink everything he thought he knew about the Americans.

Mokhtari's wife was talking about their daughter-in-law and the new baby. How she was struggling a little with this one, more than with Leyla, when his cell phone rang. He reached over and answered it as his wife immediately stopped talking mid-sentence.

"Mokhtari."

"Good afternoon, Colonel," a woman said in English. "I do hope the prognosis for your recovery is good. My name is Janelle Hayes with the CIA."

"How did you get this number?" Mokhtari asked in English as his wife looked at him puzzled.

"Oh, please Colonel, the how is irrelevant. The fact is we do have it and we have a mutual problem," Hayes answered.

"Oh really? What would that be?" he asked suspiciously.

"Well, who really sabotaged your nuclear test for one. You know, the one at the nuclear research facility your leadership said didn't exist. But that is for others to deal with. Ours is the person and organization responsible for the death of hundreds of your people," she replied.

"We know who the individuals are," Mokhtari suggested in his calm voice.

"Colonel, we both know that's not true. We're professionals so let's not try to fool each other, shall we? You already know the timeline doesn't match with your suspects. You also know whatever evidence you have was likely planted. But you weren't the only ones played here; many others were too and have responded exactly the way the saboteur expected them to, including you," she said.

"You seem to have all the answers, so what do you want from me?" he asked dismissively.

"We are simply trying to help you find the person, or persons responsible for this terror attack of course," Hayes answered.

"And why would you help us; we are enemies after all?" Mokhtari asked as he desperately tried to understand what this American wanted in return.

"Because we have a shared interest for a change. Yes, there will be something we will ask for in return but not until we have an agreement for our help in capturing your bomber," she said seemingly reading his mind.

"I know you think it was this Hamadani fellow, but it wasn't. As a matter of fact, the individual you are searching for is still in your country and still an active agent against you. And rest assured, whatever you think you know to be true, isn't. It's your choice, Colonel. So, think on this and go through the evidence again. When you are ready to close this case, call this number," Hayes finished.

"Why should I trust you? You just sent an armed force into my country to rescue two traitors and killed many of my men. That is a blatant act of war against Iran," he responded bluntly.

"Oh, you mean our response to your country attacking our allies in the Gulf and killing several innocent people who have not shown any aggression against you? Wouldn't that be an act of war? I'd say we had a proportional response, Colonel.

"My question to you is, how many more of your countrymen are you willing to sacrifice before you listen to reason? Explain that to the families of the men you will send to die for nothing. Or more importantly, look at your sons and tell that beautiful granddaughter of yours why her daddy had to die for the false pride of your government's leaders," Hayes said. "Call this number, any time of the day."

With that the line went dead. Mokhtari's wife stood there in stunned silence. He put the phone down and looked up at her.

"The Americans?" she asked.

He just nodded; his mind was racing. He wanted to discount what the American said but couldn't. On one hand they were twisting the knife, but on the other, they offered a lifeline. If they were behind the attack, then his country had all kinds of issues, and all of them bad. The advantage to the Americans was clear: a crippling of the country's nuclear ambition for several years. For Iran's enemies, the halting of their global expansion and influence in the region was reason enough, but the evidence of collusion between Saudi Arabia and Israel was so...obvious.

So, if it was an attempt at misdirection, it was the worst in history. Too many threads in this event were too convenient. Even if one could accept that one intelligence agency was simply sloppy, all of them together being equally sloppy was too much of a coincidence. All those nagging questions came flooding back.

"Jahan, why would the Americans be calling you?" his wife asked, yanking him back to the present.

Mokhtari looked down at his phone, turned it off and handed it to her.

"I need to talk to General Kamaliazad, but not on this. I don't know how the Americans got this number or if they managed to tap into our communications, but this needs to be put in a metal box. Call him and ask him to come to the hospital. And call Major Rashani, tell him I need all the evidence here by the morning; we need to go over everything. The Americans know something we don't. I need to know what that is."

Chapter 40

A Rock and a Hard Place

Mokhtari sat sweating after an agonizing physical therapy session as the light through the window highlighted the vibrant colors of the hand-woven Persian carpet in his makeshift hospital room. It took two soldiers to help him in and out of his bed to minimize the strain on his abdominal muscles and he felt like a helpless baby learning how to walk. He never really understood how much he relied on his core, but activating those muscles now meant white-hot pain.

Two days had passed since his release as his team went over every shred of evidence again. The inconsistencies that troubled him throughout the investigation hung in the air like a dense fog. It prevented him from finding the answers he so desperately wanted.

The laptop found in the dumpster was wiped clean of prints but had modest security allowing tech to easily break into it. The timeline had too many gaps that didn't align. The maintenance logs indicated Hamadani's signature at critical times, but handwriting matches were inconclusive. Electronic modules found in parts of the facility attributed to Hamadani had brass screws as he claimed, but the ones suspected in the trigger had steel.

They searched Massoud's apartment and found nothing that exactly matched any of the components, though some were similar. He gave investigators the codes to unlock his cell phone, which was clean; no calls to any of the numbers, and nothing suspicious. Though he had the clearance, access, time, and ability to do all of this, they had absolutely no evidence implicating him.

The links between Saudi Arabia and Israel were obvious. The bomb setup was highly sophisticated, but the cell phone number was easily traced to the Saudis. The gun fragment was definitively identified as Zionist. The laptop with the old Zionist encryption and conspicuous messages left on it. Saudi intelligence was not as good as Mossad but the sloppiness of both stretched his imagination. Mokhtari's wife brought him a bottle of water.

"Your Executive Officer is here to speak with you Jahan."

"Send him in," he grumbled.

She nodded and left the room. Thirty seconds later the Major came in.

"Good afternoon, sir. Are you feeling any better?" the Major asked.

"I feel like a gutted animal, so no, I feel like shit. What do you have?" Mokhtari snarled as he took a drink of water.

The Major cleared his throat.

"We found the woman from the mining company. She secretly married a miner without her father's approval. She claims her father is politically connected, so when she heard the sirens, she thought he was sending the police for them. They've been hiding at a friend's house ever since. They've been cleared.

"We've gone through everything forward and backward. We've run every possible explanation for the evidence but found nothing to link anyone else to the bombing. Whatever the Americans have, we can't find it. What are your orders sir?" he asked pensively.

"Bring me that encrypted phone over there," Mokhtari ordered pointing to his desk.

The Major retrieved the phone and Mokhtari punched the speed dial for the commander of the IRGC.

"General Soleiman."

"General, Colonel Mokhtari. Sir, we've gone through the evidence but there are too many inconsistencies that cause more questions. These inconsistencies require a level of coincidence or incompetence that doesn't track with what we know of our enemy's capabilities. Sir, I strongly feel we must contact the Americans."

"Colonel, why would we trust anything those pigs tell us. I understand your frustration, but our allies assure me we have all the information they have. If it points to an obvious suspect, then why dig up others?" Soleiman asked.

"Sir, I have no illusions of trusting the Americans so any information will be accepted with suspicion," Mokhtari responded. "They obviously have a vested interest in placing blame somewhere other than their two closest allies in the region. But given the questions I have about the evidence, it's worth the risk. Sir, if there is a mole, it could take years to ferret them out and would set our programs back decades.

"Are we to replace everyone who worked at the facility? Or execute them to prevent information leaks? If the Americans are telling us of a mole to disrupt us, then we proceed cautiously and expose them. But if they have real, actionable information, I can only assume it is a common enemy. It wouldn't be the first time they shared information sir," he finished.

There was a brief silence on the line.

"Alright Colonel, you have permission to contact the Americans but be careful. Keep me informed of everything they provide you," Soleiman instructed, and the line went dead.

"Major, bring me that metal box," Mokhtari ordered pointing to a desk in the corner of the room.

The Major brought him the box and Mokhtari turned on the phone. He pulled up the screen with the list of previous calls and did a quick calculation of time zones. It would be somewhere around four in the morning DC time, and he hesitated for a second, then selected the number and pushed the green phone icon to connect.

There were four rings and a pause, then the American woman's voice.

"Good afternoon, Colonel, I'm glad you called. Can I assume the questions you've been struggling with are still unanswered?" Hayes asked.

"Miss Hayes, we have gone through the evidence and believe we've identified the bomber and are working to identify his accomplices. We'd certainly be happy for any other information you have that helps us roll up this network," Mokhtari lied.

"Oh Colonel, I admire your confidence. So, you've arrested the person responsible?" Hayes asked in a sickly-sweet tone of voice.

"Apparently you already know we haven't Miss Hayes, but our investigation continues, and they will be arrested soon," he replied.

Mokhtari hoped to keep the American guessing as to what information he actually had.

"Well, that is good news Colonel. Then I guess there's nothing more to discuss, is there?" she answered in a polite, but dismissive tone.

"Well Miss Hayes, you extended the olive branch of cooperation. I'm just following up to see if there is any information you can add to fill in any gaps," he stated in his best poker voice.

"Colonel I'm sure you have everything well in hand. Why don't you call me back when you make an arrest and we can compare notes," Hayes replied.

There was an awkward silence on the line. Mokhtari struggled to come up with how to proceed.

"Colonel, are we done with this dick dance now?" Hayes asked, calling his bluff. "The so-called evidence you have is fabricated bullshit and we both know it. So why don't you get to the real question you want to ask."

The tone of her voice shredded any illusion she believed a thing he'd said.

"Let's start over Miss Hayes, shall we?" Mokhtari acquiesced. "We are not convinced the people you retrieved are innocent in this attack. While we agree there are others, you clearly have a piece of information that can unwind this knot we have in the evidence. What will it take for you to share that information?"

And there it was. The real question both knew they had to get to.

"You have someone in custody who's been set up like many others. We'll share what we know about this attack and the way to identify the bomber once your leaders agree to allow a single helicopter to enter your country to recover this person. If you do not agree to this in full, we will not help you capture the bomber and they will remain a threat to you," Hayes replied sternly.

"And how do we know we can trust this information?" Mokhtari asked.

"You don't, but I'll put it to you this way. I think we've proven we can infiltrate your country at will to secure anyone we believe is of high enough value. But that action often comes at a very high cost. If we wanted to recover them, we could," Hayes answered. "But we have no desire for further loss of life or the beginning of a regional war that neither government wants. So, this cooperation helps us both Colonel. Of course, we don't expect to ask for something without giving something in return. From our perspective, the information we can provide is much more valuable than what we get back."

The Americans always put a higher premium on human life than the Iranian leadership did. To them, people were a means to an end. If that meant one, or a million people had to die to achieve the objective then so be it. Of course, it was easy when none of those lives were their own or their family members.

"Who is this person we allegedly have in custody?" Mokhtari asked.

"Colonel, we're both professionals. No information without your government's full agreement with our terms. Confer with your leadership and I'll wait for your call," Hayes said as the line went dead.

Mokhtari looked at the phone, turned it off, and handed it back to the Major.

"Put this back in the box and get me the crypto phone," he ordered.

The Major handed him the secure phone then left the room.

"General Soleiman."

"General, Colonel Mokhtari. Just spoke with the Americans and they appear to know what evidence we have and what it likely shows. They insist our information is wrong. I cannot be certain if we have a mole or if they collected it from unsecure communications intercepts, but they seem to know quite a bit more than I expected.

"They claim we have an individual under arrest who was part of the set up and demand they be allowed to recover them. They propose a single helicopter to enter the country and leave with them. If we agree, they will share information about who is behind the attack and how to identify the traitor. According to them, the mole is still active," Mokhtari reported.

"Who do we have that they want?" asked Soleiman.

"They won't say until we agree sir," Mokhtari answered.

"Then can't we just look at everyone arrested around the time of the bombing?" Soleiman asked.

"Sir, we don't even know where to look. We can assume an area around Dezful, but there have been hundreds of arrests. Is it a foreigner a native? If we have them in custody, what did we arrest them for? Trying to run down one individual jailed somewhere in the country would be virtually impossible," Mokhtari answered calmly.

"Dammit Colonel, I rely on you to find these people and you're telling me you failed," Soleiman raged. "But now you say we have no choice but rely on the Americans? And who's to say this person we supposedly have isn't part of this conspiracy?"

"Sir, I never said we had no choice," Mokhtari stated in a calm, logical voice. "Just that there is information that could help us find the individuals responsible and the Americans have offered a trade--information for this person. So, our choices are to work with the Americans and find the bomber sooner rather than later or refuse in which all those issues we spoke about before still remain. Sir, there's more to this than the Americans are telling us.

"Whoever did this attack cannot be one of their allies. Since their first call I've thought, why make the offer? If an ally did the attack, they would keep that to themselves and let the infiltrator continue their work. This implies it's someone who's a dangerous enemy to them, *and* us. And if we continue that logic, it implies an organization like the Islamic Caliphate who we are both fighting.

"The Caliphate not taking credit is the puzzling part," Mokhtari continued. "I have my suspicions but not enough information to feel confident about it. If the alliance of the Zionists and the Saudis is truly just a setup, then it would suggest an attempt to start a sectarian war. Again, for what purpose I'm not sure, but it is very concerning. Especially if there remains an active operative inside our most secure areas, sir."

"I'll speak to the President and the Supreme Leader. I don't like this, Colonel. I don't like it one damn bit," Soleiman snarled as the line went dead.

Mokhtari pondered the events. The fact the Americans made the offer to begin with, so close to the attack, meant they had actionable intel, something he desperately needed. But if he followed his own logic and looked at the evidence as a setup by someone like the Caliphate, then what was the end game?

Certainly, it would cause widespread instability throughout the region on a much wider scale than Syria. That would give them the ability to make deeper inroads into Iraq and Saudi Arabia, but that had its own problems. Why risk activating full militaries throughout the Middle East, including the Zionists.

He had to consider that it was to unite the Sunni world against the Shia, but the Zionist connection would ruin that. Could it be they simply wanted to destabilize the Saudis and turn the other Sunni nations against them, but again, why involve Iran? And if broad instability was the goal, then this was the perfect setup. But to what end?

There had already been bloodshed, and unless he found another answer, the leadership would follow the evidence, no matter the inconsistencies.

"Major," Mokhtari shouted.

The Major came scurrying into the room. "Yes sir!"

"Go back to the analysts and look at the evidence from a completely different perspective," Mokhtari ordered. "Look at it as if you were running an op to create broad scale instability. Think of the evidence as steps you would take to sow division and create opportunities for us to operate more freely. What benefit do we get out of it? To what end might we be working? Go now! I want some theories before the General calls me back."

Chapter 41

Recovery

The scientist stared at the blank concrete cell wall. Although the air was warm, the thick concrete remained relatively cool, so the cell wasn't oppressively hot. A fluorescent light tube outside the cell buzzed and flickered. He passed the time thinking about the electrochemical reaction that resulted in gas particles emitting light. It was just something to fight the boredom.

A man from the Iraqi Consulate visited nearly three days before and said the Egyptian Interest Office in Tehran asked them to check on him while they investigated his claim. But the cell was better than the alternative. At least he was alive and not being tortured, though he wasn't sure how long his luck would hold.

With the sun going down on another day it just increased the chance he would be discovered. He resigned himself to the idea that the best he could hope for was a quick execution. At worst he would be doomed to a life of torture and misery for months, or years.

The distinctive sound of scraping and clicking of a metal key inserted into a metal door rang off the concrete walls. The squeal of the rusting hinges pierced the relative silence of the cell block followed by footsteps. The scientist listened carefully and guessed it was two people. It was a game of course; something to entertain his mind.

His face broke into a smile when two men emerged in front of his cell door. One was a guard, and the other was dressed in a neatly pressed charcoal colored Italian suit. The scientist knew it was Italian because he had several just like it. This man had a short, neatly trimmed beard, short black hair, and dark brown eyes behind a pair of designer black metal framed glasses. He held a package in his hands, about fifteen inches square, wrapped in plain brown paper and tied with twine.

"Al Masry step forward," the guard demanded as he opened the cell door. "This man is from the Egyptian Mission. Come with us."

The scientist complied immediately, though he struggled to hide his surprise. The three walked back down the hallway and came to a room with a table and chairs.

"In here," the guard said pointing.

Once the two of them were in, the guard closed the door.

"Hello Mr. Al Masry. My name is Shakir Youssef and I'm from the Egyptian Mission in Tehran. I'm so glad I could come to your aid, brother, and very sorry for the delay in getting here. Unfortunately, there have been tensions in the region that made travel very difficult, but I've brought you a new passport and a change of clothes," Youssef said as he looked at the scientist with a smile, then shifted his eyes up and to the left.

The scientist stood there stunned for a moment then realized there was a camera in the corner of the room in the direction the man moved his eyes.

"Yes, yes thank you sir. Waiting so long, I thought something was wrong, but you are here now, Allah be praised," the scientist replied.

Youssef handed him the package and he pulled the string to open it then put it on the table. There were some simple beige linen pants, matching tunic, pair of sandals, and on top was an Egyptian passport. And not any type of passport, but a diplomatic passport.

"As you can see everything should be in order and once you change your clothes, we are free to go. Your diplomatic clearance is fully reinstated, and we'll head to the Interest Section in Tehran. From there we will arrange transportation home. We've already sent someone to collect your things from the hotel in Basra so no worries," Youssef said.

The scientist desperately tried to act normal and began to change his clothes. The clothing was exactly the right size; even the sandals they had for him. He folded his dirty clothes and put them on the brown paper, folded it back up and retied the string. He put the passport in his pocket and gave Youssef a quick nod. Youssef knocked on the door and seconds later it opened. There stood the precinct commander.

"Thank you, Commander, for helping my countryman. We appreciate your cooperation with this very difficult and challenging situation," Youssef said.

"We still have no record of his entry. It makes me wonder how he managed to get here," the Commander said suspiciously.

"Well Commander, that is a question for the Ministry of Interior. We have a record of a request and approval for a two-day travel visa made to your Embassy in Baghdad from ours. I'm told not all of the crossings in the Basra sector have electronic confirmation systems. Certainly, none of your border soldiers would allow someone in without a visa, would they?"

"You have the appropriate documentation, you are free to go," the Commander said, dismissively.

"Thank you again Commander. Let's go Mr. Al Masry," Youssef said as he pushed past the police commander and escorted the scientist out of the building.

Outside was a black BMW Alpina B7 sedan waiting. Youssef opened the rear passenger door and motioned for the Scientist to get in. He closed the door and climbed in on the other side.

"Let's go," he ordered as he tapped the shoulder of the driver.

The V-8 engine roared to life and the car virtually leapt into the street. The driver nimbly maneuvered through evening traffic and was quickly on the highway.

"Mr. Youssef, I'm confused," the scientist said after a few minutes. "How did you get here? I'm sure you know I'm not Egyptian."

"Doctor Bashir, sorry for the cloak and dagger but the station is monitored by cameras. Your country asked for our help once they confirmed where you were being held. The Iranians don't know who you are yet, and we are working on a plan to get you out of the country.

"If they check our story, they will find no visa request, but it buys us time. It was very smart to give them your grandfather's name. It allowed us to cross check your identity. The man who visited you earlier was one of our agents to verify who you were so we could issue the passport with your current info," Youssef answered.

"But how did you know where I was? I was unable to make the contact call before I was arrested," Bashir said.

"The man you were to meet witnessed the arrest and followed the police to their station. Then the Americans monitored communications to and from the station to see if they knew who you were. The good news was, you weren't a priority, so they didn't dig very far. Once you told the police you were Egyptian and had lost your documents, they called us. Fortunately, things sort of fell into place," Youssef replied.

"So, where are we going? Are we going back to Tehran?" asked Bashir.

"No, we're heading to a safe house, The entire area around Khorramabad is closed," Youssef answered.

"Why would it be closed?" asked Bashir.

The Egyptian diplomat just looked at him, stunned.

"You don't know?" he asked.

"Know what? Nearly five days ago I woke up in an empty pitch-black warehouse. The last thing I remember before that was leaving a conference for some relaxation on a yacht that morning and nothing in between. The only contact until now was a cell phone call to my security chief who gave me brief instructions then had me turn off the phone, and your man three days ago. I've heard nothing else," Bashir replied.

"I see," said Youssef.

Youssef explained the events since his disappearance during the next two-and-a-half-hours.

"May Allah watch over their souls," Bashir said solemnly. "So, now what do we do?"

"We go to the safe house and wait for instructions. Hopefully it won't take too long," answered Youssef.

The driver turned off the highway and onto the main thoroughfare through the city of Izeh. He glided through traffic and approached an eight-story hotel on the right side of the highway, then parked in the underground garage.

The three men got out, took the elevator to the ground floor, and went to the restaurant. They sat in a corner booth and ordered dinner. Bashir noticed several other people dining. A couple in another corner booth, a man at a table for two, and another man near the window. Not too many, but then it was a bit later in the evening.

Bashir watched the man near the window get up, pay, and leave as the three were finishing their dinner. The young man and woman got up at the same time as Bashir and his escorts laughing and carrying on a bit loudly just ahead of them. The woman, about Bashir's size, wore a pair of beige linen pants with matching tunic while the man had a suit coat thrown over his shoulder. Youssef paid their bill, and they walked out to find the couple waiting for the elevator. The five people got in and the driver pushed the button for the parking garage.

When the doors opened, the couple pushed past the three men. As Bashir started to exit, Youssef stopped him. The elevator doors closed, and the driver pushed the button for the top floor. At the top floor, he pushed the button for the garage again. Bashir just stood there dumbfounded. Once in the garage, instead of turning right to head to the BMW, they turned left and walked to a light grey Mercedes AMG E53 sedan with dark tinted windows.

"Get in," ordered Youssef as Bashir complied. Youssef got into the front passenger seat. "Let's go."

The driver pulled into traffic. At Velayat Square he took the traffic circle around and got off on Chavil Boulevard. He turned right onto a side street and wound through a series of residential areas, turning and backtracking several times to ensure they weren't being followed. Ten minutes later they pulled into a gated compound with eight-foot stone walls.

"We're here, Doctor. Please follow me," Youssef said.

Youssef led him into a large house typical of the affluent neighborhood. It had a concrete stucco exterior with a curved entryway and a large arched front door. The windows were somewhat ornate with black bars on them.

As they entered, there was a dual staircase left and right of the two-story entrance that curved around to the second floor. There was a library to the left and dining room to the right. Further down the hallway toward the back of the house was a great room and a kitchen.

"Do you want some tea, Doctor?" asked Youssef.

"Yes, thank you," he answered.

Youssef nodded to the driver who disappeared into the kitchen.

"May I ask, what happened at the restaurant?" Bashir asked.

"We had someone following us from Ahvaz. We had operatives in the restaurant and switched cars. Once we got confirmation our shadow followed them, we were clear to leave. You are quite safe here," Youssef answered calmly.

"Followed? Is that normal? Were they following us because of me?" Bashir asked in rapid succession.

"Don't worry Doctor; this is common, so we were prepared. We brought you some new clothes and put them in your bedroom. I'm told we have similar taste in suits, so I got you one. Hopefully you won't have to stay here long. Unfortunately, no outside communication that can be intercepted by the Iranians and their friends. I can get a message out through diplomatic channels to someone if you would like. Otherwise, get cleaned up and make yourself at home. You can go anywhere inside the compound," Youssef stated.

"Thank you. I'm eager to get home and out of this accursed place," Bashir replied.

An hour and a half later, Bashir looked in the mirror at his freshly trimmed beard with satisfaction. The shower felt like heaven as he washed away the grime and stink from his capture and incarceration. The coolness of the marble tile floors was the perfect ending to the hot water he let flow over him for minutes on end. Youssef was correct about having everything he needed in this place. If he had to lay low, there were worse places than this.

There was a knock at the door. "Doctor Bashir, Mr. Youssef needs you downstairs now. I've laid out the gray suit for you."

"Right, I'll be down straight away," he answered as he quickly finished toweling off.

Within ten minutes he walked downstairs and into the sitting room where Youssef was waiting.

"Ah, Doctor, good. We must leave immediately. Seems our timetable has been moved up."

"So soon? I was expecting it would take much longer to negotiate my release," Bashir said surprised.

"These things are unpredictable Doctor. If you're ready, it's time to go," Youssef answered.

"Yes, yes, I'm ready," Bashir replied.

Youssef motioned toward the front door and Bashir followed him out and into the grey Mercedes once again.

Chapter 42

To Catch a Mole

Janelle Hayes put the latest intelligence analysis down and rubbed her tired eyes. While not definitive, the theory of the Caliphate initiating a sectarian war seemed plausible. The Southwest Asia section had someone playing the wargame 24/7 waiting for *Hephaestion* to make contact. He briefly came online to report the successful mission and apologize for his delayed report.

They had a fix on him in Dezful. Acting as the Caliphate handler, Karim instructed him to check in every other day to plan new targets. With luck, today would be a check-in day and Hayes really wanted Mokhtari to call before that.

Two hours earlier DDO Cavanaugh sent word that the Egyptians secured the scientist and were headed to a safe house. Fortunately, the Iranians didn't appear to know who he was. It sent a sigh of relief through the intelligence services, but they weren't out of the woods yet. They still had to get him out of the country. The fact he wasn't in custody anymore made extraction much easier.

The small tablet on Hayes' desk started ringing. It was plugged into an NSA module that opened an encrypted electronic tunnel. It mimicked a cell phone but was routed through a secure computer network. Hayes looked at the number.

"Hello Colonel, so glad you called. Do we have an agreement?"

"Yes Miss Hayes. My government agrees to one helicopter, escorted by two of our aircraft. I will coordinate entry time and call sign with you. Where will it be landing?" Mokhtari asked.

"Colonel, you will be given the landing airfield and the hand-off procedures at the rendezvous point," Hayes said. "The trust between us only goes so far. As for our part of the bargain, we need someone in Dezful on a mobile device connected to the internet.

We will share a computer screen with you when the suspect comes online. When that happens, we'll pass you their exact location so you can move in for the intercept.

"We assume you'll be using a clean smartphone, so you'll need to download the *Deskjolt* app," she continued. "It's a free open-source application that allows us to share our desktop with another user to include voice, video, and chat options. It's open-source code so neither of us can infiltrate it without the other knowing. We've created an account for you on the platform and I'll text you the logon information at the end of this call.

"We've broken a communications channel used by the Islamic Caliphate so the person you choose to track the bomber must speak English. They were the ones behind the attack and their operative has been communicating with a person he believes is his handler for the past few days. That's how we know the two we recovered were not involved. We're expecting the operative to check in today so we must move quickly," stated Hayes urgently.

"So, what is the name of this operative?" asked Mokhtari.

"Their code name is *Hephaestion*," she answered. "We need someone on the ground so we can direct them to the operative for identification. We're confident it's someone who worked at the facility and someone you've already interviewed."

"How interesting, the name of the Greek general who helped Alexander conquer Darius III and the ancient Persian empire. Seems this person has a sense of irony. And the selection as Alexander's right-hand man rather than Alexander himself, do you think that is significant?" pondered Mokhtari.

"You have a keen sense of history Colonel and as intuitive as I expected. We also believe this selection was intentional. The meaning behind it is pure speculation but seems we have a common enemy Colonel. This enemy is very patient and works deliberately to achieve their goals. Those goals appear to include sparking a sectarian war between Shia and Sunni," Hayes responded.

"Hmm, I must admit Miss Hayes, your theory seems to have some logic to it. Tell me, if you broke their communications network, did you know about the attack before it happened?" he asked carefully.

"Colonel, we've been chasing these people for decades and broken multiple communications systems, this is just one of them. Given your nuclear event this attack exposed we felt it was time to share this information for the peace and security of the region. I think we can both agree that is the primary goal here, correct?" Hayes answered.

"Miss Hayes, the United States has been destabilizing this region for years. You've tried to destroy our government since the revolution, so it is you who have threatened regional peace and security. But we welcome any mutual assistance in the capture of a member of a terrorist organization who threatens both our countries," Mokhtari said calmly.

Hayes laughed at him.

"Colonel, there are no television cameras, and this isn't a time or place for propaganda. We both know that's what your leaders feed your people to keep them in line. We could have decapitated your country's leadership long ago if we desired. You and I operate in the real world so let us deal with this threat the way it's done in our line of work. Leave the political bullshit to the fools who believe the garbage being fed to everyone else," Hayes remarked.

It was Mokhtari's turn to laugh. He was beginning to like this American CIA operative. She was right of course. The Americans could have killed the whole government multiple times over but didn't want to alienate the Iranian populace. But as more and more protests spread throughout the country, rattling the leadership, it was not out of the question the Americans would see that as justification for action.

"Yes, Miss Hayes, on that we agree. So, let's get down to business. What is the rendezvous point and time?" he asked.

"Rendezvous point is 29 degrees 10 minutes North, 49 degrees 30 minutes East. Rendezvous time is…1830 UTC. Aircraft will be an AW139, tail number November-5-6-2-Sierra-Alpha," Hayes stated.

"The pilot will radio the destination upon contact at the RZ and we'll give details for securing the package. Keep this line available but you need to have your men ready to go. We're expecting the operative to make contact sometime today. I've texted you the logon credentials for the mirroring site. And Colonel, tell your leaders if they double cross us, it will be very bad for your country. Remind your President we can repeat what happened several days ago at any time of our choosing," Hayes finished in a stern but professional tone.

"I understand Miss Hayes. I'll pass this on, and Miss Hayes, that warning goes both ways. We are both soldiers and know that trust is earned," Mokhtari answered.

"You are correct Colonel. I'll call you when we make contact; we expect him to be in the Dezful area. I suspect you've maintained your security posture there so be ready to move and move fast. I shall talk to you soon either way. Good evening, Colonel," Hayes said.

"Good day Miss Hayes," he replied.

Hayes punched the speed dial for the DDO.

"Silas, extraction is on. Rendezvous point is 29 degrees 10 minutes North, 49 degrees 30 minutes East. Rendezvous time is 1830 UTC, confirming extraction airport is Bandar Mahshahr. Estimated landing time is 1900 UTC. Tell the Egyptians to get the package ready for transport. Hold outside the airport until approach instructions are verified," Hayes reported.

"Got it Janelle. I'll make the calls. Let DoD know to get ready," Cavanaugh replied, and hung up.

Next Hayes dialed the chief of the Southwest Asia Section.

"Gerlacher," he answered.

"Zack, the extraction is on. Anything from our friend yet?" she asked.

"Not yet ma'am, but we're ready for him," he answered.

"Do we have the mirroring setup ready to go?" Hayes asked.

"Yes ma'am. Mo configured a zombie to only show the messages as text messages; no information about the game or where these messages came from. When the message comes in, it's converted to SMS then sent to the zombie. Can't say they couldn't figure out it's a wargame from the commentary, but it can't be helped. At least we're not making it too easy for them. Plus, with the number of servers and worlds it would take a while to figure it all out," he replied.

"Okay, good. Tell KZ to stay on his toes. If this goes down the same time as the extraction things could get a little dicey," Hayes stated as she punched off the line.

Next call was to the DCIA.

"Anderson."

"David, we're a go. RZ in about four hours, our friend isn't online yet, but they're ready for him," Hayes reported.

"Got it Janelle, I'll inform the President and SecDef," Anderson answered as the line went dead.

All she could do now was wait. She kept busy reading intelligence reports from North Korea. The leadership there was scurrying about in a panic with some reports of executions of a couple key leaders. The cruel dictator of the country had missed two important celebrations that he'd never missed before and the intel community for that part of the world was going a bit crazy.

She'd spent nearly an hour looking at intel from the two Five Eye countries in the South Pacific, Australia and New Zealand, when her phone rang.

"Hayes."

"Ma'am, *Hephaestion* is online. Mo triangulated his location to an internet café in Andimenshk," Gerlacher reported.

"Send me the coordinates immediately," she ordered and punched the line off.

Hayes called Mokhtari.

"Hello Miss Hayes," he answered.

"Colonel, our friend is online at an internet café in Andimeshk. I'm texting you the coordinates," she said as she hit send on the text message.

"Hold on Miss Hayes," he replied.

He came back onto the line after about a minute. "My men are moving in. Expect them to be at the café in about seven minutes. My man has logged in…says he's getting text messages. Can he see some older messages?" Mokhtari asked.

This time it was Hayes who put him on hold.

"Zack, get Mo to pull up the messages that talk about the mission so our friends can read them. Tell KZ to take his time; they are about seven minutes out from the café," she ordered.

"Colonel, your man should be getting the messages from the time of the confirmation of the mission. We are working to keep him online for as long as we can but he's smart, he doesn't stay on long," Hayes reported. "I would expect him to be positioned to see the front door."

"I agree, we'll make a tactical entry. Standby," Mokhtari replied.

The minutes moved slowly as Hayes closed her eyes and leaned back in her chair. Nothing would speed this process up and she had to be patient.

"Son of a bitch, Massoud," Mokhtari hissed. "Okay, my man is behind him." There was a short pause. "Target taken down. Thank you, Miss Hayes, we'll take it from here."

"You're welcome, Colonel. We've upheld our part of the bargain. I do hope that if you get any information from him that could help unwind his organization you will share it. Cheers," she said and disconnected the call.

"Okay Zack, your people can stand down, the IRGC has *Hephaestion* in custody," she ordered.

Chapter 43

Bloodlines

Mokhtari looked at the clock: 10:59 PM, one minute from rendezvous time. He had a radio repeater set up in his home office. The Air Force frequency was being routed to him so he could get the landing airport and hopefully move people there before the exchange. He had to know who it was that the Americans would go to such lengths for.

"Iranian Air Force flight leader this is November-5-6-2-Sierra-Alpha at rendezvous point requesting escort to Bandar Mahshahr International Airport most direct route," the pilot reported.

"November-5-6-2-Sierra-Alpha IAF Lead, confirming Bandar Mahshahr International Airport, do not deviate from route," the Iranian pilot responded.

Mokhtari picked up the secure phone. "Major, get people moving to Bandar Mahshahr. How long will it take?"

"Sir, closest units are an hour away," the Major replied. "The expected landing is in less than 30 minutes, so we'll be well behind them. We can have local police do the surveillance. The airport has a small security team onsite, and locals can increase that within ten minutes."

"Do it," Mokhtari ordered. "Not perfect but we need to know who the Americans think is so important. Secure the airport. No one to enter or leave. Tap into the CCTV system as well. Internal security override code is Alpha-One-Sierra-Seven-Seven. Look at all arrests in that area for the past week. We weren't given release instructions so if the individual is in our custody, that means they're close to the airport."

"Yes sir," responded the Major as the line went dead.

Mokhtari punched the speed dial for General Soleiman.

"Sir, Bandar Mahshahr is being secured. Unfortunately, our closest unit cannot get there before landing and we don't have release instructions yet. I've ordered a screening of all arrests close to the airport in anticipation that whoever this person is, the Americans will want an immediate release and movement to the airport."

"Good Colonel. When will you be interrogating the traitor?" Soleiman asked.

"He's in holding and psychological techniques are being applied to prepare him for interrogation," Mokhtari answered. "So, most likely tomorrow or the next day once he's been worn down. We have his wife and son in custody. She's undergoing the same psychological pressure; the boy we can use as leverage."

Known for his brutality with prisoners in using torture to get confessions for political purposes, Mokhtari had to make sure the information they extracted was accurate, not just damning. This Massoud was a religious zealot. It would be his last line of defense and Mokhtari not only had to break that down, he had to shatter it completely so there was no chance Massoud would lie. So, if that meant Massoud would watch his son rape his own mother and condemn them both to hell under the laws of Islam, then so be it.

"Okay Colonel. Let me know when we get the release details," Soleiman said and then hung up.

Mokhtari looked at the clock; twenty minutes to landing and still no information about the handoff. He was beginning to get concerned and glanced over at the cell phone he used to talk with the American. Time passed excruciatingly slow. Ten minutes before landing the cell phone rang and Mokhtari answered it.

"Hello Miss Hayes. Do you have handoff instructions for me?"

"Yes, Colonel," Hayes replied. "I assume you have locked down the airport already? The helicopter will land at the northwest maintenance ramp. There will be a light grey Mercedes AMG E53 sedan with no plates arriving at the first checkpoint gate. There is an access road to the north leading to the maintenance ramp. You will allow this vehicle to go onto this maintenance road with a challenge and reply command. Challenge command is 'Darius the Great', reply is 'Mount Behistun.'

"This car will drive to the helicopter, and you will not stop the car or anyone inside. Once it drops off its passenger the helicopter will leave on the reverse route from arrival. You will not follow the car, and anyone caught tailing it could indicate a violation of our agreement. Is that understood Colonel?" Hayes said professionally but sternly.

Mokhtari listened carefully taking meticulous notes. "Miss Hayes, you said we had this person in our custody but there are no release instructions. This could be seen by my government as a lie thus nullifying the agreement," he said in the same professional but stern voice.

Although both were intelligence professionals, this was the way intelligence negotiations went; threat and counter-threat, trust but verify. Each side understood the risks involved and so this was a deadly serious game that required nerves of steel and a willingness to back up threats with violence if necessary.

"You did, but you let them go and we recovered them," she said. "I expect you'll be getting a call about this within the hour. We have held up our end of the bargain Colonel, so you can tell General Soleiman we will respond quickly should he or anyone else interfere in this exchange."

The threat didn't have to be explained. The Americans had shown they could reach out and kill virtually anyone they wanted, at any time. It wasn't always surgical, sometimes it was very messy, but kill they could. It was a threat that was offered more than once, and to an experienced operative like Mokhtari, had to be taken very seriously. While the American President hadn't shown the backbone for violence before, the recent action in the Gulf proved he could if provoked.

"I understand Miss Hayes. I'll pass this along," he replied.

"Better hurry Colonel. I'll hold here until the exchange is complete."

Mokhtari got on the secure phone to base communications.

"Patch me to the security team at Bandar Mahshahr," he ordered.

The communications center patched him to the security team leader and Mokhtari relayed the instructions exactly as Hayes said. He was on the line with the team leader when the grey Mercedes pulled up to the checkpoint. Once the challenge and reply command was given, the car sped off down the access road.

He watched the CCTV feed from the airport. The helicopter arrived and moved to the northwest maintenance ramp and landed. Mokhtari saw the Mercedes move across the ramp when the secure phone rang again.

"Mokhtari."

"Sir, we just received some information from the Interior Ministry," the Major reported. "An Egyptian citizen was arrested with no documents in Ahvaz several days ago who said he was robbed. He said he entered from Iraq in the Basra region and was held until late yesterday. He was released into the custody of an Egyptian diplomat. Sir Interior has no record of a visa request for any Egyptian entering from the Basra region during that timeframe."

Just then a man stepped out of the Mercedes and walked quickly to the waiting helicopter. He turned and waved to the occupants of the car who sped away. Mokhtari leaned into the screen.

"Son of a bitch," he said.

The door slid shut and the helicopter lifted off. He brought the cell phone to his ear.

"Miss Hayes, you mean to tell me that Doctor Husam al Din Bashir, noted Saudi nuclear scientist was on Iranian soil at the same time as the bombing of a nuclear facility? Do you expect us to see this as a coincidence?" he virtually hissed.

"Colonel, I said we believe this person was set up just as you were," Hayes began. "He said he was kidnapped from a conference and woke up several days ago in Ahvaz. He was stripped of all identification except for a cell phone that only had two calls on it to the same cell number. We suspect it was one used in the bombing.

"Can we verify he wasn't involved, no. But that is for us to determine. He will be detained and interrogated. If there is actionable intel from him, I will share it with you. I hope you will do the same when you get information from that Massoud fellow.

"But I ask you, how would you reinforce the story of Israeli/Saudi collaboration without a real person that you can push in front of the cameras? You have evidence of an Israeli operative on the ground, all you would need is the Saudi expert to cement the story. So as professional courtesy Colonel, we will do our due diligence and get to the bottom of any conspiracy as I'm sure you'll do the same," Hayes finished and killed the call.

Mokhtari sat there stunned. If this was a Caliphate operation then Hayes was absolutely right, the propaganda value of a confession from the Saudi scientist would be the perfect spark to inflame the populous. And he certainly knew how to use propaganda. His thoughts were interrupted by the secure phone ringing again.

"Mokhtari."

"Sir, we've lost the Mercedes. After leaving the airport they turned into a dense industrial zone with several narrow alleys and just disappeared," the Major reported.

"Was it local police doing the tail?" he asked.

"Yes, sir. We didn't have time to get our people there," the Major replied.

"Dammit, find out if all of the Egyptian diplomats are accounted for and their location. The Saudi scientist was released into their custody yesterday," Mokhtari said disgusted.

"Saudi scientist sir?" the Major asked.

"Doctor Husam al Din Bashir. That's the person the Americans just picked up with that helicopter," Mokhtari said angrily. "We had him in custody for days and now the Americans have him."

"Doesn't that imply that there was a Saudi conspiracy involved in the attack on our facility?" the Major asked.

"Just get me the locations on those damned diplomats," Mokhtari ordered and slammed the phone down.

While the messages recovered from Massoud's computer implied the claim that Bashir was set was true, Mokhtari was frustrated they might have to trust the Americans to get those answers. But he still had one chance to get confirmation from the traitor. The call to General Soleiman wouldn't be so easy.

***

Mokhtari sat in his office and thought about the intelligence they'd gather in the past six months since the traitor Massoud had been captured. He sighed, opened the metal box, and pulled out the cell phone from inside. He turned it on and punched the speed dial for the CIA Deputy Director.

"Hello Colonel, it's been a long time since we last spoke. Are you fully recovered from your injuries?" Hayes said answering the phone.

"Hello Miss Hayes, I've recovered very well thank you. We have rolled up Massoud's network and have found links to at least three other groups within Iran. I was wondering if you had any more information beyond what I provided you?" Mokhtari asked.

"Yes, I saw the very public executions though I thought the suggestion of U.S. involvement was a bit overboard," she answered.

"As you said before, the politicians will be politicians. Your former President's threat was not appreciated," he replied.

"Well, nothing us operators can do about that, can we? So, we have traced nearly one hundred groups with some link to the Caliphate. There is a central command structure though we haven't identified exactly who it is yet, but there's coordination at high levels between them. You said you found three other groups in Iran? We identified at least five with the possibility of double that," she stated bluntly.

"I see," said the Colonel. "What do you think the link is between them?"

Hayes hesitated briefly before answering.

"Colonel, there is some evidence that the leader of this network is believed to be a direct male blood descendant of Mohammed," she said.

It was Mokhtari's turn to hesitate as the implications of that fact sunk in. Massoud's words when they broke him and confessed everything, confirming the American's suspicion about the Caliphate's operation now haunted him.

"I'm sorry, I'm sorry. I've failed you, my Caliph. I've failed the true Blood of the Prophet."
But the Prophet's only son had died as an infant.

"That's impossible, the Prophet had no surviving sons. Are you sure?" he asked.

"One of my analysts found a partial photocopy of a letter among documents recovered from a Caliphate safehouse. The letter was allegedly written by Mohammed himself and referenced a secret message to Abu Sayf, the husband of the wet nurse to Mohammed's son Ibrahim. The letter claimed Mohammed had a premonition of a betrayal by someone in his inner circle.

"It said that his life, as well as his son's, were in grave danger. He prophesied that one day, a descendant from his son's line would return to unite the bloodline of Allah's messenger and rule the Muslim world. He instructed Abu Sayf to find a terminally ill child that resembled his son, then send a message of the child's impending death, and hide Ibrahim. There appears to be more to the letter, but it's been cut off. So, the question is, was Massoud's plea just a belief in the existence of a direct descendant? Or was it actually a prayer to a real person, alive today?" Hayes asked.

"Do you have anything to verify this information?" he questioned.

"We've pieced some things together to suggest this Caliph merges the dual bloodlines of Mohammed and his son-in law Ali, but it's an incomplete picture," Hayes answered. "And you know as well as I there is nothing so powerful a motivator as zealotry. That is the danger here. This creates zealots on both sides of the sectarian divide toward a common goal. The Twelfth Imam, the living Imam in hiding who is a direct descendent of Mohammed according to your sect as I recall.

"That would not only threaten every Ayatollah, but every leader of every Islamic nation on the planet. What happens then?" Hayes asked. "Let's face it Colonel, nobody kills more Muslims than other Muslims. Places like Mecca, Al Aqsa, and Qom could become killing fields.

"I'm simply telling you the general consensus based on what we're seeing, and our assessment is considered plausible by experts from both sects of Islam. That is who we are both looking for Colonel. The Muslim nations of the world have a clear and present danger," Hayes finished.

Mokhtari's mind was racing with this new information. Hayes was right. If true, this would threaten the leaders within all of Islam. The prospect of the unification of the line of Mohammed and the line of Ali would be a dangerous revelation.

"Thank you, Miss Hayes," replied Mokhtari. "This gives me much to think about and much to decide on how to use our resources against this enemy. I hope we can continue to talk. I do enjoy our conversations."

"As do I Colonel. Have a good evening, and please tell your crazy little friend in North Korea too bad about his younger brother. We know he was the smart one of the family. Remind him that playing with fire can get some people badly burned, although I suspect he's not speaking with you much anymore. He's already executed the men who coordinated his brother's trip to your facility," Hayes replied and clicked off the phone.

Mokhtari looked at the cell phone and couldn't help but smile. This American had a cold sense of humor, almost as cold as his. The North Korean dictator's brother who oversaw the nuclear and missile technology transfer agreement between the two countries was incinerated when the bomb exploded beneath his feet. There wasn't even enough of him found to bury. Yes, this American was cold and dangerous, and he respected her even more for it.

Epilogue

Kirkorian stood at her kitchen island looking out the window at the bright spring morning daydreaming about the past several months, her pink and black yoga pants with matching sport bra hugging her slim muscular body like a second skin. Her recovery had been physically and emotionally exhausting in the seven months since the extraction. While her hair and clothing now covered up the physical scars from her near-death ordeal, the psychological ones would take more time. But, from the moment she awoke in Landstuhl, Naz had never left her side. They were fortunate the Secretary of Defense had personally approved Naz's assignment to her father's company as a special operations trainer which allowed him to help with her rehab.

Naz was strong but gentle, patient, and attentive not only to her needs, but her son's. When she was transferred from Landstuhl to Brook Army Medical Center in her hometown of San Antonio, her parents brought her son Joshua to see her. Naz was so good with him. He explained what happened, what the boy could expect, and that he would be there for him no matter what he needed. While it was frightening for the young boy to see his mother so helpless, she was happy that Naz and her family were there for him.

At first, Naz slept in the spare bedroom and provided her home healthcare, helped get her to and from rehab, and cared for Joshua. She was so appreciative of how hard he tried to ensure her privacy and modesty. But early on, she was helpless as a baby and there were so many things she couldn't do for herself. As her recovery allowed, he stepped back and only helped if she absolutely needed him.

Kirkorian reflected on how her Physical Therapist insisted she focus on small victories rather than the minor setbacks. That, over time, those small victories would blossom into recovery. She did her best but found herself relying on Naz when she felt depressed about her progress. He was her cheerleader without the overt rah-rah encouragement; just a calming word here and there at just the right time to lift her up or get her over an obstacle.

She didn't really know when appreciation had turned into love, but it had. And when her therapist told her she could finally start running again, she was overjoyed which led to the first time she and Naz made love. He was so cautious, trying not to hurt her. But the tenderness he showed only increased her desire for him. And when she climaxed, the tears started flowing and she had to reassure him they were "tears of joy." That the three of them together--Naz, Joshua, and her--were perfect and she had almost lost that.

The doorbell startled Kirkorian back to reality and met Naz at the bottom of the stairs as she answered the door.

"Ebrahim, Azaria, so good to see you! Come in, come in. Oh my God Azar, you look like you're ready to pop!" she said to the woman nine months pregnant.

"Any day now. Ebrahim and I have been walking every day and I've been doing that Pilates for Expectant Mothers at the gym, but it gets harder and harder to move these days," Azar said with a laugh.

Kirkorian stepped to the side as Azar entered and Naz shook Ebrahim's hand.

"How are you Shirin? You're looking pretty good!" Azar asked.

"I'm doing better every day. We run in the morning; I'm allowed to do a mile and a half, then in the afternoon I do my yoga for stretching and core strength. Trying to stick with the program but I'm getting antsy to really start pushing it," Kirkorian replied.

"Let's go out to the deck," Naz interjected. "Can I get anyone something to drink?".

Joshua came bounding down the stairs. As a tall and skinny eleven-year-old, he was just starting another growth spurt making his legs and feet seem gangly and awkward. Not much shorter than Kirkorian already, he had the height and curly brown hair of his father.

"Aunt Azaria, Uncle Ebrahim!" he called out.

Joshua ran and gave them both a hug then kissed Azar's belly.

"And you too, little cousin. I'm going outside to play Mom!" Then changing to Farsi, "Ebrahim, come kick the soccer ball with me!" and he was off to the back yard.

"I am jealous at how fast he can switch from English to Farsi," Ebrahim said.

"Well, he's grown up in an Iranian family," Kirkorian replied with a laugh. "But you're doing very well yourself. Keep working, it just takes practice."

Once in the backyard, the men kicked the ball around while the women talked on the deck. After about twenty minutes, Azar closed her eyes and put a hand on her swollen belly. A few minutes later she did it again and blew out a long breath. About five minutes later she suddenly doubled over, grabbed her stomach and let out a grunt.

"Shirin, I think I just pissed myself," Azar said.

"Azar, your water broke! Darius, get a towel out of the laundry room and put it in Ebrahim's car. Ebrahim, it's time!" she yelled as she stood and helped Azar out of her chair.

Kirkorian put her in the front passenger seat and shut the door. "Ebrahim give me the keys and go with Naz. I know a shortcut," she urged.

Ebrahim did what he was told, and the two cars sped out of the neighborhood.

"Thank you for doing this," Azar said breathlessly between contractions.

"I missed the wedding, there's no way I'm missing this," Kirkorian replied as she reached over and patted Azar's knee. "Hold on, railroad tracks."

Azar grunted in pain as the car went over the tracks in the middle of another contraction.

"Just breathe Azar, we're almost there," Kirkorian said trying to comfort her friend.

They pulled into the hospital ER drop-off and got Azar checked in. Eleven hours later Kirkorian came down to the waiting lounge to get Naz and Joshua.

"It's a boy, seven pounds, eight ounces, and twenty-one inches long. He's beautiful," she said with a smile. "Do you want to go meet him?"

Joshua immediately said yes and the three walked down the hallway to Azar's hospital room. As they entered, Ebrahim was holding his son and saying a prayer over him. Azar was smiling but exhausted.

Naz walked over, leaned in and kissed her forehead.

"And you thought combat was tough!" he whispered, making her laugh.

"That may be true, but the end result is so much better," Azar replied smiling.

"What's his name?" asked Joshua innocently.

Ebrahim looked at Azar and smiled.

"Ben Darian Hamadani. Ben which means 'son' in Hebrew and Darian means 'gift sent from heaven' in Persian," Azar answered as she reached up and held Ebrahim's hand.

"We're gonna go and let you rest. Call me anytime you need help, momma," Kirkorian said to Azar as she leaned in and gave her a hug.

The car was quiet on the way home. Normally Joshua would talk about anything but tonight he was silent and just had a grin on his face. As the three of them got in the house, Joshua grabbed his mom's hand and just looked up at her smiling.

"Why are you smiling like a Cheshire cat little man?" she asked.

Joshua looked at Naz. Kirkorian looked at the two of them.

"Okay you two, what's going on?" she asked suspiciously.

"Well, us boys had a little talk and I asked Joshua for his blessing, and he said yes," Naz said smiling.

Kirkorian stood there stunned as Naz reached out to hold her other hand. "So, my question to you is, Shirin Alisa Sabah Kirkorian, will you marry me and make us a proper family?" he asked her.

Tears welled up in her eyes. "Yes, of course I'll marry you!" she said as she pulled Naz in for a kiss and then hugged the two most important men in her life.

The End

Afterword

Ever since humans congregated into tribal communities and came into conflict with each other, terrorist activities have been used by state and non-state actors. Whether used to influence events or to force a worldview onto other communities, the purpose is the same...to create fear in a population to force them to submit. Today, the blurring of the lines between those who use terrorist tactics and those who fund them has shifted the normal political processes between nation states.

These stories are drawn from the geopolitical grey areas and those who operate in the shadows on both sides of the struggle. Where friends can become enemies and enemies become friends depending on the shifting global threat. While the goal of global harmony and peace is noble, the reality remains that we are still divided by tribal associations and beliefs. Until this goal is achieved, the struggle for dominance will continue requiring the silent sacrifices of good men and women until the forces of harmony and peace prevail.